Welcome to the Lowlife 3

Natavia

SOUL Publications

Welcome to the Lowlife 3   Natavia

*****Warning*****

This novel contains: broken English, strong language, sex, violence, and vulgar situations, which may be offensive to some readers.

SOUL Publications

Kemara

Present Day, August, 2017...

*"**C**ome on, baby. You gotta breathe. I can't lose you," my husband said as he held onto me. My vision was blurry and my body was beginning to feel relaxed; I was making peace with God. He had forgiven me for all the crimes I committed throughout my life. I was trying to hold on for the sake of my daughter. Even if He decided to take me, at least He could save her. I couldn't bare losing another child behind my actions. Beretta was a good father to Zalia and I knew he would be able to hold it down on his own. My eyes closed and blood was seeping from the corners of my mouth as I fought to breathe. My grip on my husband's hand was getting weak. As his tears fell onto my face, he whispered in my ear.*

"If you die, I'll die wit' you. I can't do this by myself. I'm afraid to lose you—I was always afraid of losing you. I know that nigga was bluffin' when he said he fucked you," he said. I tried to respond but I couldn't.

"Run inside and get somebody! Mara isn't breathing!" Beretta yelled and everything went black. It was my final moment...

SOUL Publications

Part 6:

Matrimony

SOUL Publications

Piper

November, 2011...

"**A**re you sure Kemara said I can come?" Delonte asked me while I packed my bag.

"I told her I was bringing a guest. Why are you worried? You can't be around my friends? We talked about this already," I replied.

I was packing to go to St. Croix for Mara and Beretta's wedding. I wasn't going to take Delonte until I heard Lezzi was coming with Pistol. That shit had my blood boiling, but I couldn't wait to show Lezzi's ass that I wasn't worried about her and Pistol. But who was I fooling? I wanted Pistol to be jealous because he stopped coming around that night me and Lezzi fought in my living room. Pistol was a difficult-ass nigga. One minute, he was feeling me; then the next, he regretted feeling me. I was done playing games and I couldn't wait to show off my bathing suits. It was childish of me, but I wasn't playing fair until he realized I was where he wanted to be.

"I want you to move in with me," Delonte blurted out.

"Come again?" I asked.

"I'm sayin', you should move in wit' me. You have a lot of stuff at my crib and I want to wake up next to you every morning," he said.

"Ummm, let me think about it. We're in the beginning of a relationship and I don't want us to move too fast," I replied.

"Aight, if you say so," he said and shrugged his shoulders. He went into the bathroom and I left out of the room to call Mara. She answered the phone giggling and it warmed my heart because I knew she was in a good mood.

"What's so funny?" I asked.

"Bitttcchhhh, Beretta changing Zalia's pamper and you should see him. He got one of my weave clips on his nose. Niggas go hard all day but scared of a shitty pamper," she laughed.

"I'm ready to throw her lil' ass in the trash can! She smells worse than me and I'm a grown man," Beretta said in the background.

"Who is watching Zalia while we're on vacation?" I asked.

"Pistol's aunt is gonna watch her," she replied.

"Are you nervous?" I asked.

"Yes, a little bit, but I can't wait. He's gonna be my man until the end. Hold on, Piper," Mara said.

"Nigga, I know you didn't just sprinkle baby powder all over her like she's a funnel cake!" Mara yelled at Beretta.

"I got this, shorty. Mind ya business!" Beretta said.

"I'm back. Now, what's up wit' you? You called me sounding all sad," she said.

"Delonte asked me to move in wit' him, but I don't know. I mean I like him but—"

"He's not Pistol. Why don't you just tell Pistol how you feel and stop with the nonsense?" Mara said.

"Yeah, you got all the answers even though you dragged Beretta along for years before you let your guard down," I chuckled.

"I was a teenager but we're adults now. Delonte is a good man and he's laid back. He doesn't rip and run the streets and he's legit. What more can you ask for?" she asked.

"Pistol understands me, the same way you do," I replied.

When I heard Delonte come out the bathroom, I told Mara I was going to call her back.

What am I doing? I asked myself.

"I'm ready to head out to check up on my club. I'll swing by tonight if it's not too late. What time should I be here tomorrow morning if I don't come back?" he asked.

"Be here at six o' clock. Our plane boards at eight a.m.," I replied. He kissed my lips then left.

I went downstairs to grab a bottle of wine so I could enjoy a nice bubble bath and relax. My doorbell rang as soon as I put my clothes in the hamper. It was ten o'clock at night when I looked at the clock on the wall. In frustration, I put on a robe and went downstairs to get the door. The doorbell rang two more times.

"WAIT!" I yelled out.

I opened the door and Pistol was standing in front of me looking like a chocolate Hershey bar. I wanted to drop down to my knees and bless him!

"What do you want?" I asked.

"The money out of my safe," he replied and stepped into the house. He walked past me and headed upstairs to my bedroom because his safe was in the back of my closet. I followed him into my room and sat on the bed. We didn't say a word to each other. He grabbed a few stacks and

SOUL Publications

placed it inside his pocket. He locked his safe back up then headed towards my bedroom door.

"Take all your money so you won't have a reason to come back!" I called out to him. He turned around and grilled me.

"Why, so you and that lame-ass nigga can play house?" he asked.

"Ohhhh, now I'm playin' house? What the fuck do you call you and Lezzi?" I asked.

"Yo, why do you got an attitude wit' me? You mad 'cause I walked out of here dat night? I wanted to stay but you said you wanted to go to the strip club. You already know how I feel about dat strip club shit! No man wants his shorty shakin' their ass for a bunch of thirsty niggas. Truth is, you ain't ready for a relationship and neither am I. I'm cool wit' us just bein' friends and it ain't like we can get far, anyway," he said.

"You think you can talk to me any kind of way because you're fuckin' that bougie bitch? Guess what, Pistol? I was a muthafuckin' stripper when you were in here bangin' me out wit' raw dick! You left and came back, remember that? You didn't care about Lezzi, Delonte, my job or Glock! Just get the hell outta my house," I said and got up. He stopped me on my way to the bathroom in my bedroom. I tried to snatch away from him but he tightened his grip around my wrist.

"Watch yah fuckin' mouth, shorty. When a nigga tells you he ain't ready, believe him. It doesn't mean I don't have feelings for you. I'm just sayin' dat I can't give you what you want right now and you can't fully give me what I need. You would've stopped strippin' if you were ready for me, but you too comfortable wit' makin' fast money. I'm not feelin' it," he said. He pulled away from me and I stopped him—I needed him. It wasn't easy telling Pistol to leave. I pressed my body into his and grabbed his face so I could kiss him. He picked me up and I wrapped my legs around him. He untied my robe and laid me on the bed. A deep gasp slipped from my lips when his tongue plucked at my pink pearl. My lower body raised off the bed and he gripped my hips. I was only in a relationship for one week but to hell wit' it. Maybe we weren't good for each other at the moment, but he felt damn good doing intimate things to me.

"OHHHHHHHH," I groaned as I humped his face. I gripped his hair and fucked his tongue like my life depended on it. Pistol drove his tongue into me, tasting my juicy walls. My cum ran down his chin as he ate me out from front to back. I covered my mouth to keep from squealing as my legs trembled. He pulled away from me and wiped his face off. It had been weeks since we had sex and I couldn't wait any longer. Delonte's dick was good but Pistol's dick was a masterpiece. I helped him take off his shirt then tossed it to the corner of the bedroom. He took off his shoes, pants and boxer-briefs.

He laid on top of me and pressed his dick into my opening. Pistol grabbed my face and stuck his tongue down my throat as he entered me. He sucked my lips while working his big missile into my tightness. I wrapped my legs around his waist and he sped up. He grabbed my leg and placed it over his shoulder so he could dig deeper. He knew my body and how to stroke me. Some men's strokes were in and out, but not Pistol's. He moved his dick around like he was stirring something in a pot. He pressed further into my spot and grinded harder. I screamed his name as I came all over him. He used his thumb to stimulate my clit and I lost it. I was pulling my hair and his. My essence was splashing out of me.

"That lil' pussy squirtin', shorty," he moaned.

He came with me the third time I had an orgasm. Pistol laid on my chest and I wrapped my arms around him. He lifted his head up and stared into my eyes.

"'Your naked body should only belong to those who fall in love with your naked soul,'" Pistol quoted.

"Charlie Chaplin," I said and he kissed me.

"Damn, one day I'm gonna come up wit' one you can't figure out," he said.

"I know way more poems than you," I giggled. He pulled out of me to grab his ringing cell phone out of his pants pocket.

"Go home to Lezzi. I got what I wanted," I said.

"Shut up, that's my aunt calling to tell me she got my leftovers sitting on the counter. You can ride wit' me if you want to," he replied.

"Naw, that's okay. It won't look right taking me around your family if Lezzi been around them," I said.

"Shorty, Lezzi don't even know where my grandma lives. Go shower and throw some clothes on really quick," he replied.

I took the fastest shower I had ever taken in my life. Lezzi would shit a brick if she knew Pistol took me to his grandmother's house.

****

"Don't be slamming the fuckin' screen door!" a woman yelled when we walked into his grandmother's house. A heavy-set pretty woman walked around the corner wearing a flower house robe with a bonnet on her head.

"Damn, why you yelling? Nana is sleep," Pistol said to the woman.

"She's deaf when she's sleep. Who is this?" she asked, puffing on her cigarette.

"Piper, this is my aunt, Earlene. Earlene, this is my home girl, Piper," Pistol said.

"Humph, you mean a friend wit' benefits. That hickey on her neck is bigger than your forehead," she laughed. I covered my neck in embarrassment and Pistol chuckled.

"Damn, why you tell her it was there? I wanted her nigga to see it," Pistol said and his aunt laughed. I could tell they joked with each other a lot. She looked mean but she was down to earth.

"Who is your mother, chile? I probably went to school wit' her. You look familiar," Earlene said.

"Joyce is my mother," I replied.

"That one that hung wit' that nasty bitch, Darcel?" she asked.

"Yes, that's her," I replied.

"Joyce was a sweet woman but that Darcel was an evil bitch. She took advantage of Joyce and had that woman turning tricks for her so she could get high," Earlene said.

"Damn, Earlene. She knows what her mother was doing. Mind yah business," Pistol said.

"I'm just gossiping, shit. She better get used to me if you're gonna be bringing her around. I hope you usin' condoms, baby," Earlene said.

"Where my food at?" Pistol asked.

"On the counter. I'll heat it up for y'all and bring down to you. You want a Capri Sun, too?" she teased Pistol.

"Yeah, bring five of 'em down witchu," Pistol said.

He opened up a door in the hallway and I followed him down the stairs. He cut on the light and I was shocked. The basement was set up like an apartment. He even had his own kitchen. On the wall was a big TV with a gaming entertainment center underneath. It was spotless minus the shoes he had sprawled out over the floor.

"This is a nice place," I said.

"Yeah, I still stay here. I go home sometimes but I always come back here," he replied.

"That's because you are spoiled. It's your aunt's fault," I said.

"My aunt and grandmother raised me. My mother was a stripper and they found her body in a hotel room when I was an infant. A man killed her because she was trying to steal a nigga's money while he was sleep. I don't know shit about my father. My aunt said he was a rich kid or something like that but he ain't want to be a part of my life because of who had a kid by," he replied.

"Why did you turn to the streets? You were raised in a decent home," I said.

"My grandmother and aunt were workaholics, so I started doin' me. Newtowne is only a few blocks over, so it ain't hard to fall into the trap when you're young," he replied. His phone rang and he turned it off. I laid across the couch and he threw a blanket over me. His place was so cozy, I almost fell asleep but Earlene came downstairs with our food. She cooked oxtail stew, cabbage, macaroni and cheese, fried chicken and a sweet potato casserole.

She sat the tray of food in front of us on the coffee table along with Pistol's Capri Suns.

"Aight, I'm ready to take my ass to bed. Holla at me if you need anything, and it was nice meeting you, Piper," she said.

"Nice meeting you, too, and thanks for the food," I replied. She kissed Pistol's forehead and he was embarrassed. Earlene laughed at him as she headed up the stairs.

"Come here, baby. Let Mommy feed you," I said to Pistol and he grabbed his dick.

"Naw, but I can feed you this sausage, though. Fuck outta here wit' dat bullshit, shorty," he chuckled. He grabbed a plate and sat next to me on the couch. I reached for it and he pulled away from me.

"I got dis, now open up wide, so I can see how flexible those jaws are," he said with a forkful of cabbage. I opened my mouth and he fed me.

"Damn, this is good," I said.

Fifteen minutes later, I was stuffed and could barely move. I fell asleep on the couch while watching TV.

****

"Shorty, wake up!" Pistol shook me. I sat up and looked around, realizing I was still at his house.

"What time is it?" I asked.

"Five o'clock. I gotta take you home because we have to be at the airport in a few hours," he said.

"And Lezzi is really going?" I asked.

"Yeah, ain't your old head goin'?" he asked and I rolled my eyes. I stood up from off the couch and stretched. Pistol pulled at my leggings and I smacked his hand away.

"Don't be stingy now. All I need is fifteen minutes," he said.

"I'm not messing around with you. Get your punk-ass up and take me home or should I call a cab?" I asked.

"Naw, you ain't gotta do all dat," he said, sliding my leggings down. I straddled him after he took my panties off. He tapped my butt so I could lift up; he pulled his meaty dick out of his pants. I rode Pistol until we both exploded.

Thirty minutes later, Pistol pulled up into my driveway. It was almost six o'clock and Delonte was going to meet me at my house. Pistol cut the car off and sat quietly for a while.

"Let me guess. You regret us again," I said.

"Naw, it ain't dat. I'on know how I'm gonna act wit' your bitch-ass nigga around, but he yah man so I gotta respect it," he replied. I leaned over and kissed his lips.

"We can sneak off. Just think about how erotic it'll be to fuck on a beach while everyone is asleep," I said and he smirked.

"Yo, get yah cheatin' ass out my whip," he said and playfully mushed me. I grabbed my purse and got out of his car. He called out to me as I unlocked the front door.

"Take a few stacks out the safe and treat yourself while you down there," he said.

"I got my own money," I replied.

"And? What does dat have to do wit' me, baby girl?" he asked.

"Thanks, now get outta my driveway before I climb on your lap," I said and he licked his laps.

"Aight, I'll get up witchu lata," he said. I stood in the doorway and watched Pistol back out of my driveway before he pulled off.

Damn, I love his fine ass, I thought.

I ran upstairs to my bathroom and got into the shower. When I got out, I dried off and put make-up around my neck. Delonte rang the doorbell while I was getting dressed in a sweat suit. I opened the door and he came in to grab my luggage.

"Do we have time for breakfast?" he asked.

"Not really. We can eat at the airport," I said.

He walked out the door to put my things inside his trunk. I went upstairs to grab my purse, coat and the money Pistol wanted me to have.

Damn, I know Delonte gonna want to have sex. Ummmm, maybe I can grab my tampons so he can think I'm on my period. Yup, dats what I'm fittin' to do, I thought.

Beretta

St. Croix...

"This place is beautiful!" Mara said, looking around our suite. We had a room on the beach. She opened the sliding doors and stepped out onto the patio. I went to the bathroom so I could piss. I had been holding it since we left the airport.

"BERETTTAAAAAAAAA! HELP ME!" Mara screamed as I shook my dick off. I ran out of the bathroom. Mara was standing on a chair, throwing stones at an iguana. Matter of fact, there were four iguanas lounging around in the shade. I pulled out my phone and recorded her.

"Stop fuckin' recordin' me and kill them!" she screamed.

"What's da matter, shorty? What you want daddy to do?" I teased.

"I need to pee! Please, just get it! ARRGHHHHHHHH, it's crawling towards me!" she screamed.

"They ain't gonna fuck witchu, shorty. This place got a lot of 'em so you can't be scared. Get down and walk past it. I'll kill it if it comes near you," I replied. Mara rolled her eyes at me and crossed her arms.

"I'm stayin' up here," she said and I shrugged my shoulders.

"Prove to me dat you trust me. Comere," I replied.

Mara slowly stepped down off the chair and tip-toed past the iguana. She hauled ass into the suite once she got past it. I went in after her and closed the doors.

"Listen to yah man, shorty," I chuckled.

"You just wanted to fuck wit' me," she said, fanning herself.

"You gotta face your fears," I replied.

"Practice what you preach," she said.

"I don't eva wanna face what I fear. I might fuck around and merk everybody," I replied. She got undressed and laid across the bed underneath the ceiling fan.

"What is it?" she asked.

"Losing you. That's sumthin I can't accept and you know dat," I replied.

"Don't do nothing to lose me, plain and simple. But in the meantime, bring yah ass over here and rub my feet.

SOUL Publications

My ass hasn't run like that in a long time. A bitch can't breathe," she said. I sat on the bed and Mara placed her feet in my lap.

"Squeeze it a little harder," she moaned. I massaged her feet while her eyes were closed. The Amona and Moesha situation was on my mind and I wanted to tell her, but I wasn't sure if I was ready for that. Mara would think I was a dog-ass nigga if she knew I fucked another bitch right after we lost our daughter.

"What's bothering you?" she asked.

"What you mean?" I replied.

"You have been quiet lately. Talk to me," she said and pulled her feet away from me.

"I'm straight," I lied and she twisted her lips up.

"We can wait to get married," she replied.

"Naw, I'm not havin' any regrets on makin' you my wife and you already know dat," I said and she kissed my lips.

"I can't wait to be your wife. I'm gonna Harlem shake down the aisle. Oh, babbbyyyyy, I'm showin' my ass!" she said. Mara was happy but a nigga was stressed the fuck out! I kept thinking about Moesha and her baby bump. What would I do if I was the father? I couldn't see myself being a deadbeat, but at the same time, the bitch did it on her own. I would only take full responsibility if I willingly fucked her. Mara was saying something to me but I wasn't paying attention until she slapped my shoulder.

"Do you hear me talkin' to you? Would it be too soon to call Earlene back to check up on Zalia?" Mara asked.

"You called her on our way to the resort. Yo, let her do her thing," I replied.

I ain't fuckin' another broad again! This shit is stressful, I thought.

"Come take a shower wit' me," Mara said.

She took my shirt off and I helped her with my pants. We walked into the spacious bathroom and Mara fell in love with it.

"I want a house that has this layout. Just think how lovely it'll be to feel like you're on an island twenty-four-seven," she said.

"I gotchu," I replied.

She turned the water on in the shower then stepped in. I closed the door after I got in with her. Mara got down on her knees and it had me puzzled because shorty didn't suck dick. It was a problem in the beginning, but after a while, I just chalked it up for what it was.

"You lost an earring or sumthin?" I asked and she looked at me with lust-filled eyes.

"Teach me how to do it," she replied. My dick instantly got hard. Seeing Mara on her knees for me almost made me bust one off. She held my dick in her hand, close to her pretty full lips.

"Remember those popsicles you were craving when you were pregnant with Zyira? Wrap your lips around it without using your teeth and dats it," I said. Mara wrapped her lips around the tip of my dick and closed her eyes. She was scared but I tapped her face and told her to loosen up.

"Ease it in, shorty. Yeah, just like that," I groaned. Mara put my dick a little too far back and it made her gag. I tried to pull away from her but she held on to it and tried it again. It took a while for it to feel good because she had to adjust to it. She started bobbing her head and I gripped her hair.

"FUCK!" I groaned. I played with her breasts and she moaned.

"Play with your pussy, baby," I said.

Most females would suck the skin off a nigga dick if she was turned on by it. Mara parted her pussy lips and rubbed her clit. Her mouth got wetter and she was able to put me in her throat.

"Suck dat shit!" I said, slowly pumping into her mouth. My back was against the glass wall and the steam made everything inside the bathroom foggy. Mara's breathing got deeper and I knew she was on the verge of cumming. Watching her please us made a nigga explode. My nut shot into her mouth as I pulled her hair. She kept sucking my dick and I forgot to tell her that she was supposed to stop after I came. I almost snatched Mara's head off her shoulders because she was still deep throating my sensitive dick.

"OWWWW!" she yelled out.

I wasn't done yet, though. I got down on the floor with her and pushed her legs back. She gasped when I slipped my tongue into her pussy. Mara's pussy kissed back. Her walls squeezed my tongue and I wrapped my lips around her clit. She pulled at my dreads while moaning my name.

"Stop being shy wit' it, Mara!" I said. She knew what I meant by that. I wanted shorty to ride my tongue and hold my face down in it. She pressed my face into her pussy and wrapped her legs around my neck. My lips gripped her pussy lips as I lifted her bottom up. She trembled when my tongue curved into her. Mara's pussy gushed onto my lips and down my beard. I pulled away from her then laid on top of her. She placed me inside of her then wrapped her legs around me. Her succulent breasts were pressed against my chest; her nipples were swollen.

"Baby, you feel so good," she moaned in my ear. I went deeper, pressing against her G-spot. My dick was so hard it felt like I took a Viagra. I raised up a little bit so I could wrap my mouth around her nipple. Her nails dug into my shoulders while I drilled into her. Her mouth was gaped open, but her moan got caught up in her throat and silenced her. Mara's eyes rolled to the back of her head. I fucked her harder, repeatedly ramming my dick into her spot. She spread her legs wider; she wanted me to go deeper. Mara knew that shit made her cry, but fuck it, she wanted it. I slid the rest of my dick into her and hammered shorty. Her moans got louder and my strokes got deeper. My dick was beating like a heartbeat as the blood rushed to the tip of my head. Mara's pussy squeezed me as she came. My body jerked as I empty my seeds into her.

The water was cold, so we took a fast shower. Everyone was meeting up on the beach for a boat lunch party. I wasn't in the mood to go but Mara almost took a nigga head off. All I wanted to do was sleep.

"You tired me out," I said.

"We can sleep when we come back to the room. I'm ready to get drunk and have fun. This is exactly what I needed," she said, while putting on her lip gloss. We left our suite after she was finished getting dressed. Lezzi and Pistol were in the hallway arguing about something. Mara sucked her teeth and I squeezed her hand. Mara wasn't feeling Lezzi because she didn't fuck with Piper. Mara didn't know Lezzi and Amona were related. I didn't want Lezzi to come but shorty would've started some shit if I told her she couldn't. Basically, a nigga was in a fucked-up situation!

"Y'all should've kept that bullshit in Annapolis," Mara said and I grilled her.

"Yeah, you right," Pistol said and Lezzi rolled her eyes.

"Leave your phone in the room. Why do you need it? We talked about this on the airplane. You said this trip was going to help our relationship," Lezzi said and Mara giggled. Lezzi cut her eyes at Mara and Pistol shook his head.

"You should be the last one to laugh," Lezzi said to Mara.

"And you should've stayed your ass home because we don't like you. You're not a part of this family. Far as I'm concerned, you're the picture girl. Carry on, Lezzi. You don't want me to go there wit' you. Enjoy the sun and the free trip," Mara said. Shorty's mouth was reckless and she knew it.

"This ain't the only free trip I've been on. Ain't that right, Pistol?" Lezzi laughed then walked down the hall.

"My bad about dat, bruh. Lezzi mad because Piper is wearing a two-piece outfit. She caught a nigga lookin," Pistol chuckled.

"Y'all muthafuckas are sneaky," Mara said and walked off.

"I think I'm gonna send Lezzi home in the morning. Shorty got some loose screws. I left to get a bucket of ice and was only gone for a minute. She said I went to Piper's suite and fucked her. She knows damn well, Piper got dat old ass nigga wit' her. But don't worry about her saying sumthin about Amona. I told her from the rip that I'll leave her dumb ass homeless if she starts dat snitchin' shit," Pistol said.

"Mannnn, that situation not on my mind right now. Moesha claiming I'm the father to her son," I whispered and Pistol's face dropped.

"Damn, yo. So, what you thinkin' about doin'? Calling the wedding off?" he asked.

"And embarrass Mara so Lezzi can talk about dat shit to Amona? Naw, fam. I can't do it. I'on know how to tell her," I said.

"Don't tell her until you know for sure that's your seed. Ammo said Moesha was a sneaky broad, but damn. Shorty out here trappin' niggas. Look, bruh, just marry your shorty and move on wit' yo life," he replied. The shit was easier said than done but fuck it. I couldn't turn back the hands of time and change what I did. All I could do was become a better man.

Kemara

"**W**here is Quanta?" I asked Emma.

"I don't know what's goin' on wit' him. I think he got himself in some type of street beef. He's been wearing bulletproof vests and stayin' out all night. We just got back together and now this bullshit. Look, don't worry about me. I wasn't gonna miss your big day. I snuck away and turned my phone off because he's gonna be pissed once he realizes I came by myself," she said. Piper, Thickems, Silk and Delonte headed towards us.

"Is that Emma?" Piper called out and Emma covered her mouth. Emma held her arms open and Piper hugged her. Piper hadn't seen Emma since high school. I made plans for all of us to hang out a few times, but so many things got in the way.

"Bittccchhhhhhh, what happened? Look at you," Piper said in excitement.

"I don't remember you havin' all that ass," Emma said to Piper.

"These are my friends, Thickems and Silk. Delonte is Piper's boyfriend and, everybody, this is my high school friend, Emma. Well, we go to the same college now," I said. Thickems waved and Silk snatched his shades off.

"I'm about to have another baby mama. Toes pretty, titties nice and round. Got a cute face and a bubble butt. Oh, yes, hunty! I'm goin' raw," Silk said and Emma giggled.

"I like him," Emma said.

"Chile, please don't tell him dat," Thickems said.

"Stop hatin'. You were actin' stingy, so I had to move on," Silk joked with Thickems. Beretta and a few of his homeboys walked over towards us. It was almost time to get on the boat. I introduced him to Emma and he gave her a dry "what's up." Beretta was acting different for the past week. I figured he was nervous about marrying me because it was a big step. A few times I told him we could wait but he didn't want to. Sniper and Machete brought dates with them. Machete's girlfriend was around eighteen years old. I had been around her a few times. She was quiet but very hood. Her name was Zain. She had peanut butter-colored skin and always wore her hair in braids. She also wore glasses and was a little on the thick side. Maryland niggas didn't discriminate when it came to plus-sized women. Sniper's date was Zain's sister, Kellan. She was older than Zain by two years. Zain and her sister looked like twins, the only difference was her sister was slimmer. Kellan was loud but she was cool.

"Maraaaaaaaa," Kellan sang and smacked her lips. She was always extra and dragged her words when she talked.

SOUL Publications

"Kellllaannnnnn," I mimicked and she hugged me. Kellan reminded me Shenaynay's best friend off Martin, Bonquita.

"Ugh, bitch. Why you gotta be so extra?" Zain asked and Kellan rolled her eyes.

"Because I'm on this beautiful island with some beautiful people and a bitch is vibin' right now. Look, girl, don't you start actin' like my mama," Kellan complained.

One of the staff members on the resort made us mixed drinks while we waited for the boat. It was the most fun I had in a long time, minus Piper and Lezzi throwing shade at each other.

****

The boat was big enough to hold fifty people. We had music, bottles of champagne and our food was on the table buffet-style with five waitresses serving us. I sat on Beretta's lap with my eyes closed because I was getting sea sick.

"Yo, we only been on the boat for ten minutes," Beretta said.

"I know but I had a few drinks on the beach. I'm a little tipsy," I giggled. He slipped his blunt between my lips and told me to hit it a few times so I could relax.

"Feel better now?" he asked.

"A little bit. Let me hit it again," I said and he gave me a shot gun. Me and Beretta was in our own world while everyone else was cracking jokes and dancing to the music. He slid his hand under my dress and realized I didn't have on anything underneath.

"Oh, you really tryna get turned out, huh?" he asked.

"We should go to the bathroom," I giggled.

"Yo, you know damn well you ain't tryna let all these muthafuckas hear all dat noise," he said. His hand brushed against my clit and I wanted it right there. I purposely didn't wear any panties.

"Damn, shorty. You drippin' wet," he said. I closed my eyes and he kissed my neck while his fingers rubbed my pussy.

"Ewwwww," Piper said and I smacked Beretta's hand away. Beretta threw his head back and roared in laughter.

"Yo, you worse than a hood roach. Da fuck you want, Pipe?" Beretta asked.

"I just came over here to check up on Mara. Y'all can finish dat later," Piper said and sat next to us. She pulled a blunt out of her purse and lit it up.

"Bitch, I know you ain't gonna interrupt us like dat. Go grab Pistol and take him to the bathroom or sumthin," I replied. Tears welled up in Piper's eyes and a few of them fell.

"Lezzi in the bathroom suckin' Pistol's dick. Kellan walked in on them by mistake and told Silk and he told me. I'm so mad right now! I wanna knock dat bitch over the rail so she can drown," Piper said.

"You popped a pill, didn't you?" I asked.

"You thought I was gonna be sober on a boat ride wit' Lezzi and Pistol?" Piper asked.

"Can you talk to Pistol for me?" I asked Beretta.

"Hell nawl! They shouldn't be fuckin' around, anyway," Beretta replied.

"Glock is not around and he has a woman. That's y'all niggas problem now. Always wanting the whole cake. Pistol actin' like a fuck-nigga," I said.

"How? Piper brought her father wit' her. Look at the nigga, he the oldest one here. The muthafucka chaperoning us on a field trip with those wide-ass cab driver sandals. I'm swagging like yo when I turn sixty," Beretta replied and Piper got mad.

"Fuck you, Beretta. That's why you eat cats," Piper said.

"The only cat I eat is right here, shorty. I'on know why you tryna clown my Asian roots, anyway. That shit is dead, shorty," Beretta said. He didn't like for anyone to bring up his Chinese and Hawaiian roots. Let him tell it, he was one-hundred percent black. I think it had a lot to do with Nika. It's almost like he didn't want any parts of her.

"All jokes aside. You don't see me all over Delonte," Piper said.

"Well, you betta get to it so he can feel the disrespect," I replied.

"Tit for tat gets niggas merked, Mara," Beretta warned me.

"And so does playin' wit' a bitch's heart," I spat.

"I'm not gonna argue witchu because you sound dumb right now. So, you mean to tell me, if a nigga fucks up then his bitch should cheat on him?" he asked.

"Yeah," I replied.

"Aight," he said.

"How else would he know how much damage he's done if he doesn't get the same treatment? Y'all niggas don't understand until a bitch gets ignant. We ask simple questions and y'all lie about it. So I'mma pop this pussy for a real nigga," Piper said.

"I'm ready to get sumthin to eat. You want sumthin?" Beretta asked when he slid from underneath me.

"Yeah, you can bring me a plate," I replied. He got up and walked away.

"Damn, he in his feelings. I always joke with Beretta," Piper said.

"I think he's nervous about our wedding. He's been acting strange for a week now," I replied. Thickems and Emma joined me on the lounging couch.

"Girl, this day party is lit! I needed this," Thickems said.

"Me, too," Emma replied.

Silk came over with a tray of drinks for us and they weren't mixed drinks. He brought us straight vodka shots.

"Let's make a toast to Mara becoming a wife!" Silk said. I picked up my drink and downed it. He handed me two more and they cheered me on.

"That's right, babbbbyyyyy! Get white-girl wasted!" Piper yelled out. Beretta didn't come back with my plate but I wasn't tripping. I was too busy throwing back shots.

Beretta

"**F**uck the Patriots," Pistol said.

We were chilling on the other end of the boat while the females were on the other side. Pistol brought up football and the nigga stayed in his feelings about it.

"Bruh, fuck the Redskins. You the only nigga I know dat fuck wit' dat sorry-ass team," Machete said.

"I'm an older nigga and I gotta agree wit' em," Delonte said.

"Y'all can say what y'all want because I'm ridin' with the Redskins for life," Pistol said.

"We still crushed y'all, though," I said and he brushed me off.

"Fuck all dat football talk. I can't believe bruh gettin' married," Sniper said.

"He about to be the only young nigga in Annapolis wit' a wife," Machete teased.

"Age ain't nothing but a number," Delonte said.

"Is dat why you fuck wit' shorty?" Pistol asked.

"It takes a real man to show a woman her worth. Piper is young but she's ready for what I can bring to the table. I'm a legit businessman and ain't in trouble wit' the law. I'm more than qualified, youngin'," Delonte chuckled.

"How much is her worth, bruh? Did she meet your friends or family yet?" Pistol asked.

"You got sumthin you wanna get off your chest?" Delonte asked, getting heated.

"Naw, fam. You ain't gotta get all swole and shit," Pistol chuckled.

"Fuck all that. I see the way you look at her. You got some shit you need to get off your chest?" Delonte asked again.

"Damn, nigga, he just asked a question. All we want is an answer. Did Piper meet your family yet? You older so school us on some shit. It's nothing but respect," Sniper said.

"He hurt 'cause da only family Piper met was the strippers that work for him. You ain't gotta front for me, nigga. It is what it is," Pistol replied.

"Nigga, you're a kid to me. I ain't gotta explain shit to you or nobody else. Y'all think I'm intimidated by a bunch of niggas with tattoos? Naw, y'all niggas don't know me," Delonte said and stood up. Pistol was fucking with him but Delonte got serious.

"Yo, you tryna fight or sumthin?" Pistol asked then stood up.

"Y'all niggas had too much to drink," Machete said.

"We don't know you, bruh. But ain't nobody gonna remember you if you keep flexin' on us niggas like we can't make shit happen. And as long as you got those sandals on your feet, my nigga, we can't take you seriously. Yo, just sit down and chill da fuck out," I replied.

Piper came over to our side to see what was up with Delonte.

"What's goin' on?" Piper asked.

"Your nigga had too much to drink and caught a bitch fit. Nigga sassier than Mara when she was pregnant," I replied.

"Da fuck you just say to me?" Delonte asked.

Machete and Sniper was ready to close in on him but I shook my head at them.

"We good, Piper. We were just havin' a lil' man talk and homeboy couldn't handle the question. Everybody a little fucked up, so he's straight for now," I replied. Delonte walked off and headed to the upper level of the boat. Piper cursed us out.

"I know damn well y'all didn't threaten him! Beretta, I know you started it!" she yelled at me.

"Yo, shut da fuck up. We were lookin' out for you," Pistol said.

"Where were y'all at when Glock was lyin' to me? Nobody was lookin' out for me then," she said.

"Glock is family and you don't snitch on family! Bottom fuckin' line!" Pistol said.

"Well, your loyalty ain't genuine and we both know dat," Piper replied. Pistol was heated! Those words had to cut him because he was a loyal dude, but the shit just happened. She must've realized it, too, because she apologized but Pistol wasn't trying to hear it. He walked away from her.

"I didn't mean to say dat," Piper said, feeling embarrassed.

"He'll be aight. Pistol was sippin' a little bit and you know he ain't a drinker like dat," I replied.

Mara came over to me and sat on my lap. I forgot all about her food. She was talking out the side of her neck, so I ended up chilling with my niggas to take my mind off everything.

"This boat is everything! Babe, we should get one," she said.

"And put it where?" I chuckled.

"I don't know but I'm gonna work my ass off to help get us a big house by a lake. You just wait until I finish college," she said.

See, shit like that was eating me up on the inside. No other female had a mindset like Mara. But I was saving everything she was telling me in my mind. Mara wanted a big house by a lake with a boat. That was a lot but I was gonna grind harder so she could have it all.

"You got it all figured out," I replied.

"I want it all, Z'wan," she said.

I don't know how long we were sitting there looking out into the sea but the heavy feeling on my chest was getting heavier.

"Shorty, I gotta tell you sumthin," I said but she didn't respond. I looked down and Mara was asleep.

Damn! I thought.

Piper

It was ten o'clock at night by the time we made it back to the resort. We were on the boat all day and I was exhausted. Delonte went into the bathroom and slammed the door. He wasn't talking to me and had been ignoring me since he got into it with Pistol. It was a mistake to bring him and it was selfish of me. He would've stayed home if Lezzi didn't go. I got undressed for the shower. The heat, liquor and weed smoke had me feeling dirty.

Delonte came out of the bathroom with a few of his things.

"What is goin' on?" I asked as I watched him put them inside his duffel bag.

"Answer me! Where in da hell are you goin'?" I asked.

"Home! You ain't slick, Piper. You brought me here because that little lowlife muthafucka got that bougie-ass bitch with him. What type of games are you playin'? You tellin' him our business? How does he know you haven't met my family yet? I can't get mad, though, I shouldn't be fuckin' a young bitch, anyway," he said.

"You're insecure! Pistol talks shit all the time. All of them do but I can't believe you're about to run away like some punk bitch! Stand the fuck up, Delonte, and own up to your shit. And since we're pulling cards, how about I call you out on some bullshit. The only reason you wanted me to be your girlfriend was because you felt threatened by Pistol. If you really wanted me, how are you okay with me walking around half-naked and showin' my ass and titties to everyone at YOUR club? You talk a lot of game, you know dat? You're so quick to put yourself on this pedestal but you ain't shit yourself," I replied and he laughed.

"The real hood bitch is comin' out of you, but it's all good. Now all of sudden you got morals and care about how people look at you. That's the reason why I liked you because I thought you didn't give a fuck about what anybody else thinks, including that nigga, Pistol. I guess he told you what you wanted to hear to get inside of you. Well, obviously it didn't work because he's still banging that fat bitch. You will never be more than another man's trash. You hop from one dick to another, looking for hope, but you ain't gonna find it. I was tryin' to show you but you'd rather have some drug-dealin' project baby that ain't gonna do you any good but keep you as his side bitch. That's what you want? Go ahead and go for it because I'm too old for this bullshit. Got me out here on an over-expensive island with a bunch of niggas that don't even pay taxes," Delonte vented.

"Just get outta my room," I said and walked past him. Delonte followed me into the bathroom.

"I'm sorry, Piper. I didn't mean to yell at you like that. You know that isn't me but those clowns tried to gang up on me. I'll tell you what, I'll spend time wit' you but I'm not goin' to that wedding or doin' anything else wit' them kids," he said. I closed the shower door and Delonte left the bathroom. I wanted to love him. I needed something different but my heart just wasn't in it. What was I supposed to do? Let go of a good man to get my heart broken? Pistol seemed perfect for me, but was he?

I waited until Delonte was sound asleep and snuck out of our suite. I texted Pistol's phone and told him to meet me by the large rocks at the end of the beach.

****

Pistol was sitting on a rock, smoking a blunt, when I walked up on him. He was shirtless and his chocolate skin glistened under the moonlight. The sounds of the waves were relaxing. I sat next to him and rested my head on his shoulder.

"My fault about dat shit earlier," he said.

"Mine, too. I think everyone was in their feelings because of the liquor," I chuckled. He looked at me then caressed my face with his thumbs.

"I'm leavin' Lezzi," Pistol said.

"Huh?" I asked.

"Yeah, I'm not goin' back home when I get back. I told her I'll pay the rent up for a year and her car note, but after that, she's on her own. I tried to work it out with shorty but I can't. I slipped up and called her your name while she was giving me head. Relationships just ain't my thing," he replied.

"I like Delonte and I think I should give him a chance. He doesn't deserve what I've been doin' to him," I said.

"That's what's up. I can't hold you on dat one, shorty. So, go ahead and see what's dat about first. You'll come back if it's meant to be," he said.

"What are you tryna tell me?" I asked.

"I'm tellin' you to not settle if it's sumthin better out there for you. I want you to be happy. Shit feels perfect when you're sneaking around. What if I get witchu and turn out to be the kind of man you hate? I gotta know if that's not what this is. Bomb-ass sex can make niggas think they in love and I'm tryna catch the real thing, ya feel me?" he asked.

"I was thinkin' about dat, too," I replied and he smirked.

"Go back to your man, baby girl. I'm about to roll up another blunt and enjoy the view. You don't see shit like this in da hood so you gotta appreciate it when you do," he said. I kissed his lips then pulled away from him.

"Good night, Olijah," I said.

"Be easy," he replied.

When I walked away from Pistol, it felt like I was walking away for good. I almost got choked up but I held it in. Lezzi was sitting on a lounge chair drinking a glass of wine on the beach.

"You just couldn't wait, huh? Tell me sumthin, why do hoes like you always get everything? All you're good for is spreadin' your legs. How far will stripping get you? You have a good man but you're chasing after someone else's man. You will get everything that's comin' your way. I hope Delonte sees you for the piece of trash you are," Lezzi said.

"You're so mad at me that you don't realize how disgusting it makes you look. You're callin' me a hoe but you tolerated Pistol's shit because he was payin' for your dumbness. You ain't no different than me, bitch. Only thing you're missin' is a pole. You thought because you have a job dat it means sumthin'. Honey, I neva needed a nigga to take care of me, but you do. Girl, eat a fuckin' cookie and go to bed because you tried it. Got the nerve to call me a hoe but fuckin' and suckin' for a roof over your head. Fix yo' life before you try to read me, bitch!" I said and walked away.

Delonte was snoring when I slid the door back to our suite. I dropped my beach cover-up and got into bed with him naked. I couldn't go to sleep as I stared at the ceiling fan. All I could think about was Pistol, but I had to do what was best for me by making sure I wasn't going to regret us.

Kemara

"**B**abe, wake up!" Beretta shook me.

"I just wanna stay sleep!" I replied and he pulled the covers back. He snatched them off then gave me a hard smack on the ass.

"Damn it!" I yelled out ready to fuck him up.

"Nigga, what is wrong witchu? I'm muthafuckin' tired. You had me up until five o' clock this morning," I said and rolled back over.

"That's 'cause yah ass was actin' like a lil' freak. You kept throwin' the pussy at me," he said. Beretta wasn't lying about that one. I couldn't keep my legs closed around him. The way he touched me, looked at me and some of the shit he said, sent me over the edge. He was fine as hell, too; I couldn't get enough of him.

"Boy, get gone," I laughed.

"You were ridin' my dick like you wanted a baby," he said and I blushed.

"What time is it?" I asked.

"Time to go scuba diving," he replied.

"Nigga, our black asses ain't doin' that shit," I said.

"I kicked out close to forty g's for all of this, shorty. I'll jump down a fuckin' volcano and swim wit' sharks to get my money's worth. You betta get your chubby ass up and dive wit' yah man," he said.

"My weave might get wet," I replied.

Beretta went into the bathroom and grabbed a small plastic bag.

"Want me wrap it around your head fah you?" he asked and I screamed with laughter.

"Get away from me," I said and climbed out of bed.

"Dats what I'm talkin' about, baby girl!" he said in excitement.

"You're a big ass kid," I replied.

He came in the bathroom with me and wrapped his arms around my waist. He licked the side of my neck and I tried to pull away from him.

"We ain't goin' nowhere if you keep that up," I replied. He grabbed my hair and pulled my head back. I bit my bottom lip when I felt his dick press against my ass cheeks.

"I think you slipped Viagra into my water," he said.

"Boy, if you don't hush and hurry up before I change mind," I replied.

And just like that, I was bent over the sink for our morning quickie.

****

"Where is Delonte?" I asked Piper.

We were all going on the excursion but Delonte and Lezzi were nowhere to be found. I wasn't tripping about Lezzi because her presence wasn't a good one.

"He's in the room. We'll talk about it later," she said.

"Ummm, I'm scared about this," Emma said.

"Don't be, you can stay on the boat. I don't want to do it, neither, but Beretta is too damn excited about this. I don't even know how to swim," I replied.

"Well, I'm takin' pictures. But if I see a fine ass man in the water, chilllleeeeee, you can call me the Little Mermaid. Bitch, I'm deep diving," Silk said and we laughed.

"I can't wait to see these niggas in scuba gear 'cause, hunntyyyyy, those pants are tight and they show everything! So, it's a good thing Delonte ain't coming because he walks like he got a little wee wee. No man on this Earth is wearing sandals with the strap in the back wit' a big dick. Sorry," Silk said and Piper slapped his arm.

"Delonte is packin'! Y'all just can't accept grown-man swag," Piper said.

"I thought they were classy. My father and his friends have a pair," Emma said.

"Delonte has an old soul," Piper laughed.

Two small boats came to shore to pick all of us up.

"We missin' two people," Beretta said.

"Lezzi ain't comin," Pistol replied.

"What's up wit' yah man? He comin'? We about to leave," Beretta said to Piper.

"Naw, he isn't comin'," she replied.

"Because of dat shit from yesterday? Bruh needs some flowers or sumthin?" Beretta asked, getting annoyed.

"He doesn't want to be around y'all non-tax payin' asses," Piper laughed.

"Oh, word? Fuck dat clown-ass nigga then. The government ain't gonna do shit but make life easier for rich folks anyway with our money. Fuck Uncle Sam," Beretta said before he walked off.

"Delonte said that?" I asked Piper.

"Yeah," she said.

"But his strippers don't pay taxes, neither. I guess he cool wit' dat since his lame ass makin' a profit off of 'em. And to think the whole time I was feelin' sorry for him," I said.

"Delonte doesn't know what to say. He threw the bible at me last night and read my ass scriptures but it's cool. He just gonna be lonely the rest of the trip," she replied.

"Kemara! Is that you?" a voice called out.

I turned around and was greeted by my twelfth-grade boyfriend, Carl, but his nickname was Chevy. They called him "Chevy" in school because he was fascinated with old-school Chevys. Our relationship was a short-lived one. Matter of fact, it only lasted for five months. I lost my virginity to him on prom night and afterwards, I dumped him. He didn't give me the same sparks Beretta gave me. I thought it was going to be special but it was quick sex that meant nothing to me. Chevy wasn't a hood boy, but he wasn't a square, either. He was a pretty boy that was into fashion. Chevy was a little shorter than Beretta, probably standing at six feet even. He had gray eyes, full lips and a cute gap. His hair was cut low in deep waves and he had a few tattoos. He was light-skinned but his skin had a golden tint to it.

"Oh, hey, Chevy," I waved.

He ran over to me and hugged me.

"Damn, shorty. I haven't seen you since prom night. What have you been up to? It's crazy running into you here. My bad, what's up Piper?" he asked then hugged her.

"Hey, Chevy. What's goin' on witchu?" Piper asked.

"Came here on a family vacation. We come here every year for my grandparents' anniversary. Y'all still terrorizing shit?" he asked.

"Naw, we chillin' now," I said.

"You still beautiful. You must be aging backwards because you looked older in school," he said.

"Thank you. You don't look bad yourself," I replied.

"What you doin' later? Wanna grab a bite to eat and go to the beach party?" he asked. Thickems cleared her throat and Emma's eyes were looking in another direction. Silk took off running but I wasn't surprised. Silk had issues.

"Who da fuck is dat nigga?" Beretta asked when he walked back over to me.

"Oh, um this is Chevy," I replied and he looked at him.

"The boat is loading us up now," Piper said. She grabbed Emma's arm and rushed her away. They left me standing there between my ex-boyfriend and my fiancé.

"So, I'll see you at the beach later?" Chevy asked me.

"Naw, nigga, you won't," Beretta said.

"Oh, my bad, are you her man or sumthin? I ain't know, bruh," Chevy said.

"He's my fiancé," I replied, and with that, he walked away.

"What's up wit' dat, shorty? Who is dat nigga?" Beretta asked.

"My boyfriend from high school," I replied.

"The one dat took your virginity?" he asked.

"Yeah," I replied.

"He asked you out, huh?" Beretta asked and smirked.

"Are you jealous?" I teased.

"Oh, you think dat shit funny? But I ain't trippin' because I broke dat hymen. Y'all was just pants rubbing," he said.

"Boy, come on," I said and grabbed his hand. Everyone else was on the boat but us.

****

"How many times you fucked dat nigga?" Beretta asked.

"You still talkin' about dat?" I replied.

We were getting dressed to dive but Beretta wasn't excited about it anymore.

"Yo, Mara, don't play wit' me. Dat nigga was all up in your face smilin' like y'all know sumthin else," he said and I smacked my teeth.

"It was once and it only lasted for a few minutes if that, now let it go," I replied.

Beretta took off his shirt and sweat dripped down his tatted abs. He didn't want a swimsuit. He only wanted the head gear to breathe under water. Matter of fact, all of the guys didn't want to wear the tight suits. I took my cover-up off and was wearing a two-piece shorts bathing suit. The high waist shorts covered the stretch marks I had on my stomach from my pregnancy. The tour guys that worked on the resort gave us rules before we dived in.

"Come on, Mara. Go under the water," Beretta said, holding me up.

"NO! I can't do it! Put me back on the boat!" I panicked when I saw fish swimming under my feet. Silk was sipping a margarita while taking pictures of us.

"I'm so scared. How deep is it?" I asked.

"Only four feet," Beretta lied.

"Nigga, how is it four feet?" I asked, getting mad.

"It's forty feet Mara!" Silk instigated.

"Once you go under, the fear will go away. Trust me," the tour guy said.

"Aight, close your eyes," Beretta said with his arms wrapped around me. I closed one of my eyes and he pinched my thighs.

"Close your eyes, shorty. The sun is tearing my back up," he said. The sun was beaming down on him. I told him to put on sunscreen but he didn't want to. I closed my eyes and my heart almost skipped a beat when Beretta pulled me under the water. He tapped my leg and I opened my eyes. I saw everyone else swimming around us. The feeling was unexplainable. It was almost like we weren't on Earth anymore. I grabbed on to Beretta and he pulled me down further with him. His long dreads blended in with the seaweed, blinding me. I trusted Beretta with my life. He came into my world and taught me things. Who would've thought a love like that could come from the place we grew up at? Cinderella stories were what every girl dreamed of, but realistically your prince could come in any form. He could be broke, ugly, sick or even handicapped. It didn't matter as long as you felt like you were living above the ordinary.

Poppa

"**W**here da fuck you been?" I asked Jasmine when she walked into the crib.

"I was out wit' Stone at the bowling alley. What's up?" she asked.

"I think you fuckin' another nigga," I blurted out. Jasmine rolled her eyes at me then headed straight to the kitchen. Something was up with her but I couldn't put my finger on it.

"Really, nigga? I'm always in the crib laid up wit' you! Let's not forget your hand problem. You got some fuckin' nerve accusing me of some bullshit," she said. I wanted to knock shorty's teeth out. Jasmine was obedient most times but suddenly she was talking back to a nigga and leaving out the house without her phone. I was trying to be a good dude because I ended up falling for her but I was having regrets. I checked out her outfit and she was wearing tight skinny jeans, a black leather jacket with a pair of black pumps. Her hair was braided back into long cornrows that reached passed her ass. Jasmine was a cute little shorty when I first met her but now she was bomb and giving Nika a run for her money. I was so busy sniffing up Nika's ass that I wasn't realizing the dime piece I had in front of me.

I got up from the couch and walked over towards her. Jasmine's eyes watered then suddenly she burst into tears.

"I can't do this anymore, Kamar. You have been cheating on me and abusing me for months! I'm so tired," she said.

"Yo, it ain't even like dat, shorty. I ain't fuckin' around," I replied.

My back was against the wall. I merked Tyshawn and fucked over Mara. They were the only two who was down with a nigga. Truth is, nobody else was fucking with me if it didn't have nothing to do with money. Rich was a cool dude, but I had to pay the nigga to come through for me. Nika only wanted my money and my dick but Jasmine was different. She was feeling me before she knew I had money and I was turning her against me. I fucked up big time and all I wanted to do was make it right.

"You won't open up to me! I tolerated your bullshit long enough. Look what you're doing to me. How would you feel if someone treated your daughter like this or even your sister? Would you even care? You're a disease and it's killing me. I did what I had to do for you, so find another young gullible bitch that you can corrupt because I'm not dat shorty anymore," she replied. Jasmine walked around me and headed to the bedroom. She went into the closet and pulled out her clothes.

SOUL Publications

"I thought I loved you but I woke up this morning and realized you'll never love me. All you see me as is a come-up," she said. I pushed her into the wall and a picture fell on the floor.

"You ain't leaving me. I have nobody! Do you hear me?" I asked.

"That has nothing to do wit' me! Grow the fuck up!" she yelled.

I grabbed her by the neckline of her jacket and raised my hand. She didn't look afraid. Jasmine was no longer scared of me. It led me to believe she met another nigga. I began wondering if she fell in love with a lick, the same as Mara.

"Who have you been fuckin', Jasmine? You think a nigga dumb or sumthin?" I asked. I looked at the clock on the wall and it was almost two o'clock in the morning. The bowling alley closed two hours ago.

"Get the hell away from me!" she yelled. She slapped me in the face and I slapped her back. Jasmine scratched me and bit my arm while I choked her. She kneed me between my legs and I released my grip. Jasmine went into her purse and grabbed a gun. She pointed it at my head.

"One more time, Poppa. You got one more fuckin' time! I'm tired of you!" she said. All I could do was stare down the barrel of her gun. *What happened to Jasmine?* Is what I kept asking myself.

SOUL Publications

"Put the gun down," I gritted. She put the gun back into her purse then sat on the bed.

"You don't share anything wit' me and you're always leaving out when she calls. You don't care about me," she said. I had to hurry up and fix whatever was going on between us. My money was getting low and my plan with Rich to kidnap Hope was dead. It came to a point where I needed Jasmine. All I could do was kiss her ass and promise her that I wouldn't lay a hand on her again.

"Come on, shorty. You know how I get about you. Why you trippin' on me and where did you get the gun from?" I asked.

"I keep it on me when we do our licks just in case shit gets out of hand. I'm ready to take a shower then I'm going to bed," she said. She got up and went into the bathroom, slamming the door behind her. I looked around the bedroom and realized it was a mess, so I straightened everything back up and put Jasmine's clothes back into the closet. Her purse was wide open and I noticed her cell phone vibrating. The caller hung up when I answered the phone. The number was blocked but I heard niggas talking in the background. I went through her messages and only saw messages from her female friends. When I put her phone back in her purse, I saw a thin pamphlet between her wallet.

Music, Theatre and Arts, is what it read. I shrugged it off because I figured Jasmine wanted to go to school for something else. Maybe she wanted to be a singer or some shit, I figured.

SOUL Publications

****

The next day...

"I can't come through today," I told Nika.

I was in the living room whispering on the phone while Jasmine was in our bedroom getting dressed. I told Jasmine I wanted to take her out and spend some time with her. She complained about it until I told her that I was taking her shopping.

"What do you mean, you can't come through? You must've forgotten I run this shit!" Nika yelled into the phone.

"Run, what? You ain't doin' shit but taking my fuckin' money! Oh, and dat blackmailing shit is dead, shorty. I'm spending time wit' my shorty today," I replied.

"Oh, now you wanna spend time wit' her? Okay, so I guess she can help you from now on," Nika spat.

"She been helping me while you have been doing nothing but sucking my dick!" I said.

"What about Hope?" she asked.

"You'll figure it out," I replied and hung up.

Jasmine came out of the bedroom dressed in a sweat suit with tennis shoes. She rolled her eyes at me when she saw me holding my cell phone. We had a false pregnancy test before but I was starting to think shorty was knocked up or something.

"You didn't have to hang up," she said.

"Yo, I'm tryna be nice. Don't start no bullshit," I warned her.

"Well, I'm ready to go," she said.

I grabbed my car keys off of the table and followed her out the door.

****

"I think we should move out of Maryland and start over. What do you think?" I asked Jasmine as I drove on the interstate.

"What are you runnin' from?" she asked.

"Who said I was runnin' from sumthin?" I replied.

She turned the radio down then crossed her arms.

"How can we move forward if you don't tell me shit? You know everything about me but I know nothing about you. I'm tired of lying next to a stranger," she said.

"What do you wanna know?" I asked.

"What happened to Tyshawn? You met him that night he was killed then a week later, his friend Shag was merked. I need to know what you're hiding because I don't want to be in the dark. Is my life on the line, too, because I'm involved witchu? We're a team, remember?" she asked. Jasmine knew some shit but she didn't know much and I tried to keep it that way.

"Tyshawn was tryna go to war with GMBAM, so I merked him. My sister fuck wit' them and I didn't want her to be a part of it," I replied.

"Why would he do that?" she asked.

"Because he wanted Mara for himself," I said.

"I don't know much about Mara but Tyshawn doesn't seem like her type. He should've known he couldn't get her," she said.

"Tyshawn was a wild dude. The nigga wanted to destroy GMBAM so bad dat he started fuckin' Swan," I replied.

"Ammo's Swan?" she asked.

"Yeah, she was pregnant by him. Shorty helped him set Ammo up to get killed," I replied.

"Ammo was killed by Tyshawn?" she asked.

"And Shag," I replied.

"You left the house the night he was killed. Were you there?" she asked. I looked at Jasmine and wondered if I should tell her the truth. I mean, who was she gonna tell? Jasmine was guilty by association, so her ratting me out would be setting herself up to get killed.

"I was there but I didn't kill the nigga," I lied.

"But you watched him die?" she asked.

"I didn't know he was in the house when Tyshawn wanted me to meet up with him," I replied.

"I didn't fuck wit' Ammo, anyway. The GMBAM niggas brainwashed my brother. He isn't the same anymore," she replied. I kissed the back of her hand and she smiled at me.

"I'm tired of Maryland, too. Let's get away and never look back. I can start lookin' for a place now but you gotta promise me that I pick our home this time. Our condo is too small," she said and I chuckled.

"Okay, bet. So, you changed your classes up?" I asked.

"What do you mean?" she replied.

"I saw a pamphlet in your purse last night," I admitted.

"Why are you going through my shit? I'd get a black eye if I went through your shit, though," she said.

"Mannnnn, chill da fuck out. I thought you was out fuckin'. But why you didn't tell me?" I asked.

"Tell you what? I like painting and stuff?" she asked.

"Yeah," I replied.

"I don't know. I guess it never crossed my mind," she said.

****

I dropped close to ten g's on Jasmine at the mall although I only had thirty-five g's left to my name, but I had her back on my team. It was around nine o'clock at night by the time I made it back to our neighborhood. When I pulled up, Nika's truck was parked in front of my building. I almost panicked because I didn't know how the bitch found out where I lived.

Mara probably told this bitch, I thought.

I grabbed the shopping bags before I got out of the whip. Jasmine was laughing and joking about something but my eyes were on Nika. Her driver's side door opened and she stepped out wearing a sweater dress with high-heel boots. She looked good as fuck, but she wasn't about shit.

"I hope you got me and Hope sumthin, too," Nika said. Jasmine looked at me then looked back at Nika. I knew shit was about to hit the fan. Jasmine knew I was banging another broad but she didn't know the identity of my baby mama.

"What is goin' on?" Jasmine asked.

"Oh, he didn't tell you? I'm his daughter's mother and we have been spending a lot of time together. So, are y'all gonna invite me in or leave me out in the cold?" Nika asked.

"You're Beretta's mother?" Jasmine asked in disbelief.

"That's none of your business," Nika spat and Jasmine rolled her eyes.

"Yo, what da fuck! This isn't supposed to get out," I gritted at Nika and she smirked at me.

"I don't give a fuck about that anymore. Can I come in or do you want me to make a scene?" Nika asked. Jasmine was ready to speak up but I cut her off. She grilled me when I told Nika she could come up.

"Ewwww, this place is so small," Nika said, looking around. Jasmine took off her coat and sat down on the love seat with her legs crossed.

"Our bedroom is straight to the back," Jasmine said. Nika walked down the hall and into our bedroom.

"What are you doin?" I asked Jasmine because she was being too calm about Nika in our shit.

"Bein' the good little bitch you taught me to be," she said with sarcasm. Nika walked back down the hallway then went into our kitchen.

"I gotta make sure your home is fit for an autistic kid," Nika said, looking in our kitchen cabinets. After she was finished, she sat across from Jasmine and sized her up.

"You look familiar. Aren't you Sniper's twin?" Nika asked Jasmine. I didn't know shit about Sniper and Jasmine being twins. I thought the nigga was older than her.

"I thought he was older than you?" I asked Jasmine.

"Him being born hours before me makes him older, Kamar. Let's cut to the chase, what do you want?" Jasmine asked.

"I want the time Poppa promised me. Tonight is my night and it's been that way for months. So we can either go back to the bedroom or back to my place. Make up your mind because I don't have all day," Nika said.

"Just like you to break up happy homes," Jasmine replied.

"Are you still mad about that?" Nika asked.

"What da fuck is goin' on?" I asked.

"Me and Jasmine's mother have a little history. Her mother thinks that Beretta's father is her twins' father but the DNA proved otherwise," Nika laughed. Jasmine stood up with her fist balled.

"Your friend who worked at the clinic tampered with the test! I believe my mother and she's not a liar!" Jasmine yelled.

"Then why haven't you or your brother told Beretta yet? Your mother got ahold of bad drugs and hasn't been stable for years. Don't test me, little girl," Nika warned her.

"You will reap what you sow," Jasmine said and Nika laughed.

"You're crazy just like your mama. I hope you find your daddy. All girls need their father," Nika laughed.

"I'm not fuckin' you anymore, Nika. What happened to the strip club you were supposed to open up for me? My money is gone down the fuckin' drain from fuckin' witchu!" I yelled at her. Nika went into her purse and pulled out a stack of papers along with a key. She slammed it down on the coffee table. I was sick of that bitch's games.

"What is this?" I asked and picked up the papers.

"The deed to the strip club and the key. I wanted to surprise you but you have been busy wit' this little black trash," Nika said about Jasmine.

"Don't think I did you any favors. I want Hope to have the best of everything, so I did this for her. You won't have any excuses as to why you can't provide for her once that little bitch stops selling pussy for you. Maybe you can put her on the pole," Nika said.

"Oh, and maybe you can upgrade from this shoebox. I'll let you two talk tonight but I'll be expecting yah ass at my home tomorrow," Nika said. She blew Jasmine a kiss before she left out of our condo. Jasmine stared at me with tear-filled eyes and I reached out to her. She smacked my hand away and stood up from the love seat.

"You didn't mean any of that shit you said earlier, huh?" she asked.

"Yo, I love you and I'm doin' this for us," I replied. She grabbed my face and kissed my lips.

"I'm doin' this for us, too," she said, then walked out the living room.

What da fuck just happened? I thought.

****

Later on that night, while Jasmine was asleep, I went to the club. I parked in front the empty building then got out of my whip. It needed a lot of work done but it was mine. No more robbing niggas and using Jasmine's pussy to get money. I unlocked the door and walked in. Broken up chairs and tables were spread out across the floor and the place had a bad odor. It wasn't the building I wanted but Nika said it would've cost more. She said it was cheaper to buy a fucked-up place and fix it yourself. I knew

I could get a few fiends from the hood to paint and all that extra shit for close to nothing. I heard heels clicking across the floor, and when I turned around, it was Nika.

"What do you want?" I asked and tears fell from her eyes.

"It was hard seein' you with her. I knew you was gonna come here so I waited down the street in my truck for you," she said. Nika looked like she had been crying. I didn't think she cared about me in that way.

"So now you give a fuck about me?" I asked.

"I love you," she admitted.

I thought shorty was trying to get over on me, but I developed strong feelings for her, too. It didn't take away from the fact that I fell in love with Jasmine. I was more confused than ever.

"Is Jasmine Beretta's sister?" I asked and she looked away from me.

"TELL ME!" I yelled at her and she jumped.

"YES!" Nika admitted.

"So, you're tellin' me dat I could've been fuckin' my enemy?" I replied. Jasmine was an enemy since she was Beretta's sister.

"Beretta isn't your enemy. When will you get that through your fuckin' head?" she screamed at me.

"The nigga doesn't fuck wit' me, so he's an enemy," I replied.

"I'll fix it because it's time he knows about us, anyway. I feel bad for keepin' him away from Hope because of us. I had to raise Beretta on my own and I'll be damned if I have to raise Hope and my unborn baby by myself. You got one week to leave your bitch and I mean it. I'll see you tomorrow," she said. Nika kissed my lips then walked out of the building.

Unborn baby, I thought.

I got myself into more shit than I could handle. Sometimes I wished I completed my whole prison bid. I would've got out on a clean slate but shit was too deep and there was no way out. Nika had something up her sleeve and I hoped she acted on it ASAP because it was time for me and Beretta to bury our beef. I finally had a lot to lose, especially if Jasmine ratted me out. But then again, shorty didn't even tell Beretta she was his sister, so maybe they weren't close like that. All I knew was I had to play it safe.

****

Jasmine was at the kitchen table smoking a blunt when I came home. She had puffy eyes and she looked like she had been crying. I sat across from her and she blew smoke into my face. I reached out to her and she pulled away from me.

"Let me be," she said.

"I apologize," I replied.

"Save it," she said.

"What do you want me to do? Turn the club down after I have been giving her money for it? Shorty, she ain't gonna give me a fuckin' refund," I replied.

"Why didn't you tell me?" she asked.

"Why didn't you tell me about Beretta possibly bein' your brother?" I replied.

"I don't fuck wit' Beretta because his mother tore my family apart. Sniper is cool wit' him because he doesn't know our family secret. My mother only confided in me because she realized Sniper was close to GMBAM. Nobody would believe her anyway because she's crazy. She lost her mind after my father was shot up. I'm the only one who believes in her," Jasmine said.

Good! I won't have to worry about her ratting me out, I thought.

"I love you and I got your back," I said and she smiled at me.

"I know you do," she said and wiped her eyes.

I got up from the table and hugged Jasmine and she hugged me back. She pulled away from me and told me to make love to her. I carried her into our bedroom and laid her down on the bed. She took off her panties and bra and grabbed a condom from the top drawer. I couldn't wait to slide into her wet pussy. She helped me undress and I tore the condom wrapper off. I put the condom on then entered her. Jasmine wrapped her legs around me and dug her nails in my ass cheeks while I drilled into her. It was the best feeling in the world. I didn't think about nobody but us as I gave her back-to-back orgasms. She was my rock and brought peace into my life even though I didn't act like it. Nika couldn't give me what Jasmine could give me and that was the truth.

When I woke up the next morning, my bed was empty. I called out to Jasmine but she didn't respond. I got up and searched the condo for her because she usually woke me up with breakfast. Something told me to look in the closet.

This bitch left me, I thought when I realized most of her clothes and shoes were gone. I called her phone and it sent me straight to voicemail. Nika was right, Jasmine was playing me.

Beretta

Three days later...

I paced back and forth in the dressing room and my niggas clowned me.

"Yo, would you calm down? I'm gettin' dizzy," Machete said, then passed the blunt to me.

"Nigga, stay outta grown folks' business," I replied.

"Bruh, the wedding is in thirty minutes, so I hope you chill da fuck out," Pistol said.

"She's gonna be my wife," I said and wiped the sweat off my forehead.

"Nigga, you betta go through wit' it because she'll kill you on this island if you change your mind," Sniper said. My phone rang and I excused myself to talk in a quieter place.

"Talk to me," I said.

"He admitted to being there," Jasmine said.

"And what else?" I asked.

"Your mother came to our condo last night. She almost blew my cover. This shit is gettin' out of hand now. Oh, and she got him the strip club. Nika loves him, Beretta," she said. I clutched the phone in my hand as I listened to Jasmine tell me everything she knew.

"Where is he at now?" I asked.

"He's at our condo. I'm ready to start my acting classes and I don't need this distraction. Do you want me to take care of him now or wait until you come back from your trip?" Jasmine asked with an attitude. I was ready to ask her what the problem was but I didn't have the time.

"I'll take it from here. Appreciate it," I said and she hung up. Soon as I hung up, Nika called me but I ignored her call. She called me again and I answered because it could've been about Hope.

"Make it quick. I'm busy," I said.

"We need to talk about something very important," she said with worry in her voice.

"Is it about Hope?" I asked.

"Somewhat," she replied.

"Talk then and hurry up wit' it," I replied.

"I want you to end your beef with Poppa," she said.

"Da fuck is you talkin' about?" I replied.

"You think I don't know why that girl is pretending to be wit' him? That has your name written all over it. You think just like your father, Z'wan. You're just like him and I know how he operated. You have a lot of them fooled but not me. So, I'm beggin' you to move on. Do you think Kemara will want sumthin to happen to her brother?" Nika asked. I bit the inside of my cheek to keep from lashing out, but Nika was doing it again. She was always taking sides wit' niggas who were against me. Maybe it was because I reminded her too much of my father.

"What does he mean to you?" I asked and she started crying.

"He's Hope's father and I'm pregnant again. I love him, Beretta, and he's a good father to Hope," she said.

"Good father? Nika, get off yah hoe shit for five seconds and pay attention to everything around you. What father plans to kidnap his own daughter? Hope would've been missin' if it wasn't for me. That nigga is usin' yah dumb ass! When will you realize dat nobody wants you? My father didn't even want you and that's why you trapped him. Get da fuck off my line 'cause you talkin' stupid. How da fuck you accusin' me of some shit and I'm on an island gettin' married?" I chuckled.

"You're lyin!" she said.

SOUL Publications

"See for yourself," I replied and hung up.

"FUCK!" I yelled out. Sniper stepped onto the balcony and handed me a glass of Henny.

"Jasmine just hit me up. I'll catch an early flight if you need me to," he said.

"Naw, don't even worry about it. Nika knows too much and I'on trust her. Dat bitch will have me rottin' behind bars," I replied. The more I thought about it, the angrier I became. There was only one bitch that could take me down in the blink of an eye and it was my own mother. I thought about killing her but I wouldn't be able to forgive myself because of Hope. It was something I had to force myself to get over.

"Jasmine said Poppa didn't do it but he was there when those niggas merked Ammo," Sniper said.

"I'on believe dat," I replied.

"Poppa merkin' a nigga? Come on, bruh. He ain't built like dat," Sniper said.

"Most niggas that kill ain't built like dat," I said.

"The only way you can merk him is if you merk yah mother. She'll roll on you, bruh. She knows too much shit about GMBAM and we'll all go down. I hate to say it, but this is a loss you gotta take. One thing I know is niggas like Poppa will destroy themselves. He's doin' it now by fallin' in love with Jasmine and you know shorty ain't workin' wit' a full deck," Sniper chuckled.

"I like yah way of thinkin'," I said but deep down inside I was heated!

Pistol and Machete stepped onto the balcony with me. It fucked me up because my nigga Ammo should've been there along with Nika and my daughter, Zyira. Shit was supposed to be complete for me but there was a big empty space missing. I chalked it up to the game and took another swig of the Henny.

"After today, this nigga will have a curfew, so let me take a pic in case I forget what this nigga looks like," Pistol joked.

"Yeah, aight, nigga. I'm still the man around the house. Kemara ain't doin' shit," I replied.

"I bet you won't tell her dat, though," Machete joked.

Me and my niggas was decked out in all-white and gold Versace linen suits. Kemara didn't want me to see her dress, but I wasn't tripping. I knew my shorty was going to look beautiful. I smoked a few blunts and finished the rest of the Henny before we headed down to the beach. My nerves were still bad and my stomach was in knots. Excitement and curiosity was how a nigga was feeling. We walked down the beach to the tent; the minister was waiting for us. He was an old man, probably in his seventies. Me and Mara met up with him the day before. He wanted to make sure we were serious about getting married. He damn sure made it known we were the youngest couple to get married on his island, but an average young couple couldn't afford the shit because it would've taken them years to save up for everything we had going on.

Thickems, Piper and Emma walked down the beach wearing white lace summer dresses with flower bands around their heads. I didn't see Kemara and I got worried about her. Moments later, a few others came to join us. We were all standing underneath the tent waiting for Kemara.

"Where is Mara?" I whispered to Piper.

"She's coming, damn. We have only been standing here for three minutes," she replied. Thickems nudged me and told me to look out into the sea. There was a small boat coming towards us. We waited for what seemed like forever until the boat came onto the beach. Kemara was carried by six island niggas on a litter chair with flowers around her. She reminded me of an angel. Everyone around me disappeared as I stared at her. It seemed like it was just us two on the beach. They brought her to the tent and lowered the chair. Her dress was sheer-lace and it fit her curves like it was painted on. It was see-through but she wore a neutral color leotard underneath. The bottom of the dress had feathers and it fanned out around her. Her hair was pulled up into bun with gold flower hair clips. Her make-up was natural, including her lipstick. She stood in front of me and my body seemed too heavy for my legs. Matter of fact, I couldn't feel my legs.

Damn, shorty. You got my eyes watering in front of all my niggas! I thought.

SOUL Publications

Kemara

S eeing Beretta's eyes water made me emotional. I saw plenty of weddings in movies and never understood why people cried until my wedding day. I still couldn't believe I was getting married myself but the feeling was the best feeling in the world. The way his eyes stared into mine told me it was real—we were in love. He grabbed my hand and kissed it so it could calm me, but his lips on my skin made the butterflies worse. The minister began the ceremony and we exchanged our vows, but I had my own.

"I thank God every day for you. You came into my life and showed me many things. Because of you I got to experience carrying my first child, real love and loyalty. I'll do anything for you to make me a better woman. I'm very grateful for you. You are my king," I said. He wiped his tears away and he tried to talk but his words weren't coming out. All I understood was that he loved me so much and wouldn't do anything to hurt me. He kept saying he was sorry but I wasn't tripping over him staying at Ammo's aunt's house while Moesha was there. Beretta said he didn't sleep with her and I believed him. He grabbed me and picked me up. His hands squeezed my ass cheeks while he tongue-kissed me. We had a professional photographer and I hoped he caught all our moments, including the emotional ones. Beretta showing all of his layers was a Kodak moment.

"This hoe is finally a wife!" Piper yelled and kissed my cheek. She was crying, too, but Silk had a breakdown. He yelled he needed CPR and I realized what he was doing. Silk wanted one of the guys who carried me to give him CPR. One of them ran to Silk and rubbed his back. Silk fell into the sand, grabbing his throat.

"Is Silk doing what I think he's doing?" Thickems asked.

"Aight now! Nigga you ain't gotta do all of dat!" Kellan yelled. Silk winked at Kellan then blew her a kiss while the guy continued rubbing his back.

"Silk performing gay porn at our wedding?" Beretta asked me. I made sure the photographer captured Silk's moments.

"I don't blame Silk. Them niggas is fine," Zain laughed and Machete snarled at her.

"Ay yo! Keep yah fuckin' eyes in your head," Machete said and we all laughed.

The minister shook our hands and wished us the best of luck before he walked away.

"I gotta admit, shorty. My wedding band fly like a muthafucka. I thought you was gonna come through wit' a piercing pagoda joint but this shit is icy," Beretta said, admiring his diamond band.

"I thought about it," I giggled.

"Aight, y'all, tonight is our last night here! I'm fittin' to turn the hell up!" Piper said.

"Sit yah hot ass down," Pistol teased.

"Be quiet before I sit on yah face," she said.

"Come on then," Pistol replied. Everyone else thought he was joking but I knew he was serious.

"Me and Beretta are staying for two extra days," I said.

"Ummm, y'all about to come back with a baby," Thickems joked.

While they were talking, I snuck off to go to my room to change. My dress was extremely too tight around the hips and the girdle I had on didn't make it any better. I wore a white loose spaghetti linen dress with a pair of gold sandals. I took the clips out of my bun then headed out of my room. On my way back to the beach, I ran into Chevy. He was only wearing swim trunks and swim shoes. I tried to go the other way before he saw me but it was too late.

"It's like that now, baby girl? I'm hurt," Chevy said when he walked over to me.

"What are you talkin' about?" I asked.

"I'm sayin' you ain't gotta act like a stranger. You looked beautiful earlier, by the way. We were watching the wedding from the balcony in the buffet room. My grandmother couldn't keep her eyes off your dress," he smiled.

"Thank you but I gotta get going," I replied. Chevy grabbed my wrist when I walked past him.

"Don't be a stranger, Kemara. I'm gonna send my number to your inbox on Facebook," he said and I pulled away from him. Chevy lost his fucking mind! I had just gotten married but he was still hitting on me. Beretta came around the corner and grilled Chevy when he saw us standing in the hallway. I could tell by his body language he wasn't happy about us talking.

"Yo, you gotta a fuckin' problem or sumthin?" Beretta's deep voice bellowed throughout the hallway.

"I was just tellin' your wife congrats, bruh. You're a lucky dude. Seeing her in that dress reminded me of prom," Chevy said. Two things about Chevy that caught my attention in high school, he wasn't scared to say what was on his mind and he didn't switch up for nobody. But we weren't in high school anymore and Beretta wasn't like those fake hood niggas Chevy always got into fights with.

"Nigga, you tryna fuck wit' my head or sumthin? Do you think I give a fuck about y'all's prom and the two seconds you spent between her legs?" Beretta asked.

"Beretta just chill out, please," I said.

"Chill out? Dat clown-ass nigga is tryna shoot his shot wit' my fuckin' wife," Beretta seethed.

"Yo, it ain't even like dat. I'll see you around, Mara," Chevy said.

"Da fuck was dat about? You came up here to meet him?" Beretta asked.

"WHAT?" I replied.

"Yo, don't bullshit wit' me," he said.

"We just got married twenty minutes ago and you wanna accuse me of some bullshit?" I asked.

"Whateva, yo. I'm ready to go in the room and lay down for a little bit," he said. Instead of going back to the beach with our friends, I went back to the suite with Beretta.

****

"Babe, are you okay?" I called out to Beretta.

"I'm sick," he said.

SOUL Publications

He came out of the bathroom only wearing his boxers and his lips were dry. We missed our own party because Beretta wasn't feeling good.

"Go on ahead, Mara. I'm straight," he said and laid across the bed.

"What happened?" I asked.

"I ate some shit dat fucked wit' me. The food here is too rich," he replied.

I took off my clothes and got underneath the blanket with him. He wrapped his arm around me and rested his head on my breasts.

"We partied enough. I'm tired out myself," I yawned.

"I ain't gonna lie, I would've fucked you up if you left the room," Beretta said.

"I had a little surprise for you, too," I replied and he opened one of his eyes.

"What kind of surprise? A threesome?" he asked.

"Nigga, I'll knock you clean da fuck out if you say some shit like dat to me again," I said.

"Damn, I was just fuckin' around. What you got for me, though," he said, feeling between my legs.

"Nothing, you sick remember?" I asked.

"Shiddd, I thought I was sick, too, for a minute," he said and I mushed him. Beretta sat up and stared at me for a while. He did that when he was stalling for asking or telling me something.

"Can you give me another baby?" he asked.

"We have Zalia," I said.

"I know dat but I mean our own blood baby, shorty," he replied.

"I'm on birth control," I said. Beretta looked at me like I had two heads.

"Aight, stop takin' them," he said.

"I have it implanted in me. It's not that simple," I replied.

"When did this happen?" he asked.

"After we lost Zyira. I couldn't risk getting pregnant again and things not going right. It's not that big of a deal," I replied.

"That's why you been throwin' the pussy at me like crazy lately. You knew I couldn't knock you up," he said.

"I'll get it taken out after I finish school, but right now we have Zalia," I replied.

"You are forcing her on me when the least you can do is give me my own seed, Mara. I wanna help you raise her but let's be real, it ain't the same as having our own baby," Beretta said.

"Can we talk about this at home?" I replied.

"Aight," he said and kissed my lips.

He rolled over and went to sleep. I grabbed my robe and made sure the coast was clear of iguanas before I sat on the patio. That feeling came back again—Beretta was hiding something from me.

Stop it, Mara! You are his wife now and he loves you. He will not hurt you again. You're just paranoid because everything seems so perfect now. Let the past go and focus on your husband! I thought.

He's tryna trap you into stayin' wit' him because he fucked up. He loves you and wants you to himself, but he's not loyal to you. Beretta is hidin' something from you and the guilt is eating him up. He tried to warn you but you're not paying attention, I thought.

Thoughts and scenarios were playing around in my head and I wanted them to stop. It seemed like I was losing my mind. I turned around and saw him peacefully sleeping on his back. His dreads were sprawled out on the pillow, and as the curtain from the wind blew, I couldn't take my eyes off his ring finger.

He's yours!

SOUL Publications

Piper

Two weeks later...

Me and Delonte have been on good terms since we came back from St. Croix. I guess lack of communication was the cause of everything. It was ten o' clock at night and time for me to go to the club. I was getting bored with dancing and popping pills. The fast life was becoming a thing in the past but Delonte wanted me to help him out with a few shows. Every weekend, the club had different themes and it was attracting people from all over, even some local rappers and athletes. Delonte's club was making a lot of money, not to mention, he gained a lot of Big Mike's audience after he was killed. I grabbed my backpack and headed out the door. Pistol pulled up in the driveway while I was locking the top lock. It was winter time and he was wearing a North Face coat, sweatpants and Timbs.

"My bad for stopping by unannounced. I came to get my money out da safe," he said.

"You were supposed to come by three days ago," I replied.

"I was busy. So, can I go in or what?" he asked. I unlocked the door and followed him into my house. Delonte texted me asking me where I was at because I had an opening show. I trusted Pistol in my home, so I didn't need to be there but I missed him. The last time we saw each other was at St. Croix. Pistol went into my closet and punched the code into the safe. He tossed each stack into his duffel bag. I sat on my bed and watched him.

"Soooo, how have you been?" I asked.

"Good, can't complain. How about you?" he asked with his back turned towards me.

"I'm great," I replied.

"Dat's what's up, baby girl," he said as he tossed the last stack inside his duffel bag. I couldn't stop staring if I wanted to; his lips gave me flashbacks of the times he French-kissed my pussy.

"YO! Did you hear me?" he asked.

"No, I didn't. What did you say?" I replied.

"My nigga Wesson is having a party at Fat Cat, so GMBAM niggas are gonna be there," he said.

"Okay, and?" I asked.

"Yo, what do you mean by dat? So, you really wanna show them niggas your body like dat, knowin' you fucked two GMBAM niggas already," Pistol said.

"I haven't seen you in two weeks and this is the bullshit you wanna talk about? Newsflash, Pistol! They saw me already when I was at Mikey's," I replied. Pistol dropped his bag on the floor and walked over to me. He wrapped his hand around my throat and shoved me back on the bed.

"I don't give a fuck about you havin' a nigga now, but you ain't gonna be testin' me, neither, shorty. You weren't just a piece of ass to me, so I treasure the fuck outta you. I'll never look at you the same if you get naked in front of my niggas knowing I'll be there. I'on play dat stupid shit!" Pistol gritted. He pulled away from me and I sat up massaging my throat. I tried to charge into him but he mushed me into the dresser.

"Yo, chill da fuck out! You ain't fittin' to do shit," he said, then smirked.

Nigga, I'll trap you wit' a baby if you keep on wit' da bullshit! I thought. I laughed out loud because I couldn't believe what I was saying in my head. Kids weren't in the game plan but Pistol had that effect on me.

"What's funny?" he asked.

"You don't wanna know, but okay, I'll work behind the counter tonight. I'll just tell Delonte my cycle came on," I replied.

"Ight, bet," he said. He kissed my forehead and his cologne filled my nostrils. I melted into his chest and he pulled away from me. Pistol picked up his bag of money and walked out of my house.

****

I arrived an hour late because the club was already crowded and I couldn't find a parking space. Delonte was blowing up my phone but I ignored his calls. He was beginning to piss me off already. I should've known those two weeks of peaceful bliss wasn't going to last long. When I walked into the club, Sugar was on the stage performing with another girl. Delonte stormed down the stairs and pulled me off to the side. I snatched my arm away from him because I didn't like how he was grabbing me.

"What the fuck, Piper! You're late! You were supposed to be opening the stage tonight. Niggas paid top dollar for this shit and you're slacking," Delonte drilled.

"Pump your brakes, nigga. My period came on and the flow is super heavy," I replied.

"Your period was just on," he said.

"I can't help dat I have bad fibroids. Da fuck do you want me to do? Listen, I'll help the ladies out and tell them what songs to dance to and what kind of moves to make. Have some faith in the other girls," I replied.

"But they came to see you," he said.

"Shit happens. Look, I'm cramping and my ibuprofen didn't kick in yet. I can go home and lay down with a heating pad," I replied.

"Naw, that's okay. Just promise you'll help out," he said.

"I promise," I replied.

"Okay, I'll see you around," he said and walked away. We didn't show each other affection inside the club because the girls were watching and Delonte didn't want them to think he was showing favoritism. It didn't bother me because I wasn't up to beefing with a bunch of bitches I didn't know like that. I went into my locker room and got dressed in spandex booty shorts with a half top and stripper heels. It was probably the most clothes I wore while walking on the dance floor. I went to the bar and helped a middle-aged woman named Angie out.

"You're not performing tonight?" she asked while cutting lemons.

"Naw, I'm cramping," I replied.

"Well, honey, get ready for your feet to be hurting because it's about to get packed," she said, pointing towards the door. I cursed Pistol out in my head because it was all his fault. Thirty minutes later, Thickems and Silk came into the club. I waved them over to the bar and they cut through the crowd of people that were waiting for their drinks.

"Girl, what are you doing behind the bar?" Thickems said while I made someone a margarita.

"I'm not stripping tonight," I replied and slid the drink across the bar. A guy picked up a drink and placed a twenty-dollar bill on the bar. Silk picked it up and stuffed it inside his sweater.

"Really?" I asked.

"Yup, chile, who is Delonte? He damn sure ain't cocking his PISTOL up in dat pussy the right way," he replied and I rolled my eyes.

"Kemara said she was on her way with Beretta," Thickems said.

"Girlll, Kemara and Beretta be cooped up in the house. They ain't comin' out. I'll believe it when I see it," I laughed.

"Mara know these thirsty hoes love a married man. She keepin' his fine ass in the house. Hell, I don't blame her because, chilleeeeee, when he got out of the water wearing swimming trunks! Y'all let me tell you sumthin, I'm neva flirtin' with Mara again. Dat nigga's dick width made my dick look like a bobby pin. She ain't impressed wit' my package," Silk said.

"Silk, honey, you heavy," Thickems said.

"But that nigga is my length but a little thicker. It turned me da fuck off because I know my baby Mara's walls are thinner than the ones in the projects," Silk said.

"And I'm gonna tell her everything you said, including lookin' at her man," I replied and Silk waved me off.

"Oh, honey, Mara knows how I do. Shit, I told her ass the same day I saw it and she fell out. She told me I had competition and I had to deal wit' it. Mara knows I wanted to tap dat ass one good time. Dat thing juicy," Silk said.

"Beretta is packin', though," Thickems said and Silk grilled her.

"What? I didn't mean to look but, shit, you couldn't miss his swimming trunks sticking to his piece. Mara knows her nigga is blessed and I'm sure she ain't worried about us seeing sumthin that couldn't be avoided. Plus, she shared a few stories wit' us, so we know," Thickems said.

"Beretta is like my brother, so I didn't see shit but I damn sho was eyeing Pistol's package," I replied.

"Chile, Delonte's little seahorse should've went scuba diving with everyone else to find his way back home underneath a rock somewhere. I'mma start calling him Nemo," Silk said and I threw an ice cube at him.

"Well, you know I moved on from Mara, so what's up wit' me and you?" Silk asked Thickems. Silk was smooth when he wanted to be and probably could talk any woman out of her panties, but then he had another side to him that scared a bunch of bitches away.

"Nigga, will you stop tryna fuck yah home girls. You worse than a straight whorish man," I said and Thickems fell out laughing.

Pistol walked into the club with a few girls walking behind him. One of them wore a skimpy cream sweater dress with heeled fur boats. I watched their body language and I could tell they fucked. She was whispering in his ear and his hand was resting on her waist.

"That nigga choked me while telling me to keep my clothes on yet he brings a bitch in here wit' him to flaunt in my face," I seethed.

"Girlllll, dat hoe ain't about nothing. She fuckin' everybody," Silk said.

"You know her?" I asked.

"She buys things from me here and there. Her name is Dee. I heard she be smuggling drugs in her pussy for niggas in jail. That hoe ain't you, though," Silk said.

"She damn sho ain't. That hoe got dat greasy twenty-seven piece on her head. Pistol must not be giving her no money. She's just his flavor for the night," Thickems said. I walked from around the bar and headed to the section where Pistol was chilling at. The broad, Dee, was sitting next to him with her hand resting on his leg.

"What's good, Pipe?" Machete said.

"Nothing, who are these broads? Where is Kellan and Zain?" I asked when I noticed Sniper chilling with one of Dee's friends. Sad to say, everyone and their mama knew GMBAM was nothing but a bunch of hoeing-ass niggas.

"Damn, why you trippin? We just chilling," Machete said.

"It doesn't look dat way to me," I replied.

"Can we have eight bottles of Moet and three bottles of Henny?" Dee asked me. Pistol was just sitting back smoking his blunt without a care in the world.

"She's not a bartender. That's Piper, the one on the flyer," another girl said.

"Babe, do you have some ones I can give her?" Dee asked Pistol.

"Pistol doesn't give me ones, honey. I get stacks from him," I said. Dee smacked her teeth and rolled her eyes. I went back to the bar and told Angie what the GMBAM section wanted. My eyes were on Pistol almost the whole night. It burned me up how Dee was all over him and the bitch even had the nerve to put her hand down in Pistol's pants.

Dat hoe playin' wit' my dick!

I thought about dancing to piss Pistol off but I was tired of playing the back and forth game with him. One of us was going to end up hating the other. Angie tapped me on the shoulder and told me Delonte needed me upstairs.

SOUL Publications

I went upstairs to his office and he was chilling with a few older guys. I'd seen them a few times around the club but I didn't know anything about them.

"These are my homeboys, Mark and Wylee. This is my woman I have been telling y'all about," Delonte said and pulled me down on his lap.

"How is it going?" the one named Mark asked. Mark and Wylee looked like they were in their mid-forties. They were handsome but I found them being friends with Delonte odd. Delonte was a little street but his friends were squares.

"We've been boys since college. He's a wild dude," Wylee said. Delonte scratched his head at the mention of college.

"Oh, you went to college?" I asked. Delonte told me he grew up in the streets and had it rough.

"I mean yeah I went to college. But, um, what about those Wizards? Are we still betting on them or what? Put your money where your mouth is," Delonte said to Wylee. I got off his lap when I noticed he changed the subject.

"I gotta get going now," I said to Delonte.

"I'll see you lata," he said.

Awkward, I thought.

I left out his office and closed the door behind me but it didn't stop me from eavesdropping.

"How old is she? She's young enough to be your daughter. When are you coming back to the firm? You almost made partner," Mark said. Someone was coming upstairs, so I walked away. Delonte definitely had some explaining to do but I didn't want him to know I was eavesdropping.

A fucking lawyer! This nigga is living a double life. No wonder Pistol makes him uncomfortable. He probably lied about coming from the hood, too, I thought.

The night took a turn for the worse. Dee was giving Pistol a lap dance and he was feeling up her dress. I couldn't take it anymore. Between Delonte and Pistol, I was going insane. Pistol wanted me to figure out what it was I wanted but I wanted him. Silk and Thickems were partying with the strippers but my bed was calling me. I sent in two job applications online and was waiting for someone to call me back. College was on my mind but what could I do for money if I went to school full-time? How would I pay my bills if I quit stripping? Pistol told me he'd help me with whatever I decided to do after I quit dancing but relying on a man was something I couldn't do. I'd watched Mara go through the same thing. She gave up making her own money so she could go to school while Beretta took care of her and she hated it.

"Are you leaving? It's still early," Angie said.

"How long have you been working here?" I asked her.

"Since it opened, so I'd say about five years," she replied.

"Do you know anything about Delonte other than him bein' the owner?" I asked.

"No, he's to himself. He does what he has to do for the club and treats all of us with respect. I really don't know much about him. Not even a story about him messing with a stripper and you know how these club owners get down," she said.

"How about his friends or family?" I asked.

"Nope, I only know Mark and Wylee. Why, are you interested in the boss?" she joked.

The boss is my damn man! I thought.

"Naw, I was just asking," I replied.

Silk walked over to the bar and I gave him and Thickems a free bottle of Champagne.

"Chilleeeeee, you about to get me pregnant. I'mma be fucked up in a minute and I'm taking one of these niggas home. I spotted about ten niggas in here who are on the low, but one of them caught my eye. I love an older man," Silk said.

"Really, Silk?" I asked.

"Chileee, there he goes right there," he said and pointed. I looked in the direction and Silk was talking about Delonte's friend, Wylee.

"Nooooooo," I said and stomped my feet.

"Bitch, he got money. I told you I was gonna find Amber a new daddy. Y'all hoes playin', so now I'm full-blown gay. No more lesbian in my blood," Silk said.

"You need Ritalin," I replied.

"I saw when he pulled up in his new 2012 Jaguar. Trust me, I'll be in his bed tonight, and since you don't believe me, I'm gonna call you with his dick in my mouth," Silk said.

"I'm going home, so call me lata," I said. I kissed his cheek and headed to the locker room to get my bag. Thickems stopped me on my way out the club.

"Don't let Pistol run you out of here," she said.

"It's not about that. I'm not feeding into Pistol's bullshit, and besides, the club scene is getting whack to me. I'm about to go home and read a book or sumthin," I replied.

"Okay, I'll call you when I get home. I'm getting tired myself," she said. We hugged before I left out of the door.

****

I woke up to the ringing of my doorbell. It was five o' clock in the morning. I checked my phone and had a missed call from Silk and three missed calls from Delonte. The doorbell rang again and I stumbled out of bed. I walked down the stairs and looked through the peephole.

Ugh, why is he here? I thought as I opened the door. Delonte was standing in front of me with his hands in his pockets. It was cold outside, probably thirty degrees. I stepped to the side so he could come in and he sat on my couch.

"I know what you're thinking," he said.

"About what?" I replied.

"My friends," he said.

"Go ahead and spill it because I'm tryna go back to sleep," I replied.

"Why do you always do that? You act like you don't care about shit but you really do," he said.

"The same reason why you keep hiding shit. I'm not tryna get hurt again and I don't think you realize that. Come off the shit and tell me what the fuck is up before I cancel you. You made me look like a cheap whore in front of your old ass friends. Why would you introduce me like that? You couldn't do it over dinner or sumthin?" I asked.

"Seriously? First you wanted to meet my family and friends and now it's an issue? They have seen you strip before so it wouldn't matter if it was at dinner or the club. Talk to me, Piper, because I'm trying to figure you out. What is bothering you?" he asked. I sat next to him on the couch then propped my feet up.

"I want someone to love me without being ashamed," I replied.

"I'm not ashamed of you. I admire you for your 'not givin' a fuck' attitude. I want to make you happy and you should always come to me if you want to know something. Angie said you questioned her about me," he said.

That bitch! I replied.

"That's not my fault, so I ain't apologizing," I said and he chuckled.

"I know and that's why I came here so you won't have to ask around about me. I was a lawyer but I quit because I wasn't happy wit' my life. My wife wanted me to live in this image that just wasn't me. I did a few things when I was younger like selling drugs and all that other bullshit but I turned my life around after my best friend was gunned down. This man right here is the real me so I don't like talkin' about the person I used to be because I wasn't happy wit' it. I saved up my money and busted my ass to get my club and I want you to do the same thing. Do what you want to do and be happy with it," he said.

"Is there anything else I should know?" I asked.

"My friend Wylee likes your friend, Cotton or whateva his name is," Delonte said, talking about Silk.

"Wait, so you know Wylee is gay?" I asked.

"Yeah, he came out in college. He's still my homeboy. It was hard taking it in and it took years for me to fully accept it but he's a good dude," Delonte said and shrugged his shoulders.

This is too much, I thought.

"Silk is too much for his old ass," I said and he chuckled. Delonte scooted closer to me and wrapped his arm around me.

"Fuck all of 'em. How about we focus on us," he replied and kissed my lips.

What I feared the most was letting Delonte all the way in to find out I made the wrong decision but it was a chance I had to take if I wanted to know the truth.

Beretta

Meanwhile...

"I'm down here!" a voice called out when I stepped into a house.

I walked downstairs to the basement of an abandoned house. A nigga who copped work for me named Antwon said he had something important for me. I was hours late because Kemara had to study and I got tied up with Zalia who cried all fucking day. By the time Kemara was finished, I was too tired to go anywhere. I even missed the party GMBAM had for one our niggas named Wesson.

"Nigga, I hope you called me here to tell me you got the money you owe me and you handled that nigga, Quanta," I said. A woman was sitting in a chair with a bloody pillowcase over her head. She was naked from the waist down and was wearing a Morgan State University sweatshirt.

"You mean to tell me Quanta is a bitch?" I asked Antwon. He took the pillowcase off the girl's head and I recognized shorty. It was Kemara's friend Emma.

"Please take me home! I didn't do anything!" she cried. Antwon punched Emma in the face and blood dripped onto her shirt. He was ready to hit her again, but I slammed my fist into his face.

"What da fuck!" he asked, holding his lip.

"Nigga, I said I wanted Quanta! Not his fucking bitch!" I replied.

"I told you I couldn't get to him but I knew where his shorty went to school at," he replied.

"That was weeks ago, nigga, and this is the best you could do? Do you think kidnapping his bitch is gonna put money in my muthafuckin pockets? Get yah bitch ass up!" I said. I grabbed Antwon by the neckline of his hoodie then slammed him into the wall.

"Get my fuckin' money!" I said.

"Quanta doesn't have your money!" Emma cried.

I walked over to her and kneeled so she could look at me.

"Did you know who I was when you came to my wedding?" I asked.

SOUL Publications

"Quanta doesn't tell me his business but I remember seeing Antwon. He's lyin' and you gotta believe me. Please, Z'wan, just let me go home. He tried to rape me and I'm so scared," she said.

"Where did you see him at?" I asked.

"Mannn, that bitch is lyin'!" Antwon said.

"Nigga, shut da fuck up!" I replied.

"I saw him at a mall. Quanta pulled him to the side and asked him where his shit was at and he told Quanta he was gonna deliver it to him. He's a fuckin' liar!" Emma yelled. Antwon tried to get to her but I pushed him onto the floor and pulled my gun out.

"Call dat nigga up," I said.

"Come on, yo. We can hold her for ransom and get your money back," Antwon said. I already knew what that nigga was trying to do. He thought he was covering up his tracks. Emma rambled off Quanta's cell phone number so I could hit him up. I dialed the nigga up with my gun pointed at Antwon's head.

"Who dis?" he answered and I put it on speakerphone.

"You got sumthin of mine and I want it back," I said.

"Yung, what da fuck you talkin' about? I'on know you, nigga," he said.

"You want your shorty and I want my fuckin' money! Nigga, you know who dis is," I replied. I put the phone to Emma's face.

"Baby, please just give them what they want! I'm scared, I'm so scared!" she screamed into the phone.

"You touched my fuckin' girl!" he yelled into the phone. I kicked Antwon for putting me in the middle of his shit. All I wanted was my fucking money and the nigga was running around town stealing bitches.

"Look, bruh. I didn't touch your shorty and I believe this is a big misunderstanding. I'm not about to rap to you over the phone so I'll expect you here ASAP," I said.

"You took my fuckin' girl and you talkin' about it's a big misunderstanding?" Quanta asked. I kneeled next to Antwon and he shook his head "no" because he didn't want to get on the phone. I took the butt of my gun and smacked him across his face with it. Blood got on my butter Timbs.

"Yooo," Antwon cried over the phone.

"Antwon? Yo, what da fuck is dat nigga talkin' about, yung? You playin' games wit' me, muthafucka?" Quanta asked.

"I pulled her up because I was lookin' for you," he said.

"Lookin' for me? Nigga, you got my fuckin' number!" Quanta shouted.

"I lost it," Antwon said.

"Ask him about my money, nigga," I seethed.

"Yo, umm, Beretta wants his money," Antwon said.

"Money? I'on owe dat nigga shit! Fuck is you talkin' about, slim? Tell me sumthin before I pull up to your mother's crib, nigga. I'm right around the corner. I don't want no code talk, neither!" Quanta said.

"The money I gave you was the money I owed Beretta. I gave you Beretta's money and he wants it back," Antwon admitted.

"So, you kidnap my bitch so you can pay the nigga back out of my fuckin' pockets? I don't got shit to do wit' dat, fam. Yo, what's the address where you at?" Quanta asked and Antwon rambled it off. I hung up the phone then untied Emma. I took my coat off and gave it to her and she hugged me.

"I'm so sorry. I didn't do anything," she cried.

"It's cool, but go on over there and have a seat," I said. She sat on the busted-up couch and pulled her knees to her chin. Antwon made a dash towards the stairs and I shot him in the leg. He fell down the stairs and started pleading for his life.

"Yo, I'm sorry, bruh. Come on, Beretta. I'll pay you your money back. Just give me two months," he said. I shot him in the other leg and he screamed for help. I knocked him out cold with the butt of my gun.

Twenty minutes later...

I heard heavy footsteps coming down the basement stairs. Quanta pointed his gun at me and Emma ran to him.

"I'm here, now what?" he asked.

Pistol came downstairs with Sniper behind him. They both had their guns pointed at Quanta. I texted them while I was waiting on Quanta to show up because I didn't know the nigga like that. He could've brought other niggas with him to merk me. GMBAM niggas were surrounding the house, waiting for something to pop off.

"It's about twenty niggas outside in the cut waitin' to merk you. So I'd put the gun down, bruh," I said. Quanta lowered the gun and Sniper snatched it from him. Emma buried her face into her man's chest and he held her close. The nigga was in a fucked-up situation because his shorty was exposed to his other life. I would've lost my mind if it was my wife. I felt sorry for the nigga. He probably thought nobody would be bold enough to touch his woman but niggas would do anything when their lives were on the line.

"He came by himself," Sniper said. I respected Quanta's gangsta. Not too many niggas would risk their lives for their girl.

"Y'all niggas got beef wit' me, so let my girl walk out of here," he said.

"Nobody is walkin' until I see fifty g's of my money," I replied.

"I don't have yah fuckin' money, slim," he said.

"That's not what I want to hear. I know it ain't yah fault, bruh, but I'm short fifty g's and a dead man can't pay me back," I replied.

"What do you want me to do?" he asked.

"I want your territory," I replied.

"Nigga, what!" he said.

"You heard him, nigga. He wants your territory. You can't be makin' no bread if you can't give the man his fifty g's back," Pistol said.

"It's hot right now because I'm beefin' wit' a few niggas so ain't nobody eatin'," Quanta admitted. I respected his honesty. Most niggas I came across in the streets hated admitting to being broke.

"Let me holla at this nigga in private. Take Emma upstairs and make sure she's straight," I told Pistol and Sniper. Quanta didn't want to let her go; he didn't trust me, neither.

"She's friends wit' my wife, bruh. I ain't gonna hurt her," I said.

"I'll be fine," Emma said. She pulled away from him and followed Pistol and Sniper upstairs.

"Yung, don't hurt my girl," he said.

"I ain't got no issues wit' shorty, but we can talk business. Tell me about this street beef," I replied.

"Come on, yung. You can't be serious," he said.

"Dead ass serious," I replied.

"This nigga and his goons have been knocking my squad MMN off for the past few weeks. It's only me and a few other niggas left but those niggas laying low. I ain't got fifty g's, I'm broke. The money I have saved up is to keep a roof over me and my girl's heads," he said.

"I'll take care of dat for you," I replied.

"What do I have to do in return?" he asked.

"Push my weight on your territory and we're even," I said.

"I'll forever be in debt to you," he replied.

"Look at it as a business move because the way I see it, these niggas gonna end up merkin' you, too. So, what's it gonna be, bruh? You'll be eatin', too, probably betta than eva," I said.

"I'll do it," he replied.

I handed him my gun and he looked at it.

"Merk him," I said, talkin' about Antwon.

Quanta put the gun to Antwon's head and pulled the trigger three times.

With me gaining access to another territory, I was able to push those extra bricks Chulo was giving to me for a low price. And because I didn't have to lower the price to get rid of them faster anymore, I was able to go back to selling them at full price. My wife was going to get her mansion sooner than she thought.

****

"It's eight o'clock in the morning," Mara said when I walked into the bedroom.

"I had to take care of some important shit," I replied and she rolled her eyes at me. Zalia started crying and I looked at Mara because I wasn't getting up. I spent more time with Zalia than Mara did because she was always studying or doing school work. I wasn't tripping but a nigga was missing sleep.

"Can you get her for me?" Mara asked.

"Fuck no," I replied.

"Please, Z'wan. I'll do that thing you like," she said, biting her bottom lip.

"Man, aight and you betta do it soon as she goes back to sleep, too. Go on ahead and exercise your jaws," I replied. I left out of the bedroom and went to Zalia's room. She stopped crying when I picked her up.

"Daddy's little g—," I said but I caught myself. I didn't know how I felt about calling Zalia my daughter. In my mind, it felt like I was betraying Zyira. Zalia looked at me with her pretty eyes and I rocked her. I kissed her forehead and she kicked her feet.

"You my baby girl, you know dat, don't you?" I asked and she smiled. Kemara stood in the doorway with a towel wrapped around her.

"Awww, Z'wan. You're so sweet," she said.

"I'm a sucka for kids, you know dat," I replied.

"I'll feed her. Go ahead and lay down," Kemara said, reaching her arms out. I gave her Zalia but a nigga wasn't trying to lay down.

"Naw, shorty. You said you wanted to do sumthin to me so hurry up with it," I replied and smacked her on the ass. My cell phone was vibrating on the nightstand when I walked into the bedroom. I picked it up and answered.

"Yooo," I said.

"Oh, hey, Z'wan, this is Lashonda. I got your number from Nika when I saw her at the gas station this morning. I'm calling because Moesha is in the hospital because of complications. I don't know what's going on between the two of you but she needs you," Lashonda said.

"Dat ain't my baby," I replied.

"You were laid up with her in my fucking house for three days! You wouldn't be smelling yourself if Ammo was alive. He's turning in his grave right now for how you're doing his nephew. Your wife just has to deal with it because Z'wan Jr. isn't going anywhere," she said.

"I want a fucking blood test!" I spat into the phone.

"A blood test for what?" Kemara asked and I almost dropped my phone. I hung up and sat my phone back down on the nightstand. It was time to confess everything because the shit was on my mind, and each day that passed, the guilt worsened.

"Ay yo, Mara. I gotta rap to you about sumthin," I said.

"I'm listenin'," she said, crossing her arms.

"Can you sit down and listen?" I asked.

"No, I can't," she replied.

"Moesha claimin' dat I'm the father of her seed, but I didn—," I was cut off from a hard slap in the face. Kemara wouldn't let me finish, she was swinging on me. I slammed her down on the bed and held her arms down. She tried to knee me between my legs but I pressed my knees into her thighs so she wouldn't move.

"Get da fuck off of me! I knew it was some shit wit' you! I fuckin' knew it!" she screamed.

"I don't remember fuckin' her, so calm down. Just listen to me, Mara!" I said. I held her down for ten minutes until she calmed down. I pulled away from her and she sat up with tears falling from her eyes.

"A baby?" she asked in disbelief.

"Mara, I didn't fuck dat girl. She sent me these pictures but I was asleep in all of them. I ran into her like a month ago and she told me she was carrying my seed," I said.

"So, if you were drunk, you don't know for sure if you fucked her or not!" Mara screamed at me.

"Dat's not my seed!" I said.

"You knew this before we got married and didn't say shit to me? Our fucking marriage is a fraud! Do you hear me? My nigga is a fuckin' fraud. I'm not playin' step mommy to your damn child! You played me, Z'wan. I'on trust your trifling' lyin' ass. I should've known you fucked dat bitch. Tell me everything, and so help me God, I'll kill you if I find out some other shit," she said. It was the hardest shit I had to do. A nigga felt like he was in court getting a life sentence. I told Kemara about Amona, the trip to Miami and sleeping with her. I didn't think it was that bad until I heard myself tell her the truth. The shit hurt me, too, but I had to get it all out.

"I should've killed you when we were in the hotel room. You were a lick and I fell in love wit' you. I wouldn't in this marriage if I had merked you. I hate you so much right now. I spent months in a hospital, recovering from losing our daughter and you're telling me that you were living your best life with another bitch? A bitch you claimed you didn't have no involvements with when I asked you. You got bitches laughing at me! We're married, Z'wan. I'm your wife!" she screamed. Kemara flipped the mattress over and grabbed a gun. She aimed it at my head. It wasn't the first time she pulled a gun out on me, but it was the first time I thought she was going to use it.

"You don't love me," she cried. I tried to reach out to her but she took the safety off.

"Beretta, I'll kill you if you come near me!" she said.

"Shorty, I love you and you know dat! It was just sex and that was it!" I pleaded. Kemara wasn't trying to hear shit I had to say and I couldn't blame her, but I wanted to take her head off when she told me Zyira wasn't my daughter. I charged into her and the gun went off...

Kemara

Beretta slammed me onto the floor and snatched the gun from me after it went off. I wanted to kill him, but I probably wouldn't have been able to live with myself. The bullet grazed his arm and blood was dripping on the floor. Beretta lifted me off the floor by my hair then slammed me into the wall.

"Run dat shit by me again, bitch? Zyira wasn't my daughter?" he asked. I tried to hit him again but I missed.

"Get the fuck off of me!" I screamed and he choked me.

"On God, I'll kill you! You know how much she means to me and I'll hurt anybody over her and not give a fuck! Tell me dat bullshit again, Kemara," he said.

"You lost me for good this time. I can't believe you gave another woman a piece of us! A piece I'll never get back. You can't unhurt me. I loved you so much and gave you everything you wanted from me! How could you fuck her?" I cried. Beretta pulled away from me and sat on the bed.

"Shorty, you know I love you more than anything and I fucked up as your boyfriend. But I won't fuck up as your husband and you have my word," he said with tears falling from his eyes. Beretta knew how serious I was because he felt every emotion that came out of me. He also knew shit would never be the same again because he lost my trust.

"I'm supposed to be the only one to carry yah fuckin' child! I'll never accept it. You got me fucked up if you think our vows are gonna keep me with an ungrateful, dirty dick, bastard. You were supposed to be just mine and you fucked it all up. I hope Amona has extra space for you because you gotta get the fuck outta my house," I said.

"We gonna talk about this," he said and stood up.

"We can talk in front the judge when we get a divorce," I replied. Zalia started crying and I almost forgot she was in the house. I should've known better than to pull out a gun but I was too angry... I was hurt. Keeping my game face on and pretending to not give a fuck was tiring. I wanted Beretta to see how much he hurt me.

"What's the matter wit' me? Is it because I'm not polished enough? I'm not perfect and neither are you so I thought our flaws would've made us perfect together. Our wedding was supposed to change my life so I could let go of all the hurt. I thought we finally did it! But you knew you lied the whole time and you want to look me in my fucking face and tell me you love me?" I asked. Beretta couldn't look at me. All of a sudden, he was quiet and didn't have shit else to say. I grabbed his face and forced him to look at me.

"If I ever hurt you, just remember you hurt me first. You better eat all that shit up and take it like a man because I'm tired of this shit," I said. Beretta pulled away from me and silently left the house. I went to Zalia's room and picked her up. It was time I got off my ass and got a job. I could've easily went back to robbing niggas but I had someone else to look after. Zalia needed me because she didn't have anyone else and I'd be damned if she had to grow up in the streets.

****

I turned my phone off for four days and stayed in the house with Zalia. The dishes were piled up in the sink and my bedroom still had Beretta's blood on the floor. All I could do was feed and change Zalia but I stayed in bed the whole time. I didn't eat anything or even shower. Beretta was cold-hearted but I didn't think he could be that cold. He cheated on me right after I lost our daughter. Not only did he cheat, there was a possibility Moesha was carrying his child. Her giving him his first son and naming the baby after him was a slap in the face. I burst into sobs thinking about everything. I thought he cried when we got married because of joy, but it was guilt eating him up. After all, my marriage was a ploy to keep me tied down to him and his dirt. Poppa warned me but I was in love, so in love that I lost myself.

The doorbell rang, bringing me out of my train of thought. I remained in bed, staring at the ceiling fan. The bell rang for thirty minutes before I decided to get up.

"WAIT!" I yelled from the top stairs.

I opened the door and it was Silk and Piper with bottles of wine. My hair was all over the place and my underarms were musty.

"Ohhhhh, honeyyyyy. We need to hurry up and save you," Silk said, stepping into my home. Piper hugged me and rubbed my back.

"Beretta called me and told me to check up on you. Let's sit down so I can talk to you," Piper said.

"I don't feel like talking about Beretta. Y'all can make yourselves at home. I'm going back to bed before Zalia wakes up," I replied.

"No, you're not going back to bed. We are gonna sit and talk about this because, chile, I know how you can get and we don't want that shit to happen again," Silk said.

"Beretta cheated on me and Moesha is pregnant," I replied.

"That's what I wanted to talk to you about," Piper said.

"Yeah, she has sumthin to tell you and I know you're gonna be mad but hear her out," Silk said. I looked at the both of them, pondering what they had to tell me. I became nauseous because I was afraid to find out about more of Beretta's dirt. Tears fell from my eyes and Silk hugged me.

SOUL Publications

"Oh, hell nawl! I'm fightin' Beretta!" Silk fussed.

"He stripped me from my dignity. Look at me," I sobbed.

"Thickems told me about the pictures Moesha showed her. I wanted to tell you but Pistol said Moesha took advantage of him while he was passed out. I'm so sorry, Mara, but I just wanted you to be happy. I didn't want Poppa to prove he was right about y'all because he always gets what he wants from you. I still believe Beretta," Piper said.

"You and Thickems knew about this shit and didn't tell me! Y'all watched me marry that piece of shit!" I yelled and Silk pulled me back.

"Get the fuck outta my house, Piper! Fuck you!" I screamed.

"I'm tryna talk to you. Don't let Moesha ruin your marriage," Piper said.

"If Beretta fucked Amona after I lost my daughter, what makes you think he couldn't fuck Moesha after Ammo's death? All these excuses for him ain't gonna cut it. So-fuckin'-what he was goin' through something. So was I! Beretta might have y'all fooled but he's a manipulator, just like his nasty-ass mama. We have been friends for years and you couldn't tell me my man was caught wit' another bitch? I don't give a fuck what you thought! You ain't married to the nigga, I am! It's easy for you and that bitch Thickems to say it wasn't nothing. I should fight both of y'all bitches," I fussed.

"No, we are gonna talk about this," Silk said and I snatched away from him.

"Get dat hoe outta my house before I kill her and she know I would. I got too many snakes in my grass. It's time for me to mow my lawn, and tell Thickems, fuck her, too. Fuck all of y'all," I said.

"You like being miserable. So miserable you don't know what happiness looks like. I was looking out for you. You knew Moesha was tryin' to break y'all up, so why let her? I would never do anything to hurt you. I thought my intentions were pure," Piper said.

"I don't know what happiness looks like? Bitch, you got some nerve! I guess you have the answer since you're fuckin' two niggas. I was happy! You don't think my wedding day meant something to me? What about me seeing my first sonogram of Zyira. Hoe, I was very fuckin' happy, so don't tell me I don't know what it looks like. You are my sister and I'll go to war for you but you fucked up, so own it. I would've waited to get married if I knew my nigga was out hoeing around," I replied. Piper wiped her eyes before she sat the wine bottles down on the kitchen table. She stormed out of the door, letting it slam behind her.

"I'm sad behind this, Mara. Be mad at her. Hell, I was mad at her, too, when she told me earlier but you know dat girl loves you. She made a mistake—shit, we all do, but best friends neva fold under pressure, hunty," Silk said.

"I still love Piper and she's gonna always be my sista but I don't have to like her right now," I replied.

"We rode in separate cars because I had a feelin' this wanna happen. But, chile, go take a shower. You smell like Darcel," Silk joked and I rolled my eyes.

"Listen out for Zalia for me," I replied and headed upstairs. Silk being in my company lifted my spirits because he kept me sane at times. Yelling at Piper crushed me because that was our first real argument. Beretta was changing my life, even my friendships. The nigga was just bad for me all together.

Two hours later...

Silk stayed at my home and helped me clean up. I told him I had to run out to get a few things for Zalia before I left out. My first stop was the pet store around the corner from my loft then I headed to Hanover, Maryland. It took me thirty minutes to get to the townhouse I used to live in with Beretta. His car wasn't in the driveway but the light was on in the living room. He had the nerve to bring a bitch into our home. It didn't matter that I moved out, I once lived there and still had the key. But he still had it and I wondered if he kept it for his side bitches. I unlocked the door and the place was spotless. When I walked into the living room, I saw a pair of sandals on the floor and a chef apron. Hope's toys were sprawled out on the floor and DVDs of kids' cartoons were all over the coffee table. Tears fell from my eyes because my husband was playing house with another bitch! I went upstairs to our bedroom and nothing looked out the ordinary so I assumed they spent most of their time downstairs. For some reason, I wanted to go back to our first home together. Tired of reminiscing, I left out of the house and popped the trunk to my car. I grabbed two crates and walked back into the house. I took one crate upstairs to our master bedroom and went into the closet. Boxes and clothes were in the way, so I moved them to get to his safe. When I opened the safe, Beretta had it filled with stacks of money but I could care less about his money.

"Okay, Mara, you can do this," I said to myself while putting on a pair of gloves. I opened the crate and inside were two tarantulas, one male and female. My hands violently shook as I picked up the big hairy spider. I screamed as I placed it inside the safe.

"One more to go," I said aloud, while beads of sweat dripped down my forehead. I almost fainted when the tarantula started kicking its legs. I threw the second one inside the safe then hurriedly closed it. There was one more crate, a bigger one. I said a silent prayer before I opened it. Ten rats ran out of the crate and I hauled ass out the house. Beretta was a snake to me and I was feeding his ass a year's supply of food. After I got into my car, I sped off and jumped on to the interstate to go back home.

****

"I was getting worried about you. What took you so long? You need to turn dat fuckin' phone on," Silk said when I walked into the crib. He looked at me and shook his head when he noticed I didn't have any bags.

"Where is the stuff for Zalia?" he asked.

"Huh?" I replied.

"Bitch, you heard me. What did you do, Mara? You ain't kill nobody did you because you a little cray," Silk said as he stretched his long legs. I kicked off my tennis shoes and took my coat off.

"I just had to clear my mind," I said and shrugged it off.

"I would love to stay but I gotta hotel date. You need anything before I go? Let me know now because I'm gonna be gone for a few days," he said.

"I'm good, now get outta my house," I smirked. He grabbed his pea coat and promised to call me in the morning before he left. I picked Zalia up from her play pen and headed upstairs to my bedroom. My phone was on the nightstand and I was contemplating on turning it on. Curiosity got the best of me after a few minutes. I had so many alerts from Facebook messages as soon as I turned my phone on. My blood boiled all over again because it was Moesha. Seeing your man in pictures with another woman in sexual positions wasn't easy to stomach. She was on top of Beretta kissing his lips, but I couldn't see his face because of her weave but the hoe was naked. Moesha also told me she was going to make my life a living hell until Beretta manned up and was there for her and their son.

Beretta

Three days later...

Five niggas sat on the floor in front of me with their arms tied. I promised Quanta I was going to take care of his problem and I got it done in no time. I had to keep myself busy so I wouldn't think about my wife but the shit was hard. Quanta's beef became a personal one for me because merking niggas temporarily eased my pain.

"We can take this," Sniper said. We were inside Strike's trap house. Strike was the nigga who was merking Quanta's squad and moving in on his territory. We raided their home dressed in all black with gear that resembled a policeman's. On the table was stacks of money and bricks of cocaine.

"This shit is trash," my nigga, Wesson, said about the drugs.

"Nigga, fuck you!" Strike said. I lifted my foot and gave him a swift kick to his face. He fell back on to the floor with blood dripping from his mouth.

"Yo, just take what you want!" one of his boys said.

"Nigga, I don't want dat fake shit. Who is y'all niggas' connect?" I asked.

"Don't tell him shit!" Strike yelled.

"This nigga thinks he's still running shit. Give me my knife, Sniper," I said. Sniper handed me a combat knife and I kneeled next to Strike. I pressed my knee into his neck and he opened his mouth to gasp for air. He groaned in pain and tears filled his eyes when my knife sliced through his tongue.

"Do anybody else got a fuckin' problem wit' not tellin' me what I wanna know?" I asked.

"Yo, all I know is his name is Rich. He told us to get rid of MMN by pushing our product through their turf. That's it! I neva met the nigga up close," a guy said.

"Ain't Rich the nigga Poppa fuck with?" Machete asked me.

"Come on, yung. We told you everything, so let us go," another one begged. I pulled out my Beretta and shot him between the eyes. I nodded my head, giving my niggas the "OK" to handle everything. Gunshots flew through Strike's men's bodies, blowing holes through their chests.

SOUL Publications

Blood and brain matter decorated the floors and walls of the small living room.

"What do you want to do wit' this?" Machete asked about the bloody drugs on the table.

"Burn it with the house but take the money," I replied.

"What we gonna do about Rich?" Sniper asked.

"Hit up Jasmine and tell her to take care of dat. I'm sick of these clown-ass niggas, bruh. Every fuckin' thing is always connected to Poppa's bitch ass homeboys. He's a thorn in my side," I replied.

"He'll fall like the rest of 'em," Sniper said.

"So, da nigga Rich a king pin or sum shit?" Wesson asked.

"Naw, he got a bunch of dummies to move fake weight. Some shit he probably made himself. Nowadays, niggas will sell their soul to anybody who they think can put food in their mouths. Rich knew he couldn't pull that shit in Annapolis so he came to an area where niggas don't know him," I said.

"Yo, let's burn this place up and bounce. I got a taste for some ribs," Sniper replied. I walked out the small rundown house and headed to my stolen van with fake tags. I didn't pull off until I saw smoke coming from the house and my squad walking out. They got into another van and pulled off. I headed into another direction. My townhouse wasn't too far from where I was at. I called

Pistol so he could meet me because I had to ditch the van. While waiting for him, I rolled up a blunt to calm my nerves. Kemara had a nigga having anxiety attacks or something. It was crazy how she had that effect on me. Every time I thought of the word "divorce," my heart beat faster. I couldn't deal with none of it. I hurt her so bad I hated myself. Not only was I missing her, I was missing Zalia, too. It wasn't an easy thing to adjust to, but I spent a lot of time with her. I called Kemara three times before she decided to answer the phone. It was two o'clock in the morning and she sounded wide awake. I sat on the phone for a few seconds because I didn't know what to say. Honestly, I was surprised she answered the phone.

"What do you want?" she spat.

"Yo, I, um, was wondering if I could see Zalia. I know you don't wanna see me, so can you drop her off at Pistol's aunt's crib?" I asked.

"Zalia ain't yah fuckin' daughter! Bitch, go see about your son," Kemara spat.

"Shorty, I'on wanna argue witchu. I'm beggin' you to cooperate wit' me on this. Can I please see my daughter? I miss her," I replied. I wasn't trying to hear about Zalia not being mine after Kemara gave her my last name.

"I'll think about it," she said.

"I love you, Mara. I know I fucked up bu—," I was cut off because she hung up on me. I called her right back and she sent me to voicemail. There was a knock on my window and I pointed my gun at the dark figure. I lowered it once I realized it was Pistol.

"Yo, get out before police start lookin' for this van," he said. I got out the van and walked over to his whip. I took my gloves off before getting into his truck.

"Kemara still trippin' on you, bruh?" Pistol asked as he pulled off on the dark back road.

"I think she's gonna divorce me. I ain't lettin' her do dat shit, though," I replied.

"She'll cool off. It's only been a week," he said.

"Dat bitch tryna get to me but I ain't gonna fold. Fuck her. Shorty only actin like dat because she tryna be a hoe," I replied.

"Y'all niggas need counseling," Pistol chuckled.

I smoked my blunt and rode the rest of the way to my crib in silence. Niggas didn't understand how fucked up I was feeling. Kemara was happy when we got married and I took that shit away from her. My heart started racing again, so I hit the blunt harder.

"I think I'm gettin' sick, bruh," I replied.

"Nigga, you need to get some sleep. You look fucked up," Pistol said, pulling up into my driveway. I'd been up for the past two days, ripping and running the streets because I couldn't sleep. I was practically living in a hotel room.

"Yo, when are you gonna let this crib go?" Pistol asked. I kept the townhouse because my safe was in there. I checked up on it once a week if that. I'd go in to put my money up then bounce.

"I'on know, bruh. This was my first real home with Mara," I replied. I got out of Pistol's whip and he got out behind me with a duffel bag. While I was handling Strike and his boys, Pistol was collecting money niggas owed me. I unlocked the door then punched the code in but something was off about my crib.

"You hear dat?" I asked, pulling out my gun.

"Don't start dat paranoid shit, bruh. I'on hear shit," Pistol said. Something ran past my feet. I thought I was tripping because of the kush I was smoking.

"Nigga, you ain't see dat?" I asked, walking into the living room. On the floor were black coffee beans.

"Bruh, dat look like rat shit," Pistol said.

"Rats? This ain't da hood," I replied.

Two fat rats crawled across my couch and another one was next to the fireplace. Pistol screwed the silencer on his gun and shot it. A few more rats ran across my feet.

"Fuck this crib," I said and ran up the stairs. I was going to empty my safe then bounce. After I punched the code in, I pulled stacks of money out and a big ass spider crawled up my arm. Pistol came into the master bedroom.

"Yo, you got two rats fuckin' on your kitchen counter by the bread," he laughed. The spider got down in my hoodie and I took it off.

"Da fuck is that?" he asked and I smacked it off.

"I'm gonna kill dat bitch! Kemara did this shit. She's the only one who knows the code to my safe," I said. I went back into the closet and baby spiders were everywhere and crawling on my money. I heard a loud crash and I looked over my shoulder. Pistol was running around the room while the spider chased him.

"Yooooo, this nigga chasing me!" he shouted. He shot at it but missed. A rat came from underneath the bed and grabbed the spider.

"Oh, shit, bruh. Comere and look at this shit. Bet twenty on da rat," Pistol said, recording the fight. It was funny until the spider killed the rat. Pistol rushed out of the bedroom and I followed him after I had all my money in the duffel bags. He was gagging in the driveway with spit hanging from his mouth when I walked out the crib.

"Yo, you good? I know yah bitch ass ain't scared. We had roaches in the hood bigger than all dat shit up in there," I chuckled.

"Fuck you, yo. Kemara crazy as fuck! My nigga, just take the divorce and walk away," he said, scratching. I got back into his whip because my truck was at the hotel I was staying at. I texted Kemara and told her she was foul for doing my crib like that. Shorty responded back and told me snakes eat rats and spiders are symbolic of feminine power.

I would've given you a black widow but they don't sell those at the pet store. Be grateful because they are venomous...

That's what her last text message read. In so many words, my wife was letting me know she had the upper hand.

"I think my wife got me caught up in her web and she fittin' to chew me up and spit me out," I said to Pistol.

"You gotta fix it, bruh, because she can be your downfall. She knows about your money, how you move and how to hustle. Bruh, you stuck and the only way out is if you merk her but you ain't gonna do dat," he replied.

I can't merk Mara but what if my operation is on the line? How far is Mara willing to go to crush a nigga's ego? Do I wanna go to war wit' my own wife? I knew what type of female she was and still cheated on her, so it's on me, but fuck dat. I grinded too hard to get where I am, I thought.

SOUL Publications

Twenty minutes later, Pistol pulled up to the hotel I was staying at. The nigga was still scratching and twitching when I opened the door to get out.

"Bruh, you good?" I asked.

"Yo, I hate spiders. I can deal with a few rats but that was a gigantic-ass spider. Shit was hairy, too. Fuck dat, I'm sittin' in bleach when I get in the crib. Your wife needs help, bruh, and on da real. I'on even wanna be around her anymore. Keep your marriage problems to yourself," he said. Pistol was heated!

"Shorty is trippin' but I'll get up witchu lata. Oh, yeah, Glock hit me up earlier. He said he is coming home early. He'll be out by summer time. His lawyer saw a few things wrong with his arrest so they threw one of his cases out. He only gettin' charged for the weed instead of the gun," I said.

"Yeah, I talked to him," Pistol said but I knew his mind was somewhere else.

"Yo, you ain't tell Glock about you and Piper?" I asked.

"I tried a few times but it couldn't come out. I fucked up big time," he said.

"I can't have y'all niggas beefin' over a broad. We are like brothers, nigga. Talk to me, bruh, I'm listening," I said and closed the passenger door.

"We built GMBAM on loyalty and I went against the code," he replied.

"On some real shit, I'm GMBAM all day every day for the rest of my life, but I'm not gonna let it control me. I went against all the shit I taught myself just to be with Kemara. Shorty admitted that I was supposed to be a lick. She's supposed to be dead by now according to the GMBAM code, but I love my wife. If Piper just a broad you were fuckin' then move on and don't say shit, but if you feelin' shorty, Glock will accept it because we are brothers before anything," I replied and he scratched his chin.

"I kinda love her," Pistol smirked and I chuckled.

"Nigga, stop bluffin'. You hate dat nigga, Delonte, and he ain't do shit to you. Shit, you got me side-eyeing the nigga, too," I replied.

"Thanks, bruh. I'll take your word because you are always right. I'on know how you do it," he said.

"Yeah, except when it comes to my wife. I'll fix it, though. I'll get up wit' you tomorrow," I said. We slapped hands before I got out of his whip with my duffel bags.

****

After I showered, I laid across the bed staring at the ceiling. I was straight when I was running around but laying alone fucked with me. I closed my eyes for ten minutes but still couldn't sleep. Kemara cut me off a few times but I knew shorty was coming right back; not this time. I broke her heart during a time when I should've been mending it. A tear slipped out of my eye and I hurriedly wiped it away.

Yo, man da fuck up and stop cryin' over dat bitch. You can have any bad bitch you want. Fuck Kemara, I thought. I got on Facebook and went to her page. I had a Facebook page even though I wasn't a social media type of day. My profile pic was of Newtowne and I had a random name just in case the FEDS was watching. Too many niggas were getting locked up from fucking with social media. Kemara accepted my friend request a few days ago, not knowing who it was, but knowing her, she probably knew it was me. Shorty knew me better than anybody. I checked her page and she deleted our wedding pics and changed her status to "divorced." She had pictures of her and Zalia at the grocery store. She posted it a day ago and it messed my head up because she looked happy—relieved. I had it all and lost it in the blink of an eye.

"What da fuck!" I yelled out. Dat nigga Chevy Mara used to fuck with commented underneath my wife and daughter's picture, talking about, "next time invite me." Kemara's stupid ass commented, "bet." I threw my phone into the wall and went to the small fridge to grab a bottle of Henny—a man's savior.

A week later...

"Babe, are you okay?" Larissa asked me while looking through my dreads. I went to get my hair re-twisted at this shorty's crib who had a salon in her basement. Larissa wanted me to fuck her, even offered to suck my dick, but she wasn't attractive. Matter of fact, she looked exactly like Donald Duck with a short blonde hair cut.

"Yeah, I'm straight," I replied, wanting her to hurry up with it.

"Your hair is shedding bad in the middle, it's damaged. What the hell happened? It was healthy a month or so ago," she said.

"Cut it off," I replied. She walked from behind me and grilled me with her hands on her hips.

"Oh, hell nawl! Nigga, I have been twisting your hair for years. I can't let you cut these beautiful locs off. It's no problem, I can fix it. A lot of people's hair tends to break off in cold weather," she replied.

"Yo, just cut da shit off, damn. It ain't me anymore, you feel me?" I asked.

"Aight, cool," she replied. Pistol came out of the bathroom and saw Larissa cutting my dreads off. He also came to her crib to get his hair braided.

"My nigga, what is you doin'? Me, you and Ammo made a deal when we were teens. We ain't supposed to cut our hair until the dirty thirty," he replied and I chuckled. We were young when we made that bet.

"Hair grows back," I replied.

SOUL Publications

"Fuck it, I'll get mine cut, too, then. Chocolate niggas wit' waves are in style now, ain't dat right, baby girl?" Pistol asked Larissa.

"I can't believe this," Larissa said with an attitude. Her sister, Eva, came down into the basement wearing tight sweatpants and shorty was thick. I smashed her a few times a couple of years ago before I was with Kemara. I had to cut her off because she got married. Eva was around my mother's age and Larissa was six years older than me. She rolled her eyes and me and Pistol cracked up. Shorty couldn't stand me.

"How long you gonna be? I got somewhere to be in a few hours," Eva said to Larissa.

"Not long, have a seat or sumthin," Larissa said and smacked her teeth. My phone beeped and it was Kemara telling me to meet her at Silk's crib at noon so I could get Zalia. Almost two weeks had passed and she was finally letting me see her. An hour later, I was standing in the mirror looking at my fresh cut and trimmed goatee. I pulled out a hundred-dollar bill and paid Larissa.

"Finally, he looks like sumthin," Eva said, while flipping through a magazine.

"Yo, you still trippin' over dat?" I smirked and she blushed.

"Whateva, I got a grown-ass man now. You still got breast milk on your breath," Eva said and I shook my head.

"Be nice, Eva, damn," Larissa laughed.

Pistol sat in the chair and told Larissa to hurry up and cut his hair. That nigga was bluffing. The only reason he really wanted his hair cut was because he thought spiders got into it. He washed his hair twice a day since it happened because he thought something was crawling on him. While he was getting his hair cut, I was thinking about seeing Kemara for the first time since she kicked me out her crib.

Kemara

"**W**here you going?" Silk asked, as he eyed my outfit. I was wearing a forest green, stretch, skin-tight sweater dress with brown knee-high heeled boots. My Brazilian weave stopped above my butt, styled in deep wavy curls. The leather jacket with fur around the neck set the outfit off. I was looking so good, I had to put extra sway to my hips when I walked.

"I'm goin' out to have a few drinks with Emma," I replied.

"Do you have on panties underneath dat dress?" Silk asked.

"Yeah, nigga, it ain't hot outside," I replied. He took Zalia out of her car seat and took off her jacket.

"Beretta should be on his way, so I need to hurry up and leave," I replied.

"Girlllll, don't you go out here and get a nigga killed by GMBAM, shit. You playin' wit' fire. If I can't hit it, nobody else can," Silk said.

"Whatever, thank you for everything and call me later," I replied. I kissed his cheek and rushed out the door because it was almost noon. I wasn't paying attention and bumped into a nigga on my way down the stairs. He wrapped his arms around my hips because I almost fell. The cologne was all too familiar and so was his touch. I moved my hair out of my eyes and Beretta was staring at me.

GOT DAMN! I thought.

I cut him off, kicked him out of my house, took Zalia away from him and put spiders and rats in his home. He wasn't supposed to look better than he ever did. He cut his hair off and his waves made me dizzy. I pulled away from him and fixed my jacket. He grabbed my hand and realized I wasn't wearing my ring. Beretta's jaw tightened when he saw how my dress was hugging my curves.

"Where you about to go?" he asked.

"To a place," I replied.

"When can we sit down and talk about us? I have been livin' in a fuckin' hotel for almost two weeks," he said.

"What happened to the townhouse you share with Ammonia? I saw her shit in there," I replied.

"Shorty, dat shit is old. I only go there to stash my money then leave. I'on know what's laying around in there," he said.

"Umph, well anyways. Zalia is in the house. Call me later," I replied. I tried to walk off but he trapped me in the corner of the building.

"Yo, why you fuckin' playin' wit' me?" he asked, grabbing my face and looking down at me. He pressed his body into mine and I felt the gun he had on his hip.

"I'm not playin' witchu. Now, can you let me leave?" I asked calmly.

"I love you," he said and it angered me. I pushed him away and walked out the building.

"Yo, you still my fuckin' wife!" he called out to me with sadness dripping from his voice. I got into my Range Rover and pulled out of the parking lot to meet up with Emma.

****

Fifteen minutes later, I met up with Emma downtown Annapolis at a sushi bar. She was sitting at a table in the corner of the restaurant. I hadn't seen her since my wedding. I hugged her before I sat across from her.

"You look cute. You and Beretta got a date later on?" she asked.

"We're split up right now," I replied, embarrassed.

"Like as in, broken up? Y'all just got married," she said.

"He's the reason why I haven't been keeping my phone on much. It's so much shit going on. Beretta might have a baby on the way and he cheated on me with his mother's best friend. He made me look so fuckin' stupid," I replied. A waitress came over and we ordered our appetizers and a pitcher of mojito. I told Emma everything after the waitress walked away.

"I was kidnapped," Emma said.

"WHAT!" I replied.

"It's a long story but I was leaving out of the library and some guy put a pillowcase over my head and threw me inside of his trunk. He beat me and tortured me for hours. He worked for Beretta and Beretta came there and realized who I was. I thought he was going to kill me but he untied me. It was a big misunderstanding between Quanta and Beretta but they solved it and now they're cool," she said.

"I'm so sorry to hear that. Is he dead? The guy who hurt you?" I asked.

"Quanta killed him. I don't know how I got sucked into this and it scared the shit out of me but I know too much to turn back now. You are the only person I can talk to about this because I trust you," she said.

"You gotta learn how to shoot and start keepin' a gun on you at all times. This isn't a fairytale life, baby. Sometimes, bitches gotta show their hand to gain respect because you'll get walked on if you don't," I replied and she agreed.

"What if the baby isn't his?" Emma asked.

"He cheated on me with another woman. I think he had feelings for her. It wasn't just a fuck, he was spending time with her and Beretta values his time to throw it away on a hoe he doesn't care about. I lost respect for him," I said.

"And you're still mad at Piper and Thickems?" she asked.

"I'll talk to them when I'm ready. Right now, it's all about me and what I want," I replied.

"Let him come back home," Emma said.

"Girl, have you been listening to me?" I asked.

"I have been listening but just hear me out. Why let your husband roam the streets when his home is wit' you? You don't want him getting comfortable with another woman. Let him come back home and make him live under your roof as your roommate. What about Zalia and college? It's hard studying with a baby and Beretta made sure you didn't have to stress about schoolwork," she said.

"Who told you this was normal?" I giggled.

"My mother did it to my father when he stepped out on her. He had to sleep in another room. He hasn't cheated since and they have been together for thirty years," Emma replied.

"I put a bunch of rats and spiders in our old home," I told Emma and she bust out laughing.

"Ewww, you touched that shit?" she asked.

"Honey, my revengeful heart overshadowed the fear I had for those huge spiders," I laughed. While we were talking, Lezzi and Amona walked into the bar. Lezzi worked in the building a few blocks down, so I wasn't surprised to see her, but I damn sure wasn't looking forward to seeing Amona.

"I spoke his bitch up too soon," I said to Emma. The waitress sat them at a table next to us.

"Hey, hoes," I said.

Beretta told me they were cousins when he confessed to all of his foolery. I guess him and Pistol called themselves double-dating two older bitches who was only looking for young dick.

"Ignore her," Amona said to Lezzi while looking at her menu. The waitress came over with me and Emma's food and drinks but I lost my appetite.

"So, Amona, how was dat dick you got in the back seat of my husband's car? I would've respected you more if you made him get a hotel room. Do you still love him? Inquiring minds wanna know," I asked.

"Girl, do you know how to act in public? But then again, a crackhead raised you," Lezzi said.

"Oh, bitch, don't get me started on you because your nigga wasn't even sleepin' next to you at night," I said.

"Let's just go. I don't like sushi anyway," Amona said to Lezzi.

"But you like other bitch's men, though?" I asked.

"Be happy, Kemara. You got your husband and your make-believe daughter, so you should be celebrating life, honey," Amona said. I stood up from the table and grabbed my chair. Lezzi screamed when I swung the chair and cracked Amona in the face with it. She fell on the floor and I jumped on her. I wrapped my hand around her throat and slammed my fist into her bloody face. She screamed for help and Lezzi pulled my hair. Emma grabbed Lezzi's shirt and yanked her off me. The people in the bar sat and watched until the manager came from the back.

"I'm callin' the police!" the manager screamed. Amona scratched at my face and I banged her head against the floor. I was snatched off Amona and someone helped her stand up. She almost collapsed onto the floor.

"You were in my fuckin' house! Bitch, you're dead!" I yelled. Amona grabbed a knife off a table and charge towards me. I snatched her by her weave and slung her into a table. I tried to stomp her but two waiters wrestled me off of her. Lezzi snuck me and Emma smashed a plate upside of Lezzi's head. I snatched my purse off the table and told the waiters I was leaving. Emma grabbed my arm and pulled me towards the door.

"I'm gonna catch you in da streets, bitch!" I yelled at Amona before walking out of the restaurant. Police pulled up and jumped out of their cars. The manager came outside and told them I messed up their restaurant. We got locked up, all four of us.

****

I sat at the police station for hours. The manager showed up and her story changed. She told the police Amona and Lezzi started it with me and Emma, even told the police Amona asked to sit next to our section to provoke us. I was free to go and so was Emma. Beretta and Quanta were standing outside by Beretta's truck when we walked out the station. I was sorta happy to see him, although I didn't call him. Quanta must've told Beretta what happened when Emma called him. Beretta grabbed my face to see if I had any bruises.

"I'm good," I replied and pulled away from him.

"The manager got her story together, I see," Emma said.

"Yeah, I know her. I called her up and told her what was good," Beretta said.

"You fuckin' her, too?" I asked.

"She's a fuckin' fiend, Mara, damn," Beretta spat.

"Aight, yung. I'm ready take my girl and go home," Quanta said and slapped hands with Beretta.

"I'm gonna call you later," Emma said before she walked off with Quanta. I got inside of Beretta's truck and he got into the driver's seat.

"Where is Zalia?" I asked.

"I took her to Pistol's aunt's before I came here so she could take a nap," he said.

"You can take me back to my truck," I replied.

"Sniper picked it up so you wouldn't get towed," he said. I cursed at myself because Beretta had spare keys to my vehicles.

"Can you take me to Silk's house?" I asked.

"Naw, we are going home to talk," he replied.

"Why are you forcin' yourself into my life?" I asked.

"Because you are my life. Moesha's son ain't my seed, shorty. Now with Amona, I fucked up, but I don't want her," he said.

"Was the sex good?" I asked and he looked at me.

"Yo, what?" he replied.

"Nigga, you heard me. Was her pussy good?" I asked.

"Yeah," he answered truthfully. I slapped Beretta upside his head and he pulled over on the side of the road. Sadly, I would've felt better if he said Amona's pussy was trash but he gave me what I asked for and that was the truth.

"Her pussy is good, she gave you a peace of mind and what else? What does she have that I don't? Why is she so perfect and I'm not? Tell me what it is!" I asked.

"I'on think I should tell you dat," he replied.

"You ain't gotta choice. You put us here, so I want all of the truth," I said.

"She was more passionate, nurturing. You're just like me, so some shit I needed during certain times, I couldn't get from you. It's not your fault, though, I should've told you what I needed instead of gettin' it from somewhere else," he said.

"Street niggas only want tough love, so where is all of this passionate bullshit coming from? You're a thug,

Beretta. You ain't no damn Leonardo DiCaprio from *Titanic*. How am I supposed to know you wanted that when all you showed me was the same shit you're accusing me of? Make it make sense!" I said.

"I know dat, Mara, and that's where I fucked up at. I don't blame you for nothing. You want da truth and I'm giving it to you," he replied. I didn't reply. I closed my eyes to avoid conversation. My ankles were killing me from whipping Amona's ass in heels. I hadn't been getting much sleep but Beretta's presence was soothing. I closed my eyes and took a much-needed nap.

****

"Yo, Mara! You home," Beretta said when he shook me. I opened my eyes and we were in the garage at the bottom of the building.

"I need to come in to get a few things. Is dat cool witchu?" he asked.

"Why are you bein' so calm about everything? I'm stressed da fuck out and you walking around with a fresh haircut," I said.

"I had to get a haircut because my dreads were hanging on to one strand of hair. I haven't slept for more than three hours since you put me out and I was sick as a muthafucka. Oh, and I had to spray my money with bug spray for hours because one of those gigantic spiders was pregnant and baby spiders were everywhere. Rats were fuckin' on my counter and sittin' on my couch like they pay bills and shit! And you told me I had no ties to Zalia after you named her after me! Da fuck is you talkin' about? You see me still wearin' my ring but tell me something. Why do I always gotta tell da truth? When was you gonna tell me about Nika and your bitch-ass brother or about my sister being autistic? I didn't know I was a lick until you got mad because I cheated, so if I didn't cheat, I wouldn't have fuckin' known! BOTH of us fucked up. Then you on birth control and wasn't gonna tell me about dat until I asked for another baby. We always talking about me and what I'm not doin' right but Mara don't have to say shit, huh? But I knew about most of the shit before I married you. I'm not tellin' you to accept it but I ain't as fucked up as you paint me out to be. I love you so much dat I'on know what to do. What do I have to do?" he asked and wiped my eyes.

"I don't know what we should do? Am I supposed to just take you back so you can keep doin' it?" I asked.

"Yo, let me just get a few things so I can be out," he said and got out of his truck. I got out and stepped on to the elevator with him that took us to my loft. When we got to our floor, I tried unlocking my door and he was standing behind me. His tall frame towered over me and his chin was almost resting on the top of my head. My nerves were bad and I couldn't focus on sticking the key into the hole. Beretta grabbed my hand and helped me turn the key. He pushed the door open and walked in. I headed straight to the kitchen to drink a shot of Henny. I hated Henny but I needed something quick and fast to keep me from slipping back into his arms. The nigga was addictive and had a way with words that always seemed to reel me back in. I sat downstairs for almost a half an hour and Beretta was quiet. I didn't hear him moving around like he was getting his clothes and shoes together. After I took off my boots, I went upstairs to the master bedroom. Beretta was knocked out across my bed. His phone vibrated next to him and I answered it.

"Hey, Mara. This is Nika, someone robbed me and snatched Hope from me!" she screamed.

"BERETTA!" I shook him.

"I'll leave in fifteen minutes," he said and rolled over.

"Someone kidnapped Hope!" I yelled. He sat up and I gave him the phone.

"Where is your bitch-ass nigga?" Beretta asked, going into the closet. "How do you know he ain't in on it! I told you da nigga was plannin' on kidnapping Hope to get the money back he was payin' you, now you wanna cry to me? Yo, you brought this on your fuckin' self!" Beretta yelled into the phone then hung up.

"On God, yah brother is dead!" Beretta said to me. He pulled shoe boxes from the top shelf and opened the safe where he kept a few guns. He even grabbed a bulletproof vest. Poppa was always thinking careless but was he really that heartless to orchestrate his own daughter's kidnapping for money? It seemed like I didn't know the nigga after all. I grabbed my UGG boots and Beretta looked at me.

"Where you goin'?" he asked.

"With you. Poppa is my brother and Hope is my niece. Maybe I can talk to him because I don't think he would do that," I replied.

"You probably knew about it. Did you plan this to fuck wit' me? You have been sending me slick threats with this feminine power shit," he said.

There goes the other side of Beretta, I thought.

"You gotta be a slow individual to think I'd stoop that damn low. A fucking child? Hurry up, 'cause I'm driving," I replied. I grabbed my gun case and slipped a pocket knife down into my boot. I snatched the keys to my Altima off the table and we headed out the door. Beretta told me to drive to Nika's crib and gave me the address.

****

Nika's crib was only twenty minutes away from our home in D.C. She lived in the Bladensburg Upper Marlboro area. Her brick family home was surrounded by a lot of land. She ran out of her house as soon as I pulled up into the driveway. Her eye was black, her cheek was swollen and her lips were puffy.

"Z'wan, please find her! Please," Nika cried as she pulled on his hoodie. He pushed his mother away from him.

"I told you what the plan was and you threatened my fuckin' freedom over dat nigga. This is all your fuckin' fault!" Beretta said.

"I don't believe you! Poppa loves his daughter! The kidnapper said they'd kill her if I called the police. Two men attacked me and the third one snatched Hope out of her car seat. It happened so fast while I was checking the mailbox. I think they were watching my house," Nika said.

"Do you know about this, Mara? This has your name written all over it! You did this because you found out about Z'wan and Amona. She told me everything after I picked her up from the police station," Nika accused me. She charged into me and Beretta pushed her back.

"I know this is right up her alley. Suddenly someone up and snatches my daughter after Mara finds out about your cheating ass," Nika yelled.

"If you don't shut da fuck up! You wanna blame her and not Poppa's bitch ass is what you're tellin me?" Beretta asked, although it crossed his mind, too.

"Sorry, Kemara. I just don't know what to do. They are asking for money I don't have. Half a million fuckin' dollars? They are gonna kill her. She's special needs and they are gonna take advantage of her. Let's go in the house," Nika said. I followed Beretta into Nika's crib and Amona's dumb ass was sitting on the couch with a bandage wrapped around her head. The way she looked at my husband made me sick.

"Why is she in here?" Amona asked Nika.

"Not now. I don't give a fuck about y'all love triangle. Hope is missin', so can you put everything to the side and focus on that?" Nika asked.

"You see what she did to my face? She's mad 'cause her husband wanted a seasoned woman and not some young hoodrat. I made him happy! Bitch, you practically threw him to me so you have yourself to blame for that," Amona said.

"Shorty, it ain't da right time for all of dat," Beretta said.

"When will it be the right time? You think I don't have feelings, too? You used me then tossed me away," Amona replied.

"That's what niggas do after they deal with trash," I replied. She jumped up and Nika pushed her on to the couch.

"Y'all aren't fuckin' up my house," Nika said.

Beretta left out of the living room to make a few phone calls. I sat across from Amona and crossed my legs. Nika sat next to Amona and lit a cigarette.

"I think y'all two should just squash whatever beef you have with each other," Nika said.

"You must've got hit pretty hard if you think I'm squashing something with a bitch who fucked my husband.

SOUL Publications

I don't play those type of games, and where I'm from, bitches get kilt for even sneezing on a muthafucka," I replied.

"I'm not scared of you," Nika said.

"You invited her into my home knowing she had intentions with your son," I replied.

"Cut da bullshit, Mara. Yes, my son loves you and we know that, but you knew what type of nigga he was when you got with him. A pretty face and good pussy don't keep a nigga faithful. I thought you was just gonna use him for his money but you actually thought he was gonna change for you? He's just like his father. He looks like him, talks like him and has the gift to make you do what he wants you to do. You should've got paid then walked away like most stick-up chicks but you fell in love. Blame yourself!" Nika said and Amona laughed.

Laugh all you want because you have one foot in the grave, I thought about Amona.

"I get it, you know your son, but you don't know Poppa. You are the lick and don't even realize it but you will soon. He's gonna drag you down to hell," I said to Nika.

Y'all hoes ain't laughing now, I thought.

Nika was close to Amona so it was natural for her to take her side. But I couldn't avoid how she always talked about Beretta being exactly like his father. Beretta came back into the living room.

"Where is Poppa's bitch-ass at?" he asked Nika.

"I can't get in touch wit' him. Maybe he's working at his club," she said. Nika gave Beretta the address and I stood up to leave. Amona told Beretta to be careful and I bit the inside of my cheek as I left out of the house. I got into the car and slammed the door. Beretta got into the passenger's seat and looked at me.

"You fucked shorty up," he said.

"And Nika is next," I replied.

"Do your thing, shorty. Just don't do it around Hope," he said and pulled off.

"Hope is missing and all Amona could think about was fuckin' you again. I saw the way she was lookin' at you. I wonder how good you fucked her because I don't think you gave me that type of dick yet. Dick will be the last thing on my mind if a bitch beats my ass and somebody I care about goes missing," I said and he gripped the steering wheel.

"I didn't touch her the way I touch you and I damn sure wasn't making love to her," he said.

"Let's just find Hope so I can get Zalia then go home. I have had enough festivities for the day," I replied.

"Hope ain't missing. I bet she's wit' your bitch-ass brother," Beretta replied.

"Well, if that's the case, it's not considered kidnapping. Nika probably asked for that ass whipping those men gave her. Your mother is a piece of shit. She doesn't care nothing about you but calls you when she really needs sumthin. It's probably just a custody battle because Poppa ain't got the heart to kidnap someone and hold them for ransom. He's not going to hurt his own daughter," I said.

"We'll see, but if he does, I'm gonna kill him. I let dat nigga live on the strength of you but he keeps testing me," Beretta said.

Lord, please keep Hope safe because I'll have to bury my brother, I thought as Beretta zoomed in and out of traffic.

Poppa

"**C**ome on, nigga. You know dat shit doesn't go right there!" I yelled at a fiend. There were six crackheads cleaning up my club. The place still needed a lot of work and I planned on hiring professionals after I took care of the basics. I was on a tight budget and Jasmine straight cut a nigga off. She changed her number on me and left me out to dry. I had to find her and planned on doing so after I kissed Nika's ass. The door opened and I heard a familiar voice echoing throughout the empty building. I turned around and that nigga Beretta was standing in my club and he had my sister with him.

What do this nigga want? I thought.

"Where's Hope at?" he asked while grilling me.

"With her fuckin' mother," I replied. The cat was out of the bag and it was no sense in running. Nika said she had the situation under control and I believed her but apparently shorty was slacking.

"Hope was kidnapped," Kemara said.

"WHAT!" I replied.

"Bucky, get out and take these niggas witchu," Beretta said to one of the crackheads from around the way.

"We gotta get paid, man," Bucky replied.

"Nigga, what I say? Get da fuck out!" Beretta barked. Bucky dropped the trash bag and left with the rest of his friends following him out.

"Yo, I know about you planning on kidnapping Hope, but I told myself you weren't that dumb when you realized Hope was spending time with me. What you thought I didn't know about your nigga, Rich, following Amona?" he asked.

"By law, I can't kidnap my own fuckin' daughter unless I'm restrained from seeing her, which I'm not. You still ridin' wit' dis nigga, Mara? I guess you ain't know him and Amona was playin' family with my fuckin' daughter," I said and Mara smacked her teeth.

"Grow up, Poppa, and just tell us if you know where Hope is! Nika was attacked and Hope was snatched from her. Did you have any beef with anybody?" Mara asked.

"Yeah, yah bitch-ass husband. Maybe he knows where my daughter is at," I spat. Beretta swung on me and his fist connected with my jaw. I fell on the floor with blood dripping from my mouth. He pointed his gun at me and I looked at Mara. Her facial expression said it all, the situation was serious.

"Did you ask your sister? Nigga, you playin' fuckin' games wit' me. Jasmine just up and left and Hope mysteriously goes missing? You dat mad I'm bangin' yah mother?" I asked Beretta.

"What sister?" Kemara asked.

"Jasmine! This nigga sent her to me spy on me and Nika tried to warn me but I didn't believe her. Ask yah man where my daughter's at, Mara. Your loyalty is to me and not dat nigga. I bet you can't even fix your mouth to ask dat nigga about it, even after he dogged you out and was playing house with another bitch," I chuckled.

"Is it true, Beretta?" Mara asked him.

"Why would I set up my own sister to get kidnapped, Mara? You believe this nigga?" Beretta asked her.

"I'm talking about Jasmine," Mara said.

"He knows what you're talkin' about. Jasmine hates Nika, so it makes sense on why she'd steal Hope. Nika destroyed her family so maybe it's a get-back. Yo, stay outta my business and check your camp!" I said to Beretta.

"Wait a minute. You have another sister?" Mara asked Beretta.

"No, I don't," he said. Beretta yanked me up off the floor and pushed me into the wall. I balled my fist, wanting to hit him, but he was strapped and I knew he would've merked me.

"You got one hour to bring Hope here or you're a dead man," I replied.

"I'm gonna go with him," Kemara said.

"Naw, shorty. Let your brother be a man for once. Like he said, Hope is his daughter and I have no business being around her," Beretta said.

Maybe he really didn't set it up, I thought. I was nervous and sweat beads formed on my forehead.

"You gangsta, ain't you? Merk whoever did it like how you did Ammo," Beretta said.

"I didn't kill him," I lied and he chuckled.

"You a dead man walking, anyway," he replied. He sat on a chair and pulled Mara down on to his lap.

"My niggas will be following you to make sure you ain't bluffing. I hope you got a strap because they ain't interfering wit' shit. If you don't do what you're supposed to do, you gettin' merked. So, you betta make me proud, brother-in-law," he replied. Mara tried to give me her gun but Beretta yanked her arm back.

"Naw, your prints on dat. He'll find his own," Beretta said.

"You know he won't be able to do this by himself," Mara gritted.

"A father dat loves his seed will make it happen by himself. You know where to find Hope, this nigga is bluffing," Beretta said.

I walked out the building and looked around. Two vans were parked on the other side of the street and the passenger of one van nodded his head at me. It was Machete. I'd never forget what he did to Big Mike back in the alley when he cut his hand off. I called Nika and she answered on the first ring.

"Where are you? Do you know where my baby is at? They want five hundred g's for her," Nika cried.

"I think Jasmine did it and your bitch-ass son thinks otherwise. I'm gonna find Jasmine and get to the bottom of this," I replied.

"Why would she do that?" she asked.

"To break up our family like you broke up hers," I said.

"I told you to stay away from her!" Nika screamed into the phone. I hung up when she began cursing me out. Fuck Nika! My life was on the line and she was making the situation worse. I got into my whip and pulled off. I looked in my rearview mirror and the two vans followed me. For weeks, my life was on track but that nigga Beretta always seemed to fuck up my plans. I was going to take Hope so Nika could pay me back but I wasn't going to hurt her. It was karma for even putting my daughter into that situation. I called up my nigga, Rich.

"Yooo," he answered.

"Bruh, someone took my fuckin' daughter! I need a favor from you while these GMBAM niggas are following me," I said.

"Damn, bruh. I'm not even in the area," he replied.

"Da fuck do you mean by dat?" I asked.

"I mean I'm not in da fuckin' area! Those niggas hit up my team and dat nigga Beretta have been lookin' for me. I'm laying low. That bitch Jasmine told them where my mother stays at and niggas have been watching her house ever since. Shit is real and I'm on probation. I'm not tryna go back to jail," Rich said.

"What team, nigga?" I asked.

"I was moving shit on Quanta's turf and the nigga linked up with Beretta is what I'm saying. Sorry, bruh, but I can't help you," he said and hung up. I called back and the number was disconnected. Rich was rubbing me the wrong way.

Beretta hit up your team, so you kidnap his sister to get your money back, I thought.

"FUCK!" I yelled out and punched the steering wheel. I set up the trap for that nigga to kidnap Hope. I made a U-turn in the middle of the street and went to Rich's baby mother's house. He must've forgotten he took me by there one day. I had a big problem on my hands. One, I wasn't strapped and, two, I didn't know the nigga as well as I thought I did.

****

It was six o' clock in the evening and because it was winter it was dark outside. I pulled up on the street and turned my lights off. I looked in the rearview mirror and Beretta's niggas were still behind me.

Damn, I hate dat nigga. Muthafucka got niggas babysittin' me, I thought. Someone tapped on my window wearing a white mask. Them niggas were dressed like the SWAT team. I stepped out of the car and one of them patted me down. The one that was feeling for a weapon grabbed my dick.

Homo thugs! I thought.

After he felt me up, he took off his mask and it was Jasmine.

"Hey, boo," she teased and the niggas behind her started chuckling. I fell in love with the bitch and she played me big time!

"You betrayed me," I said.

"No, I didn't. I was workin', don't take it personal. But anytime you need some pussy, call me. That dick was too good to go to waste," she said. Beretta knew all along Jasmine wasn't a suspect because the bitch was outside in the van with the rest of the GMBAM niggas.

"Yo, stop playin' and get back to it," someone said to her.

"Shut da fuck up, Machete," she spat.

"So, y'all want me to go in there with no gun? I don't even know if the nigga is here," I said.

"Nigga, we don't give a fuck about you! Beretta said it was your problem and for us to make sure you handle it. We'll be out here waitin' for you. I gotta a plastic knife in my glove compartment if you need it. Fake niggas don't need real weapons, G," Machete said. Something about that lil' nigga's voice made my skin crawl.

"Ease up on him. Poppa is a lover boy but he can whip Rich's ass like he did mine," Jasmine said.

"Wait, dat nigga was hittin' you? Muthafucka you were touchin' my sister?" Sniper asked.

"Shut up, Sniper. Y'all let me talk to Poppa, I can handle this," Jasmine said.

"Fuck naw! What you need to talk to him for?" Machete asked and the lil' nigga sounded jealous.

"Because Beretta put me on this, so y'all niggas can back da fuck up. Let me handle this," Jasmine said. They backed up and got inside the vans.

"They are gonna kill you. You're actin' real suspect right now. Beretta thinks this is all on you. Please tell me that you don't have anything to do with this. I have been underneath you for months and you're coldhearted and very vindictive. You planned to have her kidnapped before until Nika came through and bought you that building. I left you so I know you're hurting for money again. Did you do this?" she asked.

"I don't have anything to do with this! So, this is you, huh? You're GMBAM? I've been fuckin' the enemy the whole time," I said.

"You're your own enemy, Kamar. GMBAM has bigger fish to fry and you're just one lonely-ass tadpole in the way. I'm gonna help you this time but the next time you have a run-in with Beretta, I won't interfere. Stop playin' around because niggas are itching to merk you once he gives them the word. Get your fuckin' shit together because Nika can't hold Beretta off for too long," she gritted.

"This whole time you had me thinking you had sumthin against the nigga and I told you a lot of shit," I spat.

"I am my brother's keeper. I told you what you wanted to hear," she said.

"He doesn't know you're his sister," I replied.

"I'll tell him when I'm ready, but in the meantime, let's see if you're tellin' the truth," she said. I walked away and passed three houses to get to Rich's baby mother's house. Before I knocked on the door, I looked around to make sure nobody was outside on the block. It was freezing, so I rubbed my hands together to keep them warm. I knocked four more times before someone answered the door. Rich's baby mother stood there with a cigarette hanging out of her mouth. The bitch was bad looking in the face and built like a carton of eggs.

"What you want?" she asked. Suddenly, Jasmine burst into the house and hit his baby mother in the face with her gun. She fell on to the floor with blood dripping from her face. Jasmine pulled her into the living by her hair while the woman screamed.

"Get out of my house!" she yelled. Jasmine hit her with the butt of her gun again and put a deep gash in her head. I closed the door and locked it.

"I don't have any money!" the woman cried.

"Where is Rich?" Jasmine asked.

"At his mother's house!" she screamed.

"We have been watchin' dat house for a while and he hasn't been there. Where in da fuck is he at?" she asked then put a gun to her head.

"I don't know! He just texted me a few minutes ago and told me to stay by my phone because he needed me to bring him some clothes. My son is upstairs takin' a nap," she said. I went upstairs into the bedroom and Rich's son was sleeping. The lil' nigga was about six years old. I searched the top floor to make sure it was just them two in the house. Rich's baby mother was losing consciousness when I went back downstairs. Her phone beeped on the coffee table and Jasmine picked it up.

"Rich texted her his location and told her to hurry up. Let's bounce," Jasmine said. She screwed the silencer on her gun and shot his baby mother in the head. Her brain exploded out the back of her head and decorated the old flower-patterned couch behind us.

"What was da point in dat? Yo, what da fuck! Her son is upstairs," I said.

"She's a witness. Damn, nigga, do you not know about this lifestyle?" she asked, agitated.

"Yeah, but I'm tryna leave dat shit behind!" I replied.

She put the phone in her pocket and left the house with me following her. Jasmine asked for my car keys and I gave them to her.

"Get in the passenger's seat," she said.

"Where is da nigga at?" I asked.

"Pennsylvania Avenue," she said.

"He got my daughter in Baltimore City? Niggas stay getting merked on Pennsylvania Ave," I replied.

"Just be ready to merk him. We're running out of time. Beretta said one hour, and twenty-five minutes have passed already."

Damn, the clock is ticking, I thought.

SOUL Publications

****

"Okay, this is it. The house he's in is up the block. I'm gonna leave the van running. Go in and do what you gotta do and hurry up. Your time is running out, so hurry da fuck up," Jasmine said.

"I ain't gotta fuckin' gun! What if Hope isn't in there?" I replied.

"Then you'll die," she replied. I wanted to choke Jasmine but I thought better of it when I saw two vans behind us in the rearview mirror. Jasmine texted Rich's phone from his baby mother's phone.

"He said come around the back," she said.

"Okay, give me your gun," I replied.

"So you can shoot one of us and get away?" she asked.

"You think I'm gonna get away with two vans full of niggas with AK-47's behind me?" I replied.

"Get out of the car. I'm comin' witchu. I'm tryna save your life and you're not cooperating," she said.

"Bitch, you don't give a fuck about me!" I replied and she put the gun to my head.

SOUL Publications

"I'll blow your brains out if you ever in your life disrespect me again. I've tolerated enough of your bullshit and endured a lot of shit from you, and I'm still angry about it. So many times, I wanted to kill you for puttin' your hands on me, but I owe Beretta my life. He's the reason why me and Sniper didn't end up in a homeless shelter. Machete will torture you and I don't think you want dat because he's a lunatic. They don't call him Machete for nothing. He'll slice you up like deli lunchmeat," Jasmine said. She got out of the car and pulled her mask down over her face. I got out behind her and we cut through a dark alley filled with rats. She told me to get down once we cut around the corner.

"Rich is in the back of the house. Hope's life is on the line if he runs in the house. I'm gonna shoot him in the leg and you're gonna get him to tell us who all are in the da house. I'm gonna alert the others to go inside and look for Hope," Jasmine said. Shorty didn't give me a chance to respond, she stepped around the corner and Rich tried to run. Jasmine pulled the trigger and the bullet hit him in the hip. He fell on the ground and I rushed him. Rich tried to yell out but I put him in the chokehold.

"What you runnin' for, nigga?" I asked.

"Get off me!" he gasped.

I heard loud gunshots coming from inside the house when Jasmine walked in. It wasn't from her gun because she had a silencer on hers. Bullet holes flew out of the window from inside the house and I ducked. Rich tried to reach for his gun but I sent a nose-crushing blow to his face.

"Nigga, where is my daughter?" I asked.

"Fuck yah daughter. Dat nigga Beretta had my niggas merked and he took my money. This ain't about you! You could've got on the deal but your head is so far up these bitches' asses that you can't make money," he said.

"Bruh, you went behind my back and got my daughter involved in some bullshit?" I replied.

"Muthafucka, you didn't care about her, anyway. You wanted me to kidnap her," he said.

"I wanted you to safely take her away and bring her to me! But you got her around niggas with guns," I replied and punched him again. A few GMBAM niggas ran down the alley and into the house. Jasmine ran out of the house with Hope in her arms and a bullet flew past her head and went through the fence. A big black nigga came from the other end of the alley and started shooting at us. I used Rich as a shield and bullets ripped through his body. Hope screamed and reached out to me but I told Jasmine to take her and run. Jasmine picked her up and ran, as the big gunman started shooting at her. I pulled the trigger of Rich's gun and missed, but the second bullet hit him in the chest. He was holding his chest and gasping for air when I walked over to him. I pulled the trigger twice and his head burst open.

"LET'S GO!" someone called out. GMBAM niggas ran out of the house and I ran with them. Jasmine was in my car when I got into the driver's seat. Hope was in the back seat crying with blood all over her clothes. I pulled off as soon as I heard police sirens getting closer. The GMBAM vans went in the opposite direction as I sped off.

"Beretta put my daughter in danger!" I yelled out in frustration. Jasmine slammed her fist into the side of my face twice and I sideswiped a car on the side of the road.

"THIS IS YOUR FAULT! You showed Rich where Nika lived. You exposed your own daughter. The kidnapping was your idea! Take blame for your own shit for once and stop blaming Beretta for everything. If you say his name again, I'm gonna cut your fuckin' tongue out!" Jasmine screamed. Hope was still crying and Jasmine got into the back seat with her and hugged her.

"You and Nika don't deserve this little girl. Y'all don't even deserve to live," Jasmine said. I was a hard-headed nigga but Jasmine's words got to me. The whole time I thought shorty was dumb and took advantage of her, but all she was doing was playing her part because she was loyal to GMBAM. It made me think of Kemara. She would've done everything for me that Jasmine had done for Beretta but I betrayed her. For the first time in my life, I wished I was dead.

"Thank you for everything. I know you don't believe this, but I really fell in love witchu," I admitted.

"Just hurry up and get me back to Annapolis," Jasmine replied.

I have to win her over again the right way. But, first, I have to focus on my daughter, I thought as I got on the interstate.

Beretta

K emara was sitting on a chair, checking her phone. We were still inside of Poppa's club. Machete texted me and told me they were in Baltimore.

"Poppa got them niggas in Baltimore," I said.

"And you still think he has sumthin to do with it?" Mara asked.

"Dat nigga ain't in the clear yet until Rich is dead and Hope is back home. I'on trust dat nigga and neither do you," I replied.

"I don't trust niggas, period. So, what's up with you and this sister?" Kemara asked.

"Jasmine and Sniper ain't related to me. Poppa was talkin' shit," I replied.

"Sniper resembles you, he's just darker. He's also tall and y'all have the same deep, raspy voice. I see a lot of you in him," she said.

"That doesn't mean anything. Him and Jasmine would've told me if they knew," I replied.

"Maybe you should call Nika and ask her," Kemara said, scrolling through her phone.

"I guess you over there flirting with niggas on Facebook. What's up with you and dat clown-ass nigga, Chevy?" I asked.

"What are you talkin' about?" she replied.

"Yo, you know what I'm talkin' about. You couldn't wait, could you? Wearing tight dresses when it's cold outside. Putting yah lil' make-up on and shit. And where is dat fifty-thousand-dollar ring I bought you?" I asked.

"I was in a good mood today, so I stepped out lookin' fly. What you thought? I was gonna be home depressed? Hair nappy and wearing tacky clothes? Mad 'cause my bounce back was a comeback? Or are you jealous because niggas are interested and willing to treat me the way I deserve?" Mara said.

"Here we go," I replied.

"We gonna keep going there until you stop questioning me," she replied.

SOUL Publications

"I'm coming home tonight, so you can delete your social media. You too exposed and I don't like it. And take Zalia off, too. Soon, niggas are gonna start plotting on kidnapping her for ransom. We can't do shit like everybody else," I said and she rolled her eyes.

"You can sleep in the spare bedroom," she said, which caught a nigga by surprise.

"Yo, you trippin'," I replied.

"We aren't sleepin' in the same bed. If you can't respect that then you need to live someplace else," she said.

"Ight, I can do dat," I replied and she crossed her legs. Shorty was looking good. Her thick short legs and wide hips in her dress made me want to put her against the wall. Amona didn't have shit on Mara, and even though she had good pussy, it wasn't as tight as Mara's. I was in the dog house and planned on playing by Mara's rules because shorty was talking about a divorce. That word to me was a death threat and I didn't take those too lightly. She yawned and I told her to take the whip and go home.

"I'm not leaving. I gotta make sure you don't hurt Poppa for no reason," she replied.

"Mannn, get da fuck outta here. You won't be able to stop me from killing him unless you kill me. I already know won't be able to do that. You can't live without me. No other nigga out here will be able to replace me or tolerate your crazy-ass attitude," I said and she rolled her eyes. She got up and walked to the other side of the club. Mara bent over and plugged her cellphone into the charger that was hanging out of the wall. I walked over to her and wrapped my arms around her hips. She froze when I kissed her neck.

"Get away from me," she said when my hand palmed her moist center. I could feel the heat and wetness coming from between her legs. Kemara's body always betrayed her; it said what her mouth couldn't. I grabbed her full breast and gently squeezed, rubbing her pussy with my other hand. She tried to pull away from me but I turned her around and pinned her against the wall.

"GET THE FUCK OFF!" she shouted but I kissed her while holding both of her wrists above her head. I used my free hand to lift up her dress and ripped her thong off. Kemara's slit was soaking wet. A moan escaped her lips when my finger slipped into her. My thumb massaged her clit while my finger stroked her walls. She moaned into my chest as I brought her to an orgasm.

"Tell me to stop," I said, unzipping my pants.

"This isn't fair," she moaned.

"Can I come in?" I asked. Kemara pulled my face down to her lips and kissed me. The door to the club opened when I was ready to enter her. Kemara pushed me away and I fixed myself. I turned around and it was Poppa, Jasmine and Hope. Poppa put Hope down and she ran to me. I picked her up and squeezed her. She wrapped her small arms around my neck tightly. Kemara kissed Hope's cheek and Hope reached out to her.

"I gotta talk to this nigga privately," Poppa said and Kemara looked at me.

"Y'all go ahead and get in the car. I'll be out," I said. Kemara, Jasmine and Hope left out of the club.

"Can you sit down?" he asked.

"Naw, nigga, I can't," I gritted.

"I want to mend the situation between me and my sister," he said and I grilled him. The nigga was a straight-up bitch! He couldn't look me in the eyes and he fidgeted when talking to me. I hated when scared niggas talked to me. Most niggas got a kick out of having that much power but I liked competition. Poppa was a waste of my fucking time!

"Naw, you ain't mending shit with my wife. Jasmine left you so you think my wife is gonna be robbin' niggas for you again? Kemara don't need you, nigga," I replied.

"And she needs you? Yo, don't you think you tryna control her the same way I used to? She doesn't need dat shit anymore," he replied and I chuckled.

"Nigga, I'on give a fuck about your opinion. I don't want you around my fuckin' wife! You bad blood, G. Keep my mother and do what you want wit' shorty but Kemara is off fuckin' limits! But we can talk about this club," I said, looking around.

"What about it?" he asked.

"Your club is in the middle of my turf. So, you know what the fuck I'm talking about. You gotta pay up, bruh," I said.

"WHAT!" he said.

"Yeah, nigga. Da fuck you thought I was gonna walk out here skippin' or some shit? You think we cool now because you got Hope back? I'on give a fuck about dat. A father is supposed to keep his kids safe, so no points from me, nigga. You owe me your life for that Ammo shit. I can kill you right now but my wife wouldn't like that too much. So, here's what I can offer. You either give me this building or give me a percentage," I replied.

"What's the percentage?" he asked.

"Sixty percent. I would take it all but you gotta pay the IRS to keep this spot up and running," I replied.

"For how long?" he asked.

"For the rest of your fuckin' life. Pistol is gonna come through in a few days with professionals. The crackheads you got working in here is gonna make this shit fall to the ground before you open it. You need a liquor license and this shit has to pass safety and health inspections. The wiring is fucked up and I smell mildew so there is a leak in this muthafucka somewhere. Bruh, you got a lot of work to do. Oh, and the bouncers are GMBAM niggas, even the fuckin' accountant who will be handlin' the finances. I'm gonna have eyes and ears throughout this muthafucka. On God, I'll risk it all and merk you if you fuck me over," I said and Poppa nodded his head. I left out of his club and got into the passenger's seat of my whip. Kemara pulled off and we headed to Nika's house.

Thirty minutes later, we pulled up to Nika's driveway. She opened the door and ran out to the car before Kemara could park. Nika pulled Hope out of the back seat and checked her for bruises.

"I'm gonna take her to the emergency room but I need to burn these bloody clothes first. Thank you so much," Nika said to me when I got out of the whip. She tried to hug me but I pushed her away.

"Jasmine step out for a second," I called out to her. She stepped out of the car and Nika smacked her teeth.

"Not now, I gotta make sure Hope is fine," Nika said.

"All I need to know is if this is my sister," I replied and Nika tried to swing on Jasmine but I pushed her back.

"Don't you dare tell my son those lies! He's no kin to you!" Nika yelled at Jasmine.

"She didn't tell me, Nika. Your bitch-ass baby father did. You do a lot of pillow-talkin' wit' dat nigga and he exposed you. Just tell me if she's my sister and I'll stay out of your way," I replied.

"Yes, Z'wan! Happy now! Now, get that bitch away from my house," Nika said. She snatched Hope by the arm and pulled her into the house. Jasmine broke down crying as she got back inside the car.

"That bitch needs to die," Mara said when I got back in.

"If she needs to go, so does your brother," I replied and she started up the car.

Damn, Sniper and Jasmine are my siblings. I mean we're GMBAM family, anyway, but I got a brother and sister only a few years younger than me, I thought. The ride to Jasmine and Sniper's crib was a long one.

"Where are those niggas at?" Jasmine asked.

"Ditching the vans. You good?" I replied.

"Yeah, I'm straight. See y'all later," she said and got out of the car. Kemara didn't pull off until jasmine walked into the building and waved us goodbye.

"Jasmine got more heart than some of these niggas," Kemara laughed.

"Definitely got more heart than Poppa's bitch-ass," I replied.

"What a GMBAM type of day," Kemara said.

"You got dat shit from me," I chuckled and she shrugged her shoulders.

"Hope is safe and that is all that matters," she replied.

We picked up Zalia then headed home.

****

Kemara bathed Zalia then laid her down in the crib when we got home. I wanted to finish what we started back at Poppa's building but I knew shorty wasn't going for it. A nigga was just happy to be back home. She got out of the shower and walked downstairs wearing a black lace robe with a pink lace thong set underneath. Kemara was trying to start some shit. Shorty was teasing me while I was sitting on the couch watching TV.

"You petty as shit," I said.

"Nigga, I always sleep like this," she replied. She grabbed a bottle of wine out the cabinet then bent over to go in the lower cabinet. Her robe came up and exposed her meaty ass cheeks. She put body oil on her skin because she knew that shit made my dick hard. My dick was pressed against my leg, dying to slide into her wetness.

"I put some clean sheets on the bed in the guestroom. You just have to make it up," she replied.

"Can I get some pussy, though?" I asked.

"Don't let what happened at Poppa's club go to your head. You should've nutted when you had your fingers in it because I know I did. Goodnight," she said and walked up the stairs. Shorty wasn't playing because I heard her lock the master bedroom door. My cell phone rang and I answered it. It was Nika calling me.

"Hope is fine. We just got back home from the hospital. But hold on," she said.

"Z'wan, we really need to talk," Amona said.

"Yo, I thought I told you dat lil' shit we had goin' on is dead! What part you need me to break down to you again?" I asked.

"I balance out your life. You married her out of guilt for having feelings for me. We spent so much time together. Don't throw it away for something you're not sure about," she said.

"Shorty, if you fuck wit' me then let me be happy with my fuckin' wife! Get da fuck off my line and tell Nika's hoe ass don't call me no more!" I said and hung up. I went on Facebook to see what Kemara's sneaky ass was up to and shorty posted a picture wearing that tight-ass sweater dress. She took a side view picture and her ass was just sitting. The bitch had so many comments from niggas. The nigga, Chevy, commented talking about, "don't get yoked up." That nigga was trying to check my bitch.

Shorty ain't gonna have no clothes in her closet tomorrow. Her sneaky ass better start wearing sweats, I thought.

****

The next day...

"Where are my stretch jeans and sweater dresses?" Kemara asked. She wanted to go to the club and didn't have shit to wear. I got rid of her tight clothes while she was in school. She snatched the butter knife from me while I was fixing myself a sandwich.

"Yo, what are you talkin' about?" I asked.

"My fucking clothes! What did you do to them?" she replied.

"I ain't do shit to them. Maybe we were robbed or some shit," I replied and shrugged my shoulders.

"I'm supposed to be meetin' Emma and Silk in an hour and I don't have shit to wear. Why would you do this to me?" she asked and I chuckled.

"Tell them you can't go because you're in for the night. Tryna watch this movie with me?" I asked.

"Now you wanna sit in the house?" she replied.

"Yeah, what's wrong with that? Matter of fact, I'm chillin' for a few weeks. I need to get some rest," I said and she rolled her eyes. Kemara went into the living room and laid across the couch with her arms crossed. Shorty was hot!

"Aye, boo, you mad or sumthin?" I called out.

"Nope, you takin' me shoppin' tomorrow," she said.

"I'm broke," I replied.

"I bet you is since you were payin' for pussy," she spat.

"I ain't neva pay for no muthafuckin' pussy," I chuckled. I made Kemara a sandwich, too, then grabbed the bag of chips.

"What movie you wanna watch?" I asked.

"*Baby Boy*," she replied.

"Hell nawl! I'm tired of watchin' dat bitch-ass nigga and dat bicycle. All you wanna do is start some shit. Evette gonna have you in here gettin' backhanded because you gonna get in yah feelins," I replied.

"How about *Paid in Full*?" I asked.

"Yeah, so I can look at Micah Phiefer's sexy ass. Hurry up and put it in," Kemara replied then opened the bag of chips.

"Fuck dat nigga, his bitch-ass got merked anyway," I replied and she gave me the middle finger. I put the DVD in and laid back on the couch next to her. It reminded me of how we used to be a few years ago when we were just chilling. Shorty must've read my mind because she brought it up.

"I remember we used to watch movies all the time. You always had time for me back then," she said.

"I wasn't gettin' money like dat, neither," I replied.

"Sometimes I wish you were broke," she said, looking at the TV.

"Yo, don't wish bad luck on us," I replied.

"I'm not but I enjoy your time more than your money. I came from a very poor household, so I can go without. The money attracts a lot of females and has them doing stupid shit just to get a piece of what you do. Money just causes a lot of problems. I used to dream about it but now I have nightmares about what it'll do to us," she said.

"Money ain't da issue, shorty. A nigga just fucked up," I replied.

"Yeah, you did and I'm not over it right now. This hurt doesn't go right away. Even if I forgive you, I'll never forget what you did," she said.

"So, you sayin' our marriage is over?" I asked.

"Is it worth fightin' for?" she replied.

SOUL Publications

"I'll show you," I said and she rolled her eyes. Kemara thought I was bluffing but I was serious. Cheating wasn't worth the stress. I wanted to do right and be that perfect nigga for her, but nobody is perfect. All I could do was learn from it and show my wife she was the only shorty I needed. Kemara took my sandwich and bit into it.

"Yo, you do this all the time. I made my sandwich the same way I made yours," I said.

"But yours always tastes better," she replied. I hit a button on the remote and it turned the lights off in the living room. Kemara laid on my chest and ate chips. She stressed about money being the issue but I couldn't stop what I was doing at the moment. I was ready to reach my first mil' and that was only the beginning.

Piper

A month later...

I was sitting on Silk's couch, drinking rum and orange juice. It didn't feel the same without Kemara. She wasn't talking to me or Thickems. I reached out to her a few times but she didn't respond. It was stressing me out because we'd been friends for years and didn't go a day without talking to each other.

"I can't believe she's still mad at me. She forgave Beretta but didn't forgive me?" I said to Silk and he rolled his eyes.

"First of all, that's not the same. Second of all, Beretta is still in the dog house and Kemara is walking around without her wedding ring. She's not even fuckin' the man or sleeping in the same bed with him. They are raising a child together so she's stuck wit' da nigga. She'll come around eventually," Silk said.

"I heard Kemara be talkin' to her first, Chevy. He be flirtin' with her all over her Facebook page, so everyone is talkin' about it," Thickems said when she came out of the kitchen.

"They're just friends," Silk said.

"Beretta won't feel the same way," I replied.

"She can have a friend. I mean, he did cheat on her," Thickems said.

"Yeah, but we know he loves her. I just don't want them to break up. Y'all don't understand Kemara like I do. Beretta is the only one who can tolerate her and see past her flaws. Chevy is gonna get himself killed and Mara will never want him like that anyway," I replied.

"They're just friends. Don't get your panties in a bunch," Silk said.

My phone rang and it was Delonte calling. I stopped stripping for him and even found myself a little job at the post office. It didn't pay as much but it was something. Delonte called me for every little thing about his club. It was almost like he was purposely complaining to me so I could give in and tell him I was coming back to be a stripper again.

"Hello," I answered.

"Where you at? I was wondering if we could go out for dinner," he replied.

"Okay, I'm at Silk's apartment. I rode with Thickems so can you pick me up?" I asked.

"Yeah, I'll be there in twenty minutes," he replied and hung up.

Silk was staring at me when I tossed my phone in my purse.

"Ummm, trouble in paradise," he said.

"No, we're actually fine but something is missing," I replied.

"That's because you had some of dat good hood dick. Chilleeeeeee, fuck Delonte and get your boo because I'm not into y'all," Silk said.

"Really, Silk? It ain't up to you," Thickems laughed. Silk put his hand in Thickems' face.

"Bitch, I'm the overseer of my friends, hunty. We only known each other for a year and some months, but Piper and Kemara grew up in this hood with me. Dat chile don't love dat man and could care less about his lil' dick, Jehovah-wearing sandals looking ass. Mind yo' business when I'm havin' girl talk and where yo' man at?" Silk asked and I covered my mouth.

"In a grave," Thickems said and I felt sorry for her but it didn't stop Silk.

"Well, dig him up and be happy, shat. You need to get yo' shit together, too, and start dating or sumthin," Silk replied.

"Don't play with me. You know I'm not ready to date," Thickems said.

"Silk does have a point in a way. He's sayin' live your life because Ammo has been gone for over a year and there is nothing wrong with having a male friend," I replied and she rolled her eyes.

"I'm not ready. I don't want him if he doesn't act like Ammo. There was something about the way he loved me that was addictive. Sorta how Beretta is with Kemara," she replied and Silk smacked his teeth.

"Chile, you sound like you want another GMBAM nigga and if so, it's gonna make you look like a hoe. You ain't Piper, although she barely gets a pass for fuckin' friends. You actually have a baby by dat nigga and was in a relationship wit' him," Silk said.

"I'm not saying that! And why are you always in somebody's business? What about you fuckin' men and women?" Thickems asked and Silk kicked his house slippers off before he stood up.

"Sit down, Silk," I laughed.

"First of all, bitch. I fuck, suck and pluck whomever I want to. I'm not undercover with my shit. The women I fuck know I like dick, too. Sometimes, I borrow their lip gloss so it's clear I got some sugarcane in my tank. Second of all, don't get your lip busted because I'm about sick of yah slick-ass mouth! I said what I said and I'm not takin' it back. Ammo is maggot food, rotten like an old banana. That nigga doesn't care about you movin' on but I bet he'll haunt yah ass if you fuck wit' a GMBAM nigga, now debate with me so I can read yah ass, nah," Silk said.

"Silk, leave her alone, damn. You always go overboard wit' it," I said. He sat down and crossed his legs while flicking his imaginary hair over his shoulders and moving the invisible bang off his forehead.

"Don't you like extra hot sauce on yah chicken?" he asked.

"Yeah, and?" I asked.

"Exactly, bitch. I like my drama with extra spice, just like how you like yah chicken, nah," he said.

"Anyways, I'll talk to y'all later. I gotta pick up my son from Lashonda's house," Thickems said. After Thickems had her baby, Ammo's family started coming around. Well, just his aunt because everybody else still didn't want anything to do with her. Personally, I would've gave Lashonda my ass to kiss because they treated her horribly after Ammo was killed. Thickems grabbed her purse and car keys and left out the door.

"You wrong for all of dat," I said.

"Dat's yah friend. I'm only cool wit' her because you started bringing her around but I'on trust her ass," he said.

"You don't trust nobody," I replied.

"Pay attention, Piper. She wants a nigga like Ammo and I only know two other niggas that remind me of Ammo and that's Pistol and Beretta," he said.

"You just like drama but I know for a fact Thickems isn't dat type of person," I replied.

"You met her at a strip club. How well do you know her? You ain't grow up wit' her, shat," Silk said.

"I'm not listenin' to yah bullshit. You have been trippin' since Fushia got a boyfriend," I laughed and Silk gave me the middle finger.

"She don't love dat nigga because I was in her guts last night and the night before. I didn't pull out, neither," Silk said, then crossed his legs.

"I'm curious to know how you be fuckin'," I replied.

"The bed is in the back. Do you wanna find out?" he asked.

"Nah, I'm good," I bust out laughing.

"Hold on, I'll be right back," he said. Silk got up and went into his bedroom. He came back out with a DVD. He put the DVD inside his video player and the TV screen turned black. A few seconds later, my mouth dropped at the scene on the TV. Silk was eating Fushia out like there was no tomorrow.

"Yes, hunntyyyy! Dat bitch couldn't stop cumming," he bragged then turned the volume up.

SOUL Publications

"You recorded her?" I asked.

"She told me to," he replied.

I wasn't ready when Silk slid his big dick into Fushia. I also couldn't grasp the fact that Silk acted like a straight man while fucking her. My mouth was gaped open when Fushia squirted and Silk pulled out of her to catch her fluids in his mouth before he sucked the rest of it out of her pussy.

"Niggggaaaaaaaa," I replied.

"I got one wit' me fuckin' Delonte's friend, Wylee," he replied and I gagged.

"Wait, Wylee is a bottom?" I asked.

"Does Lobster turn red in boiling water?" he replied.

Delonte texted me and told me to walk outside. I kissed Silk's cheek before I left his apartment. I opened the door to Delonte's Bentley and got into the passenger's seat. He kissed my lips and rubbed my thigh.

"My beautiful woman," he said and I blushed.

"You look handsome yourself," I replied.

He was wearing a black pea coat with jeans and Timbs. The fitted hat on his head was pulled down low over his eyes.

"Where do you wanna eat?" he asked.

"Carolina Kitchen," I replied.

"That's all the way up in Largo," he said.

"I got taste for some real soul food," I replied.

"Alright, anything to make you happy," he said.

While he was leaving out, Pistol's Yukon was turning into the parking lot. My stomach got butterflies and the palm of my hands were sweating. I hadn't seen Pistol since the night he came into Delonte's strip club. He stepped out of his truck wearing a North Face coat, jeans and some kind of boots. My eyes almost popped out of my head when I noticed he had a haircut. Flo walked up to him and gave him dap and he smiled showing his diamond fronts. My pussy throbbed as I thought about his cologne and deep strokes. Delonte waited for the car to drive past before he pulled out of the parking lot. I watched Pistol in the mirror until Delonte left out of the neighborhood. I was no longer interested in Delonte's conversation about his club. Thoughts of Pistol flooded my mind because I missed him. My phone beeped and it was a text message from an unfamiliar number. The message read...

Why you ain't get out so I could get a hug? Damn, it's like dat? Pistol asked.

Now you wanna text me? I replied.

The phone works both ways, shorty. But fuck all dat, I miss you, he said.

"The heat up too high? You're sweating," Delonte said, adjusting the heat.

I'm sweating because my future baby daddy and husband just texted me, clown! I thought.

"Yeah, it's hot in here," I replied and fanned myself.

I miss you, too, I replied.

Why you wit' dat scared ass nigga for then? He asked.

The same reason why you're fuckin' nasty hoes, I replied.

Here we go wit' dat bullshit. Ditch dat nigga and come see about me later on. I'll be over my grandma's crib, Pistol replied.

Delonte talked about his club for the rest of the ride to the restaurant. I blocked him out as I thought about riding Pistol's tongue until I screamed a bunch of gibberish.

"Talk to me, Piper. Why are you so quiet? It's almost like I'm talking to myself," Delonte said.

"Because I'm bored with this conversation. Can we talk about shit outside of your club?" I asked.

"What do you wanna talk about?" he replied.

"How about my job at the post office? You haven't asked me about that yet," I said.

"Because it doesn't fit you. Come on, Piper, let's be realistic here. You're loud, speak a lot of broken English and short-tempered, and it's okay, but the post office?" he chuckled. Delonte thought he was making a joke until he realized I didn't find it funny.

"I'm just joking, sweetheart," he replied and squeezed my leg.

"Pistol would never—" I said to myself but he heard me.

"Seriously," Delonte asked and turned the music down.

"Yes, I'm serious. What nigga says shit like that to his girlfriend? You should be happy I'm tryna get my life on track," I replied.

"By what? Fuckin' a drug dealing gang member?" he asked.

"It's better than fuckin' a boring ass fake 'woke nigga,'" I replied.

"This is the shit I'm talkin' about. You're not satisfied wit' having a good man. Maybe I should catch a few charges and get tattoos everywhere in order for you to appreciate me," he said.

"Or maybe you can stop acting like a lil' dick nigga with a big ego. You practically called me stupid! Bitch, I speak slang! How do you think I got my job in the first place? You thought I acted a fool on my interview? Nigga, don't take me there because I'll slap the hell out of you. And if your club is so poppin', why you keep talkin' about it?" I asked. Delonte made a U-turn in the middle of the road and headed back to Annapolis. He was taking me home. I cursed him out the whole way there until he pulled up to my house. He threw my purse out the window and told me to get the fuck out of his car. I got out of his car and he sped off almost running over my feet. I picked up my purse off the ground and went into the house. My life was spiraling out of control. It didn't feel right not having Kemara in my corner. I got comfortable on the couch and called her. To my surprise, she answered the phone.

"Yes, Piper," she said and I burst into tears.

"We need to talk," I replied.

"I know we do. Silk just called me and ripped me a new asshole. I just needed some space but I don't hate you and you know that. But we can talk about that another time. Why are you crying?" she asked. Luck was on my side that day, my best friend answered the phone in a time when I really needed her. I told Kemara everything that happened between me and Delonte.

"I don't know what to say, Piper. I can tell you to leave him but I'm still in a situation myself," she said.

"Beretta loves you, though. I'm mad he cheated, too, but Moesha is lying on him," I said.

"You're stickin' with dat story, huh?" she asked.

"Until the day I die," I replied.

"Everything will come to light soon, but in the meantime, let's talk about this job? How is it? Any bitches you don't like yet?" Kemara asked and I chuckled.

"Yes, bitch. It's this one girl named Teresa that I cannot stand," I said.

"Umph, tell me about this hoe," she replied. I almost dropped my phone when I heard a nigga in the background and it didn't sound like Beretta.

"Mara, where are you?" I asked.

"At the studio," she replied.

"You a rapper now?" I asked.

"Bitch, I wish. I stopped through to see Chevy but I'm ready to leave," she said.

"Umm, I—" I said but was cut off.

"I know and Silk cursed me out, too. I'll tell you more in a few when I leave. He just walked back into the room," Kemara whispered.

"Umm, okay. I'll call you later on," I replied and we hung up.

I took a long, hot bath until it was time for me to get ready to see Pistol.

****

Two hours later...

I parked behind Pistol's Yukon and nervousness took over me.

"Calm down, bitch. It's just Pistol," I said to myself while looking in the mirror to make sure my make-up was intact. When I got out, the front door of his grandmother's house opened and it was Pistol waiting for me.

"Hurry up, girl! I'm letting the heat out," he said but I took my time because I wanted him to study the movement of my hips. He pulled me into the house when I got to the top step.

"What's good witchu?" he asked and wrapped his arms around me. Pistol picked me up when he hugged me then kissed my neck. I inhaled the smell of his cologne and closed my eyes. He pulled away from me and helped me take my coat off.

"You hungry?" he asked.

"Yeah, what did Earlene cook?" I replied.

"Turkey wings, stuffin', greens, potato salad and yams," he said and my mouth watered.

"Yes, to the Lord!" I said and rubbed my hands together. Since I stopped popping pills, my appetite increased. I followed Pistol into the kitchen and realized the house was really quiet.

"Where is Earlene and your grandmother?" I asked.

"They left for Florida a few hours ago," Pistol replied. Pistol had family in Florida and he told me his aunt always went down there, especially close to the holidays. It was only a week before Christmas. Holidays were depressing for me since I didn't have any close family, so I rarely celebrated. We went into the kitchen and I sat at the dinner table while he heated up my food. He was quiet so I picked his brain.

"So, what have you been up to?" I asked.

"Nothing, much. Just chillin', but I told my nigga, Glock, about us," he said.

"Really? What did he say? Was he mad?" I asked.

"He asked me if I smashed and I told him the truth. It's been on my mind for a minute and I had to get dat burden off my shoulders, you feel me?" he asked.

"I'm sorry. It was hard to resist," I replied.

"The nigga asked me if I love you," Pistol said. My stomach was going insane. It was so bad it felt like I was getting bubble guts.

"We don't have to talk about this," I nervously said.

"It's sumthin we gotta talk about, baby girl. Anyway, I told him I love you," Pistol admitted. I almost fell out of my chair because my body went limp.

"Please don't tell me that," I said.

"He said he was cool wit' it as long as I wasn't tryna bag his wife," Pistol said. To sum it all up, Glock was basically telling Pistol he was just smashing me so he didn't care because he had a wife.

"Now what?" I asked.

"I'm tryna figure it out because I'on know if I can be a good nigga. Like seeing Mara and Beretta go through their shit just opened my eyes up to relationships," he said.

"Are you sayin' you can't be faithful?" I asked.

"I'm sayin' dat I'm not tryna find out yet until I'm ready to take dat step. My life consists of hustling, partying and bitches. Yeah, it's fucked up, but it's a habit. Almost like you stripping. It might not be easy for you to just stop," he said.

"I quit stripping over a month ago. I work at the post office now," I replied.

"Oh, word? Damn, baby girl. Congratulations, now I gotta get my shit together," he said.

"That you do, now hurry up with the food," I replied. I was a little disappointed but I had to respect his honesty. I couldn't pretend like Kemara and Beretta didn't have an effect on everyone else close to them. The shit they were going through opened our eyes to relationships and made us yield to things we weren't ready for. Hell, it should've stopped me from being with Delonte but I thought he could offer me something different since he was more mature and had his life together. Pistol sat my plate in front of me and I waited until he was done heating up his food before I dug in.

"I like your haircut. What made you cut your hair off?" I asked.

"Kemara's crazy ass. Shorty put rats and spiders in Beretta's crib. I'm not talking about small spiders we get in the corner of the wall. I'm talking about those big, hairy, built niggas. Anyways, shorty snapped. I couldn't stop scratching my hair and when Beretta got his cut, I said fuck it and cut mine, too," Pistol said.

"Wait a minute! Kemara's ass is crazy!" I screamed, laughing.

"He should've beat da fuck outta her, too. Nigga talkin' about roaches in the hood bigger than rats so it didn't fuck wit' him. Dat nigga makes excuses for shorty but I don't. Kemara needs help," Pistol said and I couldn't stop laughing.

"Naw, on da real, though. I feel bad for my nigga. I know for a fact he loves his shorty but just got put in a bad place," he said.

"They'll get through it. I know Kemara. She raises hell and gets out da gate but she's not leaving Beretta and we all know that," I replied.

"Yo, just don't get no crazy ideas from her," he said.

"This food is so damn good. I'm going to sleep after this," I replied. It was Saturday and I was off on weekends. All I wanted to do was cuddle with Pistol and turn my phone on vibrate. After we finished eating, I followed him to his apartment downstairs.

"You waste no time, huh?" he asked. I stripped down to my bra and panties before I climbed into his bed. I grabbed the remote and put it on the Lifetime channel.

"Fuck no! Come on, shorty. I want to watch the sports channel," he said, getting agitated.

"Come cuddle with me," I replied. He took his clothes off.

I miss all that fine dark chocolate. Yes, baby! Slide your fine ass right in this bed, I thought.

He slid in next to me only wearing his boxers. I melted into his arms when he wrapped them around me. Our lips met and he slipped his tongue into my mouth. It was like electricity going through my body. Not even on a drunk night did Delonte's lips feel that good. He rolled over on top of me and deepened the kiss. I wrapped my legs around him and he groaned from the heat of my pussy against his hard dick. I missed him so much it was insane. It sounded corny when I thought about it, but his love was like a drug and I wouldn't mind overdosing. He reached behind me and took my bra off. My pussy dripped when he pulled my nipple into his mouth. My hips thrust upwards and my clit swelled from the hardness of him rubbing my pussy. He pushed my panties to the side and freed himself. I bit my lip when he entered me.

"Ummmm," he groaned when my walls squeezed him. He sucked on my neck and licked behind my ear. It was my spot and he knew it.

"Baby, fuck me," I panted. I hadn't had a good dicking down for a while. Pistol pulled out of me and slid my panties off. He placed a pillow underneath my ass and I remembered Kemara telling me Beretta did that to her and she felt everything. I bit my bottom lip to keep from being loud. Pistol went deep in my pussy!

"Wait a minute!" I said and placed my hand on his stomach but he smacked my hand away. He stuck my panties in my mouth and pounded away. It almost felt like he was going to blow a hole through my back. My pussy gushed and wet noises from him splashing in and out of me echoed throughout the room. My hair was stuck to my face and sweat dripped down my cleavage. My body convulsed and my legs violently shook when he repeatedly slammed into my G-spot. He pulled the panties out of my mouth and kissed me.

"Pisttooolllll, baby!" I groaned. He pulled out of me so I could ride him. He laid back on the bed with his dick coated in my cum. He gripped my hips when I slid down his length. With my feet pressed down on the mattress and my hands on his chest, I bounced on his dick like my life depended on it. His chest muscles tightened and he bit his bottom lip. The nigga was even fine while making fuck faces. The way he looked at me made me cum again. He palmed my breasts and squeezed them as his dick jerked inside me. He kept me in place and pumped into me as he let out a deep groan from exploding. I fell onto his chest and he kissed my forehead.

"Straight put da pussy on a nigga," he said and I blushed.

"I missed you," I said.

"You missed this dick," he joked and I playfully bit him. Pistol rubbed my back then massaged my ass cheeks while I was still lying on top of him. I fell into a deep sleep.

****

The next day...

"Yo, please hurry da fuck up," Pistol said while we were in Nordstrom's.

"Wait a minute, nigga. I can't decide if I want the purple pumps or the red ones," I replied.

"Please get both. I caught a Charlie horse in my leg from sitting here. You keep picking up shit and putting it back," he complained.

"I swear you can't go shopping wit' niggas," I spat.

"It took me five minutes to get everything I needed, but you still tryna pick between two heels when it's like fifty different pairs in the store," he said.

"Okay, so imagine me dancing for you naked with only heels on. What color would you want them to be?" I asked.

"Red looks good on your skin," he said.

"See, that's all you had to fuckin' say," I replied.

"That's all you had to ask," he said. He went into his pocket and pulled out ten large bills to give to me.

"Nigga, you couldn't call me back!" a female said when she walked up on Pistol. She was funny-shaped and her edges were completely bald. I cringed because I could see her sew-in pulling at her edges. She had a cute face but her lipstick was lumpy.

SOUL Publications

"Yo, Yoshi, chill da fuck out," he whispered in embarrassment.

"Naw, nigga, I won't! You left me in a hotel room in D.C., and I didn't have a ride back, bitch! And who is this?" she asked, pointing at me.

"Whew, chile," I said aloud.

"Whew, chile, shit. What are you doin' with my man?" she asked. To be honest, I wasn't surprised to run into one of Pistol's jump-offs. For years, Pistol has been the hoe out of his crew and that's why it was hard for him to be in a relationship. If he was my man, I would've slapped the both of them.

"I need to know who this bitch is," Yoshi replied.

"Excuse me, ma'am, you have to leave," one of the salesclerks said to her. Yoshi was every bit of hoodrat and I couldn't believe how busted she was.

"I'll leave when I find out what I wanna know!" Yoshi yelled at the salesclerk. The salesclerk left to get security. Pistol bit the inside of his cheek as Yoshi made a big scene inside the store. She even read text messages between them out loud.

"That shit is from two weeks ago, though," Pistol said. I walked away and paid for my shoes. I left out of the store and Pistol left out behind me with Yoshi and her busted-ass friends.

"Bitch, da nigga said he don't want to be bothered!" I said, getting annoyed.

"Oh, naw, Yoshi! Hit dat bitch!" one of the girls said. Pistol stood between us and pushed Yoshi back.

"Shorty, I'll get someone to fuck yah lil' ass up if you don't chill out! Bitch, get gone," Pistol barked.

"Girl, let's go," one of her friends pulled her. Security came out of the store and went over to Yoshi and her friends. Pistol grabbed my hand and pulled me away.

"Nasty-ass nigga," I said and he chuckled.

"Mannnn, shorty caught a nigga on a late night after a party. I got da room then da head from her before I bounced. She ain't 'bout shit," he said. We walked into a jewelry store and Pistol slapped hands with a white guy behind the counter.

"How's it going, Olijah? What can I help you with?" he asked Pistol.

"Piper, this is our jeweler, Mison. Mison, this my lil' shorty," Pistol said and Mison nodded his head at me.

"She wants a GMBAM chain with pink diamonds or something simpler?" he asked and I chuckled.

"Naw, she doesn't need a GMBAM chain. Maybe we can do that pink diamond choker with the handcuffs in the middle," Pistol said, pointing in the case.

"Handcuffs in my chain?" I asked.

"Cuffing season, shorty," he replied and I giggled.

Mison handed me the necklace and Pistol hooked it for me. It was cute, although I wasn't big on wearing jewelry. I always kept it simple with earrings and a bangle here and there.

"Yeah, that's nice," Pistol said.

"I have the bracelet and earrings to match. I can knock off a few numbers if you want them," Mison said.

"Aight, let me see," Pistol said.

"How much does this necklace cost?" I asked.

"Twelve thousand," he replied and I looked at Pistol. He had given me money in the past but twelve g's for a necklace was too much.

"Umm, I'm good," I replied and Pistol chuckled.

"Ring me up, bruh. We don't need no boxes. She's gonna wear it out of the store," Pistol said. Mison smirked, probably happy he was getting rich off the GMBAM squad.

"Yo, next time mind yah business and don't question me about a price. If I'm gonna get it then that's just what it is, and plus, it's a gift because I'm happy for you. Shorty done got a job," Pistol smirked. I pecked his lips before he went over to Mison to pay for my jewelry. My phone vibrated in my purse and it was Delonte. It was his third time calling me and he wanted to apologize according to the texts he was sending. Pistol came over to me with the bracelet and earrings and I put them on before we left out of the store.

"I'm getting tired," I yawned. We'd been shopping for hours—well, shopping for me I should say. Pistol had one bag and I had six. He was spoiling me but it wasn't a surprise because he was doing it before things got serious between us. My concern was him getting the wrong message from me. I loved Pistol because of how he made me feel, not because of what he could afford for me. We left the mall and I was riding in the passenger's seat of his truck thinking about us.

"I love you for you, not your money," I said and he looked at me.

"Oh, so you love a nigga now?" he smirked.

"Yeah, but you knew that. Stop playin," I replied.

"I knew for a minute and I also know you ain't worried about my pockets. You always held yourself down. You and Kemara was probably the only shorties in the hood who didn't give a fuck about niggas' pockets. So we can nip dat in the bud and enjoy what we have now," he said.

"Well, what do we have?" I asked.

"The beginning to something deeper," he said.

"I'm cool wit' it," I replied and he squeezed my leg.

****

Three days later...

I spent the next few days with Pistol. As soon as I got off from work, I went to his grandmother's house. I forgot all about Delonte. All I needed from him was the clothes and shoes I left at his house. Most of my things were at his loft and I didn't want all of it, just the stuff I had recently purchased. I had a house key so when I got off from work, I stopped at his house. Delonte wasn't home and that was even better. Pistol wanted to come with me but I told him I didn't want shit to get out of hand. So, the nigga only gave me fifteen minutes to get everything.

"I just pulled up, Pistol," I said into the phone.

"Yo, don't be havin' dat clown-ass nigga begging you to stay, neither," Pistol said.

"Now you jealous?" I asked, parking my car.

"Naw, I ain't jealous but you gotta explain shit to dat nigga. I'm ready take care of sumthin so hit me soon as you walk out the door," Pistol said and I hung up. I got out of my car and walked into Delonte's building. I caught the elevator to the top floor and his home was at the end of the hall. Voices were coming from the other side of the door and I got annoyed because he was home even though I didn't see his car. I used the key to unlock the door and was greeted by a little brown-skinned girl who looked to be around eight years old.

"Who are you?" she asked me.

"Where is Delonte?" I replied.

"DADDDYYYYY!" the girl called out. Delonte came out of his room and stood by the rail on the top level looking down at me with confusion.

"What are you doing here?" he asked.

"I came to get my shit, but why you didn't tell me about your daughter?" I replied.

"You gotta leave, Piper!" he said.

That nigga had the nerve to give me a key and told me to move in but was hiding shit from me. Delonte was a fraud. Now I understand why I couldn't force myself to love him.

"Okay, I will, but can I get my things first?" I asked.

"They're not here," Delonte said.

"My mommy threw your clothes and shoes in the dumpsters," the little girl said. I looked at her arm and noticed she was wearing my diamond gold bangle that Kemara bought me for my twentieth birthday a few years back.

"Can I have my bracelet?" I asked the little girl.

"No, it's mine!" she said and ran upstairs to her father.

"So, you just toss my shit out and have your daughter steal my shit? Nigga, if you don't give me that bracelet back!" I yelled. Delonte came down the stairs and tried to get me to leave out of his loft.

"Listen, I'll explain everything later, but right now isn't the time. I didn't know she was comin' home," Delonte replied. He tried to push me out the door but I slapped him in the face.

"Get my fuckin' bracelet before I have to snatch it off her arm!" I yelled.

"Sarah, please give this woman her bracelet back!" Delonte said.

"It's mine! My mommy said I can keep it," Sarah said.

"I'll call the police on all of y'all muthafuckas! Y'all stole my shit and I have a key to this place, so I know they will work in my favor! You cannot toss my shit out and get away with it!" I yelled.

"Sarah, give her the damn bracelet!" Delonte yelled.

"NO!" Sarah yelled back.

Delonte ran upstairs to Sarah and she darted away from him. I shook my head at his clowned-out ass.

"Get back here, Sarah!" Delonte said. I sat on the couch and waited for that nigga to smack his daughter on the hand or something. Sarah was out of control and even called her daddy a "punk." The front door opened and a woman walked into the house with two boxes of pizzas. She snarled when she saw me. She was pretty but I could tell she was way older than me, perhaps in her late-thirties, early-forties.

"You must be Piper," she said and slammed Delonte's keys down on the counter.

"Yes, and who are you?" I replied.

"I'm his wife. Wow, he goes younger and younger. How old is this one, Delonte? Eighteen like the last one?" she asked him and I looked at him.

"It's not the time right now, Mariah. Piper wants her bracelet back then she'll leave," Delonte said.

"No, let her stay so she can eat with us. I want to know all about this one," Mariah said.

"Look, I don't have shit to do with y'all but I want my bracelet. You already tossed my shit out but I'm cool. Just tell your daughter to hand it over before I call the police," I said.

"Call the police? Honey, you're the intruder," Mariah said.

"And you're supposed to be dead, bitch. Don't pretend like I knew this nigga had a fuckin' wife with a kid," I replied and stood up. Mariah looked at Delonte and he scratched his head.

"I just came home from prison. Tell her why I went to prison," Mariah said.

"Don't do this right now, Mariah!" Delonte yelled at her.

"I went to prison for stabbing a bitch he knocked up. My mother raised my daughter in Arizona. Delonte is very manipulative. First, he pretends to be the perfect gentleman, then after he gets you where he wants you, he changes. He becomes verbally abusive and he's also a cheater. He has five other baby mamas and he's older than you think. He keeps a bald head so we won't see the gray. Oh, and he has a knack for young, ghetto strippers because he thinks they are easier to manipulate. He pays them to keep their mouths shut and sometimes moved them out of state so nobody will know about his dirty games. I did five years in prison and I came home to him having a bitch's clothes in my house! He didn't know I was getting out early until I surprised him. My father warned me about him but I didn't listen. I stayed with the piece of shit. Every stripper he has slept with has the same story. It always starts out as a private dance. He plays the innocent man who lost his wife so they feel sorry for him. Then he goes to tell them how he lived in the projects and how he had to hustle to go to college but it's all a fuckin' lie! Delonte's parents are both judges and they moved in a mansion in California. He's a spoiled rich brat who always gets what he wants and plays with women's feelings," Mariah said.

That's how it all started with Delonte. I gave him a private dance and one thing led to another. No wonder he was so secretive at the club; he was probably sleeping around with other strippers.

"You nasty son-of-a-bitch!" I screamed at Delonte.

"Mariah, this isn't fair. You know I asked for a divorce a few months ago! Listen, Piper, I was gonna tell you but we kept arguing and it made it hard for me," Delonte said.

"Wow, this is the first time I saw him shaken up. You might have the best pussy of them all," Mariah laughed.

"How old are you Delonte?" I asked.

"He's forty-six," Mariah laughed and Delonte hung his head down in shame.

"His oldest son is about your age, but Delonte doesn't want anything to do with him. He lives in the same city and refuses to reach out to him," Mariah said. Delonte being almost fifteen years older than me was pushing it but to hear he was twenty-four years older than me sickened me. He violated me and I figured he was lying about something but nothing as big as his wife still being alive and him having a lot of kids.

"Who is your oldest son, Delonte?" I asked and he put his head down.

"Pistol," he admitted. I jumped on Delonte and couldn't stop fighting him. That piece of shit was trash! No wonder Delonte felt so uncomfortable around Pistol. Delonte fell onto the floor after tripping over the coffee table. I picked up the lamp and bashed him in the face with it. Sarah screamed when she saw the blood and Mariah just sat and watched. I stopped hitting Delonte because I wasn't a murderer but I felt like killing him.

"You knew I was in love him and sat back and said nothing! How do you think I feel knowing I fucked a son and his father because you lied about your whole life! But too bad your secret isn't gonna keep me away from Pistol because I'm gonna be with him. He's more of a man than you! And he fucks wayyyy better, too! Let dat marinate, bitch!" I yelled and kicked him in his stomach.

"Delonte really loves his whores," Mariah said, eating a slice of pizza.

"Oh, bitch, fuck you! You should question your pussy if your man is out here ruining lives!" I replied. I grabbed Sarah and snatched my bracelet off her arm. She ran to her mother and Mariah jumped up and tried to charge into me but I sent a gut-crushing kick to her stomach and she flew over the couch.

"Y'all dysfunctional niggas can go to hell!" I screamed before I left out of the house. I ran downstairs to my car like my life depended on it. My phone rang but I couldn't answer it. I wasn't in the mood to talk to anybody. As soon as I made it home, I unlocked my door and fell out on the floor in the living room. I screamed from frustration and cried because I would've been fucked if I gave Delonte my all. He would've ruined my whole life and drained me. An hour later, someone knocked on the door. I wiped my eyes and got off the floor. Pistol was waiting for me at his grandmother's house so I figured it was him wondering what happened to me. When I opened the door, two police officers were standing in front of me.

"Piper Stephens, you're under arrest for attempted murder and burglary," an officer said, then began reading me my rights. I couldn't believe it! Just when my life was looking up, it was taken away from me. Who would've thought Delonte would be the cause of my downfall?

Kemara

I t was almost midnight as I followed Amona through the streets of Annapolis. I had been keeping tabs on her for a few weeks so I could thoroughly carry out my plan. Earlier that day, I was at the studio with Chevy listening to some rap song he wanted to put out. Chevy was an okay rapper but the thing I hated about his style was he rapped about street life and selling bricks. Chevy was never exposed to that type of life, so it was hard for me to listen to it. We'd been talking on the phone a lot and I hung out with him and his friends a few times at the studio. It was just something to do because I wasn't sure how me and Beretta's marriage was going to play out. Lately, we had been on good terms as far as communication but we slept in separate beds and wasn't having sex. I was so tempted to give him some on many nights when he walked around the house only wearing baller shorts without boxers.

Amona was on her way to Lezzi's house. She went there every night when she left work, and some nights she stayed. I was tired of waiting around to kill her. I could've done it sooner but it would've been too obvious that I was responsible. Besides, Christmas was around the corner and

I wanted her dead by the holidays so Nika could drown in depression. I parked up the street and cut the lights off to the hooptie I purchased with fake tags for five hundred bucks. My clothes were all black and baggy. My hair was tucked under my hat which was pulled down low over my eyes. I went inside the glove compartment and pulled out a pair of black leather gloves. I grabbed my gun from underneath my seat, under the carpet and waited until Amona got out of her car before I got out. She walked up the stairs to Lezzi's house and I crept up behind her. Lezzi opened the door and I grabbed Amona around the neck and pointed my gun at Lezzi.

"Scream and I'll blow her fuckin' head off," I said. Lezzi's hands trembled when she opened the door wider for me to step inside. I hit Amona with the butt of my gun when Lezzi closed the door.

"What do you want? We don't have any money," Lezzi cried and got down on the floor next to Amona. I pulled the trigger and a bullet pierced through her forehead. Her body hit the floor in a loud thump and Amona screamed. I kicked her in the side when she reached out to her cousin.

"What did you do?" she cried. I snatched her up by her hair and dragged her upstairs. She reached for the rail but I smashed her fingers with the butt of the gun. I took her into a bedroom.

"Let me go!" she screamed. I hit her in the face with my fist and she fell onto the floor with her nose bleeding.

"Take whatever you want! Please, just take it!" she cried as tears fell down her face. I lifted my hat so she could see my eyes. She covered her mouth in shock.

"You thought I forgot about you?" I asked.

"Kemara, please don't do this! You need help," she sobbed.

"You can beg me all you want to but it won't keep me from killing you. What you think, I was gonna let you walk after seeing me shoot Lezzi in the head? Bitch, you really dumber than I thought. Do you know how I feel about you and my nigga? And did you ever stop to ask yourself how it would affect the other woman? You felt nothing because you didn't give a fuck! You're a fuckin' coward! You fucked my man while I was in the hospital! Save those side-chick tears, bitch, because I'm like you, I'on give a fuck about nothing," I said.

"So, you think I played a hand in this by myself?" she asked.

"I know what you're doing but it ain't working. Beretta is reaping what he sows but you on the other hand just need to go. Then you had the audacity to eye-fuck him in my face? Nika isn't here so where is the tough girl act now?" I asked.

"I'm so sorry, I didn't think it was gonna be like this. Please don't waste your life on this. You can go to jail," she said and I laughed.

"Why do you love him?" I asked.

"Stop doing this!" she yelled and I pointed my gun at her head.

"Why do you love him?" I replied.

"He's, he's, he's..." she kept repeating.

"He's what, bitch! Tell me why you love my husband!" I screamed at her and she jumped.

"He's gorgeous, nice physique and he helped me with my bills," she said.

"Wow, unbelievable! So, you're telling me you were lusting behind a man and willing to destroy his marriage because of his looks and money? You know, I would've respected you if you said he made you feel like you'd suffocate if he left you. What about him holding you and giving you the kinds of butterflies that make your knees weak? How about he makes love to you that brings tears of passion to your eyes or even makes you a better person? Did you picture giving him babies or walking down the aisle to carry his last name? Did he stare at you while he thought you were sleeping with a smile on his face because he knows no other woman could make him happy? What about his personality? Did it match yours?" I asked and she sobbed. I kneeled next to her while she cried in the palm of her hands.

"See, all those things I just asked you I experienced with him. I love him! I can take Beretta handicapped, sick and broke and still love him the same. Do you see the difference between us now? I'll kill to keep that happiness

SOUL Publications

because it's all I have to fight for," I said. She reached out to me but I shot her twice in the head. I raided the drawers and flipped mattresses over in the bedroom while I was upstairs. I threw clothes and shoes out of the closet to make it look like a robbery. Lezzi had a few pieces of jewelry on her dresser and I put them in my pocket. I went inside Amona's purse and took cash out of her wallet and left it on the floor. I left the house out of the back door.

****

After I burned my clothes and ditched the car I was driving, I walked a few blocks to a nearby restaurant and caught a cab from there. I was dressed in the clothes I had on earlier which was a puffy coat with fur around the hood, jeans and riding boots. My weave was flowing down my shoulders and my make-up was refreshed like nothing ever happened. The cab driver took me to my truck which was parked in a casino garage.

"Twenty dollars," he said. I handed him a fifty-dollar bill and told him to keep the change. I got out of his cab and got into my truck then headed home to D.C. It took me twenty-five minutes to get home and it was a little bit past two o'clock in the morning. I tried to sneak into the house but I was greeted by Beretta sitting at the kitchen table running his money through a money machine while drinking out of a bottle of Henny. He had two trash bags full of money sitting on the floor.

"Where da fuck you been at?" he asked.

SOUL Publications

"Out," I replied.

"Out, where?" he said.

"Let's not start that bullshit right now. Where is Zalia?" I asked.

"In her fuckin' crib, sleepin'! This is what you want, Mara? Me sitting in da fuckin' house waitin' on you to come home like I'm some bitch-made nigga who can't handle his wife?" he asked.

"There is da door," I replied.

"You fuckin'?" he asked and I rolled my eyes at him. I was on my way upstairs but he grabbed me by the hood of my coat and dragged me down the steps. I yelled for him to get off me but he put his weight on me. He unbuttoned my pants and I tried to fight him off but I was missing. Beretta slapped me in the mouth and I scratched at his face. He stuck his hand in my panties and one of his fingers entered me. The nigga had the nerve to smell his fingers to see if I smelled like sex. Satisfied with the outcome, he stood up and walked away from me.

"You're crazy!" I spat and he continued counting his money like nothing happened. I stood up and touched my lip to see if it was bleeding.

"I ain't smack you dat hard but da next time I will. Yo, on God, I'll beat da fuck outta you if you keep disrespecting me. How are we supposed to make this shit work if I'm the only one trying?" he asked.

"I'm going to bed," I replied and walked upstairs. Zalia was sleeping peacefully in her crib when I walked into her room. Beretta bathed her and washed her hair. I rubbed her fat little stomach and she woke up. Her smile was the cutest because she had four teeth. She kicked her feet and began babbling, so I picked her up. I took Zalia into my bedroom and sat her on the bed. Beretta came upstairs and walked into my bedroom.

"It took me three hours to get her to go to sleep and you just woke her up," he said.

"She'll go to sleep in a few," I yawned.

"Want me to run your bath water or sumthin?" he asked and I blushed.

"Yes, please," I replied and he walked into the bathroom.

"Daddy just tryna get some," I said aloud and Zalia babbled like she knew what I was saying. Beretta came out of my bathroom and laid across my bed with Zalia.

"You gotta sign for the mattress that's coming tomorrow. I'm not gonna be home," Beretta said.

"What mattress?" I asked.

"A good mattress for the guest room. That shit hurts my back," he said and I felt bad.

"You didn't have to do all of that," I replied.

"I'm not askin' to sleep witchu anymore. Shorty, we ain't nothing but roommates. I looked at a few cribs earlier today, though. Maybe you'll feel better if I got my own crib. I can keep Zalia during the day then you can get her at night so I can handle my business," he said. My chest felt heavy because I wasn't ready for Beretta to move out.

"We had a deal," I said.

"Yeah, but I ain't gonna keep kissin' yah ass, neither," he replied.

"Why can't you fight for me? You're supposed to deal wit' all of this to prove to me you'll neva do it again," I said and he shook his head.

"Put dat ring back on your finger and I'll do anything I gotta do, but you showin' me that I'm fightin for a shorty dat is not tryna see I wanna do the right things. You want to walk around here like a single woman, so how does that help us?" he asked. I went over to my dresser and opened my jewelry box. I grabbed my wedding ring and band then placed it on my finger. Honestly, I didn't think it meant that much to him but it did because he always brought it up. I looked at his hand and he was still wearing his wedding band.

"Thank you, damn," he said and I giggled.

"Aight, you can get out of my room so I can take my clothes off," I replied. Beretta laid back on the bed and laid Zalia on his chest.

"Go ahead, let me see a titty or sumthin. I'm tired of beating my dick," he said and I covered my mouth.

"Ewwwww, Z'wan," I said.

"Yeah, and a lot of nut came out, too. My balls heavy and my dick stay hard at the wrong times. I was chillin' wit' my niggas earlier and caught a boner. Let me taste it at least, damn," he said.

"I'll think about it," I replied and he grilled me.

"See how Mommy do?" Beretta asked Zalia who was going to sleep and I smacked his leg. I took my clothes off and he licked his lips.

Nigga, I'm gonna give you the business if you keep lookin' at me like that, I thought.

Beretta took Zalia to her room and closed the door behind him. I went into the bathroom and sat in the tub. The water was soothing and the aroma of lavender and spearmint almost put me to sleep. A smile crept across my face when I thought about Amona and her tears.

I need some dick, I thought. Lord knows I wanted to have Beretta inside of me. I understood Amona's attraction to him because at one point I was smitten by his looks, too. I used to look out my bedroom window and stare at Beretta all day shooting dice and talking shit. His loud deep voice used to echo through the building. It was just something about him that was hard to resist but lust and love were two different things and I had both of them.

SOUL Publications

An hour passed, and I stepped out of the tub after washing up. I grabbed a towel and dried off. It was four o'clock in the morning and I heard Beretta's TV on in his bedroom. I dropped the towel on the floor and headed towards his bedroom. I pushed his bedroom door open and he was sleeping peacefully on his back with the sheet down to his waist. My pussy throbbed while staring at his dick print. I slid the sheet back and laid on top of him. My tongue outlined his sexy full lips and he palmed my ass.

"Shorty, you betta not be teasing me," Beretta whispered against my lips. I kissed him and he rolled on top of me. A deep gasp came from between my lips when he stuffed my breast inside his mouth. He worked his way down to my center. His tongue parted my lips and dived right in. I missed his dreads because I used to pull on them or control his head movement but with them gone he was able to do what he wanted.

"Ohhhhhh," I moaned as my clit throbbed. He pressed my legs into the mattress and covered my peach with his mouth. Beretta was treating my pussy like he was eating a pudding cup and didn't have a spoon. I clutched the sheets and wrapped my legs around his neck but that didn't stop him. He sucked and flicked his tongue across my clit. A tear slid out the corner of my eye while he took my body through a realm of pure ecstasy. My nails dug into his shoulders and my hips moved in the direction of his tongue.

"UGHHHHHH!" I screamed when I exploded into his mouth. My body lazily fell into the bed and Beretta pulled away from me with my essence plastered all over his face.

He got out of bed and went into the hall bathroom to wipe his face.

"Why you ain't leave it on there?" I called out while laughing.

"'Cause it'll dry up and have my beard stiff!" he replied. He came back into the bedroom and laid next to me. I looked at him like he was crazy because I wanted some.

"Z'wan, don't play with me," I replied.

"Naw, I'm tryna save dat lil' pussy because the way I'm feelin ain't the same as how you feel. I'm backed up so you already know a nigga straight smashing," he replied and it made me hornier. I sat up and crawled to the end of his bed and arched my back so my ass could be sitting up. My mound was exposed for him and I wanted him to enter.

"DAMN!" he said. He got to the end of the bed and gripped my hips. My heart raced when he rubbed the tip of his head against my opening. A moan slipped from his lips when he eased himself in. I was tight—very tight, so he had to adjust. Seconds later, Beretta was digging my pussy out and I took all of it. He grabbed my weave and pulled my head back.

"You cummin' already, huh?" he asked then smacked my ass cheek. It wasn't an easy task but I threw it back anyway. I used to think females exaggerated when they bragged about feeling it in their stomach but it was nothing but the truth. He was hitting a spot inside of me that made me feel like I was ready to pee. Whatever that spot was, it was magical because I was squirting and couldn't stop cumming. Sounds of him diving into my wetness was louder than my moans.

"Yo, you so fuckin' wet, umph! Baby, throw it back again," Beretta groaned while pulling my hair. I squeezed my pussy muscles together and slammed my ass against his pelvis. He palmed my ass and slammed me onto his dick and I shrieked. He pulled out of me and snatched me off the bed. He swiped everything off our dresser and picked me up.

"UUUUUMMMMMMMMM!" I cried out when he pinned my legs back and slid all the way into me. He gripped my hips and slid me up and down his girth. I squeezed my breasts and bit my lip while he passionately fucked me. The muscles in his chest flexed and I wanted to run my tongue over his body. He pulled out and smacked his dick against my clit and it jumped. The feeling was indescribable, but it made my essence splash against my inner thighs.

"Put it back in," I panted.

"Can I sleep witchu again?" he asked then sucked my lips.

Nigga, you can sleep inside me! I thought.

"Yessssssssss," I hissed when his head entered me.

"Look at yah freak ass," he teased while pounding me. He went deeper and his dick was harder. Beretta jerked inside of me and wrapped his hand around my throat while stroking between my walls. He moaned my name and I scratched at his sweaty chest as we both climaxed. His heavy body leaned into mine and I wrapped my arms around him. I missed him so much it was killing me. He pulled away from me and stared into my eyes.

"Why did you come in da house late?" he asked.

"I killed them," I admitted.

"Who?" he asked.

"Lezzi and Amona," I replied. He pulled out of me then sat on the edge of the bed.

"Do I need to get one of my niggas to get rid of their bodies?" he asked.

"No, it was a home burglary gone wrong," I replied.

"Did anybody see you?" he asked.

"I drove a hooptie with fake tags and burned it with my clothes. Are you mad?" I asked.

"Her life means nothing to me but yours does. On da real, I just can't risk you doin' crazy shit and getting jammed up for it," he said.

"Just say you mad because I offed your bitch," I replied.

"You want me to argue with you so bad but I'm not goin' to, so get back on your childish shit and ignore me for another month. I gave you what you wanted so you can go back to your room and continue on thinking about how I ain't shit. Do you even know if there were cameras where you were at? Come on, shorty, you gotta know this type of shit. Did you do it at Lezzi's house? Pistol had cameras installed when they were living together. I don't know if he took them out," Beretta fussed and grabbed his cell phone.

"Keep your dick in your pants then," I replied and left out of the room. I took a quick shower before I got back into bed. Beretta came into my room twenty minutes later.

"Mara, sit up. I got some good news and bad news," he said and I hurriedly sat up to listen.

Please don't tell me those bitches had cameras in the house, I thought.

"What happened?" I asked.

"Pistol took the cameras out before he moved out," Beretta said.

Whew, I thought.

"Okay, what else?" I asked.

"Piper is locked up on an attempted murder charge," he said.

"WHAT!" I screamed.

"She sent dat nigga Delonte to the hospital from beating him with a lamp and she stole something from his daughter," Beretta said.

"Daughter? Wait a damn minute!" I replied, getting worked up.

"Her bail hearing is later on today," Beretta said. I got up and went to my purse for my cell phone but it wasn't in there. I figured I left it in my truck.

No wonder I didn't hear my phone ring, I thought. I threw on some clothes and Beretta asked me where I was going.

"Naw, shorty. You ain't leavin out this late," he said.

"I need to get my phone so I can call Silk or Thickems. They might know more. Piper was probably trying to call me," I said.

"I'll go get it," Beretta said and walked out the room.

My shit list keeps growing. Now I'll have to hurt Delonte because he got Piper into some shit, I thought.

We couldn't win for losing. It was always something, and no matter how much we tried to escape it, trouble followed us. I wished there was some type of time travel button so we could start all over again, but the lowlife was our daily dosage...our environment.

Beretta

I looked through Kemara's truck for her phone and couldn't find it. Kemara was always misplacing her phone or it ended up falling out of her purse. Shorty just be thinking a lot and don't be paying attention to shit. I reached underneath her driver's seat and felt around until I found it.

"What da fuck is this?" I asked myself. I flipped the phone open and it was a prepaid phone. Kemara had an iPhone, so I figured it wasn't hers until I clicked on the messages. Shorty was using it to talk to a nigga. I punched the driver's side window in her truck and it cracked. I was heated!

Yo, just calm down before you go upstairs and merk dat bitch! I thought. The last message was from the nigga telling her she left her cell phone at the studio. Shorty was out with a nigga before she merked Amona. I called her six times and she didn't answer. That little bitch was playing me, but she warned me. In St. Croix, she told me if a man cheats then he deserved to be cheated on, too. Everything was a game to her and I was done with it! Kemara was a good shorty but she had some shit with her that I couldn't grasp. We were too much alike and it was a good and bad thing—it was dysfunctional. Two negatives didn't make a positive. I went back into the crib and she was sitting on the couch with a robe on.

"Did you find it?" she asked.

"Naw, I ain't see it. You probably left it somewhere," I said and went into the kitchen to grab a bottle of water.

"I'm worried about Piper. I talked to her earlier and we were supposed to meet up tomorrow with Silk," she said.

"Yeah, you'll see her soon," I replied and headed upstairs to my bedroom. I took off my sweatpants and hoodie before I got back into bed.

Focus on your bread and forget about shorty. She'll come around eventually, I thought.

****

Eight hours later...

"I can't believe they won't let her out on bail," Kemara said, riding in the passenger's seat of my Benz. Zalia was in her car seat fussing about something and kicking her feet.

"Wait a minute, Zalia. We're almost home," Kemara said. Zalia was hungry and she wasn't trying to hear that, so she started screaming. Kemara handed her a bottle and Zalia snatched it from her.

"Delonte's parents are judges so I think they called in a favor. Piper's charges are bullshit and the system is working overtime against her. They act like she killed the nigga, plus she stole what already belonged to her. She'll be aight because we are gonna find a good lawyer, so don't trip," I said to Kemara.

"But Piper can't do jail time. What am I gonna do without her? This is so fuckin' foul. I blame myself because I told Piper to work it out with Delonte. He seemed like a good man but now look at her. I swear niggas fuck bitches' lives up," Kemara said and I looked at her.

"What?" she asked.

"Nothing, I'm gonna drop y'all off at home because I have to take care of a few things," I replied. She was ready to say something but the ringing of my cell phone interrupted her.

"Yooo," I answered.

"BERETTTAAAAAA!" Nika cried into the phone.

"What's up, Nika? Hope straight?" I asked.

"Amona is dead! Lezzi's mother found them this morning with gunshots to their heads. Someone robbed them!" she screamed into the phone and Kemara giggled.

"Sorry to hear dat, Nika, but what you callin' for?" I asked.

"You know why I'm calling! I know you have your connections to the streets so find out who did this to her so justice can be served," she replied.

"Yah baby father got connections to the streets, too, so what you calling me for? What is dat nigga good for besides keepin' you pregnant?" I asked.

"Are you mad at me about Jasmine and Sniper? Did you hurt Amona?" she asked.

"Yo, get off my line asking me some police-ass shit. Maybe the same niggas who kidnapped Hope robbed her. They were watching y'all, remember? Go figure dat shit out yah self. I keep tellin' you Amona ain't my concern. She ain't my fuckin' wife, Nika. Don't call me about dat girl no more," I replied and hung up. Nika called back three more times but I let the phone rang.

"What do you have to do after you take us home?" Kemara asked.

"A few things," I replied.

"Are you mad at me about sumthin? Please don't tell me you're trippin over Amona," she said.

"Mannnnn, you know I'on give a fuck about dat," I replied.

"What is it then?" she asked.

SOUL Publications

"Nothing, shorty. Everything straight," I replied.

"Can you come home early so we can talk?" she asked.

Now this lil' bitch wanna talk after I have been kissing her ass for almost seven weeks. Chevy's bitch ass must be slacking, I thought.

"Yeah, I can," I replied and she grabbed my hand.

"You find yah phone yet?" I asked.

"No, I'll get another one later," she replied.

I took them home then headed back to Annapolis. When I rode through Newtowne, I saw the lil' nigga Carlos standing on the corner talking to a little girl. I parked my Benz and got out of my whip.

"The king of the city!" Flo said, then slapped hands with me.

"What's good witchu?" I replied.

"Shit, chilling. Waiting for this bitch-ass nigga to bring me my Bentley back. I told that nigga to take my car and get it washed but that was five hours ago," he said and I chuckled.

"Oh, word? You got a Bentley? Damn, nigga I ain't know you was getting it like dat," I said and he scratched his chin.

"Yeah, I'm gettin' dat bread like you," he bragged.

"My nigga Beretta," Carlos said when he walked over to me.

"What's up, youngin'? You got a lil' shorty or sumthin?" I asked.

"Yeah, she phat, too. Where Pretty Girl at? I want a shorty like dat when I get older," Carlos said and rubbed his hands together.

"You checkin' my wife out, lil' nigga?" I chuckled and he smirked.

"Naw, she cool, though," Carlos said.

"What yah grades lookin' like?" I replied and he put his head down.

"I got all C's and D's," he said.

"Start takin' yah ass to the community center so they can help you with your homework," I replied.

"Okay," he said and I slapped hands with him. Flo shook his head when Carlos walked off.

"That lil' muthafucka wanna be just like you. He calls himself Nine," Flo said.

"Yo, stop playin'," I replied because Flo lied about everything.

"For real. The lil' kids around here call him Nine like the 9mm gun," he said. Pistol pulled into the parking lot and parked his truck next to my whip. Him and Machete stepped out of the truck. I told Flo to walk off so we could talk and he left. Flo was a cool nigga but I didn't say shit around him or near him. The nigga couldn't hold water and was always mixing up information.

"What Flo's bitch-ass talkin' about? His Bentley?" Machete laughed.

"That nigga got a Bentley emblem on an Elantra," Pistol said.

"What we gonna do about this Delonte nigga, bruh? Say da word and I'll catch a flight to California where his parents live," Machete said.

"We gotta play this one smart because Delonte got a feeling of how we get down. I can see his bitch-ass now saying one of us did it. They'll investigate us and killing two judges will go public," Pistol replied.

"I'm heated, too! Shorty just got a job and was chillin' and dat fuck-nigga pulled her into some bullshit. I should've merked his ass when we were in St. Croix," Machete said.

"Threw his body over the boat and made it look like he drowned by accident, but Piper will be straight," I replied.

"I hope so because she was crying on the phone when she called me and it fucked me up," Pistol replied.

Sniper walked down the street and dapped us up. He'd been quiet since he found out we were brothers. I paid for me, Jasmine and Sniper to get a blood test and a week later the results came back. I wanted to talk to him one-on-one but the lil' nigga was always on the move.

"Take a walk wit' me, Sniper," I said to him. He put his hands in his coat pocket and walked down the sidewalk with me.

"Yo, everything good? You mad at me about sumthin?" I asked.

"Naw, neva dat. I'm just feelin' some type of way because Jasmine was tryna tell me for the longest time but I thought she was talking out of her head," he replied.

"I feel you but we always been like brothers, but us being blood brothers is even better," I said and he smirked.

"Yeah, my big brother," he chuckled then his face got serious.

"You got any pictures of ou—our father?" he asked.

"Naw, but I might can get you one," I replied.

"I always wanted to know what da nigga looks like but the people I asked said you look just like him. My mother got rid of all the picturs of him," he said.

"I ain't neva checked for da nigga. For years, Nika lied to me and pretended he manipulated her but she trapped the nigga by lying about her age," I replied. Machete walked over to me with his phone.

"Yo, Beretta, is this yah wife?" he asked. He showed me a video on Facebook. It was that nigga Chevy recording some bullshit while he was in the studio and my wife was sitting on his lap smoking weed with him. Sniper took the phone from him and looked at it.

"Naw, bruh. Dat can't be Mara," Sniper said.

One thing about keeping your position is you have to be on your toes at all times. Muthafuckas was going to start questioning me if they knew I couldn't control my bitch. Kemara was exposing herself to a lot of situations that could fuck up my name and I couldn't have that. It wasn't a good look for me and shorty was about to have every nigga in the city laughing at me because she was chilling with a clown.

"Yo, Beretta, don't do nothing crazy," Pistol said.

"I'm straight," I replied and my niggas looked at me.

"Yo, I'm Gucci. We gotta shipment coming in tonight so I need y'all close by," I replied. I was on grind mode but on the inside, I was raging! My calmness wasn't good a one, though. A nigga was ready to blow off some steam.

Nigga, stop being the nice guy. Go back to dat nigga you used to be when you were merking niggas for disrespecting you, I thought.

Naw, I can't go back. I want to be a different nigga. Less killings, drug wars and more money, I thought.

Niggas don't care about dat! They are gonna take your growth for weakness, I thought.

I was constantly battling between the man I used to be and the man I wanted to become to make my wife happy, but the shit wasn't working. When I got into my whip, I called up someone who could help me solve my problem and fast.

****

It was one thirty in the morning when I walked into the house. Kemara was sitting on the couch watching TV. I knew she was waiting up for me because she called me over twenty times. She looked worried about something, probably the situation with Piper or the video of her chilling in the studio with a nigga; perhaps it was both. She sat up on the couch and I sat across from her.

"I don't want to fight anymore," she said.

"Me, neither, shorty," I replied. I pulled the papers out of my back pocket and slammed them on the coffee table.

"What's this?" she asked, picking up the papers.

"Your walking papers," I replied.

"An annulment?" she asked.

"Like we never been married. Don't worry, I told my lawyer everything. He knows I cheated and I told him about the situation with Moesha and how we're sleeping in separate rooms. Sign them so I can be on my way," I replied. Kemara stood up from the couch and walked into the kitchen to pour herself another glass of wine.

"Yo, sign da fuckin' papers!" I yelled out.

"I can't!" she yelled back.

"I don't want you, Mara. I can't fuck with a bitch who is gonna treat me like I'm her enemy and take my kindness for weakness. Yo, it's takin' everything in me to not strangle you to death and blow your face wide open. Sign the fuckin' papers!" I said.

"Z'wan, I'm not signing those papers," she said. She reached into her purse and pulled out a small pamphlet.

"I wanted to talk to you about a marriage counselor. I've gone too far, I should've left so I could sort things out but I wanted you to feel the pain I was feeling. I'm not signing those papers. We can work it all out," she said. She tried to hug me but I pushed her away.

"I know you have been following my Facebook page. Something told me that profile was you, so I've been flirting with Chevy to make you jealous. I've been spending time with him at the studio and talking to him on a prepaid phone but I didn't sleep with him. I don't know how to deal with pain so I replace it with vengeance. Please, just stay home so we can fix this," she said. Seeing Mara cry was probably one of my weaknesses, but shorty was doing too much.

"I'll be back tomorrow and I want those papers signed," I replied. She grabbed the papers and ripped them up.

"I'm not signing a fuckin' thing," she said. I balled up my fist and swung, punching a hole in the wall next to her face. Mara was a little shaken up because she thought I was going to hit her even though I wanted to. Controlling my temper wasn't easy but I was forcing myself to for the sake of her life. My fist was bloody but I punched another hole in the wall and she jumped.

"STOP!" she said but I used my left hand and punched another one. Who else could I have taken my anger out on? By the time I was finished, both of my hands were bloody with skin pulled back from my fingers.

"I saved yah life," I said and went up the stairs.

"I'll get Zalia ready then we can go to the hospital," Kemara said, following me upstairs. I rinsed my hands off in the sink and Mara wrapped a towel around them.

"Go to sleep, Mara," I said.

"No, I'm gonna clean you up," she replied with her hands still shaking. She grabbed the peroxide and poured it over my hands. It didn't look bad after she cleaned them up and I was still able to move my fingers even though they were starting to hurt. I left the bathroom and laid across the bed.

"We will be happy again. Life just caught us at our worst when we got married, but no man out here can make me feel the way you do. I know there's people who went through more shit than us and found a way and so can we," she said. I closed my eyes and said a silent prayer to God. Crazy how I was starting to talk to Him lately but I thanked Him for showing me a better way because I was going to kill my wife that night.

Kemara

One week later...

Me and Beretta wasn't fully on good terms. It didn't take long for the rumor to spread about me and Chevy. I didn't know his homeboy was recording us when I was in the studio and of course Chevy didn't see any fault in it. Truth be told, I wanted my marriage to work because I couldn't imagine myself with anyone else. Christmas had come and gone, Zalia wasn't old enough to understand Christmas, but we opened gifts with her anyway. It was silent between us that day while we exchanged gifts. I tried to talk to Beretta but he kept the conversation short. Everything was falling apart but I don't remember it being well put-together in the first place. My phone rang, bringing me out of my thoughts.

"What do you want, Chevy?" I asked.

"Aye, yo, Mara! Where you at?" he asked.

"I'm home and I thought I told you not to call me anymore. I'm working shit out with my husband," I replied.

"And I told you I don't have shit to do with that!" he slurred. I knew he was drunk and possibly high. Chevy lived the average twenty-three-year-old life. He was always partying, drinking and smoking.

"You're drunk," I replied.

"Tell me sumthin, shorty. You used me to get back at dat nigga, didn't you?" Chevy asked.

"No, I didn't. You kept coming on to me and messaging me on Facebook. We were just chilling together but you knew my situation, so don't play that good guy bullshit with me. I didn't lead you on and I told you upfront I just needed someone to talk to and now you're pinning the blame on me?" I asked.

"I asked around about dat nigga and someone told me he got another bitch knocked up. It all makes sense as to why you were spending time with me," Chevy replied. Chevy knew I was having problems in my marriage but I damn sure wasn't pillow-talking to another man about my husband. Chevy kept asking about us and I told him "it was complicated" every time. The fact that he was asking around about Beretta was going to send him to an early grave if word got back to Beretta about Chevy. Matter of fact, Beretta was too quiet about the situation with Chevy; it was almost like he forgot about it even though I knew it was heavily on his mind. The front door unlocked and I hung up on Chevy. Beretta walked into the loft and his cologne breezed past my nose. He gave me a head nod and walked straight to the kitchen. His hands were wrapped up in bandages because of the open wounds he had from punching the wall. It crushed my spirit to know my husband wanted to hurt me that much but took it out on the wall instead. The clock on the living room wall read eleven forty-five. It was almost midnight and he was home early.

"How was your day today?" I asked when I went into the kitchen.

"It was straight. What about yours?" he asked.

"Okay, I feel a little better since I talked to Piper earlier. She's going through so much and I wish I could do sumthin about it," I replied.

"Nobody can do anything because dat bitch-ass nigga filed a police report saying Piper was a part of a gang and he feared for his life. If anything happens to dat nigga, Piper's case ain't gonna look good at all," Beretta said.

"I shouldn't have told Piper to give that lame-ass nigga a chance," I replied.

"Yeah, 'cause you definitely the spokesperson for lame-ass niggas," Beretta said. He grabbed a V8 vegetable juice out the fridge then headed upstairs to his bedroom. I followed him and he grilled me.

"What's up, Mara?" he asked.

"Our appointment with the marriage counselor is tomorrow and I hope you come," I said and he chuckled.

"I might stop by," he replied. I wanted to yell at him but I was too tired. Nobody knew how drained I was from the past year of my life. When I talked about it, I felt like nobody was hearing me. It always seemed as if I wasn't allowed to be sad or emotional because of the type of female I painted myself out to be. I was a depressed and sad individual that hid behind the person everyone thought they knew. My soul felt like it was burning in hell and the devil had his hand over my mouth so I wouldn't cry out for help.

"Okay," I replied and walked out of his bedroom.

I went into my bedroom and laid across the bed.

I wondered how my life would've been if I had both parents in the same house and we lived in a nice middle-class area. Soon as I come home from school, a hot meal would be on the table and my mother would ask, "how was your day at school and do you have any homework?" My father would come into the kitchen and place his briefcase on the table before he kissed my mother on the cheek, I thought. I wiped my eyes before I drifted off to sleep.

The next day...

"I appreciate you for keeping Zalia for me. I'll be back as soon as we're done," I said to Pistol's aunt, Earlene. She became a big help with Zalia because I didn't trust nobody else to watch her.

"Anytime. I gotta pretend this is my grandbaby since Pistol ain't having any no time soon. Good luck, Kemara," Earlene said.

"What if he doesn't show up? We haven't been talking much since he saw that stupid video," I replied.

"Then it's his loss," she said. Pistol walked into the house with a snarl on his face.

"What's the matter wit' you?" I asked him.

"You ain't bring no shit in here witchu, did you?" he asked.

"Seriously?" I laughed and he grilled me. He took Zalia from Earlene and kissed her forehead.

"Where is Beretta? He wasn't home when I woke up this morning," I said.

"I haven't talked to da nigga yet," Pistol said.

"Chile, you know they stick up for each other. He wouldn't had told you anyway. Call me later because my Judge Joe Brown is about to come on and I don't wanna miss nothing," Earlene said and took Zalia from Pistol. I kissed Zalia's forehead and thanked Earlene again before I left out of the house. My phone rang from an "Unknown" number and I answered it because Piper called from private numbers. I answered and nobody said anything so I figured it was Chevy. He was clingy in high school when we were together but I figured it was because I was his first girlfriend. I thought he would've outgrown it, but him acting insane reminded me all over again why I broke up with him.

"Chevy, you really lost your fuckin' mind callin' my phone!" I yelled into the phone. I only heard breathing over the phone followed by muffling sounds then the caller hung up. I shrugged it off thinking they had the wrong number. An hour later, I was pulling up to a small business building. I sent Beretta the address again just in case he deleted my text messages. For some reason, I was nervous because I didn't know the outcome from the session. I fixed my hair in the mirror before I got out of my truck and headed towards the building. When I stepped in, I was greeted by a white girl who looked to be in her thirties. She told me Ms. Baker was in a session and I had to wait for ten minutes. I didn't mind because I was early and Beretta wasn't answering my text messages. While I was in the waiting area, I looked around at the pictures on the walls of married couples. Underneath each picture was a small story of the couple's battle and how they overcame it.

"You're gonna love Ms. Baker. She's saved a lot of marriages," the front desk girl said to me.

"I've read a lot of great things about her on the internet," I replied.

"How long have you been married?" she asked.

"A few months," I replied, feeling embarrassed.

"Ohhhh, I see. Well, good luck and my name is Jane by the way. There are some refreshments on the table, so help yourself," she said. I looked at the time on my phone and checked my messages and still nothing from Beretta. Our session was only two minutes away. A black middle-aged couple walked out of the back room and the wife was in tears. The husband looked angry about something as he stormed out of the office. The wife ran out of the office calling out to her husband.

"I can't do this," I said aloud and grabbed my purse. It seemed like the best thing to do but I was afraid to expose our truth. I stepped out of the door and Beretta's Mercedes was backing up into a parking space. My palms started sweating although it was freezing outside. He got out of his car and I had butterflies.

"Yo, you sent me the wrong address. Took me straight to an abortion clinic. I thought you was tryna tell me sumthin," he said.

"You probably read it wrong," I replied.

"Naw, those long-ass nails probably hit the wrong zip code," he said and opened the door for me. Ms. Baker was at the front desk talking to Jane when we walked in. Ms. Baker was around sixty years old with pretty silver hair that hung past her shoulders. She was a petite light-skinned woman with big cat eyeglasses and small freckles on her face.

"Good morning, Mr. and Mrs. Jones. Follow me to my office," she said and grabbed her leather notebook off the counter. We followed her down a long hall and into a large room with huge glass windows. Her office was very clean and had a homey feel to it. It reminded me of our living room at the loft. She told us to take a seat on the brown leather couch and she sat in front of us in a recliner chair. Ms. Baker pulled out a few papers and scanned over them. They were the forms I submitted online.

"I have to admit, you two are the youngest married couple I've seen and I have been doing this for twenty-five years. It says you just got married a few months ago and have been in a relationship for only two years. Sorry for your loss. I see here you lost a baby this year," she said, flipping through the papers.

Damn, she might charge us double, I thought.

"So, let's introduce ourselves. What do you do for a living?" Ms. Baker asked and Beretta was uncomfortable, so I answered first.

"I'm a full-time college student," I replied then she looked at Beretta.

"Home Improvement," Beretta replied.

"Okay, that's a start," she said, then sat her notebook down.

"First, tell me how you two met. Z'wan, you go first," she said and crossed her arms.

"I met shorty, I mean, I met Kemara from our old neighborhood," Beretta replied.

"By all means, feel free to express yourself in your language. I want to understand you two. Tell me how you felt about Kemara when y'all were younger," Ms. Baker said.

"Shorty had a smart-ass mouth and was always poppin' slick but it was sumthin about her. I couldn't understand it at first because she wasn't fashionable like the other girls around the way. Her clothes were too big and her hair wasn't done, but she was the prettiest girl in da hood. It wasn't just her looks, though, she was different from all the females. But, what made me really like her was her mind; she's intelligent," Beretta said and I looked at him.

"What's the matter, Kemara? Are you surprised?" she asked.

"Sorta, I knew he liked me back then but I wasn't aware of how much he paid attention to me," I replied.

"Tell me what attracted you to Z'wan?" she asked.

"It's hard to explain. Z'wan wasn't the easiest boy to talk to. He used to pick on me and call me names, but there was something about the way my body acted when he was around. I felt like I couldn't breathe and the butterflies were uncontrollable. He used to stare at me but not in a weird way. Like he said, my clothes were a mess due to financial problems, so not too many boys were checking for a busted girl. But he looked past that. I couldn't stop thinking about him and even became obsessed with the idea of being with him," I replied.

"Tell me something about Z'wan that needs improvement," Ms. Baker said.

"Communication," I replied and Beretta grilled me.

"Communication goes both fuckin' ways, shorty," Beretta spat.

"Did her statement make you angry?" Ms. Baker asked Beretta.

"Yeah, her statements always fuck wit' me. Kemara thinks she doesn't do shit. Shorty walks around with a stick up her ass," he replied and I wanted to pinch him.

"This is why we're here! You get mad when I call you out on your shit!" I yelled at him.

"Look, let's get this shit over with 'cause I got sumthin to do," Beretta spat.

"I sense a lot of hurt and pain in this marriage," Mrs. Baker said.

"That's because he cheated on me while I was recovering from the loss of our daughter. I had to go to rehab to learn how to walk again and this nigga was fuckin' another bitch! A bitch that came into our home. He spent money on her, took her on a trip, too. I have every right to be angry because I can't get over it. He married me anyway. Months before I lost our daughter, his friend was killed and Beretta couldn't grieve in front of me because he thought it wasn't the manly thing to do. So, you know what he did? He went to his friend's aunt's house and spent three days there with a female he had relations with! Every time our back is against the wall, he finds solace in everyone but me!" I said.

"Tell me about these other two women, Z'wan. What did they have that Kemara couldn't offer you?" Ms. Baker asked.

"The one she said I spent three days with was nothing to me. I was drunk and she's right, I didn't want Kemara seeing me fucked up dat way. I'm always on my toes around her, her protector. I didn't want her seeing me cry like some little bitch. I thought shorty would look at me in a different way if she thought I was soft and couldn't protect her. Da shit sounds stupid, but at that time, I wasn't used to any of that shit," he said.

"Tell me about the woman you had an affair with and what she was like," Ms. Baker said. I squeezed my purse and closed my eyes because I didn't want to hear that shit all over again but it was too late to turn back.

"Me and Kemara already talked about it," Beretta said.

"You're sitting in a marriage counselor's office, Z'wan. Therefore, I can't help if you don't tell me what I need to know because from the looks of it, it seems to me you two have a lot of work to do. We've only been in here for five minutes and a lot has been said which means a lot has happened in a short span of time," Ms. Baker said. Beretta leaned back into the couch and scratched his chin.

"Amona is my sister's nanny. She was bringing my sister to me behind my mother's back because my mother didn't want me around Hope. Anyway, shorty was throwing herself at me. I wasn't trippin' about it because my concern was Hope, but after my daughter died, being around her and my sister gave me the family I wanted with my wife. I told Kemara to stay away from her mother and she didn't listen to me. Her mother caused her to crash her truck which killed our daughter. I held my daughter, staring at her lifeless small body, thinking how that shit could've been avoided. She's supposed to be here! What was so important that she had to leave outta the fuckin' house at eight and half months pregnant? But I saw how broken up she was about it, so I forced myself to let it go. The way Amona cared for my sister attracted me to her because she had a motherly instinct, something I blamed Kemara for not having because she pretended for a while that Zyira never existed," Beretta admitted. I jumped off the couch and Ms. Baker rushed over to me.

"I'm out of this muthafucka. You brought me here so we could talk about shit and you can't handle it!" Beretta said. I told Ms. Baker I was fine and she told me to sit on the other couch. My nerves were bad and my hands were shaking.

"Express yourself, Kemara," Ms. Baker said.

"I blame myself, too, and I thought about suicide so many times. It's just so hard losing a baby that way. She was killed from my actions and I'm trying very hard to focus and move forward but something is pulling me back. Imagine going through a darkness alone. I loved her so much and I begged God to take me instead when I was trapped inside of my truck. I never got a chance to hold her and tell her goodbye. It was either I tried to forget about her or take my own life because I knew it would've drove me to the edge if I grieved the way everyone was expecting me to," I sobbed. Beretta wrapped his arms around me and Ms. Baker left the room to give us a little privacy.

"I'm sorry, shorty. I didn't know you was feeling dat way," he squeezed me.

Beretta's tears fell onto my shoulders as he rubbed my back. We were detoxing ourselves from all the pain and hurt we endured. Ms. Baker came back into the room minutes later and sat back in her chair.

"Tell me about your mother, Z'wan," Ms. Baker said.

"I don't have a mother," he replied.

"Father?" she asked.

"He's dead," Beretta replied.

"Who raised you?" Ms. Baker asked.

"Nobody," he replied.

"How about you, Kemara. Mother? Father?" Mrs. Baker asked.

"They are dead, but my mother was a crackhead when she was living, so my brother had to raise me," I replied.

"What's the relationship like with your brother?" she asked.

"We're not on good terms because he doesn't get along with Z'wan. Z'wan's sister is my niece. My brother slept with his mother," I replied.

"I would like to talk to you two separately. Before I was a marriage counselor, I was a therapist. I can come to your home and I'll do it free of charge," she said.

"I don't need a therapist," Beretta said. Ms. Baker closed her notebook and took her glasses off. She crossed her arms and looked at us the way a parent would if their child was misbehaving.

"Y'all don't need a marriage counselor, Z'wan. You two have personal issues that's affecting the marriage and they need to be resolved before it sends y'all down a dark path. Couples come in here with issues like falling out of love so they seek help to get that love back. But you two love each other, y'all just don't love yourselves. Imagine you putting twenty bricks into a barrel and Kemara puts in thirty. Along the way, you put five bricks and she adds six more. Pretty soon, the barrel will be too heavy to pull. The key is subtracting, not adding. Without help, you two will be so worn down from pulling that heavy barrel that you'll give up. You two might walk away from each other not realizing you are your own problem. Broken homes, no guidance and the fact you had to raise yourselves hurts me because so many people that grew up that way can't find a way out. And the ones who do get out, are not always okay. I'm not forcing it on you but if you want this marriage to work, you have to put your pride aside and get help," Ms. Baker said. She grabbed a card off her desk and handed it to me.

"I'm free any day after 5pm. I look forward to hearing from y'all soon. Please just think about it," Ms. Baker said.

"What's your schedule looking like 'cause a nigga free tomorrow at 6pm," Beretta said and I giggled.

"Is he always like this?" Ms. Baker laughed.

"Yes, one of the reasons why I love him," I replied and Ms. Baker chuckled. I thanked Ms. Baker before we left out of her office. Earlier, it looked like it was about to rain, but the sun was shining when we walked outside. It seemed as if it was shining for us.

"Ms. Baker was talking about bricks like she was tryna tell me sumthin. You think shorty be hustling?" Beretta asked and I bust out laughing.

"I can't with you," I replied.

"I'm serious, though, Pretty Girl. Ms. Baker an old G," Beretta smirked.

"You do know we saw our real selves in her office. We were just Z'wan and Kemara. Do you think we will be okay?" I asked and he moved my hair out of my face.

"Yeah, we'll be straight but only my wife can see me because the world doesn't need to know, Z'wan, you feel me?" he asked.

"That's all that matters, but in the meantime, you can take me out to brunch," I said.

"Oh, now you want a nigga to take you out on a date?" he asked.

"There is a restaurant right around the corner," I replied.

I knew that our relationship was going to be stronger than ever because everything we were going through, we went through together. My husband held my hand as we walked to a restaurant and I stared into his handsome face as he joked around. His smile was contagious and his deep laugh warmed my heart. Beretta didn't look like the murderous king pin I was used to. He seemed like a normal guy in love with a normal girl.

Part 7:

I'll Hold You Down

SOUL Publications

Piper

July 2012...

I smiled when I saw Kemara sitting down in the visitation room. I was at the women's facility in Glen Burnie, Maryland. I hugged her and she squeezed me. I was facing eight years but Pistol got me a good lawyer who worked her ass off and a few charges were dropped. I had to do sixteen months for assault on Delonte, his wife and daughter. Delonte told the police I snatched his daughter's arm so they showed up at court with Sarah wearing a sling. I hated that whole damn family. I cried about the sixteen months but it was damn sure better than eight years.

"So, what's new? Any bitches fuckin' with you in here?" Kemara asked.

"Naw, I stay to myself and write sweet poems to my baby, Pistol," I replied.

"Speaking of Pistol, he told Beretta y'all are officially in a relationship," she said and I blushed.

"Yup, he asked me to be his girl two days ago. I can't wait to get out, though. I miss everyone," I said.

"We miss you, too. But look on the bright side, you ain't never gotta worry about fuckin' with niggas like Delonte anymore," she replied.

"But nobody is going to hire me," I said and she smiled.

"Don't speak too soon. Something better awaits you," she replied. Kemara was glowing and it was good to see she was at a happy place in life.

"How is Zalia?" I asked.

"Spoiled. She follows her daddy through the house. We go to court for Moesha in a few weeks," Kemara said.

"That hoe still in the picture?" I asked.

"Yeah, she's been stalling, though. The bitch keeps harassing Beretta so I'm taking her to court because we want a blood test. She wants money for a baby that we aren't sure if it's his. For months, I have been dealing with her harassing messages on Facebook. It's time to end that shit," she replied.

"Moesha just wants some money because she knows Beretta has it like that," I said and Kemara grabbed my hand and squeezed it.

"I wish I didn't waste time on being mad at you," she said.

"Girl, if you don't let it go. It was only for a month. Now months or years would've caused me to whip your ass. You didn't know I was going to end up here and neither did I," I replied.

"I'm taking this class with Emma and they talk about peace, love and forgiveness. Emma talked me into it and I thought she was crazy but it's so relaxing. We light these special herbs that detox our bodies from negative energy. You have to try it when you get out of here," Kemara said.

"Bitch, that sounds like a crack house," I replied and bust out laughing.

"I told Emma the same thing when she said it to me, but it's meditating," she replied.

"Who are you and what have you done to my sister? You're glowing, talking about meditating and your vibe is so refreshing. Awww, I'm getting emotional, Mara," I said with tear-filled eyes. I'd known Kemara all my life and had never seen her this happy. Usually, her face was in a scowl like she was mad at something or in deep thought, but she sat across from me looking angelic and showing her cute dimple.

"I'm here just tryna get myself together so I can spread the love in my marriage," she replied.

"How is Beretta?" I asked and she blushed.

"He's good and we're so close now. The nigga even got a schedule like he got a real nine-to-five. We took Zalia to the park yesterday and she had a ball," Kemara said.

"Beretta gettin' all soft and shit," I joked.

"Oh, honey, that part of him is only for his wife. Piss him off and you'll see ain't shit change much," she replied. We talked for an hour until the guard told me my visit was over. Kemara blew me a kiss and she got teary-eyed when they took me away. I cried like a baby when I got to my cell because I was missing my friends and Kemara's happy moments. The hate I had for Delonte was so deep that I wanted to get out and risk it all just to kill him. I sat on the bottom bunk and grabbed my notebook off the raggedy stand in the corner of the muggy room. Poetry was the only way I could escape my sadness but I knew something good was going to come after it all. They said sometimes storms weren't a bad sign because they moved things out of paths by washing them away. It seemed like that was me and Kemara's problem since birth because our lives were filled with bad weather.

I can't wait to see the sun, I thought as I continued to write.

SOUL Publications

Poppa

I stood over the banister inside my club and it was filled with GMBAM niggas. My club opened three months ago and it was already hittin' but I couldn't deny GMBAM's help. Those niggas had connections to everything, including hiring some of the baddest strippers I'd ever seen in my life. Beretta came up with the layout of the club. Matter of fact, it seemed like it was his club with my name on it. Niggas was pushing weight, pills and other shit right before my eyes but what could I say? I was still getting paid, and quite frankly, I didn't have a choice because I would've been buried underneath cold soil. My cell phone vibrated inside my pocket so I went inside the small office to answer it.

"What da fuck is it?" I asked Nika.

"Can you come home? I'm having contractions," she said.

"Yo, you keep lying about dat shit! Naw, I'm not coming home right now and don't call me no fuckin' more tonight. Bitch, I'on give a fuck about your pregnancy!" I yelled into the phone.

"Poppa, I'll come to that fuckin' cheap-ass club and set it on fire!" she yelled into the phone.

"Get yah hoe ass off my fuckin' line," I spat before I hung up. I moved in with Nika a few weeks after her dumb-ass roommate Amona was killed. Nika begged me to live with her because she was afraid of being in the house alone. It was cool for a little bit until she started getting needy. I had never been around a shorty while she was pregnant so I wasn't used to the mood swings. Shorty just needed to disappear because I no longer needed her and her pussy wasn't even the same. Maybe it was because I was missing Jasmine like crazy. I saw her a few times but shorty didn't even look my way. There was a knock on the door and a stripper named Staxx walked into the room.

"What do you want, shorty?" I asked. She locked the door and pushed me against the desk. Staxx was stacked like Waffle House pancakes. Shorty was dark skinned with smooth silky skin. The Pocahontas wig she wore made her look like a goddess. The gold and blue eye shadow gave me Indian vibes. She was gorgeous and I was fucking her. Hell, I barely spent time with Nika but I made sure I checked up on Hope. Staxx got on her knees and unzipped my pants. She pulled my dick out and I grabbed her wig.

"Fuckkkkkk, baby! Suck dat dick, shorty," I coached as I fucked her mouth. On the verge of nutting, someone banged on the door.

"Open, da fuckin' door, Poppa!" Nika yelled. I thought dat bitch was home but she was probably sitting in her car outside of the club. Staxx stood up and wiped the spit off her chin. I straightened up my clothes before I opened the door. Nika stormed into the office with her round belly. The sight of her was making me sick, not to mention, she wasn't bad like she used to be. Her face was round and fat and she had bags under her eyes. Nika gained about one hundred pounds and I wasn't tripping about the baby weight but she didn't put no effort in looking good anymore. Shorty wasn't even going to her restaurant to check up on shit so she hired a manager to look after everything. All she did was sit in the house and call me.

"Who is this bitch?" Nika asked, pointing at Staxx.

"I'll see you downstairs," Staxx said to me. She looked Nika up and down with a smirk on her face before she left out of the office. Nika slapped me in the face and pushed me into the desk.

"I want your sorry ass outta my fuckin' house! How fuckin' dare you treat me like this after all I've done for you. My son would've killed you if it wasn't for me! I went against Z'wan because I thought you were a changed man but you were only kissing my ass because you wanted this piece-of-shit club! Your slow ass couldn't have done it without me," Nika said.

"Bitch, take your sloppy old ass home. You know betta than to fuck a young nigga, anyway. What you thought, your looks and good pussy was gonna have me stuck forever? Shorty, you almost forty years old. All you got on me is Hope and the lil' nigga you're pregnant with. Beretta knows about me, so you can't blackmail me anymore. Tell me why you're so important now? All these young lil' pretty bitches walkin' around here and you expect me to come home and lay next to those sag bags?" I laughed. Tears fell from Nika's eyes and I shook my head at her.

"It's Jasmine, isn't it? You have been dogging me out since she left you," Nika said.

"You know da answer to dat, so why ask? Go home and I might see you tomorrow," I replied.

"I want your shit outta my house!" she yelled.

"Damn, Ma, nigga cuttin' up already?" a voice asked from behind Nika. She turned around and it was Beretta standing in the doorway with a backpack.

"Mind your business," Nika said and wiped her eyes.

"Most definitely, shorty. Wrap this up, nigga, I ain't got all day," Beretta said.

"Leave, Nika," I said. She looked at Beretta and he smirked at her.

"You picked him over yah son, so you gotta deal wit' it," he said.

"Y'all must be fuckin'," Nika cracked slick and Beretta chuckled.

SOUL Publications

"Go home, Nika, before your restaurant burns down to the ground in the morning. Say some gay shit to me like dat again," he replied. Nika wobbled out of the office and I felt a tinge of guilt but shorty wasn't trying to let a nigga breathe. Beretta threw the backpack on the desk and I opened the safe under the carpet underneath the desk. I grabbed the backpack and filled it up with stacks of money. It was around one hundred g's in the safe but eighty of it belonged to Beretta.

"How is Jasmine?" I asked as I handed him the backpack and he grilled me.

"Da fuck you wanna know what's up wit' my sister for?" he spat.

"I know we don't see eye-to-eye but I love shorty," I replied and he chuckled.

"You loved shorty when you were beating her ass, too, huh?" he asked.

"Come on, bruh. Don't act like you ain't do shit to Mara that you ain't proud of," I replied.

"Nigga, you gettin' too fuckin' personal when this ain't even about dat, muthafucka," he said and walked out of my office with his backpack.

Damn, I miss Jasmine, I thought as I poured myself a shot of Patrón. I know shorty was pretending but I deep down I felt a connection to her. The day Hope was kidnapped showed me how Jasmine was feeling about me.

She didn't have to ride for me like she did and no matter what, I was grateful for her.

****

I stepped out of my new two-door Mercedes coupe and leaned against my car. While I was waiting, I lit up a blunt to calm my nerves. Matter of fact, I didn't know why I was nervous. It seemed like forever until Jasmine walked out of a building wearing a half long-sleeve top, stretch jeans and a pair of Jordans. Her hair was in a Chinese bun with a swoop bang. She looked more mature and I couldn't keep my eyes off her hips. Some nigga walked over to her and she laughed when he whispered in her ear. The shit had my blood boiling because she was mine! She stopped smiling when she saw me. Jasmine said something to the guy then waved him off as he walked away. She took her time walking to me but I wasn't tripping because I enjoyed the view.

"Nigga, you must want me to put some heat to yah fuckin' dome! How in da fuck you gonna roll up on me while I'm at school? What's up witchu, huh? Do you know what we had was fake? Seriously, Poppa, you need to stop calling me and texting me all hours of the night!" Jasmine yelled. I pulled a velvet box out of my pocket and gave it to her.

"I don't want shit from you," she said.

"Please don't do this, shorty. I'm sorry for puttin' my hands on you. I was insecure and a lame-ass nigga for dat but I promise I won't do it anymore if you give me a real chance. I'm damn-near begging," I replied and she crossed her arms.

"You know you can't put yah hands on me because I go harder than most niggas, including you, so I'm not worried about dat. Do you realize I saw da real you when I was living with you? Plus, I was sleeping with niggas to rob them. Do you think I want a nigga who saw dat side of me?" she asked.

"That's even better. We all fucked up out here tryna survive and I'on give a fuck about how many niggas you let smash. I can't help how I feel about you," I replied. She snatched the velvet box out of my hand and opened it. It was a diamond tennis bracelet with matching earrings. Jasmine held it up in the sun to see if the diamonds was hitting.

"Shorty, dat shit is blingy as fuck," I said.

"I had to make sure," she replied.

"Can we go out to eat or sumthin?" I asked.

"Maybe tomorrow. I'm in this play and I have to go to rehearsal," she said.

"Can I come?" I asked.

"Baby, you know I can act so what you need to watch for?" she asked and I smirked. I wasn't into smart-mouth ass females but Jasmine was different.

"'Cause I miss you," I replied, pulling on her belt loop. She fell into me and I wrapped my arms around her. I inhaled the scent of her perfume and squeezed her tighter. She pulled away from me and a smile crept across her face.

"Okay, you can come to watch," she replied. I followed her into a building next to the one she came out of; it was a small theatre. I sat in the back row and my phone vibrated in my pocket. It was a text from Nika telling me she was going into labor. I should've got up and went to her but I didn't want to blow any chances with Jasmine. Nika gave birth to Hope without me so she didn't need me there for my son. It was a fucked-up way to think but I had no attachments to Nika's pregnancy. Hope was the only one who mattered to me. I told Nika to get an abortion when she slipped into a depression because of Amona's death. For some reason, I thought the baby wasn't mine. My phone rang and it was her again. I turned my phone off and stared ahead at my future.

****

Two hours later, Jasmine was finished with rehearsal. It was about a single mother losing her son to the streets. The shit touched my heart because Jasmine played her part. Her cries and screams as she held her son's body sounded so real. Shorty had pure talent and it made me fall for her even more.

"Yooo, dat shit was crazy," I said to Jasmine while leaving out of the building.

"It's crazy when you have to act like something you see every day. I didn't have to read the whole script," Jasmine said.

"I'm proud of you," I replied.

"What's da deal, Poppa? I mean you won't let me go and you're acting like some nice ass nigga when we both know how grimy you are," she said.

"I'm a fucked-up nigga but I had come across so many scenarios where I could've lost my life, so I'm tryna live right. Besides, GMBAM is on a nigga's ass. I feel like I'm on probation around them niggas," I replied.

"Serves you right, Kamar. I don't feel sorry for you but it's good to see you maturing," she said. We talked on our way to her whip and shorty was riding in a brand new black Cadillac Escalade with pink trim around the black rims.

"Damn, this shit is phat," I said.

"Beretta bought it for me two weeks ago. He's so into being a big brother and I wanna tell him I'm grown but I don't wanna hurt his feelings. He's wayyy stricter than Sniper," Jasmine chuckled.

Dat nigga is always tryna control some shit! I thought.

"He's yah big brother so I understand, but what do you want?" I asked.

"I want to be fuck-nigga free," she replied.

"Oh, it's like dat?" I asked.

"I don't trust you yet. I will have to get to know you all over again. If you let me down, Beretta will be the least of your worries. I'll bury you myself so I know you ain't ready for a bitch like me," Jasmine said.

"We can take baby steps then. I'll work for it," I replied. She pecked my lips then wiped her lipstick off.

"You gonna be working yah ass off, and if you don't, I don't even want it. I'll let you decide because I'm not changing to accommodate your needs. Take me like this or stop calling me, plain and simple," she said.

"I love you so I'll do whateva," I replied.

"See you lata, Poppa," Jasmine said, unlocking her truck door. I stood in the parking lot watching her pull off. My phone beeped when I turned it back on and I had mad text messages from Nika's dumb ass. I called her back and she answered on the first ring.

"Where are you?" she cried into the phone.

"On my way to the hospital now," I replied, getting inside my whip.

"Hurry da fuck up! I'm still in labor!" she screamed then hung up.

SOUL Publications

I hope that stupid bitch gets her tubes tied after this, I thought as I drove to the hospital.

****

When I got to the hospital, Nika was still in labor. She was screaming and crying but refused the epidural. Shorty was doing too much extra shit and I wanted her to just die or something.

"I feel like I'm about to dieeeeeeeeee!" she cried.

"Hurry da fuck up then. Get the epidural!" I yelled at her.

"It's too late," a nurse said and I threw my hands up in frustration.

"You're almost there! Push!" a nurse told Nika. I sat in the chair dressed in a hospital gown with a cap on my head like I gave a fuck about what was going on. Nika was screaming for me to help her and the doctor told me to be more passionate towards Nika to make the delivery smoother.

"No offense to none of you hard workers but shorty is too fuckin' old for this bullshit! She should've gotten the fuckin' epidural instead of pretending like she can push a baby out of her twat. Fuck all dat, I ain't have shit to do with that so I'm chilling," I replied.

"I HATE YOU!" Nika screamed as she pushed.

"Glad I could help," I replied when the doctor told her the head was out. Seconds later, small whimpers filled with the room. Suddenly, the dislike I had for Nika went away because she gave birth to my son but I knew the feeling wasn't going to last long. Nika was possessive and it should've been a red flag because most bitches bad as her had a man but she didn't. I was caught up on having an exotic-looking chick but I realized looks didn't mean shit if shorty couldn't help me better myself. The nurses cleaned off Omario before they gave him to Nika. She wanted him to be a Jr. but I lied about having a son with my name already. I took a blood test a few months ago for two kids that was supposed to be mine and they came back negative. Ain't that some shit? It's crazy how females pin babies on niggas when he's on the come-up but in reality, I only had two kids, both by Nika. Honestly, I wanted a blood test for Omario, too, which was another reason I didn't want him to have my name.

"Awwww, he's so cute," Nika said and I scratched my head.

"I, umm, I want a blood test," I replied and she grilled me. Nika told the nurses and the doctor to give us some privacy.

"You heartless muthafucka! He hasn't been out of my pussy for five minutes and you're already starting shit. Let's not forget the support you haven't been giving me during the pregnancy and you embarrassed me while I was in labor. After everything you put me through, you want a blood test?" she asked.

"It shouldn't be an issue if there isn't nothing to be worried about, right?" I replied.

"Kemara warned me about you. The raggedy little bitch told me you were gonna get what you could from me before you start showing your true colors. I knew you wasn't shit but I thought you changed! I thought we had a family," she said.

"I'm not in love with you, shorty. I was attracted to you because I thought you was one of the baddest bitches I fucked and your sex game is off the chain but that's it. I tried to be with you like dat and even moved into your crib but then you started putting your nose into my business. I'll continue to take care of Hope and I'll be in Omario's life, too, if he mine but this shit between us is dead," I replied.

"I can take that club from you, then what? I molded you, and if it wasn't for me, Jasmine would still be selling her stale pussy to help you rob niggas. What you think you're GMBAM now? They will never accept a punk ass nigga like you," she said.

"Shorty, I don't wanna be a GMBAM nigga, and besides, you can't take dat club. You'll be fuckin' over a lot of niggas and I don't think your son will let you live. Don't forget the bridge you burned with dat nigga," I chuckled.

"Don't go to war with me, Poppa. What you think really happened to Beretta's father? He tried to take my son from me and guess what? He ended up shot up in broad daylight. I have connections so mark my fuckin' words!" she gritted. I kissed my son's forehead.

"I thought I was fucked up but shorty you're cold. Get some rest," I replied and walked out the hospital room.

****

I swung by Nika's crib to get most of my clothes and shoes. Hope was sitting on the floor with a nanny. She was an older woman, around age fifty and she was from Nigeria. Her name was Odimau. She was a sweet lady and kept the house clean and food on the table. Nika had a nanny like we were millionaires and all shorty had was a restaurant.

"Daddy," Hope said in sign language. She wasn't good with speaking so we had to learn sign language. I still didn't know how autism worked and I didn't understand how she could learn something which was harder than actually speaking. Sign language was hard for me to learn but I was getting there.

"I love you and I'm gonna come back for you, okay?" I replied in sign language.

"Take me with you," she said.

"Baby, I can't right now," I replied and she slammed her Barbie down on the floor and ran to her room.

"I'm ready to get our things together and go to the hospital. Why are you leaving? You're supposed to be the man of this household," Odimau scolded.

"Me and Nika aren't getting along and I think it's best to leave now before I get stuck. I'll be back," I replied. I went into my pocket and pulled out a wad of money for Odimau. It was a lot of money but I didn't mind giving her more than what I was supposed to because she sent it back home to her village in Africa.

"I'm gonna pray for you, Kamar. You have dark clouds over yah head. Have you made things right with your sister yet?" she asked. Odimau knew a lot about me because I told her about my childhood growing up. Nobody knew how painful it was to be made fun of in school. All my life, I was against the world because it turned its back on me. I had learning problems and it fucked me up that my little sister was smarter than me. I was twelve years old and she was helping me with my homework at nine. Tired of the embarrassment, I quit school. My mother never showed up to my teacher and parent conferences. She could've gotten me the help I needed but she teased me instead. I wondered if me being a crack baby did something to my daughter.

"Her husband doesn't want me around her and I'm cool with dat. Mara is an angel and she doesn't need to be surrounded by niggas like me," I replied.

"She will forgive you if you show her a positive man," Odimau said.

"Naw, I'm good on dat. I'm happy for Mara from afar," I replied. I picked up my bags and left out of the house. A sense of relief came over me but I couldn't ignore Nika's threat. I wondered if she really had Beretta's father merked.

****

A week later...

"Why are we walking through the park?" Jasmine asked.

"That shit ain't romantic to you?" I replied and she chuckled.

"It's okay. So, what's up with you and that bitch, Nika? Congrats on the new bundle of joy," Jasmine said.

"I moved out her crib," I replied.

"That's a start," she said.

"Remember when I told you I wanted to get away? I was serious about dat. I'll leave with the clothes on my back right now," I replied.

"You can't run away from your fears, Poppa. The best way is to fight those problems you're battling. I can't leave because I have family here and my mother needs me," Jasmine said.

"Bring her with you," I replied.

"I don't know, Poppa. My mother is a little crazy. She got ahold of bad drugs and hasn't been right since. She's a lot of work and I'm the only one who can deal with her because Sniper doesn't have the patience. My mother may be a lot of things but I believe everything she says about Nika," Jasmine said.

"What did she say?" I asked as we sat on a bench.

"My mother was Raynoldo's woman. They were sorta like Kemara and Beretta. Raynoldo was the king of the city and my mother was his down chick. A family moved into the neighborhood where Raynoldo kept his trap houses and it was Nika's family. My mother said she felt bad for Nika because her father was molesting her and her mother didn't believe it. Nika has an older sister but she moved away from the family and cut ties with them. I think the father was molesting her, too. But, anyways, my mother took Nika in and treated her like a little sister but she invited the wrong bitch into her home. My mother didn't know Nika was fourteen because of her body—she was well developed for her age and acted grown. Nika was telling niggas that she was eighteen. Make a long story short, my father fucked Nika and she got pregnant with Beretta. She bribed my father and made him pay her. Said she'd tell the cops he raped her because she was underage. Sadly, I think my father caught feelings for her because he could've gotten rid of her but he didn't. My mother said he loved his son more than anything and he gave her an ultimatum: she stays and deals with Z'wan or leaves. My mother loved my father so of course she stayed. Nika lost it after my mother gave birth to me and Sniper. She was telling my father lies about my mother sleeping with his enemy. My father wanted a blood test because just so happens, his enemy was a twin. You know they say twins are hereditary but anyways he took a blood test and it came back negative. Nika knew someone at the DNA testing facility and they gave my father someone else results with our names on it. Back in the day it was easy to tamper with shit like that. Make a long story short, Nika's obsession got out of hand when my father didn't stop messing with my mother. She started fucking my father's enemy and she set him up to get killed for ten g's. Ten fucking g's! Anyways, my mother ended up getting on drugs. I hated her for being so weak for a man who couldn't keep his dick in his pants, but love is toxic. Love can break you or make you but it destroyed her. Me and Sniper had to raise ourselves and our mother, but no matter what, we have each other," Jasmine said.

"Damn, that's some deep shit," I replied.

"Nika knows I believed my mother and that's why she can't stand me. I couldn't bring myself to tell Beretta his mother killed his father. After figuring out how men could ruin a woman's world, I decided to rob them muthafuckas and take everything they have because I'll be damned if I end up like my mother," Jasmine said and I kissed the back of her hand.

"A pretty face and good pussy can be poisonous," I said.

"It's okay to go for the average girl," Jasmine replied.

"I think you're beautiful," I said and she laughed.

"Nigga, get da fuck outta my face," she replied.

SOUL Publications

"Seriously. I mean I thought you were cute at first but when I caught feelings, shit changed," I admitted.

"Well, I'm not attracted to you at all," she lied.

"Shorty, I'm handsome. Fuck is you talkin' about," I said.

After we chilled in the park for a few hours, I went to Jasmine's crib which was only a few blocks away. She lived in a two-bedroom condo downtown. Jasmine's crib was spotless, almost like the crib we had together but bigger. I kicked my tennis shoes off and got comfortable on her couch. She brought me a glass of Patrón and it reminded me of old times. Jasmine went into the kitchen to cook dinner, something Nika didn't know how to do. My cell phone rang and it was Nika. I answered it because she wasn't responding to me whenever I asked her about Hope.

"What's up, Nika? I know you saw me calling you," I said.

"I was busy taking care of a newborn baby by myself," she replied.

"Do you want Hope to stay with me or something for a little while?" I asked.

"No, I want you to bring your ass back home so you can help raise the kids you helped me make! If it's not about that then you don't need to be calling me. Just remember I don't make threats, I make promises. And tell that nappy-headed black fatherless bitch I said she should watch her back!" Nika said and hung up.

"This bitch is crazy," I said aloud and Jasmine came back into the living room.

"She seems to be taking it lighter on you compared to the stories my mother told me about her. Maybe she really does love you," Jasmine replied and I shook my head. I scooted closer to Jasmine and wrapped my arm around her shoulder. She froze when I touched her. It was almost like she hated it and loved it at the same time.

"I'm makin' you feel uncomfortable?" I asked.

"Be honest with me. Would you think I was weak if I gave you a chance after how you beat my ass? I mean, I have been in a lot of fights with niggas so it ain't a thing but this between us is different, Poppa. I don't know if it's right," she said.

"I'll leave," I replied and stood up. Jasmine pulled me back down on the couch then straddled me.

"But you know I'll bust one in yah ass now so I ain't gotta worry about that sucka shit anymore. I'm tryna figure out why I have feelings for you that won't go away," she said. Jasmine leaned in and kissed me. I hadn't felt shorty's lips in months. Instantly, my dick was pressed against my jeans and Jasmine felt it. She stood up and pulled her leggings and panties down. Her pussy wasn't completely bald but that's how I liked my pussy with a trimmed Mohawk. She unzipped my pants and reached into my boxers for my dick. Shorty straddled me and those sweet, tight and wet walls gripped my dick. I grabbed her ass as she rocked her hips back and forth on me. She pulled her shirt over her head and unclasped her bra so I could suck her titties. Jasmine gripped the back of the couch as she rode me faster. Her meaty ass cheeks slapped against my legs when she bucked her hips like she was riding a bull. I closed my eyes and enjoyed the ride she was taking me on.

"Slow down," I groaned but she dug her sharp nails into my neck and choked me. She bit my bottom lip and I was on the verge of busting. I was weak for an aggressive female in the bedroom.

"UMMMMMMMMMMMMM!" Jasmine moaned when her pussy creamed on my dick. Her shit was thick and soapy like; it reminded me of bubbly from champagne and I had to stick my tongue in it. I pulled out of her and laid her on the couch. She held her legs up for me and spread her pussy lips. Shorty grabbed my head and pressed it into her pussy. My fingertips dug into her inner-thighs while I ate her sweet fruit. Jasmine ate a lot of fruit so I wasn't lying when I said shorty tasted good. She screamed she was about to come so I pulled her clit into my mouth and tongue kissed it. Her legs trembled and her pussy splashed on my chin. After she was finished climaxing, I pulled her onto the floor and took the rest of my clothes off. When I entered her, she wrapped her legs around me and placed her breast into my mouth. Shorty wasn't shy, she wanted everything she could get.

"Baby, go deeper," she moaned while I was hitting her spot.

"Hold your legs behind your head," I replied. She held her legs up and I did everything she told me to. I had that juicy tight twat gushing, erupting like volcanoes as I hammered away. The food was burning in the kitchen but Jasmine dared me to pull out. My cell phone on the coffee table rang and it was Nika's dumb ass again. Jasmine grabbed the phone and answered it but only for Nika to hear it.

"Come in this pussy, babyyyyy!" Jasmine squealed as my dick filled her up. Nika was yelling through the phone but there wasn't shit I could do. Fuck Nika! My loyalty was with Jasmine—finally.

Beretta

"**S**uck dat dick, shorty. FUCK! Slob on it a little bit," I groaned while my wife was topping me off with morning head. Kemara was treating a nigga like a king! She wore sexy lingerie every night and she was blessing a nigga with some crucial head. She moaned, too, while she was doing it and something about my shorty's moans was enough to make me bust. Everything about her was perfect, even her teeth. Kemara had straight white teeth, no gaps. She swallowed my seeds after I released down her throat. She went into the bathroom to brush her teeth and wash her face.

"I'll let you know when breakfast is ready," Mara said while putting on her robe.

"What time is it?" I asked.

"Seven o'clock in the morning," she replied then left out of the bedroom. I stepped into a pair of jogging pants and went into Zalia's room. She was sitting up in her crib watching cartoons.

"Dada!" she screamed in excitement. She held her arms out and I picked her up. I kissed her forehead and she squeezed the fuck out of my nose. Zalia was chubby with fat cheeks. Kemara had diamond earrings in her ears and she was wearing small gold bracelets around her wrist. Mara thought Zalia was a toy or something because shorty was doing too much. I took the bracelet off of her and sat it down on the dresser.

"Mara! When is Zalia supposed to be using the toilet?" I called out.

"I think they start potty-training around two!" she yelled from downstairs. I tickled Zalia's stomach while I was walking down the stairs and she was giggling so hard her cheeks turned red.

"Yo, Mara, da fuck is this?" I asked, looking around the living room. Kemara was sitting in the middle of the floor with candles lit around her, burning some type of stick. Her eyes were closed and she was whispering about something.

"Shorty, you bringin' evil spirits into our crib or sumthin? Don't call me when one of those niggas you killed emerges from the smoke," I said. Zalia tried to reach for Kemara's burning stick but I tapped her hand.

"I'm meditating. Come sit down next to me. I'm just burning herbs to keep our home purified," Kemara said.

"Me and Zalia hungry, though," I replied.

"Sit down Z'wan so I can focus. I'm almost done," she said.

Kemara was on some other shit but not in a bad way. Everything she was doing made her happy so I went with it. Her fucked-up attitude she used to have was gone as well, but Ms. Baker helped a lot with that; she helped me, too. I was able to connect with my wife on any level and it made her open up to me more. I gave shorty the same in return.

"Yah mommy trippin, Zalia," I said and she smiled. I sat on the couch and turned cartoons on. Zalia was crying out to her mother so she could hold her.

"I can't Zalia, you might burn yah self. See, look what you did. That was why I left her in the crib. I was gonna get her up after I was done," Kemara said. She blew her candles out and rolled up her yoga mat.

"Aye, you mad at me?" I chuckled and she playfully gave me the finger.

"I was trying to last night but you stopped me," I said.

"I'm on my cycle," Mara said with her nose frowned up.

"And? I saw a lot of bloodshed. All we need is a few trash bags on the bed," I said.

"Nigga, you just nasty!" Mara bust out laughing.

"You sayin' dat shit like you ain't let me run the red light a few times," I said.

"But I'm flowing heavy, those other times were yellow lights," she laughed and I waved her off.

"How do you feel about us opening up a strip club in D.C.? That shit would make us a lot of money. I'm telling you, Mara. Strip clubs are a quick and easy investment. Why do you think a lot of niggas be opening up strip clubs, barbershops, laundromats and hair salons? We can use it for proof of income and buy a bigger house because this loft is getting small already. Zalia got toys everywhere," I said.

"Babe, we have been on a good track. For six months, we haven't argued and everything has been so perfect. I don't want my husband around a bunch of naked thirsty bitches, Beretta. Why take me out of my peace box?" she asked.

"Peace box?" I replied.

"Yes, that's what I call this aura we're living in. You know bitches gonna try to fuck you and they'll do anything just to say you gave them your time. I know how strip clubs work and most of the owners do shady shit with their strippers. Look at how Delonte did Piper," she said.

"So, you're sayin' I'm gonna cheat again?" I asked.

"No, but I had to learn how to trust you all over again and I'm happy now. Money attracts bitches and haters," Kemara said.

"I got too much money sitting around with nothing to do with it. If I get busted, all that shit will be gone and we won't have nothing to fall back on. Look, I know this nigga that's into the loaning business. He can give us a loan so that way the FEDS can't say I used drug money to get my spot. I'm gonna take out a small loan and buy the shittiest spot and remodel it. I saw this place for fifteen g's and it's in the hood but we know it'll be lit," I replied.

"A loan for fifteen g's? Baby, we have that on the dresser," Kemara said.

"I'm supposed to look like I don't have it like that. If I purchase a building with straight cash over twenty g's, the IRS will be in my business. I gotta move like a broke nigga so I won't get caught," I replied.

"I understand but Beretta a strip club? I don't want them hoes on my husband. Can I think about this?" she asked.

"Ight, Mara," I replied.

The thing about marriage was that I couldn't just up and do shit without my wife knowing. I wasn't thinking about any strippers and I damn sure wasn't trying to cheat, but a bigger house and businesses in the future was a step for us. Kemara was going to school for a degree but I hoped my wife didn't have to use it because I didn't want her working for nobody. I wanted her to be in a place where she could live comfortably and help run our businesses. I had the money and a lot of it. I could go out and cop us a big-ass house by the lake with his and hers Bentleys but niggas was getting jammed up balling without a legit paper trail. I'll be damned if I get jammed up for riding a half a mill whip.

"Are you mad?" Kemara asked and I brushed my hand down my waves.

"I'm not mad but I'm tryna figure out why you have to think about it. I can't help but feel like you don't trust me," I said.

"We've been in a dark place, Z'wan, and we're seeing the light now. How often do you think you have to be at the club?" she asked.

"Shorty, I won't know dat until I get one," I replied.

"Okay, do it then," she said, but I could tell she was saying it to make me happy. I put Zalia down on her play mat before I went into the kitchen.

"We ain't doin dat shit, Pretty Girl. Don't tell me sumthin because you know dat's what I wanna hear because it'll end up biting you in the ass," I said.

"I know but I don't want you to think I'm being selfish," she replied. I grabbed her robe and pulled her into me and she blushed.

"Cut it out!" She tried swatting my hand away as I palmed her ass and kissed her on the mouth.

"We can talk about this later, ight? Just tell me you'll think about it instead of rambling shit off because you think dats what I want," I said.

"Okay, I'll think about it inside of my peace box," she said, then bust out laughing.

"Yo, you weird as shit," I replied.

"You still love me, though," she said.

"Always!" I called out as I headed out of the kitchen. Honestly, I was a little pissed off because shorty didn't trust me. No matter what I did, Kemara will always hold that against me.

****

Hours later...

"Bruh, this party is gonna be lit!" Machete said in excitement. Glock was coming home in a few days and we were having a party for him at the strip club. We were inside of Poppa's club going over the boxes of liquor to make sure we had everything I ordered. That nigga, Poppa, was sitting down on the phone sweet-talking a bitch. I wanted to know if that nigga was talking to my sister. Jasmine was grown but I didn't want her fucking with a bitch nigga like him. I had to make sure someone could protect her if me and Sniper wasn't around, and Poppa wasn't it. The only nigga in GMBAM that talked to Poppa like that was Wesson because the rest of us ignored him unless it was time to pay up. It was pretty much my club but my name wasn't on shit because we had a lot of illegal shit going around inside the spot. The club I wanted Kemara to think about was going to be clean as a whistle. You can't eat where you shit.

"Nigga, you better be on good behavior before yah shorty tries to stab you again," Sniper chuckled.

"Yeah, whateva, nigga," Machete said.

"Nigga can never keep his dick in his pants. Zain caught him fuckin' her hairdresser when she showed up at her house to get her hair done. I told this nigga he was gonna get caught, now he depressed," Sniper said and Machete grilled him.

"You were smashing her hairdresser, though?" I asked Machete.

"It wasn't even like dat. Zain's hairdresser used to be my lil' shorty in high school, so we already had a little history. I still had feelings for shorty but I'm not leaving Zain for none of these bitches, bottom line," Machete said.

"Kemara probably told shorty to kill yah bitch-ass," Pistol chuckled.

"Probably did because she's always calling Mara up, asking her for advice. I told her ass don't be gettin' any crazy-ass ideas. I might have to slice my shorty up and y'all niggas think it's a game until she ends up on the news channel," Machete said.

SOUL Publications

"Crazy-ass nigga," Sniper said.

"Call me what you want but if Zain call herself fuckin' another nigga, it's a body count nigga, on God," Machete said.

"Yo, did you take yah meds this morning?" Pistol asked.

Everybody knew Machete was bipolar but the nigga wasn't trying to take meds for it. Kemara wanted me talk to him because Zain couldn't deal with him and his mood swings. I talked to Machete twice and the little nigga wasn't trying to hear it.

"I'on need dat shit," Machete replied.

An hour later, we were leaving the club. I called out to Machete before he got on his motorcycle. All my niggas were like my brothers, and even though I was the one who came up with GMBAM and the operation, my brothers helped keep it alive.

"What's good witchu, bruh?" I asked.

"Mannn, I'm stressing," he admitted.

"Talk to me," I replied.

"I fucked up big time. Yo, Beretta I ain't share this with anybody yet but I got a six-month old son by the bitch I was cheating on Zain with. She caught us fucking but she doesn't know shorty's son is mine," Machete said.

"Damn, bruh," I replied.

"What you think I should do?" he asked.

"Let shorty know what's up then give her some space 'cause, nigga, dats deep. She caught you fuckin' another broad? Nigga you trippin," I admitted.

"Cheating ain't fun when you get caught, though. Niggas don't even be thinking about their shorty's feelings until they see them crying. I was out here smashing bitches like I didn't have a girl," he said.

"Most niggas cheat, bruh. It's fucked up but even good niggas slip up sometimes but you gotta learn from it and make it better. Don't be out here giving these bitches yah seeds, though. We all came from broken homes, yah feel me? I'm gonna live in the same house as all my kids. Fuck all that single mother shit," I replied and he nodded his head.

"Good looking out, bruh. Much love. I can't let Zain get away like how I let Jasmine get away," he said.

"What Jasmine?" I replied.

"Yah sister, nigga. Jasmine was the reason why I broke up with my baby mama back in da day. Shorty had my head wide open. I was out here catching bodies for shorty and all dat. But then I cheated on Jasmine with Zain and this is what she did," Machete said lifting up his shirt and showing me a nasty scar on his stomach.

"Da fuck," I said.

"She stabbed me, bruh. Almost killed my ass. Me and Sniper got into a fight behind dat shit and stopped talking for a month. Glock the only one who knew because he broke it up. Matter of fact, we were fighting the night Glock got locked up. Shit was all bad," Machete said.

"This shit with you and Jasmine dead, though, right?" I asked.

"No doubt. Me and shorty cool like it never happened," he replied. My phone beeped and it was a message from Ebo telling me to meet him at a small diner across town. The nigga was in Annapolis for a few days on a business tip. Ebo was one of my biggest buyers. He was copping mad weight and taking it down to Virginia. He was Moesha's ex-nigga but I wasn't a bitch-nigga to run my mouth about his shorty. Me and Ebo was only cool on the business tip—nothing personal.

"Ight, I'll get up witchu lata." I slapped hands with Machete.

I got into my whip and pulled off. While I was pulling off, I saw Jasmine's Cadillac Escalade pull up to the club and Poppa's bitch ass walk out and get inside her truck. But it wasn't shit I could really do if Jasmine caught feelings for the nigga. Poppa's bitch-ass wanted to fuck any female who was important to me. The nigga had two kids by my mother and was fucking my baby sister. Thinking about him knocking up my little sister almost caused me to swerve off the road.

Fuck all dat! I'll kill him if he knock Jasmine up! I thought.

****

I walked into the small diner called Honey Bee's in Glen Burnie, Maryland. Ebo was sitting in the back having a heated conversation with someone over the phone. He told the caller he'd call them back when he saw me walking towards him. I slapped hands with him before I sat down.

"I know you ain't gonna wanna hear this but I didn't come here on a business tip," Ebo said.

"Why am I here then, nigga?" I asked.

"Word around town is you fuckin' my baby mama," he said.

"If your baby mama ain't my wife, this conversation is dead, fam," I replied.

"Look, Beretta. Man to man, just be honest with me. I found these papers in her purse, so tell me what da fuck is up!" he said and slammed the papers on the table. I glanced at them then chuckled. Ebo was a pussy-whipped ass nigga if he couldn't see through Moesha's bullshit.

"Yo, why do you need to take a fuckin' DNA test for my son!" he said.

"The same shit I said to my wife. But check this out, yah bitch has been interfering in my marriage for a while. Shorty accused me of knocking her up and even came at my wife on Facebook with pictures of me sleeping and shit. I guess yah bitch ain't tell you how she's been begging for my dick and sending me pictures of her stale-ass pussy. I got to go to court for dat bitch in a few days because she is claiming that boy is mine and wants me to give her money, but I ain't doing shit until I know if dat lil' nigga is mine, which I doubt. When she went into labor, her aunt called me. Every time dat lil' boy gets sick or sumthin, Moesha sends crazy shit to my wife from fake pages on Facebook telling her I'm a deadbeat father," I said and Ebo bit the inside of his cheek.

"So, you're telling me my bitch wants you to father my son?" he asked. I kinda felt sorry for the nigga. I could only imagine the attachment he had to his son and his baby mother was trying to fuck it all up over a nigga who had bigger pockets.

"What it sounds like?" I asked. Ebo showed me a picture of his son on his phone and it was my first time seeing the baby. The lil' nigga looked nothing like me! I had a feeling Moesha was bullshitting, which was why I wasn't feeding into it. What I hated about the situation was that shorty was harassing my wife and sending her bullshit for no reason. Ebo's son looked just like him.

"You ain't gotta worry about dat DNA test, fam. I'm gonna make sure she doesn't bother you again," he said.

"Yo, handle dat so my wife can stop thinkin' I got another baby out here. What's his name, anyway? Moesha claimed she named him after me and she got her aunt in on it, too," I replied and he nodded his head.

"His name is Eric, after me. The shit is on his birth certificate," Ebo said.

"Good lookin' out," I replied, and stood up to leave. The nigga could've asked me that shit over the phone but if it was me, I would want to see the nigga's face, too. I thought back to the night where I had a talk with Chevy face-to-face. Everybody thought that nigga was missing but he was swimming at the bottom of the ocean. Niggas knew that if you fucked with a gang member's wife, you'd get merked. Chevy slipped up and put that shit in his verse. I was probably the only one who read between the lines when he said,"No nigga can touch me, ask the gun. I finger-popped his wife just for fun."

I didn't listen to the nigga but he was on a track with a nigga I supported around the way. When he said, "ask the gun," the nigga was talking about my street name. Kemara didn't know I merked him and she didn't ask me about the missing person signs with his face on it around the city.

Five months ago...

I waited outside the studio for Chevy's bitch-ass to come out. He was inside with a few niggas and I thought about walking into that bitch and airing all of them niggas out but that would've been too hot. Mara called me and asked me why I was still out at five o'clock in the morning but I told shorty I had some very important business to take care of. She knew the rules so she didn't question me further about it over the phone.

"I'll wait up for you," she said before she hung up. At six o'clock, niggas came out the studio and Chevy was the last one walking out. He dapped his niggas up before he got into his Dodge Charger. Since he was the last one to pull off, it made it easier for me to follow him. Thirty-five minutes later, we ended up in Bowie, Maryland which wasn't too far from my crib in D.C. Chevy pulled up into a driveway and I pulled up behind him. I got out of my whip and he dropped his keys and a backpack. He put his hands up.

"Yooo, I ain't got shit!" he said. I had a white mask over my face so the nigga thought I was ready to rob him but the only thing I planned to take was his life. I smacked him in the head with the butt of my gun and he fell into his car. I hit him again and cracked his nose. The nigga went to sleep from the impact and fell on the ground. I dragged him down the driveway and popped the trunk to a stolen Lincoln Towncar. The street was quiet and I looked around to make sure nobody saw me before I picked him up and put him in the trunk. I hurriedly got into the whip and sped off. There was a lake underneath a small bridge down Route 214 so I headed there. Fifteen minutes later, I drove through the woods and over to an old train track to get to the lake. I turned the lights off on the car after I parked.

There was slight movement coming from the trunk so I grabbed my machete off the back seat. I popped the trunk and Chevy was balled up in a fetal position.

"Please don't kill me," he mumbled and I lifted up my mask. Fear settled in his eyes and he tried to climb out of the trunk but my machete sliced through his arm and he screamed. I grabbed him by the neckline of his shirt and snatched him out of the trunk. He hit his head on a rock when he went crashing onto the ground.

"I didn't fuck yah wife," he cried.

"Tell me sumthin, bruh. You thought you could diss me in a rap verse and put out videos of my wife sitting on your lap? Nigga, do you know who da fuck I am?" I asked.

"GMBAM," he mumbled.

"So, you knew the consequences," I said.

"Nigga, it was just a fuckin' verse! She wouldn't let me fuck her!" he said. Him admitting that he wanted to fuck my wife made me angrier. I stepped on his wrist, pressing my Timb down until I heard the bone crush. Chevy swung on me and hit me in the knees. I brought my machete down on his arm and blood squirted on the tags on the back of the car. I cut the nigga until his body was dismembered. Years ago, we killed a nigga for shooting at us after school. We cut his hands off and pulled teeth out of his mouth so his body wouldn't be identified by dental records or fingerprints. I stuck a rock into Chevy's mouth to keep it open. There was a small tool box in the trunk of the car. I searched through it and found a pair of pliers. It took

a long ass time snatching that nigga's teeth out of his mouth. After I finished, I cut his hands off. I dragged his body to the lake and watched that nigga float away after I tossed his teeth into the water. By the time they found his bitch-ass, he was going to be bloated and faceless. I took off my jumpsuit and tossed it inside the car along with his hands. Seconds later, I set the car on fire and didn't walk away until it blew up...

As long as I had air in my lungs, no nigga on Earth was going to test me and get away with it. The anger I harbored over the years turned me into a nigga that saw death as a way to solve a problem. After sitting down with Ms. Baker, I realized I was fucked up in the head and so was Kemara. Two crazy muthafuckas falling in love was a deadly combination, but at the same time, I needed her to function. Without Kemara in my life, I probably would've been dead by the streets because before her, I didn't give a fuck about nothing!

Kemara

"**W**ait a minute, hoe. You still ain't forgive yah husband yet?" Silk asked while I was sitting on his couch.

"I forgave him but I don't want a nasty-ass stripper fuckin' up my peace box. I hope to God Beretta ain't thinking about going through what we just went through again. Bitches want my husband so bad I hate it but what can I do about it? Nothing! Y'all hoes ain't married, so don't school me, baby," I said to Silk and Thickems. Zalia was playing on the floor with Silk's daughter, Amber, and they were fussing about something.

"I know Zalia ain't just call my daughter a hoe," Silk said.

"Shut the fuck up, Silk. They are just babbling," Thickems said.

"And where is yah son at?" Silk asked and Thickems rolled her eyes. Thickems rarely had her son but it wasn't my business to ask her about it. She hadn't been the same since Ammo was killed, so I figured she was still going through something. Silk thought it was because her son looked just like his father and it was hard to look at him. Whatever the reason, I prayed for her and even gave her some white sage to burn around her home.

"He's with my grandmother," Thickems said.

"Do you need some more sage?" I asked Thickems and Silk bust out laughing.

"I need to stop hanging around y'all negative asses," I spat.

"Chileeee, we need to stop hanging around your voodoo ass," Silk said.

"Bitch, shut up with yah loose insides and stale-ass feet. Piper would've put you in your place if she was here so I'm doing it for her, nah. And just so y'all hoes know, meditating is very relaxing. Why y'all tryna come for me? Don't make me put my ski mask on," I said.

"Mara is always talking about popping a bitch like she's about dat life," Silk laughed and sipped his wine.

"Boyyyyyyyyyyy, just count your blessings and thank God you aren't on my bad side," I replied. Thickems' cell phone rang and a smile spread across her face.

"Ummmm, who is dat?" Silk asked.

"I can't speak on it too soon because we just started talking. I'll let y'all know if it gets serious. I'm not trying to jinx it," Thickems said and I rolled my eyes.

"But you know all of our business, though," I said.

"It's not like that. Y'all know how I am about this dating shit. Why talk about the nigga if he can't keep my interest for more than a week? Trust me, I'll tell y'all if he makes it past stage one," she said.

"You must be talking about the stage you used to strip on 'cause, chile, dat funky-ass attitude ain't even gonna get you a hot dog pretzel," Silk said and Thickems rolled her eyes.

"I have standards, hoe," Thickems spat and Silk put his hand in her face.

"No you don't, you just want a man who is like Ammo. And, baby, you ain't gonna find him," Silk said.

"That's what you think. I probably already did soooo boop boop be gone," she said, putting her hand in Silk's face. My phone rang and it was Nika calling me which was surprising but I answered it because of Hope.

"What do I owe for the pleasure of this call, Ni-ill-ka?" I asked.

"Kill the bullshit, Mara. I know you put Poppa up to leaving me and my kids," she said. I pulled the phone away from my ear and looked at it to make sure I was speaking to the right bitch.

"Ummm, come again?" I asked, uncrossing my legs.

"Mara done uncrossed the legs! Somebody is fucking up her peace box," Silk said.

"Poppa hasn't been the same since you threatened me and told me he'd get what he wanted from me then leave me. I know you had something to do with this because Beretta couldn't keep his dick outta Amona!" Nika slurred. She sounded like she was drunk or high off something.

"Chile, Amona is the least of my worries. Wherever she's at is too far to travel for my husband's dick," I said and Silk screamed in laughter.

"Hello, Jesus. Put Amona on da phone. Tell her it's Shirley," Silk said.

"See, y'all playing too much," Thickems said.

"Jesus, put Ammo on three-way," Silk said.

"Mara, give me the sage for this fool's apartment," Thickems said.

"Well, wherever she's at, I'm sure she's holding your fuckin' daughter, bitch! I know you killed Amona and turned Poppa against me. I hope you die a miserable and lonely death, bitch! Mark my words, hoe! I have something for all of y'all hoodrats," Nika screamed into the phone before she hung up.

"I'm dragging dat hoe on sight," I said, calling Beretta.

"What's good?" Beretta answered the phone.

"Nika is going to get her ass whipped! She called me and accused me of turning Poppa against her when I haven't talked to Poppa in months and she keeps bringing up our daughter's name like dat shit is cool. Get your mother before I get to her. That hoe is tryna to take me there, Z'wan," I said.

"Fuck, Mara, let me call you back. 5-0 is pulling me over," Beretta said and hung up. I started getting worried, hoping he wasn't riding dirty which he never did, but he always kept his Beretta on him. Sweat beads formed on my forehead and my legs started trembling. My best friend was in jail and my husband could possibly go to jail, too. With my nerves out of order, I ran to the bathroom and puked into the toilet.

"What happened?" Silk asked with concern.

"Beretta got pulled over by the cops. What if he goes to jail?" I asked.

"He ain't dirty, is he?" he asked.

"No, but he's always strapped," I replied and Silk covered his mouth. My phone beeped and it was a text message from Beretta. He said they were taking him in and told me not to worry.

"This is all bad! We've been on good terms for six fuckin' months and now look at us. Why can't I just be happy?" I vented out loud. Silk gave me a washcloth so I could clean my face off.

What if it's about Chevy's disappearance, I thought.

Beretta didn't tell me he was responsible for Chevy's disappearance but I knew my husband. I believed he was trying to be a bigger person about the situation because after counseling, we sat and talked about it. But Chevy put a verse in his song disrespecting Beretta and at the end of the day, my man was a street nigga and couldn't walk away from that. I sat on Silk's couch in a daze, wondering if they found Chevy's body.

Naw, they didn't find him. Beretta is too smart to get caught like that, I thought.

"Go home, Mara and leave Zalia here with me and Thickems. I'll keep her until you figure out what's goin' on with yah husband," Silk said.

"Zalia can be a handful sometimes. I can take her with me," I replied.

"Bitch, do you know how many bad-ass hood kids I've watched growing up? Let's not forget all the kids my mama had. Zalia's lil' spoiled ass will be fine right here. Amber can have someone to play wit'," Silk said. I picked Zalia up and kissed her forehead. She wrapped her small arms around my neck.

"Mum-ma," she said.

"Mommy's gotta go, Zalia. Be good for Uncle Silk," I said.

"Auntie Silk," he said.

SOUL Publications

"You ain't confusing my baby like that," I replied. Silk's daughter called him Mommy and Daddy depending on her mood. She had an attitude just like his and all the babysitters she had canceled on her after a week. I was worried about leaving Zalia with Amber.

"Make sure Amber keeps her hands to herself," I warned Silk and he rolled his eyes at me. Silk took Zalia from me so I could leave without her screaming. When I walked out of his apartment building, I spotted Pistol standing on the corner talking to a few niggas.

"Pistol, come here," I called out to him. He dapped the guys up he was talking to before he came over to me.

"What's good?" he asked.

"Beretta got locked up," I said.

"Da fuck? What for?" he asked.

"I don't know. Did you hear about Chevy's body being found? I'm tryna figure out why the police was tailing him. It couldn't have been a traffic stop. They don't take you in for that. What if he was riding dirty?" I said.

"Naw, Beretta ain't riding dirty. You think he had a gun in da whip?" he asked.

"Beretta always has a gun in da whip," I replied.

SOUL Publications

"Damn! This shit is all bad," Pistol said. I told him about Nika calling me and he wondered if she had something to do with it.

"Go see what's up with him and I'll go holla at Nika. She's just as dirty as us, so I hope dat bitch ain't dumb enough to get on some rat shit," Pistol seethed. Pistol told me to call him and let him know if I needed anything before he walked away. I headed to the police station in Annapolis. Maybe I was being too dramatic but I almost passed out when they told me my husband wasn't there. I cursed myself out when I got to my truck because I didn't know what area Beretta was in when he got locked up. We were trying to get on the right track, trying harder than ever, but nothing worked. No wonder I was so screwed up in the head. Life kept knocking me down. I started my truck up and headed home to wait for Beretta's call. Tears almost stung the brim of my eyes as I thought about the police beating him while he was handcuffed or shooting him just because of the color of his skin.

Stop crying, Mara. You always get over these obstacles. You're stronger than you think and that's a fact, I thought. I wiped my eyes and turned the radio up in my truck. Beretta was everything to me and I didn't give a fuck what he did or if he had to do time because I was going to ride for him. I'd kill a bitch or a nigga for him if I had to. Whatever he wanted me to do, I was going to do it regardless of the shit he had put me through.

****

It was midnight and still no phone call from Beretta. In order to calm my nerves, I popped the bottle of his Henny and took it to the head. Meditating didn't work at all. I realized it was only to keep the peace in my life but it damn sure didn't fix anything when I actually needed it. I called almost every nigga in GMBAM to see if they heard anything and nobody knew shit! Tired of waiting downstairs in my living room, I went to the master bedroom to take a nice hot bath. While I was getting dressed, I heard the door downstairs unlock. I grabbed my robe and hauled ass down the stairs. Beretta was walking down the hallway and I ran into him, almost knocking him over. I stood on my tippytoes and kissed his face all over.

"Baby, what happened?" I asked. He grabbed my hand and pulled into the living room. I sat on the couch and he sat on the ottoman in front of me. He looked stressed, like he had the weight on the world on his shoulders.

"Why she hate me so much, shorty? I didn't ask her to bring me here," he said.

"Talk to me," I said.

"I'm being investigated for a murder I committed when I was eighteen years old. The tip came from an anonymous caller. My mother trying to take life away from me again when she never really gave me one in the first place. I hate dat bitch so much I wanna kill her!" he said with tear-filled eyes. My husband had a sensitive side and his childhood was one of them. He wanted a relationship with his mother but she kept betraying him, and no matter what she did, I knew he loved her.

SOUL Publications

"Who is the person?" I asked.

"This nigga named D-money. He stole my money out of my bedroom. He was Nika's boyfriend at the time, but anyway, I pistol-whipped him in her bedroom. My niggas came over and we took him out the house. You can figure the rest out," he said.

"What happened to his body?" I asked.

"We burned dat nigga up but someone found him a week later. Nobody knew who did it besides my niggas and Nika," he said.

"What da fuck is her problem?" I asked.

"I'm paying for my father's sins. Shorty, I know I don't fuck with my mother like dat but I don't think I can take her away from Hope and my little brother. She was a fucked-up mother to me but she's a good mother to them. I'on know what to do," he said.

"Your mother is about to ruin your family. She's gonna take you away from me, Zalia and your friends. Nika doesn't care about you, so it's time to handle your shit or I will," I replied.

"I can't go near Nika. She filed for a restraining order. If anything happens to her, it will make this case solid. It'll be too obvious. Nika has been dealing with street niggas for so long that she knows how to maneuver her way out of shit," he said, rubbing his temples. Beretta got up and went upstairs. I grabbed my phone off the coffee table and texted a person I thought I wouldn't have to ask for anything again. Beretta would've probably choked me if he knew I was getting Poppa involved but when a king is down, it's the queen's turn to reign.

Beretta was sitting in the corner of the bedroom in a lounging chair, smoking a blunt.

"Where my daughter at, Mara?" he asked.

"Silk's house," I said.

"WHAT!" he yelled.

"I went to the police station looking for you but you weren't there and I didn't know what was going on, so I came home and waited for your call in case you needed me," I replied.

"I was with the county police, not city. My lawyer came and those niggas finally released me but them not having solid evidence doesn't mean anything. Those pigs are going to be in my business. They searched my whip, too. Something told me to leave my burner home. Intuition is a muthafucka," he said and took a long drag off his blunt.

"I'm not worried about dat nigga D-money. Them nosey-ass pigs gonna be trailing me trying to figure out where I get money from and unnecessary shit," he said.

"I think you should open up that strip club," I said and he shook his head.

"Yo, don't feel sorry for me. You okay with it now but it's gonna be a different story after all of this blows over," he said.

"I'm serious, Z'wan. You were right and we can't live like this forever. I also want to get a job," I said. If looks could kill, I would've been dead.

"Yo, don't play with me right now," he said. I dropped the subject and headed to the bathroom to take a shower. My cycle was gone off already and I didn't understand it. It came on the night before and it was heavy but my tampon was clean when I took it out. I was no longer on birth control. My IUD fell out two months prior. I was thinking about getting another one but maybe it was God's way of telling me something, so I decided to stay off birth control. Beretta walked into the bathroom naked and I flushed the toilet. He stepped into the shower and I stepped in behind him. The water ran down his chest and down the V-shape in his lower abdomen which led to his big dick. I pulled him into me and he pressed my body against the shower's wall. His full lips pressed against my neck and my nipples hardened against his chest. He whispered in my ear how badly he needed to be inside me. He lifted up my leg and entered me. The love was slow and deep. Beretta wasn't fucking me like he used to but, instead, he made passionate love to my body in ways I could never imagine. My orgasms took my breath away and the pounding in my clit beat like a drum. His hands touched my body like I was a frail piece of glass he didn't want to break. How was it possible to fall deeper in love with someone when you thought it couldn't get any better? Beretta was no longer a young man, he was more than that. He changed for me and I became transparent to him. He throbbed inside of me, on the verge of spilling his seeds. Beretta was ready to pull out because he knew I was no longer on birth control.

"I'm ready to nut, Mara," he groaned when I wrapped my legs tighter around him.

"I want it, Z'wan," I replied, staring into his eyes. He squeezed my ass while pumping his seeds into me. After he was finished, I got down on my knees and blessed him for another round. I wanted him to know that I appreciated him and if he lost everything, he still had his wife.

Poppa

The next day...

The bartender sat a glass of Patrón in front of me. I was at Applebee's in Crofton, Maryland. It was a low-key spot and I didn't have to worry about running into niggas from Annapolis. Kemara came into the restaurant and sat next to me. I didn't know what to expect when she texted me and told me she had to talk to me.

"What's good, baby sis? I know that text wasn't about us being cool again," I said.

"You're absolutely right," she said. I called the bartender over and Kemara ordered a top shelf Long Island. Something about her was different and that was a good thing. Kemara was relaxed and she looked like life was treating her better than before. She also seemed older than she was but that wasn't nothing new. Shorty grew up fast right before my eyes a long time ago.

"Does your husband know you came to meet me? Dat nigga will put a price on my head if he knew about this," I said.

"I'll worry about that. I need a favor from you and just remember all of what I did for you before you even fix your mouth to tell me no," she said.

"Come on, Mara, and spit dat shit out," I replied.

"I want you to make it right with Nika," she said and I laughed.

"Get da fuck outta here. I'm working on something with Jasmine," I replied and took a sip from my drink.

"I need Nika to be happy for a while so she can stay the fuck out of my husband's life. If Beretta goes down, we all go down, and don't think I don't know about what's going on in your strip club. Nika knows too much about everyone and that's not good for any of us," she said.

"Go back home then what?" I asked.

"Get into her head. See what it is she wants so she can undo the bullshit she's trying to start," Mara said.

"So, you want me to help you out?" I asked.

"You can't possibly think Nika will let you mess around with Jasmine and not do anything about it. The bitch is crazy and you know it. It's only a matter of time before she starts messing up your life. A happy Nika is a happy life for all of us," Mara said. Mara wasn't lying about Nika, she was a thorn in my side. I wished I would've known the bitch was crazy but it was too late because she was the mother of my kids. The baby was my son according to the blood test. I was heated but I had to deal with it.

"What am I gonna do about Jasmine?" I asked.

"Do you really love that girl or you love what she can do for you?" Mara asked.

"I'm tryna change," I replied but she didn't believe me. Kemara finished her drink and slammed her glass on the table.

"Prove it to me by making this shit right because you made that bitch insane. Whatever you did to her, undo it. Go home, Poppa," Kemara said. She grabbed her Birkin's bag off the bar and I knew that shit cost a lot of stacks.

"I hope you did change for the better so I can forgive you and move on with my life," she said before she walked away. It fucked me up because I missed my sister. I paid the bartender for our drinks then left out of the restaurant.

Damn, I gotta go back home to dat bitch, I thought.

****

I was sitting on Jasmine's couch, watching TV, while she was in the kitchen venting about some girl in her class not reading her script right.

"Poppa, do you hear me talking to you?" she asked.

"Naw, shorty. What happened?" I replied.

"What's wrong witchu? Why are you so quiet?" she asked.

"We gotta talk about something," I said. Jasmine gave me a dirty look like she was wishing death on a nigga.

"Nigga, you betta not fuckin' play wit' me!" she said.

"Damn, whatchu gettin' all hyped for?" I asked.

"'Cause I know you with da shits. See, I should've shot yah ass and been done wit' it. What is it? Another baby or sumthin?" she asked.

"I'm going back to Nika," I replied. Jasmine rocked me in the face and shorty lost it from there. She was throwing combos and I grabbed at her hands. That crazy bitch head-butted me and almost knocked me out.

"Get da fuck outta my house, hoe! I thought you changed and I even downplayed myself to be wit' a nigga like you. What happened to all dat shit about you loving me and shit? Where da fuck did dat go? Nigga, answer me!" she yelled. I don't know what it was but I was always sticking my dick in crazy chicks.

"You didn't let me finish," I said, holding my shirt to my bloody nose.

"Finish then and hurry up," Jasmine said.

"Some shit is goin' down with Nika. She knows too much and Kemara thinks she's gonna rat some niggas out because of the beef she got with Beretta. I'm doin' this for my sister, I got to. Now, you can either ride with me or we end here but I'm not changing my mind. You'd do the same shit for your brothers if you were me," I said. Jasmine sat on the love seat and crossed her arms.

"Nika is very manipulative, so I hope you play your cards right," Jasmine replied and I was relieved.

"I'm gonna be faithful to her. This shit is hard, shorty, because we just got back on good terms and I fell for you. You snuck up on me but we gotta chill out," I said.

"Cool," she said. Jasmine kissed my forehead and went back into the kitchen. It was no use for me to stay at her crib since I broke the peace, so I grabbed my car keys and headed towards the door. Jasmine called out to me and I turned around.

"I respect you for this, but at the same time, don't think I'm gonna be waiting around for you. I still have a life to live," Jasmine said.

"You tellin' me you're gonna be fuckin' another nigga?" I asked.

"Nika ain't gonna let you go so I hope you stay for good," Jasmine said. I felt like slapping the shit out of Jasmine but putting my hands on her would've definitely got me killed because her role was over.

****

Two hours later....

I used my key to Nika's crib and the house was peaceful and quiet. When I walked down the hall and into the living room, Nika was sitting on the couch with a glass of wine. My son was sleeping in a bassinet by the couch.

"Where is Hope?" I asked.

"With the nanny," she replied dryly.

"Can we talk?" I asked.

"About what? Talk about how I heard you fuckin' dat bitch when I called your phone. What do you gotta say to me? You moved your clothes and shoes out before I came home from the hospital and you call the house to talk to Hope but hang up when I get on the phone. I don't have shit for you Poppa, so kiss yah son then get your scrub ass out of my house," she said.

"I apologize for treatin' you like dat but you have been smothering me, shorty. Stop treatin' me like I'm yah fuckin' son then you won't have to worry about me fuckin' bitches my age. All you do is walk around with a fucked-up attitude like muthafuckas owe you sumthin. I'on owe you jack shit! I want to be here for my kids and change my life around but you keep bringin' me down and I'on need dat type of shit, Nika. So, what's up? You gonna let me wear the pants in this relationship or do you want me to leave for good?" I asked.

Bitch's hair ain't even done! Mannnn, shorty looks old now. I'mma have to hit her from the back when we fuck 'cause ain't no way my dick will get hard, I thought.

"I was stressed out. The death of Amona, the pregnancy and you fuckin' them strippers, sent me overboard. I wish I had never helped you get that club because you turned your back on me the minute I put those keys in your hands. How did you let Beretta and his niggas take over shit you worked hard for? And how can you let him disrespect me like that? I'll treat you like a man when you start acting like one," she said and grabbed the wine bottle off the table.

"My business with GMBAM is none of your concern. You bought me a piece of shit building and pocketed the rest of the money. Beretta helped me fix it up but he did it so I could take care of Hope. This ain't about me trying to be a GMBAM nigga. This is about me having my own money without robbing niggas for it," I said.

"I don't want you around Beretta. He killed Amona, I know he did. My son ain't right in the head. He ruins everything in my life. People who love me, he takes them away from me. Look at you, Poppa. He's startin' to rub off on you. Him and that trashy-ass wife of his. I bet her crazy ass helped him kill Amona. Her death had GMBAM all over it and you're just like them now," she said.

"Yo, you on sumthin if you think I'm thuggin' it out like that. Me and Beretta will never be cool on dat tip and you know dat," I said.

"Well, it doesn't matter now. He'll be locked up soon," she replied.

"Da fuck is you talkin' about?" I asked.

"You heard what da fuck I said!" she slurred.

"Tell me what you did," I replied.

I didn't give a fuck about what I did in my life but snitching ain't never been one of them. Nika snitching on Beretta could affect me, too, because he was pushing weight through my club. We'd all go down, including Mara since she was married to him.

"You know what I did but don't worry about it. I filed for a restraining order, and in case something happens to me, they'll get his ass. Kemara wants to be a down bitch so she can do the time with him and that bastard-ass baby they are toting around like it's theirs can go to foster care because she damn sho ain't coming here," Nika said, then lit a cigarette.

"Do you not understand what you just did? You snitched on a fuckin' king pin, dummy! The whole fuckin' team will go down, including me!" I yelled at her and she laughed.

"You've been to jail before," she said and stood up.

"Jasmine will be going down with 'em, too. Get yah commissary money together for her black ass!" Nika shouted out as she walked down the hallway.

I wanna kill dat bitch! I thought.

Nika was trying to take down Beretta, Kemara and Jasmine at the same time and the only way she could do that was by snitching on GMBAM so everybody could go down. I had to figure out a way to fix it because I was either going to end up in jail or dead. But I couldn't make it so obvious by sucking up to her all of a sudden because she would catch on.

Think, nigga, THINK! I thought.

Bingo!

I picked up my son and took him upstairs so he could lay comfortably in his crib. Nika didn't change him, he was soaking wet. I laid him back down after I cleaned him up. Nika was sitting up in bed, watching TV and smoking a cigarette.

"I gotta tell you sumthin, shorty," I said and she grilled me.

"I was fuckin' Amona," I said.

"WHAT!" Nika screamed.

"Yeah, it happened twice. We went to a hotel room a few times. She told me you were fuckin' some nigga from out of town and that's why I didn't think my son was mine. Amona wasn't rocking with you like dat, shorty. Why you think she was sneaking behind your back to take Hope to see Beretta? She didn't give a fuck about you," I said and Nika had tears falling from her eyes. The only reason I lied to Nika was so she could stop hating Kemara over Amona and start hating her, too. Shit, I didn't know what else to do without looking suspicious of something.

"HOW COULD YOU? I put that bitch in my will in case something happened to me. I trusted her with my daughter!" Nika said and threw a picture off her nightstand at me.

"Shit, it just happened. I thought you was out being a hoe and when you told me you were pregnant, I didn't know what to believe. Honestly, I still think you're fucking another nigga. I wanted to ask you but I couldn't throw shorty under the bus like that, knowing I smashed her," I said. Nika got off the bed and went to the bathroom. She slammed the door then locked it. I heard her dumb ass crying in the bathroom but she brought it on herself. Her phone vibrated on the bed and I picked it up. It was a text from Wesson. I opened the message and read through them. The only reason I was interested in who Nika was texting was because the bitch was up to something.

Ain't this a bitch, I thought as I read the thread. Nika was fucking a GMBAM nigga.

No wonder he was the only one of them niggas who talked to me. The nigga wanted to feel me out because he was fuckin' my baby mama. I bet the nigga was telling her about the strippers I was fucking in the club, I thought. Beretta had a snake on his team. I took a picture of the messages and hurriedly put her phone back. Two minutes later, Nika came out of the bathroom.

I hated GMBAM niggas for years and now I'm caught up in their shit, I thought. Honestly, I wouldn't have been in the situation if I didn't stick my dick in Nika's hoe ass. That broad was on my case about me fucking Jasmine but was banging a nigga who worked in my club while she was pregnant with my son. Shorty had more issues than anybody I came across and I came from a fucked-up poor neighborhood that was infested with crackheads.

"Where do we go from here, Nika?" I asked.

"I want my kids' father under the same roof so we can be a family," she said.

"Be honest with me, Nika. I told you everything so now it's time for you to talk. What nigga have you been fuckin', and don't lie to me? You want a family but you gotta be honest with me so we can start over," I said.

"Amona was lyin', Poppa. You believed her?" she asked.

"Yo, call me when you stop playin' games," I replied, fronting like I gave a fuck. I left out of the bedroom and Nika ran after me.

"I wasn't fuckin' nobody!" she said.

"I'll be back later on," I replied and kissed her lips. Nika was a smart female when it came to the streets but she let the wrong nigga fuck her brains out and her head up. It didn't matter if a nigga was a bum, dumb and a straight-up lame. I guess the saying was true, a nigga with a good sex game could bring a bad bitch down to any level. Nika used to be on her shit but I had her running around looking like a fifty-five-year-old couch potato. I chuckled to myself when I got in my whip and pulled off. Shit was getting out of hand but a nigga's ego was on one-hunnid. Glock's coming home party was later on and I had a feeling some shit was going to go down.

Beretta

Hours later...

Kemara walked out of the bathroom wearing a tight-ass black dress and leopard pumps. I slid my hand up her dress and she smacked it away.

"Yo, go put something on!" I said.

"You don't want to slide off in the bathroom in the club?" she asked and licked my lips. I squeezed her meaty ass cheeks and pressed my erection against her.

"Let me slide in really quick," I said and she pulled away from me.

"Nigga, I'm looking good. I don't have time to be playing around with you," she said. She grabbed her necklace off the dresser and handed it to me so I could put it on her. I had a lot of shit on my mind and being pulled over because of some stupid shit was one of them. It was a traffic stop—the officer said I ran a stop light. That was bullshit but those pigs hated seeing a black nigga driving clean. He took my license and went back to his car. Five minutes later, the nigga came back and told me I was connected to a murder. That shit kept playing over and over in my head. I had more work coming in and had to figure out a way to get to it in case those pigs were following me. My lawyer told me I could file a complaint because those niggas had nothing on me, but fuck that because niggas be making themselves look guilty. Kemara was asking me something but my mind was all over the place.

"Z'wan, you hear me talkin' to you?" she asked.

"Naw, what you say?" I replied.

"Do you think I should wear red lipstick?" she asked.

"Naw, I'on like dat shit. Yah lips look good the way they are and will look even better when you wrap those pretty muthafuckas around my dick tonight," I said.

"I can't stand you," she giggled.

Earlene was downstairs in the kitchen fixing a snack for Zalia.

"Thanks for coming over to watch Zalia," Mara said.

"Anytime, shit. This place is beautiful. Soon as she goes to sleep, I'm gonna get comfortable on the balcony and watch the city. I brought my book with me and my wine," she said.

"You need some smoke?" Mara asked.

"Ohhhh, what you got for Aunt Earlene?" she asked. Mara went into her purse and pulled out two fat bags of kush and sat them on the counter.

"Oh, honey, this smells better than my greens with neck bones," she said.

"You brought some with you, right?" Mara asked and Earlene nodded her head.

"You fattening up my wife to make me jealous, huh?" I asked Earlene.

"And making me look thick in my clothes. Don't pay him no mind. Beretta don't want me wearing nothing but sweat clothes," Mara said. Shorty wasn't lying. Mara couldn't wear certain shit if we weren't together and that wasn't going to change. I'd merk a GMBAM nigga for looking at my wife's ass. Glock hit my phone and I answered on the second ring.

"My nigga!" I said into the phone.

"What's good, fam? My bad for not hitting you up earlier but a nigga was backed up. I had to bust down my wife a few times," he said.

"Yeah, nigga. You still a clown for not telling me you married a shorty, though," I replied.

"Yo, you would've clowned me if you knew I wifed Bridget. You know shorty was a little hoe back in the day," he said. Glock wasn't lying about that. Bridget and her little preppy friends were fucking every thug nigga in the city. I smashed a few of them back in the day. Matter of fact, it was my first threesome when I was eighteen years old. That night was wild.

"Yeah, I would've, so I now I gotta make up for lost time. Sorry, bruh, it wouldn't be me if I didn't," I replied.

"Ight, don't get mad when I start clowning Mara," he chuckled.

"Yeah, whateva, nigga. Welcome back, bruh," I replied.

"Appreciate it and thanks for havin' niggas look out for Bridget and my kids while I was locked down. It's all love on my end, bruh," he said.

"Bet, I'll rap to you when I see you," I replied and hung up.

"Y'all be safe and keep an eye on Olijah for me so he can stay out of trouble," Earlene said.

"Oh, you ain't gotta worry about that. Pistol better be on good behavior while my sister does her time," Mara said and I looked at her.

"This family don't snitch," I said.

"Say what you want but Pistol better not leave the club with nobody," Mara said.

"You going to the club like that?" Earlene asked me.

I had on a black Gucci collared shirt, black jeans and black Timbs. The only jewelry I had on was my Rolex and thick gold diamond chain.

"What's wrong wit' it? This ain't the nineties. Niggas don't go clubbing with church clothes on no more," I replied. Kemara put my diamond Cartier shades on my face then took a picture.

"My husband shittin' on these niggas, Earlene," Mara bragged and I tapped her up.

"Speak for yah man, shorty," I said and Earlene shook her head.

"That's what's wrong wit' y'all bad asses. Back in my day, we were strutting through the clubs decked out in fancy shit. Y'all don't know nothing," she said. We kissed Zalia before we left out of the crib.

"I wish Piper was home. I'm not used to going out without her," Mara said when we stepped onto the elevator.

"I'on know, shorty. Piper being home probably would have niggas beefing. Glock and Pistol cool right now but niggas sing a different tune when they start drinking and smoking," I said.

"Well, hopefully Glock will be over it by the time she comes 'cause I support Pistol and Piper. Glock is a fraud-ass nigga," Mara said.

"Chill out wit' dat shit. That's my brother," I replied and she smacked her teeth.

"Well, I'm not feeling him or his racial slur-throwing bitch. That hoe called me Shanaynay. She must think all black girls are ghetto or some shit but meanwhile she's fucking a hood nigga, or do Glock get a pass because he's bi-racial? I'm telling you now, Marsha Brady better not even look at me," Kemara said.

"You startin' already," I replied, unlocking the door to her Range Rover. I took the tags off the whip I got pulled over in so I could sell it. My niggas told me I was too paranoid but I was trying to play it safe. I wasn't owning anymore vehicles for a while.

****

Started from the bottom now we're here
Started from the bottom now my whole team fucking here

I walked through the crowd with my wife, holding her hand. Bitches was giving my shorty all types of looks. Some I fucked back in the day and some who I didn't know who wished they were her. Upstairs was the VIP section and my niggas were popping champagne bottles already.

"Damn, nigga! Da fuck you been eating?" I asked Glock when we dapped each other up with a hug. The nigga got swole but it wasn't muscle. He was almost Ammo's size when he was alive.

"Y'all niggas had my commissary stacked so a nigga was eating," he said.

"Welcome home," Kemara said dryly and I grilled her. Glock hugged Kemara and she patted his back. My wife be tripping sometimes.

"Damn, Mara. It's like dat?" Glock asked.

"I'm not trying to get make-up on your white shirt," Mara lied.

"Y'all niggas could've waited until I came home to get married. I wish I was there, though, no lie. I'm still hot about dat," Glock said.

"We weren't invited to your wedding so don't feel bad," Kemara said and walked off.

"Damn, Mara still got dat nasty-ass attitude?" Glock asked.

"Stop frontin' like you don't know what's up. You had Piper out here looking like a groupie and Mara wasn't with it. But you home now so fuck all dat shit. Enjoy yah night, fam," I replied.

"Speaking of shorty. Is she straight? You think it would be outta line if I go see her and apologize to her?" Glock asked.

"Yo, let it go. That's Pistol's shorty now so I'on think that's a good move unless you get his permission. But in the meantime, it's yah party so live it up," I said. Glock slapped hands with me again before he went back to the table. My niggas had the VIP section lit. Kemara was off to the side talking to Jasmine. I was ready to pop a bottle of Henny but Poppa's bitch-ass walked over to me.

"I gotta holla at you about something," he said. We went into his small private office. I didn't know what he called himself doing, but that nigga had a desk in there like he was a school principal.

"This betta be important," I gritted.

"You got a snake in your grass," he said.

"Everybody knows Nika's a snake. Tell me sumthin worthy of my time, muthafucka," I replied.

"Wesson is telling Nika about your operation," he said. He gave me his phone and showed me a picture of messages from a cell phone. Nika was definitely texting that nigga.

"You think tellin' me this is gonna give you a bigger cut, nigga?" I asked.

"This is my club and if Nika knows shit, I'm going down wit' y'all niggas, too," he said.

"That's your bitch, so handle it. Did you tell anybody about this?" I asked, reading the messages.

"Naw," he said and I deleted the picture.

"We neva had this conversation," I said and walked out of his office. Wesson was chilling with two bitches on his lap when I went back to the section. Wesson was a rat and I had to be careful because the wrong move would have me behind bars.

"Yo, you good?" Pistol asked when I sat next to him.

"We got a snake in our camp," I replied.

"You sure?" he asked. I couldn't believe it myself because GMBAM was about loyalty and Wesson was our nigga for years. He was a little older than us but we could always count on that nigga to make sure the bricks made it to Annapolis on Chulo's fish boat. The nigga was eating off of me and even put his shorty up in a big house but he was selling me out for disloyal pussy.

"Nigga, when am I not sure?" I gritted.

Glock's wife and a posse of her friends came into the section and two of them I smashed years back. Nobody was expecting Bridget to come to a hood strip club with her friends.

"Bruh, Glock's ass is trippin. He got all his hoes in here tonight," Pistol chuckled. Wesson kept looking at his phone and it was making me uncomfortable, so I told Sniper to keep an eye on him. It was just a normal night at the strip club; usually niggas were shooting dice in private rooms or trapping out the VIP sections but the shop was closed. I kept my eyes on my wife and she was chilling with Jasmine and they were watching Bridget and her friends.

"Heyyyyy, Beretta. Remember me," Bridget's friend asked when she sat on my lap and I hurriedly pushed her off. Kemara's head was turned but shorty was asking to get merked.

"Ashley, remember that night we had? I think we should do a part two," she said to the girl we had a threesome with. My phone beeped and it was a text from Mara.

You got 0.5 seconds to get those bitches away from you!

"Kemara about to go ham. Look at shorty," Pistol said.

"Yeah, nigga, she is watching you, too," I replied.

"I already know. I'm leaving shortly anyway so I can get up in time to visit Piper in the morning," he replied.

Come over here and sit on my lap then, I texted back. Kemara walked over to me and got comfortable on my lap.

"She can join us, too," Bridget's friend said and rubbed Mara's thigh. Mara slapped shorty and she fell into the table where the liquor was at. That shit was hilarious because shorty's left cheek was red.

"What did you do that for? She was just trying to have fun," one of them spoke up.

"Tell her keep her hands to herself! I don't play those types of games," Mara said. Bridget jumped up and Glock grabbed her hand and pulled her back down.

"Is she trying to fight me?" Mara asked.

"Chill out, Mara. Those broads are drunk," I replied.

"I want to go home," Mara said. I didn't want Mara to come to the party but I invited her anyway so she wouldn't think I was up to no good.

"Ight," I replied. I was happy my homeboy was home but the scenery before me just wasn't my style anymore. Stuntin' out in VIP sections, getting head from strippers and popping bottles all night was lame. My nigga, Pistol, wasn't even feeling it and the nigga was always going broke throwing money at strippers. Technically, we outgrew the fast life so at that point, it was all about making more money and stacking so we could be secure forever.

"Yo, where you going?" Glock asked.

"Home, bruh. It's getting late," I said.

"Nigga, da fuck is you talkin' about? It's only one o'clock. Bruh, we used to party until eight in da mornin'," Glock said.

"He's married now, what do you expect?" Mara said.

"Damn, I come home to this bullshit. Niggas changing up on me. It feels like y'all niggas wish I was still locked up. I should've known what it was when my right-hand man started fuckin' my bitch," Glock slurred.

"Fuck is you talkin' about, muthafucka? We bought you a fucking G-wagon and gave you stacks, so you can chill out for the rest of the year and you trippin' because I'm not feeling this lame ass shit? My nigga, you got muthafuckas up in here partying witchu like they family. We did this shit when we were broke! Niggas ain't movin' like this anymore, fam," I said.

"Nigga, you started this shit and now you think it's beneath you? Muthafucka, we don't bang with Poppa, so why is that nigga walkin' around here? What happened to you? You got soft on us? I should've known dat shit when you let Ammo get merked. I'm ready to start callin' you Z'wan 'cause this ain't Beretta," he said.

"Yo, you fuckin' trippin!" Pistol said.

"Nigga, fuck you, too! All y'all niggas bogus," Glock said.

"Babe, he's drunk. Let's just go home," Mara said.

"Yeah, go home, bruh. Your shorty got you out here lookin' soft," Glock said. I picked up the champagne bottle off the table and cracked that nigga upside the head with it. The strippers ran out the section and my homeboys were trying to pull me off of him but I wouldn't let up. Glock's wife jumped on my back and Kemara snatched her up and swung her down the stairs.

"Yo, chill out!" Sniper said as my fist slammed into Glock's face. Pistol wrestled me off but I wanted to take Glock's fucking head off. That nigga had the nerve to speak ill shit on me when all I did was make sure his family was straight. I ain't forget about him but he wanted me to be the same nigga I was before he got locked up. It hurt knowing your homeboy who was like a brother couldn't respect your growth. I'd never pressure my niggas to do nothing they didn't want to do.

"Yooo, we're supposed to be a team," Wesson said. I rocked that nigga in his grill and he fell down the stairs. Kemara was yelling for me to stop but I was already down the stairs stomping Wesson. I remember when Wesson's family was homeless and all of us stayed outside trapping for two days straight just to put that nigga in a hotel room. I was broke at the time, too, but I was loyal to niggas who I thought was loyal to me. Four niggas wrestled me off Wesson but I wanted to kill the nigga.

"FUCK GMBAM!" I said when I pulled away from them.

"Yoooo, what?" Machete asked.

"Nigga, you heard me," I replied. I grabbed my wife's hand and pulled her through the crowd. My shirt was ripped and I had blood on my hands.

"Yo, mind yah fuckin' business when I'm talking to my homeboys! You always got yah mouth up in sumthin and don't know what da fuck is goin' on," I yelled at Mara when we got outside.

"I told him what you couldn't! Glock was too fuckin' comfortable with all them hoes up there. It's crazy how he automatically assumed you were gonna be partying with him and those bitches! He had to know that you're a married man now and can't be out all hours of da fuckin' night!" Mara screamed at me.

"I'm not arguing with yah dumb ass right now," I said, taking my shirt off.

"Fuck you, too," Mara said. I wanted to snatch shorty up by her neck and choke the shit out of her. It was a time and place for everything and shorty spoke up at the wrong time. I gave her the keys so she could drive and she snatched them away from me. She got in the driver's seat and slammed the door while I was getting in the passenger's seat. I didn't give a fuck about her attitude because I was used to it.

"I'm sick of this life," Kemara said, breaking the silence.

"You married to the game, shorty. I was a street nigga when you married me so don't act like I'm supposed to drop everything because I'm in love and shit. We had this talk before, I'm not doing it forever, but in the meantime, you gonna ride it out with me. Shit ain't change," I said.

"That's what you think," she mumbled.

"Yo, shut da fuck up! You wanted me to nut in da pussy just a few days ago but now you talkin' stupid. You ain't goin' nowhere, so kill the noise," I replied. Kemara was quiet the rest of the way home while I smoked a blunt.

****

Earlene was knocked out on the couch when we walked into the crib. Kemara went upstairs to Zalia's room and I went into our bedroom. I started wondering if more of my niggas felt the same way Glock was feeling. My phone was ringing off the hook and it was my lil' brother, Sniper, calling me.

"Yooo, what's good?" I asked.

"Everything straight?" Sniper asked.

"I'm good," I replied.

"Naw, bruh. You ain't good. You went ham on those niggas and you said fuck GMBAM. Nigga, we family and you can't let two ungrateful niggas fuck up the foundation. Give me da word and it's done," Sniper said. He was letting me know he'd merk Wesson and Glock if I wanted him to.

"We'll talk," I replied.

"Machete and Pistol got into it after you left. Pistol was tryna help Glock's bitch ass up off the floor and Machete told Pistol leave him there because he ain't fam," Sniper said.

"Everybody had too much to drink," I replied.

"Aight, bruh. I'll talk to you later," he said.

"What you got planned for the end of the month?" I asked.

"Nothing, why what's up?" he replied.

"I wanna take you and Jasmine on a trip. Just us three," I said. Since I found out they were my brother and sister, I hadn't really been chilling with them outside of GMBAM. Jasmine was a female so I was always giving her money and spoiling her but Sniper was different. The nigga wouldn't even let me gift him on his twenty-first birthday. He reminded me of myself because he believed he didn't deserve it if he couldn't get it on his own.

"Okay, bet. I'll holla at you lata, bruh," he said and hung up. Mara came into the bedroom and shorty was struggling to unzip her dress but was too mad to ask me for help.

"Yo, you need help?" I asked.

"No, I got it," she lied.

"Cool," I replied and took my clothes off for the shower.

"Okay, fine! Take this off for me," Mara said.

"Damn, where yah manners at?" I replied.

"Please," she pouted. I sat on the bed and she stood in front of me so I could unzip her dress. Mara had a tattoo of my name underneath her ass cheek with gun smoke next it. She tried to snatch away from me when I kissed her ass but I pulled her onto my lap.

"Stop playin' wit' me," I said, licking her neck.

"Nigga, you cursed me out," she said.

"That's what we do but look at us now. We gonna fuck, take a shower then watch a movie," I replied and she bit her bottom lip.

"What about eating my pussy?" Mara asked.

"That, too," I replied. She turned around and straddled me and I unhooked her bra. She pushed me back on the bed and sat her pussy on my mouth. I was about to nut from that bold shit. Shorty could sit on my face while I was asleep and I'd still suck the soul out of her. I stuck my tongue in her and she rode my face. Pre-cum dripped from the tip of my dick. Kemara knew what time it was, so she turned around and took my dick in her mouth while I sucked on her pussy lips. Shorty was a freak, she let me slide a few fingers in her ass, too. That shit made her cream so much and I was addicted to it.

"Damn, Mara! FUCK!" I groaned when she sucked my nuts.

Me and Mara went at it all night until we were stretched out on the bedroom floor passed out.

****

Two days later...

"Damn, nigga. You scared me. Wh- what you doin' here?" Wesson asked. I was sitting on that nigga's couch when he walked into his crib. I wasn't going to kill the nigga because shit was too hot but I had to let him know what was up.

"Have a seat," I said.

"Look, bruh, about the other night—" he said, but I cut him off.

"I said have a fuckin' seat!" I barked and he sat across from me. He was eyeing my black gloves and black jumpsuit. Wesson knew I only dressed in all black for two occasions: funerals and merking niggas.

"How long have you been down with GMBAM?" I asked.

"Ten years," he replied.

"And when have you ever seen a nigga go against the grain?" I asked.

"Never seen it," he said.

"So, that makes you a special GMBAM nigga then, right?" I asked.

"What you mean?" he replied.

"It means you the first nigga to turn into a fuckin' snake, nigga," I said.

"Who told you this? I'mma fix this shit right now," he replied.

"You fuckin' Nika?" I asked and fear settled in his eyes.

"Look, bruh, your mother came on to me. I was going to her restaurant and chilling at the bar. She kept flirting wit' me and one thing led to another," he said.

"You tellin' Nika GMBAM shit?" I asked.

"Come on, fam. You know I took an oath," he replied.

"Naw, nigga. Nika knows shit that she shouldn't know and it definitely came from a GMBAM nigga. Just be honest with me, tell me what you told her," I asked.

"She only knows about the deal between you and Poppa, how you ended up with Zalia," he admitted and I cursed myself. Wesson, Sniper and Machete went to the house Mara killed her mother in to burn down the evidence. That fuck-nigga dragged my wife into it. I didn't tell them Mara merked her mother but it was obvious because I wouldn't have left that house without burning it down.

"Look, man. It wasn't like that. Nika ain't gonna say shit," he said. My phone vibrated in my pocket but I ignored it. It was Glock calling me for the tenth time. He wanted to talk about that shit that happened at the party but I wasn't in the mood to hear what that nigga had to say. I grabbed a gun off the couch and gave it to Wesson. He held it in his hand in confusion.

"What's this?" he asked.

"The gun I merked D-money with. Now we can do this the easy way or the hard way," I said, then called out to Machete. Machete came downstairs with a long machete in his hand. He was dressed in all black, wearing a white mask.

"The easy way would be you gettin' pulled over with that murder weapon, which has your fingerprints on it because I never touch my weapons without gloves. The hard way would be you getting chopped up and thrown into the Severn river. Oh, and I know you don't want to rat to the cops because fuckin' with me will be fucking with my connect's pockets. The Mexican cartel's reach is so far that nobody will be able to save you. They'll slaughter your family right down the whole fuckin' family tree," I said and Wesson had tears in his eyes.

"No need to cry now, bitch. You shitted on us, bruh. You were my nigga but the shit you pulled could've had us all doing FED time," Machete said.

"I'll do it," he said.

The gun I gave Wesson had twenty bodies on it, all from me but that nigga was going to make sure the police didn't have a reason to even look my way. Machete checked Wesson's pockets to take his phone so he wouldn't call nobody. I handed him keys to the stolen pick-up truck Machete drove to his crib.

"Jail is better than death, nigga. You made a mistake, so you gotta fix it," Machete said. Wesson was sobbing and I wanted to knock that nigga out. Machete pushed him towards the back door to watch him get in the truck. I texted Sniper who was parked outside, letting him know to follow Wesson so he wouldn't do no dumb shit. Machete called Jasmine and told her to call the police and give them an anonymous tip on a stolen truck.

"Damn, bruh," Machete said. He was in his feelings because Wesson was close with him and Sniper.

"Like you said, it's better than death and the heat will be off our backs but we still have to chill out for a little bit," I said and he nodded his head in agreement. We left out of the back door and Jasmine was pulling up in a Hyundai Sonata. Machete got in the front and Jasmine smacked her teeth.

"Damn, it's like dat now?" Machete asked Jasmine.

"Nigga, shut da fuck up before I slap you," Jasmine replied.

"Fuck all dat, when we gettin' married?" he asked.

"I'll eat pussy before I marry yah cheating ass," she replied.

"Mannnn, dat shit is old, fam. Let me make it up to you by sucking yah toes or sumthin," Machete said.

"You can suck on the bitch I got in my purse while I pull the trigger. Shut up and ride! Call one of your bitches up. What happened to Zain's dusty ass?" Jasmine asked.

"She ain't messing with me," Machete replied.

"You cheated on her, huh? Serves her right 'cause she damn sure didn't care about our relationship," Jasmine said.

"Whateva, shorty. Meanwhile, your nigga couldn't even help you out in a shootout. Tell yah brother how you had to act like Rambo when they kidnapped Hope. That nigga kept saying 'how I'mma get my daughter if I don't have a gun' and 'what if they shoot me.' I would've died for mine, fuck asking questions. Don't worry, though, baby girl. Daddy will come save the damsel in distress. You still my baby mama," Machete said.

"Nigga, what you talkin' about 'baby mama'?" I asked him. I was quiet because I was trying to call Mara back. They must've forgotten I was in the whip.

"Huh?" Machete asked.

"That's what yah ass get!" Jasmine yelled in frustration.

"Jasmine got a baby?" I asked.

"She got an abortion," Machete replied.

"I didn't get an abortion, dummy! It was an ectopic pregnancy," Jasmine replied.

"How long ago was this?" I asked.

"Like three years ago," Jasmine replied.

"Jasmine was my shorty since she was running around outside with no shoes on and a lil' ass ponytail," Machete said.

"Nigga, I was twelve years old," Jasmine laughed.

An hour later, Jasmine pulled up to my crib.

"Take dat nigga straight home, too," I said, talking about Machete.

"We goin' out to grab something to eat," Machete replied. I slapped hands with him before I stepped out the whip. My phone beeped and it was a message from Sniper. The police had Wesson's bitch-ass. When I walked into the house, Mara was studying at the kitchen table with her friend, Emma. It took me a minute to let shorty have muthafuckas over our crib but Mara wasn't having it. Once a week, I'd come home to seeing Silk, Thickems or Emma. Most of the time, it was all three of them.

"Ummm, babe. Silk and Thickems are on their way over so I'm giving you a heads up," Kemara said.

"Tell Thickems to bring her son. I haven't seen him in months," I replied. If Ammo was alive, Thickems wouldn't be pawning her son on everyone. I didn't know what shorty's problem was but she was whack for that. We were giving Thickems money for Jonah but I told my niggas to stop because we were basically taking care of her dumb-ass. I told Kemara but of course she hit me with the, "Thickems is going through something and taking care of a child alone is hard."

I went upstairs and rolled a blunt. Hopefully 5-0 could stay off my back but every time one door closed, another one opened. Moesha stopped harassing Mara. It was almost as if shorty disappeared after Ebo found out about her money scheme. I thought shit was going to be great after that, but Wesson ended up being a snake. It was only a matter of time before something else happened, but I couldn't sit around and dwell on the shit because it was the life I chose to gamble with.

Part 8:

Welcome Home

Piper

August 2013,

One year later...

When I walked out of the correctional facility's fence, I almost kissed the ground. Jail taught me a lot and honestly it made me wake up to a lot of shit. I was running around not paying attention to the destruction I was doing to my life. It also gave me the chance to experience real love. Pistol and Kemara held me down while I did my small sentence. Silk and Thickems visited me, too, but Kemara came more than once a week.

"Over here, shorty!" Pistol called out and there he was, leaning against his Bentley coupe. I ran to him and he picked me up and spun me around. He pressed me against his car and slipped his tongue down my throat. I pulled away from him and tried to fix my hair. I looked a mess and my hair was done in two French braids. When I came in, I was a size twelve but my ass done blew up. My titties got bigger and my hips were rounder. Pistol didn't care because he couldn't stop hugging me. He opened the passenger door for me and I looked around his car. Pistol was driving a 2013 Bentley. GMBAM niggas were definitely getting paid and the bitches in jail couldn't stop talking about them. One girl I had to check because she was bragging about how she sucked Beretta's dick years ago. Everyone was looking for a come-up and I understood why Kemara was a little insecure at times. Hell, I was feeling insecure the moment I walked out of jail to a handsome paid nigga when he could've been giving his time to someone else. Pistol said he was faithful but seeing him looking better than ever made me realize I was back in the real world and had to deal with the bullshit.

"You hungry, shorty?" he asked.

"I'm not going out with my hair looking like this. Kemara brought me this outfit but I still feel like a bum," I said and he kissed the back of my hand.

"You look good as fuck to me. Umph, look at these, though, shorty," he said, squeezing my breasts.

"I haven't had sex in a long ass time so don't be touching me like that until I get my pussy waxed," I replied. My legs were hairy, my underarms were hairy and so was my pussy. I was feeling like wolverine. The showers in jail didn't do it for me so I felt dirty, and the soap they gave us irritated my vagina so bad I was scratching my pussy like I had crabs.

"Chill out with that, shorty. It still gets wet, don't it?" he asked and handed me a iPhone with a blingy rhinestone case.

"This is mine?" I asked.

"Yeah, Kemara picked it out. She told me to tell you to call her as soon as you get it. I already stored your friends' phone numbers in there," he said. I dialed Kemara's number and she answered it, yelling into the phone. It brought tears to my eyes because she never left my side. We argued, cursed each other out, but she always had my back.

"BITTTTCHHHHHHHH! Where you at? Tell Pistol to bring you over to my crib ASAP. I cooked so much food for you. Catfish, greens, corn, potato salad, shrimp salad, crab cakes, lobster tails and so much other shit. I bought bottles of 99 Bananas so we can take it back to when we didn't have shit. Remember we used to sit on the step with Silk and drink that? We fittin' to do it again," Kemara said and I got excited.

"I'll be there as soon as I get myself together! Love you, Mara," I said.

"Love you, too, now hurry up. Tell Pistol to give you some dick later 'cause you'll never make it here," she said and hung up.

"Glock is gonna be there," Pistol warned me. One day, when Pistol came to visit me, he told me how Glock got drunk and started tripping on him and Beretta. Kemara told me more about the situation and how Beretta whipped Glock's ass because he was drunk and being disrespectful. It took Beretta two months to talk to Glock again but I was happy they were all back to being brothers.

"Why he gotta be there?" I asked.

"We ain't got shit to hide, so why not?" he replied.

"I'm cool with it as long as it doesn't make you uncomfortable," I said. It was summer time but it was below eighty degrees. I was dying to wear a maxi dress with a plain bun. My hair had grown a lot and reached past my shoulders. The only thing I didn't like about it was that it wasn't thick. My hair was on the thin side which is why I always kept it cut.

"Never dat, baby girl," he said. There was something about the way Pistol drove with the seat all the way back and one hand on the steering wheel. Everything he did was just perfect.

"Oh, yeah, I got something for you," he said. He reached into the back seat and gave me a jewelry box. I opened it up and it was the jewelry set he bought me before I got locked up. The police took it and claimed it was lost. Those muthafuckas knew it cost more than their salaries and was trying to get paid off from it. Pistol got his lawyer involved and had to show proof that he purchased it and it was his. I cried in my cell for a week when the police told Pistol they didn't have it. It meant a lot to me, it was the beginning of our relationship.

"Thank you for everything," I said.

"I gotta thank you, too, because you opened my eyes to a lot of shit and I was able to experience it with you. You had me waiting at the mailbox for those letters and poems you were writing me. That one poem, 'Eat me till I come' was some freaky-ass shit. I had to jerk off five times dat day," he said and I giggled. Everything was perfect except for one thing. I didn't tell Pistol Delonte was his father because my ego wouldn't allow me to look like a slut. Thinking about sleeping with best friends and my man's father was downright trifling, although it wasn't my intention. I had no idea about Delonte's crazy ass but it still wasn't a good look.

"Where we gotta stop at first?" he asked.

"To get a good waxing. Everything else can wait," I replied.

****

Two and a half hours later...

I was inside Pistol's big brick townhouse putting make-up on. The hair cuttery next to the spa clipped my split ends so I could wear a cute high bun. The white and tan off-the-shoulder maxi dress I wore clung to my curves. While we were out, I was able to get a quick pedicure so I could wear sandals. Pistol came up behind me and wrapped his arms around me.

"'When peoples care for you and cry for you, they can straighten out your soul,'" Pistol whispered against my neck.

SOUL Publications

"Langston Hughes," I replied and he kissed me.

"I'm impressed," he chuckled.

It took everything in me not to push him on the bed and ride him until I couldn't take it anymore. When he brought me to his home, he gave me a key and told me it was my home, too. I was amazed at how much stuff he bought and had put up in the closet for me. It seemed as if I was living there the whole time because he had my make-up on the counter in the bathroom along with my hair supplies. A silk robe hung behind the bathroom door with matching fur slippers. I wasn't surprised when he told me Kemara helped him out.

"Yo, you ready? Kemara keeps blowing up my phone," Pistol said.

"Yeah, let's go. I'm getting lit tonight and please don't say nothing to me. I'm smoking big blunts and drinking cheap alcohol," I replied.

"Hoodrat shit," Pistol teased.

I grabbed my purse and we headed downstairs and out the door. Pistol pressed a button on his keys and a garage door came up. Inside the garage was a black Ferrari with purple leather seats and a big purple bow on the hood of the car. I dropped my purse and fell on the ground screaming. Pistol tried pulling me up but my legs were weak.

"Is that mine?" I asked.

"Yeah, you said you wanted one, right?" he asked.

"I was just saying it," I cried.

"Shorty, if you don't get your spoiled ass up," he said. I got up and Pistol brushed the dirt off the back of my dress. Who in the hell said hood niggas couldn't be romantic? My man was everything! He gave me the keys and took the bow off for me.

"I can drive it now?" I asked.

"Yeah, shorty. Drive this muthafucka full speed on some Fast and Furious shit," he said. I got in the driver's seat and he got in and showed me what to push. The engine sounded so beautiful when I started it up.

"Wayment, before you pull off. I gotta put my seatbelt on 'cause this is too much power for you," he said but it was too late. Pistol was holding on to the dash board when I took off down the driveway and did a 360 spin in the middle of the street. He was cursing me out but it was drowned out as the tires screeched.

Welcome back to Naptowne! My fuckin' city! I thought.

****

"What's this place? Kemara lives in D.C. unless she moved and didn't tell me," I said, looking at the three-story historic brick townhouse in Baltimore. It was an area in Baltimore I had never seen before. The streets were quiet and there were small stores on the strip. People were outside eating in front of restaurants and couples of all races were holding hands and eating ice cream. Pistol got out of the car and told me to come on. I got out and followed him up the brick stairs to the row house. The name of the place was called Queen's Den.

"Kemara is waiting for me," I said to Pistol.

"This will only take a second, I promise," he said and opened the door. Everyone screamed "surprise" and I screamed with them. Kemara ran to me and kissed me. She was so excited I don't think she realized she grabbed my face and kissed my lips. Silk and Thickems hugged me, too. There weren't too many people, just GMBAM niggas and their girlfriends.

"Who dat?" Beretta asked, eating a piece of fish while smiling at me.

"Nigga, don't you start dat bullshit! Come over here and give me a hug," I said and hugged him. My welcome home was bigger than I expected. Glock gave me a hug and, surprisingly, I hugged him back, but I was happy with Pistol so there was no reason for me to dislike him.

"Welcome home," Glock said.

"Same to you, too," I smiled.

"Show her around, Pistol, while we set the food out," Kemara said. We walked upstairs to the middle level and it was a huge space with a bar on the side and lounging couches and chairs.

"What is this place? Y'all rented it out for me?" I asked.

"Remember when you told me you wanted your own lounge? Nothing too big, something with a homey vibe to it? Well, I was listening to you. This place is yours. The top level has a small stage for entertainment. Beretta found this spot for me and was able to help me get the liquor license for it and all that. He went half with me because you're loyal to Mara. So, what do you think?" he asked.

"I love it," I replied with butterflies fluttering around in my stomach. There was a bathroom past the bar area so I went inside to get my feelings together. My mascara was running down my face and I couldn't go back out there looking a mess in front of everyone. Pistol came into the bathroom and locked the door. He turned me around and pressed my body against the sink, lifting my dress up to my hips. No words were exchanged, we communicated with our lustful stares. He pushed my thong to the side and picked my leg up. Our hands fumbled across each other while I was unzipping his shorts. He freed himself and there was that big chocolate dick I dreamed about every night in my cell. All I needed was two minutes of him until we got home.

"Damn, shorty, this shit too tight. Hol' on," he said. He used the wetness from my center to rub across his dick head so he could fit better. I closed my eyes and winced in pain from it feeling like I was losing my virginity all over again. Pistol was only half-way in but that was good enough because my legs were shaking from cumming. He placed his hand over my mouth when he drilled my walls.

"Ssshhhh, someone might come up here," he said, hitting my spot. I bit his hand when he sped up to keep from screaming like I was being murdered. We had a lot of great sex, but that was the strongest orgasm I'd ever had. My body was slipping off the sink but it didn't stop Pistol from destroying my guts. He let out a deep groan and I covered his mouth while he pumped his seeds into me.

"I needed dat, shorty," Pistol groaned into the crook of my neck. Reality hit me as I looked around. We were inside the bathroom while people were downstairs waiting for me.

"Now I gotta take a hoe bath," I replied, grabbing paper towels.

"You'll be ight," he replied, fixing his shorts.

About eight minutes later, we were back downstairs and Silk was giving me the side-eye.

"What?" I asked.

"Ummm hmmm, you have been gone for a long time," he said.

"That's because she was gettin' her pussy busted opened," Thickems replied. We went to the back of the home-style restaurant and sat at a table.

"So, spill the tea because I know you floating right now. Your man went above and beyond to make sure everything was perfect. I'm gonna be honest, I wasn't with it at first but, honey, I'm here for it now! I'll even help him pick out a suit for y'all's wedding," Mara said.

"You two do make a beautiful couple," Emma said and I thanked her.

"But, honeyyyyyyy, so much has happened since you left. Glock's wife divorced him, took his kids and moved to Colorado with a white man, chile. It was all over Facebook. I guess her ass couldn't deal with him because he was fucking everything in the city. I wouldn't be surprised if he had something," Silk said, sipping his wine.

"Glock was always a sneaky hoe, but what happened to him? He doesn't look the same," I replied.

"He gained a little weight but being in love be having every nigga looking funny," Mara said. Thickems' phone was going off and she excused herself to talk privately. Silk rolled his eyes and Mara slapped his arm.

"Don't do my friend like dat, Silk," I said. Thickems was my friend and I introduced her to Mara and Silk. The three of us were very close and Emma was cool, too, but she was more Mara's friend and didn't come around me, Silk and Thickems like that. Silk made people feel uncomfortable at times.

"Dat hoe has been fucking with a nigga for over a year and we still have yet to see who the fuck he is!" Silk said.

"Maybe she doesn't want us to know," Mara said.

"Or maybe it's someone in this click's man," Emma said and it caught me off guard.

"Wait a minute, Emma. Thickems ain't like dat," I said, defending her.

"Soon as Thickems got up to walk outside, my man went into the bathroom. This happened a few times while all of us were together. He's lucky I don't know the fuckin' passcode," Emma said.

"Maybe Piper can talk to her since she invited her into the circle," Silk said.

"Thickems isn't like dat. Maybe Quanta is banging someone else. That's a strong accusation to make," I replied.

"Yeah, but women's intuition is a muthafucka," Kemara said, taking her friend's side.

"Mara, you know damn well Thickems ain't like dat," I said, getting agitated with them. Thickems looked out for me when we were stripping at Big Mike's club together when she didn't have to and I'd be forever grateful for her. I wasn't feeling how they were coming at her, especially Emma.

"I'm not saying it's the truth but Emma knows her nigga better than we do, and besides, we don't know how Thickems was before we met her. Yeah, she's our friend, but her and Emma ain't besties so we can't rule it out.

Welcome to the Lowlife 3   Natavia

Now, I don't believe she'd try anything with my nigga or yours," Mara said and Silk agreed.

"Can we just enjoy this time? It's been a while since all of us were able to sit back and talk," I replied. One thing about being locked up is you have to adjust to situations when you come home. It seemed to me my friends were becoming a little judgmental and I didn't know how to feel about that. Thickems came back in and sat next to me. Quanta came out of the bathroom and Emma snatched her purse off the table and left as Quanta ran behind her.

"Ummmm, umph. Let me just sip this wine," Silk said.

"I'll be back," Mara said and got up. Silk got up, too, and they both went outside.

"What happened, what I miss?" Thickems asked.

"Talk to me. What have you been up to? Like really up to? New man?" I asked.

"I'm sorta seeing someone," she admitted.

"Okay, who?" I asked.

"Promise me you won't tell nobody. Mara and Silk have been dying to know but I feel comfortable telling you," she said.

"Who is it?" I asked.

"Quanta," she replied and I almost choked on my drink. Emma was right, they all were right!

"Why would you do dat knowing Emma is Mara's friend and we be around each other?" I said.

"She's cool but she ain't technically my friend and, honestly, I didn't know she was his girl until after we slept together. I met Quanta when I was in Philly over my cousin's house. We were in this club and one thing led to another. Look, Piper, I know it's fucked up but I was lonely and Quanta filled that void. It was supposed to be a fling but it's been a year and a half now, so I don't think I can leave him alone," Thickems said.

"Nooooo, bitch I was just rooting for you! Emma has a feeling y'all fucking around and that's why she left. I told her you ain't dat type but obviously you are. How in da fuck can you smile in her face and fuck her nigga?" I asked.

"Are you judging me now? Come on, Piper. What you did was foul, too, but I supported you because that's what friends do. Did you tell Pistol about Delonte being his father? We all got fuckin' secrets but, anyways, welcome home. I still love you but I'm finally happy with my life," Thickems said. She grabbed her purse and left. I got up from the table and mingled in with the rest of the small crowd. Thickems and her drama wasn't going to stop me from enjoying myself.

Poppa

I woke up to the smell of breakfast cooking coming from downstairs. My head was pounding from partying the night before. I stepped into my pajama pants and went downstairs so I could put something in my stomach. Nika was cooking—well, she was trying to cook. I honestly didn't know why I was there because shorty didn't make me happy. Kemara told me to come back to my family so I could persuade Nika to stay out of GMBAM's business and believe it or not, the shit worked. The bitch didn't bring up nothing about Beretta, Amona, or Kemara. Wesson's bitch-ass got hit with life and it was one of the biggest write-up's I'd seen in the *Capital* newspaper. The gun he had was tied into a lot of murders and they labeled him as a serial killer. Nika got scared after they threw the book at Wesson because the police had no reason to question Beretta. Those niggas were getting richer. Driving Bentleys, buying properties and Beretta was funding a Boys and Girls club for our old hood to give back. Everyone loved that nigga and Nika hated it but there was nothing she could do. My son crawled into the kitchen and I picked him up. Hope was sitting at the table reading a book. Her communication skills were still poor but she was a smart kid. They were the reasons I stayed. I complained about my childhood and how I didn't have parents to guide me and was doing the same shit by neglecting my kids. It didn't stop me from fucking different bitches, though. I was just doing it in a way Nika couldn't find out. Shorty was forty and was back looking young again but it cost hella money. Nika got her body done and you couldn't tell shorty she wasn't hot. We still had a nanny but she went home for the summer to be with her family in Africa.

"Yo, you still can't scramble a fucking egg?" I asked and she smacked her teeth.

"This is for the kids, not you," she replied.

"Cool," I said. I put Omario in his high chair and kissed Hope on the forehead before I made my way upstairs to the bathroom. While I was taking a shower, Jasmine crossed my mind. We hadn't talked since I told her I was going back to Nika. There had been many times I wanted to ask Beretta or the other niggas who were associated with GMBAM that worked inside my strip club how Jasmine was doing. Me and Kemara talked occasionally but I only sent her text messages out of respect because me and her husband still wasn't cool. After a long shower, I got dressed in a wife beater and baller shorts so I could hit the gym. I left out of the house without saying a word to Nika. We had sex once a month, if that. I remember a time when I couldn't go a day without fucking the bitch. It was scorching hot outside and the females were out. Booty shorts, maxi dresses and short skirts were my weakness. I saw a bad-ass broad walking down the strip. It looked like she was on her way to the nail salon.

SOUL Publications

"Aye, shortyyyy!" I called out before she walked into the nail salon. She looked at me and rolled her eyes. I got out of my whip and walked over to her.

"Damn, shorty. What's up witchu?" I asked.

"Nothing, what do you want?" she replied.

"Your name?" I asked.

"Fushia, and yours?" she replied.

"Kamar," I replied and held my hand out to her. I kissed the back of her hand and she blushed a little. She wasn't the type I normally go for because I liked hood girls. Fushia was a little more polished and somewhat plain but she was drop-dead gorgeous and didn't have on any make-up. She had a mole underneath her left eye and her hair was brushed into a high ponytail. I checked out her purse and sandals to feel her out. Fushia was carrying a white Chanel handbag with matching sandals.

"Well, it was nice meeting you but I have a nail appointment," she said.

"Are you free after your appointment?" I asked.

"I might be but come back in an hour and find out for yourself," she said. I opened the door for her and watched her walk in and her ass cheeks were jiggling.

I can't wait to get in them guts, I thought.

I got back in my car and drove a few lights up to where the gym was at. Since I got out of jail a few years ago, I'd been keeping my body in shape. Sometimes, I trained people so they could get in shape, too.

"Good morning, Kamar," a girl at the front desk greeted me.

"What's up?" I asked.

"Nothing much. What's going on witchu? I haven't heard from you since last week," she said. I fucked her in the office last week on a late night after the gym closed. She was the only one working and we were flirting until one thing led to another.

"Yeah, my bad. I've been busy. Maybe you can come through my club later and bring your friends with you. Drinks on me," I replied and she smiled.

"Okay, will do," she said.

Females liked when a nigga was on time, so I worked out for forty-five minutes then left to go meet up with Fushia. I couldn't have Jasmine the way I wanted her, so fuck it. A nigga was out enjoying his twenty-seven years of life and being tied down to one bitch wasn't my thing.

****

I went back to the salon and waited for Fushia on the hood of my car. My Facebook page was booming because a lot of hoes were sending me pictures of their pussy and ass. Some I responded to and some I didn't. Shorties knew I was the nigga with one of the hottest strip clubs in the city. A nigga named Delonte had to sell his club, Fat Cat, because they lost business once my club, Cheeks, opened up. Beretta bought it and turned it into a recreation center. When Fat Cat closed, my club started seeing triple the money and got to the point where Beretta getting his cut no longer hurt my pockets.

A white Jeep Wrangler with white rims pulled up behind my car. I couldn't see the driver because the windows were tinted. The door opened and Jasmine stepped out looking good! Shorty was wearing a short jean romper with tie-up sandals. Her long weave stopped at her hips and the tips of it was blonde. Her pink lipstick matched her pink nails and she had big diamonds in her ears. Her perfume reached my nose while she was hitting the alarm button on her truck. I got off the hood of my car to greet her and she smirked when she saw me.

"You get bigger and bigger every time I see you. What have you been up to?" she asked.

"Nothing, just chilling," I replied and hugged her.

"That's good. Are you staying out of trouble?" she asked.

"Yeah, I ain't fuckin' around. What about you? You still going to school?" I asked.

"Yeah, I'm leaving in a few weeks to go to Atlanta. I'm gonna be in this little hood movie they are filming down there. It's something small but you gotta start from somewhere," she replied.

"I'm proud for you. Where ya man at?" I asked and she rolled her eyes.

"I'm single and happy. But, anyways, it was nice seeing you. I gotta go in here and get my nails done," she replied.

"Ight, be safe," I said.

"You, too," she replied and walked away. Something was still there between us but I knew whatever it was wasn't strong enough for us to be together. Fushia came out of the nail place like she was surprised to see me.

"You're early," she said.

"'Cause I'm interested," I replied.

"That color looks nice on you," I said, talking about her short peach nails.

"Thank you. It's a small deli a few stores down. We can go in there," she said.

"Ight," I replied and followed her.

Fushia ordered a Reuben sandwich and I ordered a veggie wrap with a smoothie.

"Are you a fitness trainer?" she asked.

"Naw, but I do weight training sometimes," I replied. We sat at a table in the corner of the shop and waited for our number to be called.

"Tell me about you. What do you do?" I asked.

"I'm a manager at Neiman Marcus in Chevy Chase and I help out at my father's church during my free time," she said.

"Your Pops a pastor?" I asked.

I bet she's a virgin waiting for a nigga to marry her so he could smash, I thought.

"Yes, he's a pastor. I grew up in a church but I'm not holy if you know what I mean. I still believe in the bible, but I want to live my truth and nobody else's. How old are you and do you have any kids?" she asked.

"I just turned twenty-seven, and I have a boy and a girl," I replied.

"Interesting, you look older. I'm twenty-seven and I have a daughter. She'll be four soon," he said.

"That's what's up. How about her father? He ain't gonna trip about this, is he?" I asked.

"My daughter's father is alllllll over the place. I've been through a lot but the final straw is when I caught my cousin coming out of his apartment. Apparently, they had been fucking for years, even before I came in the picture. But, anyways, we co-parent and I'm fine with that," she said.

"Same here, I'm in my kids' lives but I'm not with their mother," I half-way lied. Me and Nika lived together but we were roommates more than anything. Nika only wanted me there so she wouldn't be a single parent. She had this image she wanted to live out which was a big house, nice cars and businesses. Nika had everything she wanted except for my love. Our number was called and I grabbed our food. Fushia was a cool female so I wasn't trying to come on to her that way so soon. I mean, I still wanted to smash but I had to go about it in a better way. If she was a hoe, I would've kicked some good game to her then invited her to my club so she could get the special treatment. By the end of the night, I would've had her bent over in one of the private rooms.

"Thank you," she said when I sat her food in front of her. We talked and ate, getting to know each other better. I decided to hold off on the pussy because hours later, Fushia was able to open my mind to a lot of things. Her vibe was calming and her giggles were contagious. She sorta reminded me of a bougie-ass nerd, but I also had a feeling she could turn up in the bedroom if she wanted to. We exchanged numbers and I told her I'd text her later before we went our separate ways.

Kemara

"**H**ey, Ms. Baker. How are you doing? I love that dress by the way," I said when I opened the door for her. Ms. Baker checked up on me and Beretta once a month but she always called before she came. She helped us a lot, especially when I had a miscarriage a year ago. Beretta was out of town with Sniper and Jasmine when it happened. I didn't know I was pregnant. Matter of fact, I was getting periods although they were abnormal. It was a painful experience and I didn't know what was going on with me. I was cramping badly, so bad, it caused me to fall down the stairs in my house. I had to crawl to a phone and call 911. Beretta cut his trip short and came home the next day. He was heart-broken when I told him there was a possibility I couldn't give him any kids because of the car accident. All I could think about was us going down that road again after I lost Zyira and I didn't want that, so I asked Ms. Baker to continue seeing us.

"Thank you, Kemara. I bought this little thing for ten bucks at Marshalls. It's quiet in here. Are you the only one home?" she asked.

"Yes, Z'wan took our daughter to the park," I replied.

We went into the living room and sat on the couch. There were refreshments on the coffee table, like cookies, homemade lemonade and small sandwich rolls.

"Your home belongs in a Better Homes magazine. It's so lovely," she said and I thanked her.

"So, how is everything? You look great and your skin is glowing," she said.

"I'm fine. I had a nightmare last night. It was about five o'clock in the morning when I woke up sweating. I wasn't able to go back to sleep," I replied.

"Tell me about this nightmare," she replied and crossed her legs.

"I was walking down this dark hallway and I could hear someone walking behind me but nobody was there. There were these doors, and every time I opened one, I ended up right back in that dark hallway again. It's sorta like my life. No matter what I do, I always end up in a dark place. I'm happy now but it never lasts," I replied.

"Nothing lasts forever. Our happiness is only temporary sometimes but we seem to focus on losing happiness instead of gaining it back. You were looking for a way out in your dream by opening doors. You can't run from whatever is chasing you. All we need is light on our situations to help guide us down the dark hallways and reveal the problems that are chasing us," she said.

"That makes sense. I keep assuming Z'wan will leave me if I don't give him a baby. Lately, I have been trying to get pregnant and every time I think I am, I take a test and it tells me it's negative. He didn't say it but sometimes I wonder if he still blames me for the accident and the reason why I'm not fertile. All I want to do is give him a baby. I'm tired of being let down. I got back on birth control to keep myself from taking pregnancy tests," I said.

"So, you're trying to find a way out instead of facing the problem?" she asked.

"I'm doing it to keep myself from being let down," I replied.

"But you're also keeping yourself from finding out the truth. Shed some light on this situation, baby. You're stopping a blessing from happening. You could be pregnant right now but you wouldn't know because you cheated yourself out of the truth. Those nightmares are your conscious and they won't go away unless you face your fear the natural way. How does Z'wan feel about the birth control?" she asked.

"He agreed because he was tired of getting excited for no reason," I replied.

"That's not a way to solve a problem like this. Have you tried a fertility clinic or went to someone who could look further inside of you? That doctor could've told you that from assumption. Maybe your womb needs to heal completely. What if it's not permanent? You should've looked further into it," she said.

"I know that but I'm scared. I don't think I'm ready to hear that I can't have kids. I'm only twenty-four and to hear those words would ruin my life and my marriage," I replied.

"You gotta let that mentality go because problems don't go away if they aren't being solved. With the technology we have today, you can go other routes but you got to figure out what's really going on before you make that decision," she said.

"We talked about a lot of stuff and you know how I feel about things. Nothing ever works in my favor so I feel like they will tell me I'm damaged and can't have kids at all. My husband gives me so much love, support and he makes me feel beautiful by the way he looks at me. Till this day, the man still gives me a bad case of butterflies and I want him to feel appreciated by giving him something he really wants," I replied.

"And that's why you must find out the truth because he deserves to know the answer. He might be upset, sad or even angry but we must appreciate the truth instead of living a lie," she said and I agreed. Ms. Baker stayed for another hour before she left. She was a big relief and I could always talk to her about things my friends wouldn't understand. I looked at the time on the clock on the wall and it was going on two o'clock in the afternoon. Silk was having a cookout in Newtowne on the old baseball field and I promised him I was going to help out.

****

SOUL Publications

Three hours later...

"Oh, no you don't! Cockroach Loretta ain't gettin' a damn thing from here. You better not fix her a hotdog," Silk said to me.

"Stop it, Silk. How in the hell you gonna have a cookout for the hood but don't want nobody to have a damn plate? Go have a seat and let me do this," I replied. I was behind a white picnic table fixing plates for everyone. Piper was making drinks and Thickems was handing out cotton candy to the kids. The violence wasn't as bad as it used to be and kids were able to play outside in front of their buildings without getting hit by a stray bullet.

"First of all, you know these crackheads ain't gonna do nothing but take their plates back to the streets and sell them for five dollas. Hell, I need to start charging since they making money off of our money. You can't be nice to these muthafuckas. Look at her, that bitch trying to steal the cooler," Silk said. When I turned around, a fiend was trying to wheel one of our coolers away.

"PUT IT BACK!" I yelled out to her. Carlos was walking down the street and snatched it out of her hand.

"Ma, what da fuck are you doin'?" he asked the woman.

"Wait, Carlos's mother looks that bad?" I asked Silk.

"I heard she got da bug, honey. That nigga she was dealing with got her strung out," Silk said. Carlos reached into his pocket and gave his mother some money. She snatched it away from him and disappeared around the corner of the building. He came over and hugged me. At fourteen years old, he was taller than me. Maybe it was his upbringing but Carlos looked around eighteen years old.

"What's good, Mara. You look nice," he said.

"Thank you. Are you staying out of trouble?" I asked.

"A lil' bit," he said.

"Tell Mara how you were driving around in dat stolen Range Rover wit' yah lil' bad ass," Silk said.

"Nigga, shut yah gay ass up. I wasn't talkin' to you," he said to Silk.

"Bitch, I'll beat your lead paint havin' ass like you stole sumthin. Keep on fuckin' with me, yah hear? Little bad-ass fucker," Silk said.

"I can't stand dat overgrown female-ass nigga," Carlos said.

"Have some respect, Carlos. Make yourself useful and go help Thickems out with the cotton candy," I said.

"Ight, I'm only doing it for you, though," he said and bopped off.

"He reminds me of Beretta," I chuckled and Silk rolled his eyes.

"He'll be lying under a white sheet before he turns twenty-one. Hell, probably sooner than that. All these lil' boys around his age is scared of him and you can't tell these lil' girls nothing. Cockroach Loretta's daughters were throwing down in the middle of the street last week fighting over Carlos. Apparently, he was fuckin' both of them," Silk said.

"You lying," I said.

"Umph, that's what you think. What time is it, my friend is supposed to be here?" Silk said. Silk was seeing someone who we hadn't met yet. He was messing around with Delonte's friend but he cut Wylee off when that shit went down between Delonte and Piper. I didn't know what Silk was doing to these females and males but they all couldn't leave him alone. Wylee was stalking Silk, sending flowers to his job and buying him a lot of name-brand stuff. It all stopped when Silk called Wylee's job and told them a lawyer from their branch was stalking him and threatening his life.

"We finally get to meet your friend? About damn time because you and Thickems were getting too secretive for me," I replied and he rolled his eyes.

"That bitch is fuckin' Emma's man and I'on give a damn what anybody say," he said. I was suspecting the same thing but I kept it to myself because I wasn't sure. Emma knew her man better than we did so I couldn't see her assuming it was Thickems out of all people for no reason.

"Time will tell but let's hope we're all wrong," I said. Emma pulled up in the parking lot. I walked over to her truck to help her with the sodas. We were running out so she went to the store to get more.

"It's soooo damn hot out here," Emma said.

"Tell me about it," I replied.

Beretta pulled up with Zalia in the back seat. He told me to get Zalia out of her car seat and he grabbed the sodas. I opened the back door and Zalia was a mess! Her hair was all over her head and her clothes were dirty.

"What in the hell," I said.

"Let it go, shorty. Zalia was playing and I let her do her thing. You be scared to let her have fun because you don't want her getting dirty. Stop buying her expensive clothes 'cause all she's gonna do is fuck it up anyway," he complained.

"But you knew we were coming to a cookout," I said.

"So, these kids around here running around the same way. Look, she doesn't even know she look a mess," Beretta said. I wanted to laugh because he was right. Zalia was smiling and trying to talk to Emma.

"Heyyy, pretty girl," Emma said to Zalia and tickled her stomach.

"Hi," Zalia waved. Zalia was around three years old, I assumed. I didn't know her exact birthday, so we always celebrated on the day I brought her home which was two years ago. A two-door BMW pulled up next to Beretta's car and it was Sniper's girlfriend, Kellan. She got out of her car wearing coochie cutters and a half-top.

"MARRAAAAAAA," she sang and hugged me.

"Sniper let you out the house like that?" I joked and she twirled around.

"Sometimes, I have to be a little bad girl. He'll show his ass later," Kellan said.

"Maybe I should start showing off my ass," Emma mumbled as we walked down the sidewalk.

"Where is Zain?" I asked Kellan.

"Who knows. She doesn't come out much since her and Machete broke up. I hate Machete for what he did to my sister. How in the hell he have a baby on her and expect her to deal with it? Niggas are sick," Kellan said. I didn't know too much about Machete's situation but I did know Zain was creeping with Machete when he was with Jasmine. Jasmine and Zain couldn't be in the same room and when they were, Jasmine didn't stay around long. She really hung out with the guys while all the girlfriends hung out with each other. We were all like family despite the drama. Zalia wanted to get down when she saw Amber so I let her go on the playground and sat on a bench to keep an eye on her. Emma sat next to me and I noticed the bags under her eyes. She wasn't the same jolly person anymore.

"Talk to me, Emma," I said.

"I've come to the conclusion that Quanta doesn't love me. I have dealt with so much of his shit. I went against my parents for him and everything else I believed in. This lifestyle ain't for me, but I love him, so I dealt with it. I have been kidnapped, beat up and almost raped, and do you think he cares? He's a piece of shit," she said.

"Leave him," I replied.

"I know but it's not easy to walk away from a man you gave years to. I have been with him since I was eighteen years old, fresh out of high school. Honestly, I feel stuck in this," she said.

"You want me to give you Ms. Baker's number? She helped me and Beretta a lot. Give Quanta an ultimatum: he can either go to counseling with you or you'll leave him and not look back. If he loves you, he'll try to fix it. But, if he comes up with an excuse as to why he can't get counseling then you'll have your answer," I replied.

"I admire you. You're a strong woman and I know sometimes you don't see it, but others do," she said.

"Awwww, don't make me get emotional," I replied and hugged her.

"I'm mushy, you know that," she giggled.

Emma didn't belong in our circle. Growing up in the hood was one thing, but to be pulled into a lifestyle you're not accustomed to is another thing. I noticed on a few occasions, Emma would act like one of the hood girls when she was around me and my friends. I told her to be herself but she thought they wouldn't accept her if she did. Emma was worried about them thinking she was too good to be there. Her parents had money and lived in the suburbs and that wasn't something to be ashamed of but she was because of the lifestyle her man exposed her to. I had to tell her that we all wished we had the type of upbringing she had and to appreciate it. It made me think of Ammo and Swan. Swan was like Emma, they had the same background. I'd never forget the day she warned me about GMBAM. She said they'd change me and that they were all the same, down to the cheating. Ammo turned Swan into a conniving female and she was the reason why he was dead. Someone was going to get hurt and I prayed it wasn't Emma.

While we were talking, Silk and Piper brought us over some mixed drinks.

"Where is your date?" Emma asked Silk.

"This fool knows damn well he ain't dating nobody," Piper said.

"Go directly to jail. Do not pass go, do not collect two hundred dollas," Silk said to Piper and she mushed him.

"Is that Monopoly?" Emma asked.

"Yup, 'cause this hoe thinks it's a game. She betta stop fuckin' with me." Silk rolled his eyes. A Dodge Charger pulled up in the parking lot blasting Future's song "No Love." A young and cute light-skinned boy stepped out wearing a jersey, shorts and Jordans with a fitted cap. His long hair was in two braids and Silk waved him over.

"Wait a minute, that's you?" Piper asked and we were all staring.

"Yes, bitch, nah. What you thought?" he asked. The boy came over and hugged Silk but I noticed something. The boy had breasts! I almost fell off the bench because I wanted to laugh so hard I had to pee. Silk was really a stone-cold freak and didn't discriminate.

"Y'all this is Roneisha. Roneisha, these are my good-good girlfriends," Silk said proudly. Piper laughed and it made us all laugh.

"Bitch, stop being rude," Silk said and popped Piper on the back of her head.

"I'm sorry, Silk, but we're confused. You're dating a lesbian?" I asked.

"I'm bi-sexual," Roneisha said.

"We're both bi-sexual. It's spontaneous and I love it. We met on a dating website for people like me and we have been hitting it off ever since. I brought her here so I could tell y'all we are in a relationship and moving in together," Silk said.

"Chilleeeeeee. So, who is getting pregnant this time?" Piper asked and I wanted to scream. Emma's face was red with tears in her eyes. She had her mouth covered with her hand but we could still hear her squeals from laughing. It was the funniest thing I'd ever seen. Silk was dressed in tight shorts with a half-top and his girlfriend was dressed like a man, but I was happy as long as he was happy.

"Nice to meet you, Roneisha, and don't pay us no mind. You're family now and this is what we do all day, talk shit to each other," I said. I stood up to hug her and she squeezed me a little too hard.

"This da pretty one with da big ass, right?" Roneisha whispered to Silk and I hurriedly pulled away from her.

"Yeah, that's my sexy Mara," Silk said.

"I smell swingers," Piper said.

"That's the stripper and this is the nerd who can't twerk," she said about Piper and Emma.

"SILK!" I yelled, because he gave Roneisha messed up descriptions about us.

"Where is the one who doesn't have her son?" Roneisha whispered to Silk.

"She over there by the grill," he whispered back.

"Oh, hell nawl. Your man-girl is messier than you," Piper said and Silk blushed.

SOUL Publications

"Chileeeee, ain't she wonderful. Let's walk over here so I can introduce you to everyone else," Silk said and grabbed his girlfriend's hand.

"Why shit like this wanna happen after I stop popping pills?" Piper asked.

"What just happened?" Emma asked, trying to breathe.

"Silk found someone who is very compatible and I don't like it," Piper said.

"Be happy for him," I giggled.

"I would love to be a fly on the wall when they fuck. I'm gonna have front row seats at their baby shower," Piper said.

"I think Silk is the man and she's the woman when it comes down to that. Silk might be feminine but he deep strokes like a straight-up nigga. He showed me a video and I was bothered," I replied.

"Roneisha will be pregnant soon. Silk is a fucking freak and they will be living together, too. This is some good drama. My release from jail has been a very great one. Let me have dat," Piper said and took my drink. Pistol walked over to Piper and whispered something in her ear. She fanned herself when he walked away then guzzled down the rest of her drink. Piper was drunk and high.

"Well, I'll be back. I gotta go to Pistol's truck and get sumthin," she said and scurried away.

"She gone to get some dick," I said and Emma agreed.

****

It was ten o'clock by the time I made it home. I didn't waste no time putting Zalia in the tub. She was sound asleep by the time I put her pajamas on. Beretta was still out so I took a bath to relax. Suddenly, my eyelids got heavy and I dozed off...

"Mara! Wake up," Beretta said and I opened my eyes.

"Huh, what happened?" I asked.

"Yo, I was tryna call you but you weren't answering. Emma is in the hospital," he said.

"WHAT!" I screamed.

"I took Quanta home because the nigga was too drunk to drive. We found Emma on the floor," he said. I rushed out the tub and my body was still wet.

"What da fuck happened? We were just together," I said with my hands shaking as I threw some clothes on.

"After you left the cookout, some shit went down. Thickems and Emma got into it and Thickems told her she was pregnant by Quanta. That nigga got pissy drunk afterwards," he said.

"Emma left before I did," I replied.

"But she came back 'cause Quanta wasn't answering her phone calls. Go see about your friend and I'll stay here with Zalia," he said. I looked at the clock on the wall and it was going on one o'clock.

"Call me when you get there and let me know what's up," Beretta said. I kissed his lips then grabbed my keys and rushed out the door. Tears fell from my eyes because she was going through a lot, probably more than what she told me. It took me almost forty minutes to get to the hospital. I rushed into the emergency room and her parents were sitting in the corner. Her mother had tears in her eyes. Quanta was sitting in the corner looking lost and I wanted to put a bullet in his head.

"How is Emma? What happened?" I asked her mother.

"You all are what happened! Emma was fine until she started hanging out with ghetto trash. My baby was a good girl and y'all poisoned her!" she yelled at me.

"Emma is my friend," I said and her mother stood up and got in my face.

"Her real friends are in law and medical school. My daughter isn't the same and it's because of you and that piece of shit right over there. Leave and don't come back. You two can't visit her and I already informed the hospital that we are the only ones who are allowed to go back," she said. I was always being reminded of the ghetto I came from no matter what I did with my life.

"You ain't gotta talk to her like dat!" Quanta said when he walked over to us. Emma's father got in Quanta's face and they started arguing. I knew it was serious when Quanta threatened to put a bullet in his dome.

"Nigga, fuck you! Let's walk outside so you can tell me dat shit!" Quanta said to Emma's father.

"Let's just go before they call the cops," I said to Quanta. We walked outside and I let him have it after he told me Emma had a heart attack.

"Yung, you don't know me! Fuck all of dat shit you're saying," he said.

"Nigga, I don't have to know you, but I know Emma! I was there when she caught you over your sister's friend's house a few years ago and she took you back because she thought you changed. You knocked up Thickems? Someone she hung around? What in the fuck you thought was going to happen? Then y'all were being spiteful in her face. Muthafucka, I ain't gotta know you to know you're a punk bitch! I hope she fucks and sucks the next nigga she meets so good that'll it make her forget about your whack ass, bitch! Fuck you! It's because of you why her parents don't want me around. You ruined her life and almost killed her. You don't deserve to breathe and take Thickems' hoe ass with you when you die," I said. Quanta got in his truck and sped off.

SOUL Publications

****

Beretta was sitting on the couch when I came home. I told him everything that was happening and I got mad when he admitted to knowing about Quanta and Thickems.

"You knew and didn't tell me?" I asked and pulled away from him.

"Everyone knew, Mara, shit I thought maybe you knew, too. And why would I snitch on my nigga? That ain't my business," Beretta said.

"She had a heart attack," I replied.

"I'm sorry dat happened but it ain't shit we can do about it," Beretta said.

"So, that's it? GMBAM sticking together like dat? Quanta not even GMBAM," I replied.

"Yo, you know Quanta is GMBAM. What you think I was gonna put a nigga on who ain't? And it's not about dat, my business is in this household and not nobody else's," he said.

"Y'all are sumthin else when it comes down to cheating," I replied.

"Yo, don't take your frustrations out on me. You think I give a fuck about what the next nigga doing with his dick.

The only way I would care is if one of my niggas was fucking you and that ain't happening," he said.

"I guess you wouldn't understand because the woman always has to carry the burden when the nigga cheats. I'm fuckin' disgusted," I said and walked upstairs. Truthfully, there wasn't nothing Beretta could do but I was still angry. He came into the bedroom and got in bed. I took off my clothes and got in bed with him. Beretta was sleeping peacefully but I couldn't sleep. All I kept thinking about was Emma and the conversation we had at the cookout. I wished I would've stayed so she wouldn't have had to go home alone with that type of pain. Another woman was carrying her man's child and that was the type of betrayal that could kill someone.

****

I left the house while Beretta was getting Zalia's breakfast together. He thought I was going to the grocery store, which I was, but I had to make a stop first. Thirty minutes later, I was pulling up in Thickems' neighborhood. I got out of my truck and walked into her building. It was fucked up what she did and how she did it. I accepted her into my circle and the least she could've done was be a woman about the situation. Fucking my friend's man was one thing but a baby was on a whole other level. I banged on her door and seconds later she opened it.

"Hey, Mara, what are you doing here?" she asked, closing the door.

"You pregnant by Quanta?" I asked.

"I guess everyone knows now," she said and sat on the couch.

"Bitch, you don't even have your son by Ammo like that, so what are you going to do with another baby?" I asked.

"Bitch? Mara don't come over here with yah bullshit because you don't know how I'm feeling right now," she said.

"I hope you feel like shit! How would you feel if Emma was fucking Ammo if he was alive? But what gets me is that you really don't give a fuck about what you did. What happened to you? You're still trying to fill Ammo's shoes?" I asked.

"And what is wrong with that? Everyone is happy and shit. Who do I have?" Thickems yelled.

"YOUR SON!" I yelled back at her.

"Go home, Mara. Go home to your husband and be happy in your palace. Your man is alive, even after all the grimy shit he did. Why did Ammo deserve to die and not Beretta? You think Ammo didn't tell me shit? Beretta gets away with everything," she said.

"You sound like a rat. What goes on in GMBAM, stays there, bitch! Ammo should've told you that, too. And since we're taking it there, only the strong survive and the weak get caught. Ammo was still fucking Swan and she set him up. Are you mad because Beretta didn't get caught up with Amona and Moesha? You know, I felt sorry for you back then because I thought you didn't know about Swan but something tells me you did and if so, you got him killed for fucking another bitch's man. Niggas enjoy side pussy until they get caught. You'll be a single mother to two kids. And you wanna know what else? Quanta might be a cheater but he ain't dumb enough to leave a woman who knows everything about his life. You know the game and you know that's why Ammo didn't leave Swan because she had too much dirt on him. Quanta is stuck with Emma," I said.

"Well, at least you admit to why Beretta is still with you being as though you can't have any kids. I bet he wishes Moesha's baby was his now. You're stuck, too, Mara, so let's not make this personal," Thickems said. All I saw was a dark cloud when I pulled my knife out of my pocket. I jabbed it into her leg and she was ready to scream.

"You make one sound and I'll slit your fuckin' throat. Bitch, I fought for you against Ammo's family while I was carrying a child, so watch what you say. You don't know me like that and I don't give a fuck how many times you came to my house. I'll kill you twice," I replied and turned the knife into her leg. Tears fell from her eyes while she held her leg. I snatched the knife away then wiped the blood on her robe.

"Have a nice day and you already know what happens to snitches. You wanna play dirty then get ready for a mud bath because, bitch, we are enemies now. Don't say shit to me when you see me and I mean that," I said, then left out of her condo. Thickems didn't have to worry about me again because I was done with her. A woman messing with someone else's man was something I couldn't stomach, especially since I'd been through it before. Knowing your man shared intimate moments with another is enough to make a sane person explode. Thickems probably didn't care what she was doing to Emma, but she damn sure knew the consequences, and I hoped she got all the karma that was coming her way.

Piper

Two months later...

Mara, Kellan and Silk helped out at Queen's Den during the week and Earlene did all the cooking. I told myself I wasn't getting anybody I didn't know to work at Queen's Den since I wanted it to be a family thing. I wouldn't have been able to get anything done if it wasn't for Kemara. She was more organized than me and stayed on top of ordering the things we needed as far as food, liquor and other supplies. She was also keeping track of the money. I didn't want to overwork her because she did the same thing for Beretta by making sure his businesses' books were accurate. On top of that, she was still going to school and I always told her to go home but she would bring Zalia with her and spend the day helping me out. Pistol talked me into letting Kellan help out with the bar area because she was a bartender a while back for a sports bar. I didn't know how true it was but I heard Sniper told her he wasn't giving her no money until she got a job because she had an outrageous shopping problem. Kellan was cool but she was too loud and ghetto at times. We all were but she didn't know how to turn hers off. Thickems and Mara weren't speaking. Matter of fact, Thickems refused to be anywhere near Mara so she called me every now and then. They didn't tell me much about their falling out other than they got into an argument about Emma. I couldn't believe she was pregnant by Quanta, and after the situation with Emma being hospitalized, Quanta was ducking Thickems. Thickems called me crying when Quanta paid her to get an abortion but she refused it so he told her he was done. There was nothing I could do but listen to her vent whenever she called because she put herself in that situation.

"When are you going to perform one of your poems?" Mara asked while setting drinks on a tray Kellan made.

"They are reserved for Pistol," I said.

"Girllll, if you don't get your ass up on stage and give us some beautiful words," she replied.

"I'm shy," I said.

Mara passed Silk the tray and he took it to a table with four college students. Queen's Den wasn't far from a library, so a lot of college students hung around. Some of them even had little study groups inside my lounge and what I loved about it was that it was multicultural. Earlene came from the back with two plates of sandwiches and fries and Mara took it to a couple sitting in the corner.

"This place came along well. I'm proud of you," Earlene said.

"I can't take all the credit. Everyone pitched in to help," I replied.

"Now all you have to do is get married and give me some nieces and nephews. Zalia ain't gonna be a baby for long," Earlene said.

"Me and Pistol didn't talk about that yet," I replied.

"It's coming, I can tell. That smart-mouth muthafucka ain't never bring a woman around his family. Not even that girl he called himself living with. What's her name again? The one who was killed in a home robbery or sumthin," she said.

"Lezzi," I replied.

"Yeah, her. I had to find out about her at the hair salon," she said.

The phone rang behind the small bar and I answered it.

"Queen's Den," I said. I had to work on sounding professional because sometimes I answered the phone like it was my cell phone. The caller hung up and I shrugged it off. As soon as I put it back down on the receiver, it rang again.

"Queen's Den," I answered.

"Piper, is that you?" the caller asked.

"Who is this?" I asked.

"You don't recognize my voice? It's Delonte," he said and I got nauseated. Delonte was the past and I wanted him gone.

"What in da fuck are you calling me for?" I asked.

"So we can talk. We ended up on the wrong foot and I just wanted to apologize for sending you to jail. Well, my wife was the one who called the cops. Listen, I live in the area and perhaps we can go somewhere and have lunch," he said.

"Bitch, suck an AIDS dick and die!" I said and hung up.

"Who was that?" Mara asked from behind me.

"Delonte," I said.

"What did his punk ass want? How did he know you were here?" she asked.

"Probably my Facebook page. I have been doing a lot of advertisement on there. He said he lives in the area," I replied.

"You gotta tell Pistol. Delonte lost his club and Beretta bought it. He might be on some sneaky shit," she said.

"I'll have to tell Pistol Delonte is his father," I replied.

"Take it from a bitch who knows about keeping secrets. It's best to tell him before another source tells and gets it all screwed up," Mara said.

"But my reputation is on da line," I replied, getting light-headed. All I wanted was for Delonte to go away. He popped up at a time when I was happily in love. The nerve of that punk-ass bitch.

"People gonna think what they want and you know that," Mara said.

"I'm gonna tell him," I replied.

"And we can jump him if he acts like he doesn't want you anymore," she said and winked at me.

Jesus give me strength, I thought.

****

Pistol was pulling up in the driveway the same time I pulled up. It was one o'clock in the morning and I was exhausted from being on my feet all day. He opened the car door for me and the heels I was wearing were making my feet hurt badly.

"Yo, you good? Why you don't wear flat shoes or those round shoes with the little heel," he said, talking about kitten heels.

"Eww, I'm not wearing those. You know I gotta look good while I'm working but Lord knows I wanna wear some shorts and a half top," I said and he shook his head.

"Dats what you think," he said, helping me out of the car. He unlocked the front door and deactivated the alarm so it wouldn't go off. I kicked my heels off and went straight to the living room. My body sank into the plush couch and I was ready to close my eyes.

"You bring me home sumthin to eat?" he asked.

"Oh shit, I forgot," I replied.

"Cool, I'll fix myself a sandwich then for the tenth time," he said and I opened my eyes.

"Wait, you mad?" I asked.

"Naw, I understand you be busy and shit but all I'm asking is for some leftovers or something. I be starving when I come home. You know I smoke kush all day and be having the munchies," he said.

"I'll fix you a sandwich," I replied, feeling bad. It was hard trying to juggle between the lounge and Pistol. It was something I always dreamed of having and I was doing everything I could to make Queen's Den perfect. My lounge wasn't big or bringing in a lot of money yet, but it could get there with hard work and dedication. The fridge was empty and the only thing left was a carton of orange juice and a stick of butter.

"We don't have any food," I said, ashamed.

SOUL Publications

"It's been like dat for a while. I be busy and you be busy, so nobody got time to go to the store, although grocery shopping ain't my thing," Pistol said.

"I'll go tomorrow morning," I replied.

"You said that yesterday and the day before. I'll ask Earlene if she could swing by the store for me, it ain't a big deal," he said.

"You betta not ask her. I said I'll do it," I replied and he shrugged his shoulders. I searched the cabinets and found two cans of salmon. We had bread so I figured I could make him salmon cakes. My man did so much for me and all I could do was fix him some dry salmon cakes because I didn't have all the ingredients.

"Pistol!" I called out to him but he didn't answer. I called out to him again and still no answer. He was stretched out on the couch, so I woke him up.

"I fixed you some salmon cakes," I said and he sat up. He went to the hall bathroom to wash his hands then came back to the living room. He stared at the dry cakes on the plate and hard bread.

"Yo, I bet you ate betta than this when you were locked up. Damn, shorty, I don't want to offend you but how I'm supposed to eat this?" he asked.

"I tried," I replied. He bit into the salmon cake and I covered my mouth because he started choking. I ran to the fridge and grabbed the orange juice and he guzzled it down.

"I'll order something. The pizza place stops delivering at two so we got time," he said and my stomach growled. Pizza loaded with sausage, sardines, onions, peppers and chicken sounded so good. I told Pistol what I wanted and he gave me the side-eye.

"What?" I asked.

"When you start eating sardines?" he asked.

"A week ago. Oh, and tell them to add mushrooms," I said, rubbing my hands together.

"You hate mushrooms," he said.

"Nigga, just order the pizza," I replied.

"You betta eat all dat shit, too. I hope you shit yah self tomorrow while you're stuck in traffic, too," he chuckled. I went upstairs to take a shower. There wasn't any more shower gel so I went underneath the sink to get a bar of Dove soap. I noticed I had a box of tampons and a pack of pads I hadn't used. I was home for over two months and hadn't gotten a period.

Ohhhhh shit! I stopped taking birth control when I got locked up. What if I'm pregnant? Damn it! I'm still getting settled in, I thought. If I was pregnant, it explained my crazy appetite and nausea throughout the day. My nerves were all over the place. Pistol still didn't know about Delonte and then there was a possibility I was pregnant. I got emotional when I remembered the two times I had been pregnant and got an abortion. The first time was at sixteen by Poppa then the second time by Glock. They said the third time was a charm but I damn sure wasn't getting rid of my baby, although I wasn't ready. Pistol came into the bathroom and saw me sitting on the floor naked.

"What's good? Why you cryin'?" he asked.

"I have been home for over two months and haven't gotten a period," I replied. He sat on the toilet seat and didn't say anything for a while. I was getting worried that he was going to tell me he didn't want a baby. Matter of fact, Pistol never talked about having kids.

"So, you don't want it if you are?" he asked.

"No, I'm not saying it like that," I said.

"Da fuck you crying for then?" he asked.

'Cause if I'm pregnant that means I slept with my baby's grandfather, I thought. I pushed Pistol off the toilet seat and threw-up as soon as I lifted the lid. After I was finished, I stepped into the shower and the doorbell rang. Pistol went downstairs to get our pizza. Ten minutes later, I was out the shower and drying off. Pistol brought the box of pizza upstairs and it bothered me he was eating on clean sheets.

"I changed the sheets this morning and the grease is dripping," I said.

"Shorty, climb up on this bed and eat this pizza. It doesn't taste that bad with sardines. Maybe 'cause I'm hungry as shit, too," he said, folding big slices in half and eating it like a sandwich. He passed me a slice and I bit into it.

"Ummmmm," I said, chewing with my eyes closed.

"I'm gonna be fucked up in the morning, but we need to talk. I wanna know how you feel about this if you're knocked up," he said.

"I wanna keep it," I replied and he smirked.

"Good, 'cause I would've body slammed you if you said otherwise. Lately, I have been thinking about starting a family but I wasn't expecting it to be this soon. I'm not saying I'm mad, though. You know you're special to me, right?" he asked, cupping my chin so I could look him the eyes.

"Yeah, I know," I replied.

"And we gonna raise our seed together no matter what because I didn't have a father or mother in my life. I don't want to be like them muthafuckas," Pistol said.

"We'll be better than our parents," I replied.

Twelve minutes later, the box of pizza was gone and I was stuffed like a pig. Pistol took a shower then came back to bed with me. My stomach was bubbling and a fart slipped out onto his leg while were lying in a spooning position. Sweat beads formed on my forehead because I was hoping he didn't smell it but he did.

"Yo, what da fuck is that?" he asked, lifting up the covers. I was hella embarrassed.

"I farted," I replied and he fell out. Pistol's deep laugh echoed throughout the room.

"Nigga, that's not funny," I said.

"Them buns jamming," he chuckled.

"Oh hush! I got gas, shat! You know cheese messes me up sometimes," I said. He got out of bed and sprayed air freshener.

"Yoooo, you smell worse than Ammo and that nigga gave me asthma," Pistol said.

"You too pretty to fart like dat," he said and I gave him the finger.

Pistol got back in bed and wrapped his arms around me. I melted into his chest, and as crazy as it might sound, it was the safest place on Earth. He was the best thing that ever happened to me and I would've never known it if Glock didn't get locked up. Sometimes you got to put your pride to the side and realize how things happen for a reason. I call them blessings in disguise.

****

I made a doctor's appointment as soon as I woke up and I only had an hour to get dressed. Pistol tossed a screen tee and a pair of leggings on the bed.

"What are you doing?" I asked.

"Yo, I know you. You'll take all day if you picked out your own shit and I'm tryna get there in the next twenty minutes," he said. He was anxious to find out if I was pregnant or not. I took a quick shower and got dressed in the outfit he laid out for me. It was late-September, so I needed a jean jacket. Pistol was already dressed and rushing me while I was putting on my shoes.

"Nigga, you about to get slapped. I'm tired, shat!" I fussed.

"Shut yo ass up. You tired 'cause you had gas all night," he chuckled and I rolled my eyes. He wasn't lying about that because I had it bad. So bad, he went downstairs to sleep. My stomach was sensitive to dairy products. Five minutes later, Pistol was practically pulling me out the door.

An hour later, we were sitting in the doctor's office and I had to fill out new forms. I was nervous and my heart was beating fast.

"You nervous?" he asked.

"Yeah, a little. Everything is happening so fast," I said.

"That's 'cause your life was on pause when you got locked up. Don't trip, baby girl. We gonna be straight. If you ain't knocked up then we can use protection til' you ready. Naw, neva mind about dat 'cause I need to feel everything," he said. A nurse called my name and we went to the back. I had to pee in a cup before they put us in a room. Pistol was making a few phone calls and I was texting Mara about it. She called me right up and started screaming in my ear.

"Aren't you supposed to be in class?" I asked.

"Honey, I walked out! Bitcchhhh, you got knocked up at your welcome home party, huh? Those eggs were waiting for dat nut," Kemara said.

"Filter your mouth, Mara," I laughed.

"Not today! I'm excited. Ohhhh, I'm gonna be a god mommy. Text me as soon as you find out. I gotta get back to class, love you. Oh, and tell Pistol's big head ass, congrats, too," she said and hung up.

"Mara loud as shit," Pistol said.

There was a knock on the door before the doctor came in and just like I expected, I was knocked up. He told me to get undressed and gave me a gown so he could examine me. Pistol couldn't stop smiling during the sonogram. I was going on ten weeks. My blood pressure was a little high so the doctor gave me a small packet on eating healthier and prenatal care. Once the doctor left, I texted Mara a picture of the sonogram.

"Let me see that packet," Pistol said and I rolled my eyes.

"Oh, you really about to show yah ass now, huh?" I asked.

"Yeah, I'll go to the grocery store from now on," he replied.

Great, this nigga about to have me eating spinach sandwiches with miracle whip, I thought. But I wasn't complaining. I'd do anything for a healthy baby.

One month later...

It was the end of October and we were having a Halloween party at the lounge. I was dressed up like Tinkerbell and Pistol was Jason. Beretta's crazy ass was Mike Myers and Machete was dressed up as Leatherface from the Texas Chainsaw movie. After seeing their costumes, I wasn't surprised to see Sniper as Freddy Krueger. Kemara was Queen Cleopatra. Silk was dressed as RuPaul and his girlfriend, Roneisha, was supposed to be Beyoncé. I almost went into premature labor when they walked through the door. Roneisha had a banging body but she hid it underneath baggy clothes. We thought Silk was lying when he said she had a phat ass.

"Look at dat bitch dancing on my nigga?" Kellan said. Sniper was chilling on the couch and some girl wearing a naughty nun costume was grinding on Sniper's dick like they were fucking.

"Don't start no shit, Kellan. I know how you get when you're drinking. Whatever you do, take it outside," I said.

"Fuck dat nigga," she said, then threw a shot back. I invited Thickems but she said she couldn't make it. It was time for her and Mara to hash out their issues because it was stressing me. I was used to all of us partying together like we used to a few years back. Pistol told me to stay out of it because Kemara was stubborn and she'd talk to Thickems when she was ready.

The DJ played "Some Type of Way" by Richie Homie Quan and the crowd got hyped. All I could do was a cute little two-step because I felt bloated. But Kellan's drunk ass got up on the stage and started twerking. She was a stripper for Halloween. Kellan had on a black fishnet bodysuit with a thong and see-through bra on underneath.

"I'll fuck the shit outta her, chilleeee. She's in heat," Silk said and I slapped his arm.

"She looks a mess," Jasmine said. Jasmine didn't like Kellan or Zain and they didn't like her, neither.

"Look at you looking all scrumptious," I said. After staring at her for a while, you could see how she resembled Beretta around the cheeks and lips. Jasmine was dressed like Kitana from Mortal Kombat.

"Thank you. I heard there's a bun in the oven. Congrats," she said.

"Appreciate it," I replied. Kemara hugged Jasmine and kissed her on the cheek.

"You started traveling and forgot all about us," Kemara said.

"I know but I love it. I might be getting a big role soon, so keep y'all's fingers crossed," Jasmine said.

"My bitch gonna be in the theatres and we're going to be right there watching with a purse full of junk food. I don't care how much money I get, I'm never buying shit from the movie theatre," Kemara said.

"I'll be happy when my brother dumps dat money-hungry bitch. Look at him letting his side-piece dance up on him. Kellan knows it, too, but she's gonna put up with it because he spoils her dumb ass," Jasmine said.

"Wait, that's the girl Sniper creeping with and he brought her here knowing Kellan was going to be here?" Kemara asked.

"Yeah, why not? She ain't gonna do shit but slash his tires and cut up his clothes. Don't let dat girl fool y'all. The only reason she's around so much is to keep tabs on him. Look at her dying for attention. A few years ago, Sniper would've dragged her off the stage and slapped the taste outta her mouth," Jasmine said.

"The tea, hunty. All I need is some lemons," Silk said. We watched everything go down and Sniper disappeared with his side-chick out the back door. Kellan didn't even notice it. Machete walked over to us and Jasmine tried to walk away but he grabbed her hand.

"I wish y'all would just make up already, lordt," Kemara said.

"Ewww, this dirty penis nigga. I'll pass," Jasmine replied.

"I'll take his yellow pretty-eyed ass. I heard Machete's dick got diamonds on the tip, chile," Silk whispered to me and I elbowed him.

"Back it up on me, Jasmine. Nobody can work dat ass like you, shorty," Machete said.

"Yah girlfriend's sister is gonna snitch on us, so I think you need to walk away," Jasmine said.

"Fuck dem hoes. Zain left me, so I'm single," Machete replied.

"Boyyyy, get outta my face," Jasmine said and pushed him.

"I'll be back over here," Machete said, then bopped off.

"You know you like him," Mara teased Jasmine and she smirked.

SOUL Publications

"We're just friends, trust me. Machete is like dat annoying ex that can be yah best friend at times. I'm not fooling with him. He'll have me out here slicing bitches like birthday cake," she replied.

"I know that feeling," Mara said.

The party went on and we ran out of napkins so I went downstairs to the basement to get some. I heard footsteps coming down the stairs while I searched the shelves.

"You just couldn't wait until we got home, could you?" I asked Pistol. We always snuck off to the basement to get a quickie in whenever he was at Queen's Den. It was a kiddish habit we had. Matter of fact, we did quickies wherever we were at. He wrapped his arms around me and the smell of his cologne threw me off. I knew my nigga and knew damn well he didn't wear Calvin Klein, but Delonte did. I turned around and he had on a vampire face mask. He took it off and smiled at me.

"What are you doing here?" I asked.

"We need to talk. I've been calling you and sending you messages for a month and no answer from you. Just let me explain myself. I missed you so much. I really loved you. We can be a team again. I got this little spot across town and you can dance again," he said. He tried to kiss me but I pushed him into the shelf. I tried to make a dash up the stairs but he grabbed my leg and pulled me down the stairs.

"Calm down! I'm not trying to hurt you!" he said with his hand over my mouth. I scratched his face then kicked him in the stomach. The door to the basement opened and Delonte ran out of the emergency exit which made the alarm go off.

"PIPER!" Pistol called out to me as he walked down the stairs. I was sitting on the bottom step trying to catch my breath.

"What happened? You opened the emergency door?" he asked.

"Yeah, I needed some air. Tell everyone that everything is fine," I said, trying to catch my breath. Pistol grabbed the napkins off the shelf. He stared at me, trying to figure out what was going on.

"Yo, why you breathing like that? I gotta take you to the hospital?" he asked.

"No, I'm fine. I'm just exhausted. I need to go home," I said and wiped my eyes.

"Why do I feel like you keeping something from me? Tell me what da fuck is up!" he said.

"Leave me da fuck alone, Pistol! I said I'm fine!" I yelled at him.

"Fuck you then," he spat and headed upstairs. I texted Mara and told her to come to the basement ASAP. Seconds later, Mara rushed down to the basement.

"He was here, Mara. Delonte was in this building and he followed me to the basement. I don't know what to do," I cried.

"Did he run out the back door? Is that why the alarm went off?" she asked and I nodded my head.

"We gotta tell Pistol. That fuckin' nigga is stalking you. He's bold coming up in here. I'm gonna kill him," Mara said and I shook my head.

"I can't risk you doing that. Delonte's parents will never let his case go. That's why GMBAM backed off of him because Pistol was going to kill him when I got locked up," I said.

"We just have to figure out a better way but dat nigga is canceled! I'll do it myself if I have to, I just want him dead! Sending you to jail was enough and now all of a sudden, he wants you back?" Mara asked.

"He wants me to come back and work for him like he's my pimp. All he cares about is getting a main attraction for his club to put him back in business," I replied.

"You gotta tell Pistol before this blows up. This is very serious, Piper. You're pregnant and that nigga is taunting you," Mara said.

"Okay, I'll tell him tonight," I replied.

"Do you want me to be there with you?" she asked.

"No, I'll tell him by myself," I said.

"I'll walk you to your car so you can go home and wait for Pistol. I'll stay back and make sure everything is cleaned up," she replied. Mara helped me up and I limped up the stairs because the fall sprained my ankle.

I don't want to tell him but I have to, I thought as we made our way through the crowd.

****

It was two thirty in the morning when I heard the front door unlock. I'd been on the couch for an hour and a half staring at the wall. My nerves were a wreck and my stomach felt queasy. My throat was dry and I was light-headed. He took his shoes off and dropped them on the floor in the foyer. I called out to him and he came into the living room.

"We need to talk," I said. He sat on the couch across from me.

"Ight, what's up?" he asked with one eyebrow raised. Maybe he sensed nervousness in my voice or maybe it was my body language. Whatever it was gave him bad vibes because he looked agitated and confused. Or he could've been upset about the way I talked to him at the party.

"I wanna tell you about that day at Delonte's loft and what made me attack him. Delonte lied about his age, he's in his forties. His wife told me he keeps his head shaved to hide his gray hair and she also told me he has other kids.

He confessed to everything and said that you were his son. I wanted to take it to my grave with me but he has been calling Queen's Den for a month and leaving notes on my car. Tonight, he got into the party because he was wearing a mask. He followed me into the basement and he was the one who opened the emergency door when he heard you coming," I said.

"Yo, stop playin'," he said and chuckled.

"I'm not playing," I said. He picked up the centerpiece from the middle of the coffee table and threw it against the wall.

"You tellin' me you were fuckin' me and a nigga that's supposed to be my father? A year and a half later and you just telling me this bullshit? Bitch, you lost yah fuckin' mind! Then you talkin' about taking it to your grave. That's some selfish shit! This ain't about me knowing da truth. I bet you thought keeping the secret wasn't gonna make you look like a tramp, huh? You couldn't have muthafuckas knowing you fucked homeboys and your nigga's father," he said.

"I didn't know he was your father!" I cried.

"But you knew da truth and ain't tell me. All the times we wrote each other and not one fuckin' word about dat nigga. How do I even know if you're telling the truth now? You probably been knowing dat bullshit. My fuckin' seed is connected to dat nigga. Now I'on even know if I want this. I told you shit about not having a father. You laid right next to me, listening to me tell you how I wanted to know my father and you knew. So, the nigga stalkin' you and now you wanna tell me what's up? But this is what I get for fuckin' my homeboy's side-bitch. I ain't even mad," Pistol said and walked out the living room. Tears wouldn't stop falling from my eyes. They said the tongue is a weapon and it wasn't a lie because his words cut me deeply.

"Please, just listen to me!" I sobbed as he walked up the stairs.

"Yo, I'm good on dat, shorty. Fuck yah guilty tears! Got me walking around here looking like a fuckin' clown. Dat nigga was around me da whole fuckin' time probably laughing at how he was knockin' down the same shorty I fell in love with. Fall in love with a hoe and she'll turn you into a circus clown. I should've used a condom or made you swallow. Sad-ass bitch," Pistol said. I covered my mouth to keep from screaming as I cried. I'd been through a lot in my life and nothing, not even the death of my mother, hurt me more than Pistol's words. Delonte was like a fungus in my life. I was losing everything because of him and he didn't care. He took advantage of me because I was young and naïve. He didn't care about anything else but me making him some money. Pistol came back downstairs with a Louis Vuitton duffel bag.

"What are you doing?" I asked.

"I got a few things to take care of," he said. I grabbed his arm to pull him away from the door and he pushed me into a picture on the wall.

"Yo, don't beg for me to stay. Dat shit ain't even cool," he said.

"That's it? You're just gonna leave me?" I asked.

"Honestly, I wouldn't have knocked you up if I knew dat nigga was my father. I would've had an option if I wanted to further our relationship. Face da facts, shorty. This isn't some shit a nigga can just wake up to the next day like everything is all gravy. Da fuck you thought love and a pregnancy was gonna make me forget?" he asked.

"I knew you were gonna leave me if I told you da truth," I sobbed.

"That wasn't yah choice to make!" he shouted. He put on his shoes then grabbed his bag.

"I love you soo much and I didn't mean to hurt you. Can you just stay home so we can talk?" I asked. He opened the door and slammed it behind him. The picture next to the door fell and the glass shattered across the floor. I slid down the wall and cried my heart out. My life shot a bullet at me for the sixth time, but this time, it pierced through my heart.

SOUL Publications

Beretta

I woke up to my cell phone vibrating on my nightstand. I looked at the clock on the wall and it was four thirty in the morning. It was a text from Pistol telling me to walk outside. Not knowing what to think, I hurriedly got dressed. Pistol ain't never pop up on me unannounced, especially that early in the morning. Kemara sat up in bed and rubbed her eyes.

"Where are you goin'?" she asked.

"To holla at Pistol really quick. Go back to sleep," I replied. She didn't argue with me and laid back down instead. I rushed down the stairs and out of the door. Instead of using the elevator, I took the stairs because the elevator was slow as shit. When I got outside, Pistol was sitting on the step and the nigga had tears in his eyes.

"Yo, what da fuck happened?" I almost shouted. My heart was beating and I was trying to prepare myself for the bad news of somebody getting merked.

"Piper told me Delonte's bitch-ass is my father. Can you believe dat shit? That clown-ass nigga knew the whole time and didn't say shit to me. I'm fucked up, bruh. Shorty betrayed me and I don't know if I'm ready to be a father myself. How can a nigga be around his seed and don't even say shit to him?" he asked.

"How is dat nigga yah pops? He ain't dat much older than us," I said.

"He lied about his age to Piper. The nigga really in his late forties. The only reason why shorty said sumthin was because dat nigga is harassing her. He was at the party and he caught her in the basement. I went down there and asked her what happened and she lied to me with a straight face, bruh. Shorty told me the alarm went off 'cause she needed some air. Mannnnn, Beretta, I'on even want her. I was busting her down raw, knocked her up and shorty knew my seed was going to be his grandchild," he said.

"Yo, dat's wild. Shorty was trippin' with dat bird shit she pulled. But how do you know he yah pops for a fact, though? Da nigga could've been just talking shit," I said.

"I went to my grandmother's house before I came here to get my birth certificate out of my mother's boxes that's in the attic. I never had a reason to look at that shit until now. But, anyways, da nigga name is on there. My aunt mentioned his name before but I didn't think nothing of it because he lied about his age. I mean it ain't like I got dat nigga's last name anyway," he said.

"Yo, you can't be like yah pops. Whateva shorty did is on her but yah seed is yah seed, regardless, fam. A dead man can't be a grandfather, anyway," I said, hinting for him to merk the nigga.

"I know, bruh. I said some fucked-up shit to shorty but it wasn't her decision to tell me what I should or shouldn't know. If she cared, she would've told me just on the strength dat she loves me," he replied and I agreed.

"Yo, you gotta be there for yah seed, though. It'll eat you up if you don't. If you ain't feeling shorty then fuck it, don't go back. But yah seed ain't got nothing to do with his or her mother makin' childish-ass decisions," I said and he nodded his head.

"You right, I was speaking out of anger, but fuck shorty. Yo, my bad for coming here. I just had to talk to somebody and I'on trust niggas like dat to be knowing my personal life. Glock probably thinking I deserved the shit, so I'on want him knowing shit, you feel me?" he asked and I nodded my head.

"Aight, bruh. I'm ready to go check into my room and chill out for a bit," he said.

"Piper gonna be bugging my wife because of you. Get ready, bruh, because even though shorty fucked up, they are gonna treat you like you fucked another broad or sumthin," I said and he shook his head.

"A nigga gonna be in the dog house and gettin' dirty looks from all her friends. Fuck it, though. I can't force myself to be around shorty, so it is what it is. Do me a favor, tell Mara to hit her up to see if she's straight," he said and we slapped hands. Pistol told me he was going to hit me up in a few days before he got in his whip and pulled off.

Kemara was sitting up in bed running her mouth on her the phone when I went back into the crib. In the beginning, me and my niggas only had one thing on our minds and that was money. We got older and solved the money problems and ended up having woman problems.

"Tell Piper to go to sleep," I said, taking my clothes back off.

"Don't do me right now. Y'all niggas stay acting up when a bitch gets pregnant. Pistol didn't have to go off on my sister like that. Wait till I see him," Mara said.

"Yo ass ain't doing shit! Damn, da nigga hurt and y'all insensitive and evil-ass bitches tryna plot on him. What da fuck? Tell Piper dumb-ass stop acting like da nigga was fucking other bitches and take her ass to bed," I said and Mara covered the phone with her hand.

"Who you callin' a bitch, Z'wan? Don't play wit' me, muthafucka. Pistol knows damn well Piper had a good reason for hiding the truth," she said.

"She hid da truth to cover her own ass. I can't let y'all sit here and clown my nigga out when he ain't do shit but love and spoil dat dumb-ass broad. Tell shorty go bed and let dat baby in her stomach sleep," I replied.

"You ain't gotta be a rude jackass about it," Mara said.

"I'm not, y'all just don't like hearing the truth. Piper was wrong, bottom line. We can agree to disagree but those are facts! She lucky he ain't knock her head off," I replied. Mara got up and went downstairs to talk to Piper. As soon as I got comfortable in bed, my phone rang and it was Sniper's shorty.

"Yooo," I answered.

"Hey, Beretta, I know it's late but is Sniper wit' you?" Kellan whispered into the phone.

"Y'all broads can't keep a nigga or sumthin?" I replied.

"Someone broke into my house and I'm hiding in the closet. I can't call the cops because it's a lot of guns in here. Look, please tell him to come home right now because I'm scared," she panicked.

"Ight, I'll hit him up," I replied and hung up. Sniper's phones were off, he was probably banging his side-piece out. Matter of fact, I called all my niggas up and they weren't answering the phone. Mara came into the bedroom and asked me who I was calling.

"Kellan hit me up saying some niggas done ran into her crib. She can't call the police because Sniper got guns and money in there. Shorty don't want them searching her home. Mann, this is a fucked-up night!" I said, getting out of bed.

"Be careful, Beretta. I'm gonna call her and see if I can keep her on da phone until you get there," Kemara said. Truth be told, I knew Mara wasn't going to trip about me leaving the house. My family was important to me, and although Sniper was messing around on shorty, that was still his girl and his home. I went into the closet and grabbed my Beretta and a bulletproof vest.

"Text her phone before you call her in case she doesn't have it on silent," I told Mara.

"Okay, please be careful," she said. She kissed my lips before I left out of the crib. I tried calling Sniper again and the nigga's phone was still off.

****

Twenty-six minutes later, I pulled up on Sniper's block. I parked four houses down and got out of my whip with my gun tucked into my pants. The doorknob to his front door was loose and a few screws were missing. I been told that nigga to get an alarm system but he said he'd rather take an "L" than to have police getting involved if the alarm went off. Sniper was the only nigga that kept shit in his home. I walked into the house and it was fucked up. If Kellan wouldn't have called me, I would've thought the FEDS raided their shit. Glass was everywhere and the big screen TV Sniper had in his living room was missing. I crept upstairs checking the bedroom closets but Kellan wasn't there. The master bedroom was at the end of the hall and I heard a mumbling noise. I rushed into the bedroom with my gun drawn and shorty was balled up on the floor naked with a bruise on her cheek. I pulled the sheet off the bed and wrapped her body up. Sniper called my phone and I answered.

"Yo, where da fuck you at?" I barked into the phone.

"I'm just leaving the hotel. We went to a Halloween stripper party. Yo, is everything good?" he asked.

"Some niggas ran up in yah crib and stole some of your shit. I think they took advantage of yah shorty," I said.

"I'm on my way!" he said and hung up.

"He doesn't care about me. He would've been here if he did! It was two of them and they had on Halloween masks. I couldn't make out their voices and they tried to rape me, but they must've heard your car pull up because they ran downstairs and I heard the back door in the kitchen slam. I was so scared, Beretta," Kellan cried into my chest and wrapped her arms around my neck.

"Yo, you straight now. Calm down, baby girl," I said. I took the sheet and wiped her eyes.

"Why can't Sniper be like you? You'd never leave Mara in da house like this. I could be dead if it wasn't for you. I owe you my life," she trembled.

"I'm gonna step out the room so you can fix yah self," I said. She grabbed my arm when I pulled away from her.

"Noooooo. Stay here. I'll go in the bathroom," she said. I helped her up and walked her to the bathroom in the bedroom. She closed the door and I sat on the bed. My phone rang and it was my wife calling.

"What happened? Is everything okay?" she panicked.

"Naw, shorty fucked up badly. They were tryna rape her but ran when they heard my car pull up. They took the TV in their living room. Sniper was at an after-party," I replied.

"What is wrong with everybody? Pistol trippin' on Piper and Sniper's cheating ass running around town leaving that girl in the house. He should've taught her how to shoot or sumthin," Mara said.

"Not everybody cut like dat, shorty," I replied. My wife was a different type of female because she'd bust her gun before some street niggas would.

"Yeah, I'm taking her to the gun range wit' me if she wanna keep puttin' up with Sniper's shit. I'm gonna wait up for you so I'll see you shortly. Love you," she said and hung up. My eyelids were getting heavy but I couldn't leave Kellan until Sniper came home. Ten minutes later, Kellan limped out the bathroom wearing a robe. The left side of her face was puffy and she had a cut above her eye.

"I'm done wit' Sniper after tonight," she said.

"Look, shorty, I came here to make sure you were straight. Whatever is between y'all ain't got shit to do with me, ya feel me? So, the less I know the better," I replied and she rolled her eyes.

"Y'all GMBAM niggas stick together so of course you don't want to hear it. Why not teach them how to be like you and Mara?" she asked.

"Because y'all females aren't like Mara," I replied.

"What does that mean?" she asked.

"It means what it sounds like, baby girl. It's only one Mara so I can't teach niggas how to treat their shorty how I treat my wife," I replied. Someone was running upstairs and Kellan's eyes almost popped out of her head. I ain't never seen someone so scared in my life. Sniper burst into the room and ran to Kellan.

"Yo, did those niggas rape you?" he asked, checking her face out. She pulled away from him and started sobbing all over again.

"It's all your fault! You were so busy fucking that bitch and forgot all about me. Almost every night you leave me in the house with all this illegal shit. No phone call, text, nothing! FUCK YOU, TIKO! If it wasn't for Beretta, I would've been getting gang-raped!" she screamed. Kellan slapped Sniper and he stepped away from her.

"Yo, we about to do this right now? It's cool when I'm busting bitches down witchu but it's a problem when I wanna fuck by myself? That same bitch you keep talking about is the same bitch who was making you cum months ago. And you wanna know da fucked-up part about it? You introduced me to shorty, you brought her here on your own. That was yah girl, too, but you ain't tryna tell nobody dat, huh?" Sniper asked.

This nigga got two bitches? Damn, what da fuck! I thought. Maybe it was something in our DNA that we inherited from our father because I had two broads years ago, Lolly and Takeda.

"So, what! I come first in case you've forgotten. I was with you before you had all of this and then Brittany comes along and you forgot all about me! Nigga, don't forget you were corner hustling and penny pinching, too. You had no car, no name brand shit, so you were just another nappy-headed crab in the hood with a crackhead mama," Kellan said.

"And your pussy still smelled like piss, bitch! You must've forgotten how you and your sister was living in a shelter when I met you. Now you wanna look down on me because you wearing name brand shit and driving foreign cars that I paid for? Bitch, you crazy! You mad at me because I spend more time with my other girl? Start giving me what I need and I wouldn't have to nut in another bitch's pussy!" Sniper yelled at her. Kellan burst into tears and ran into the bathroom.

"Yo, you see this shit? That bitch just dogged my childhood out then got mad when I reminded her where she came from," he said.

"Look, bruh. I gotta go home. Y'all niggas trippin. Two girlfriends, though?" I asked.

"Yeah, it was fun in the beginning. Seeing my girl getting her pussy ate from a bad lil' broad while I'm hitting it from behind was the best feeling in da world. She begged me to fuck da both of 'em. At first, I ain't wanna do it because that's not sumthin you wanna do with yah girl. Anyway, I gave in when Kellan let Brittany go down on her. I been sucked in ever since. Shorty lying to everybody about us and that's why I don't entertain it. Brittany lived here, too, but shorty moved out 'cause Kellan beat her up and dragged her out da crib. Kellan's jealous 'cause I took Brittany on a vacation and left her home but shorty don't know how to act," Sniper said. Kellan came out the bathroom and told Sniper to get out of her house.

"This is my crib. Come on, bruh. I'll walk you out," Sniper said.

"So, what's up?" I asked Sniper when we got outside.

"I think I know who did this. Brittany's ex-nigga been sending fade my way for a few weeks now. That's the only nigga I know who got beef with me but I'll handle it," he said.

"Yo, I keep telling you dat you don't eat where you shit. A gun or two in da house but, my nigga, you got all kinds of shit in yah crib. Come on, bruh, think. Niggas gonna test you by going to yah shorty. That shit never gets old. You gonna have to move, bruh," I replied.

"Yeah, I feel you. I didn't think a nigga was bold enough to fuck wit' me," he said.

"Use your brain, bruh. Hit me up lata," I replied and we slapped hands.

"Appreciate you, bruh. Shorty get on my nerves but I'll lose my mind if sumthin happened to her, you feel me?" he asked.

"Yeah, no doubt. I'll get up with you later," I replied. Sniper went back into the crib and I headed home. It was almost seven o'clock in the morning when I got there. Mara was on the couch wrapped up in a blanket but her ass cheek was hanging out from underneath her baby doll top.

"Pretty Girl," I shook her and she woke up rubbing her eyes.

"Kellan okay?" she asked.

"Yeah, she's good. Her face a little swollen but she still can run dat mouth, though," I replied. Mara sat up and stretched and I wasn't tired anymore. Her nipples were nice, round and hard.

"Why you lookin' at me like that?" she asked.

"'Cause I want some," I replied. Kemara stood in front of me and got undressed. My dick was trying to burst through my sweats. Kemara pulled it out and I took my hoodie and wife beater off. I relaxed my head back on the couch as soon as the tip of my head graced her pretty full and wet lips. Shorty's head game was so crucial, she could suck cement through a straw. She liked when I cupped her chin and gently fucked her throat. Mara moaned on my dick as she played with her pussy lips. Her moans got louder and I knew she was cumming on her fingers. I leaned forward so she could slip her drippings into my mouth.

"Come up here," I said and pulled her up. Shorty straddled me and I held my dick so she could slide down on it. She was tight, warm and sloppy wet. Mara instantly creamed on my dick when her walls pulled me all the way in.

"Ssshhhhitttttt," she squealed when I gripped her hips and dug in her guts.

"OHHHHHHHH!" she moaned. Her breasts bounced in my face so I caught one with my lips and she dug her nails into my back. Mara used to run from the dick, but shorty took all my inches like a pro. Her hair fell into her face and I gathered it all together and held onto it while she rode me.

"I'm ready to bust. Damn, baby! Squirt on this muthafucka!" I coached while I played with her clit with my free hand. Her eyes fluttered and her mouth was gaped open as we exploded. Mara's pussy gushed on my shaft but she wasn't finished. I laid her on her back and made love to her during the second round. If I could stay inside my wife for the rest of my life, I would never pull out. Shorty had me wide open.

An hour later, we were stretched out on the couch in a spooning position. Mara was quiet, and usually when she tuned me out, it was because she was overthinking something.

"What's up, Mara?" I asked.

"Sooo, I have been thinking and I want to get off birth control. Ms. Baker said I can see a specialist to get a real answer. What if we're cheating ourselves out of having another baby?" she asked and I sat up.

"I'm cool with just Zalia and plus I think we should wait awhile," I replied.

"You don't want a baby anymore?" she asked.

"Naw," I replied and she got off the couch.

"It's okay to be skeptical about this. I don't want to go through another miscarriage but what if the third time is a charm?" she said.

"Shorty, I see what you saying but I don't want a baby right now. If you get off birth control, just let me know and I'll use a condom," I replied.

"Wowww, Z'wan. A fucking condom? Married people don't use no damn condoms. Nigga, you acting like I'm a side-piece or sumthin," she said.

"I don't want to see you go through dat shit again. We lost two kids within two years and you think dat shit is cool? I can't do it and you shouldn't want to, neither. I don't want a baby, Mara," I replied.

"I'm ready to take a shower then I'll fix breakfast," she said. I got off the couch and reached out to her.

"I'm not tryna hurt yah feelings," I said.

"I know, you're protecting them. It's cool," she said and weakly smiled. She kissed my lips before walking away but deep down I think it was better that way. I grabbed my pants off the floor and stepped into them. Zalia was up and I could hear her fussing about something on her cartoons. I went into her room and she smiled at me with her hair all over her head. A lot of people thought she was my blood daughter because we had the same complexion and she resembled Kemara a lot.

"Daddy, take me to da swing," she said, talking about the park.

"It's too early, baby girl. Daddy needs to go to sleep. You gonna hang wit' Mommy today. What you want Mommy to buy you?" I asked.

"I want a pink pony," she said.

I wonder if Kemara can buy her a pony and spray paint it pink, I thought. Zalia deserved the world and I wanted to give it to her.

"For your third birthday party," I said, then tickled her.

I had to appreciate what I had in front of me instead of hoping for something that might not happen. Hopefully my wife could understand where I was coming from because I already made my mind up.

Piper

Two weeks later...

Things were out of control since Pistol left. He didn't call me or come home to get a change of clothes. I stopped texting and calling him after a week. My stomach was growing; I was a week away from being four months pregnant. Kemara and Zalia spent all their time with me when she wasn't in school. They even spent a few days at my house and Beretta acted like he was going to die without his daughter and wife for two days. Me and Kemara needed each other because she was trying to sort some things out herself. Earlene and Silk was at Queen's Den so I could rest a little bit. Kemara was sitting on my couch drinking wine and Zalia was on the floor having a tea party with her baby dolls. Kemara's phone rang but she didn't answer it.

"Beretta is getting on my nerves," she said.

"He misses y'all. Go home, I'll be okay," I said.

"No, you can't be pregnant in this big-ass house by yourself. You heard what happened to Kellan, didn't you?" she asked.

"Yeah, but didn't Sniper find out who did it? Plus, we have cameras and an alarm system in here," I said.

"He found out the next day who it was. Apparently, his other bitch's ex-boyfriend wanted to retaliate against Sniper for stealing his woman. The cat is out the bag now, Sniper has two girlfriends and Kellan was down with it, too. Silk gave me the scoop this morning," Mara said.

"Kellan was acting like dat when she was fucking the same bitch, too? Money makes people try anything. I ain't sharing my man with nobody," I replied.

"I might have to share my husband. We need an extra pussy so he can have the babies he wants," she said.

"Put down the wine, Mara. You'll kill a bitch before dat happens," I said.

"He doesn't want a baby now. He didn't tell me he'd think about it or nothing. It was just a flat out 'no.' I'm gonna sit here and enjoy your pregnancy with you, shit, at least your womb ain't fucked up," Mara said. I got up and snatched the wine from her and took it to the kitchen sink to pour it out.

"I have another bottle in my trunk," Mara said when I came back to the living room.

"I miss Emma. I wonder how she's doing," Mara said.

"She'll come around when she's ready. A heart attack at her age is scary," I replied and she nodded her head.

"I know but it's possible. Ms. Baker told me her aunt died from a heart attack because her husband was messing around on her. Some women really can't deal with that type of heartache. I'm telling you, love can either make you a happy or miserable bitch," Mara said.

"I don't think Pistol is coming back," I replied.

"Chilleeee, that nigga is coming back, trust me. You should know by now that a man's heartache ain't the same as ours. We can cry about it for a few days then our friends will come over and make it sorta go away. But men don't like talking about shit so he's probably keeping all his feelings in while walking around mad at the world. His ego won't let him reveal his emotional side. Beretta was the same way but it slowly goes away after y'all be through so much that his feelings will become transparent. This is y'all's first real argument so you just have to figure out his defense mechanism," she said.

"Bitcchhhhh, layman's terms, please," I replied.

"You have to figure out the techniques he uses to avoid showing his emotional side. Once you break that down, he won't have a choice but to stay his ass home and talk about it," she said.

I heard the front door open then shut. My heart was beating out of my chest because of fear and excitement.

Pistol came into the living room and he reeked of alcohol and weed.

"Ummm, call me later. I have to see what my husband wants," Mara said. She grabbed Zalia and scooped up all her toys before she left the house.

"I have to get something from the bedroom. Is dat okay wit' you?" he asked.

"Where have you been these past few weeks? I had a doctor's appointment and you didn't show up," I replied.

"Just chilling," he said, then went upstairs. I followed him into the bedroom and he went into his pocket for his ringing cell phone. A magnum fell out of his pocket and landed on the floor and he hurriedly picked it up.

"Ohhhh, I get it. You went out and fucked another bitch to make yourself feel better," I said.

"Yo, you don't know what you're talking about and stay outta my business," he said. He went into the closet and opened his safe where he kept a few stacks and his very expensive jewelry.

"I can't do this. I'm not gonna argue with you or beg you. So just get what you came to get and leave. It's obvious you don't want to be a part of this," I said and he chuckled.

"I ain't fuck nobody, but if I did, what you worried about it for?" he asked. I was dying on the inside. The thought of Pistol sleeping with another woman made my stomach turn. How could he do that to me? I know I fucked up but I didn't deserve all of what he was throwing at me.

"You were with another woman? Just tell me da truth," I said.

"I'll tell you da truth in two years. It'll only be fair, right?" he asked. He pulled out a few stacks from his pocket and placed them inside the safe along with the Rolex he was wearing. He took off his clothes and tossed them in a hamper. Pistol walked past me and went into our bathroom to take a shower like everything was normal. I knew stress wasn't good during the early stages of pregnancy, so I was trying my best to keep from lashing out at Pistol and turning into that crazy hood bitch he didn't want to see. He left his cell phone on the bed so I went through it, seeing if I could find anything. There wasn't nothing in his phone but that still didn't mean anything.

What did he need a condom for? I thought.

Ten minutes later, Pistol walked out the bathroom with a towel wrapped around him.

"Yo, I didn't fuck another broad. I went to a strip party last night. A shorty took me in the back room and before I went, Flo gave me a condom. When I got back there, I couldn't do shit so I left shorty in da private room. You happy now?" he asked.

"Naw, I'm not fuckin' happy! You have been gone for two weeks. No phone call, text, nothing!" I said.

"The only thing I'm gonna apologize for is some of what I said to you before I left out the house dat night. Some shit I said was fucked up but I'm not apologizing for cutting you off for two weeks," he said. He dried off and lotioned his body. Pistol stepped into a pair of boxer-briefs and went downstairs. I took a shower then got into bed. Mara texted me to see if everything was okay and I told her Pistol was talking to me but there was still a lot of things to work out. I almost fell out the bed when she said Beretta told her she couldn't go nowhere for a week like she was punished. Pistol came upstairs with three sandwiches, a bag of chips and a liter of Coke.

"Glad to see you went grocery shopping," he said and got into bed.

"This isn't normal. You can't just come home like this and pretend we don't need to talk about what happened," I replied.

"This is my house, too, so I don't have to explain why I'm here. Secondly, I'on wanna talk about dat shit. And I didn't fuck no bitch or none of that other shit you wanna accuse me of. Did you find anything in my phone?" he asked.

"I didn't look in yah phone," I lied.

"Lying again. How my phone go from the bed to the nightstand? My shit got legs now?" he asked.

"Whatever," I replied and turned my back towards him. My man was home and I was relieved. It didn't matter if he was talking to me or not because there was still some hope left in our relationship.

****

A week passed and it was still the same between me and Pistol. We only talked about the pregnancy, anything else was a no go. He didn't hold me at night like he used to and it had been almost a month since we had sex. It was seven o'clock at night and I was cooking roast beef, mashed potatoes, string beans with ham and cornbread. Pistol was greedy and I knew he wasn't going to turn down a meal. My cell phone rang and it was Silk calling.

"Hellooooo, make it quick. I'm cooking for my man," I said.

"You mean yah ex-nigga, but I'll let you be great," he spat.

"Don't do me right now, bitch," I said.

"Sike naw, baby. I'm just kidding witchu. What do you got on? I hope you're cooking with some bad-ass pumps on," he said.

"Yup, and a see-through teddy, too. Now, what do you want?" I asked.

"Did you watch the news? Hunnnnttyyyyyyy, they found Delonte's body in a hotel room. Said he overdosed and it might have been suicide. Where in da hell have you been and when are you coming back to Queen's Den? I'm here more than I'm at my own damn job," he complained.

"I'll be back soon. I'm tryna fix this situation between me and Pistol. And fuck Delonte. He should've died with an AIDS dick in his mouth," I said.

"I'm calling heaven right now to speak to him, Amona and Lezzi to ask them is their stay five-star worthy. Umph, fuck dem hoes. I'on play about my babies, but anyways, call me tomorrow. Oh, and the key to a man's heart is not through his stomach, it's through a peephole in the back door. Suck his dick really good and when he lifts his legs up, slide yah tongue right in. You'll thank me lata," Silk said.

"Nigga, I'll be dead fuckin' around witchu. Pistol doesn't even want me grabbing his ass when he's on top," I said.

"Umph, you got one of those manly men 'cause niggas like me will wrap legs around a bitch's neck really quick while throwing that ass to her face. Look, I gotta go fix these drinks," he said and hung up. Silk was a big help at Queen's Den because he set up small events and one night was gay night. Earlene said the place was so crowded they closed early because it was a safety hazard. I wished I was there but I was home in bed crying over Pistol.

I checked on the roast beef and it was almost done. While waiting, I made a small batch of homemade banana pudding. The door opened and it was Pistol. A few hours ago, I sent him a text telling him to be home by seven thirty for dinner and he was early. That nigga wasn't turning down a meal. He came into the kitchen and washed his hands before he sat at the table. Pistol didn't acknowledge how good I looked. My weave was styled in big, loose and bouncy curls. My make-up was on point and my lingerie set was enough to make a nigga beg for it, but Pistol wasn't biting.

"How was your day?" I asked.

"It was straight? How about yours?" he replied, looking in his phone.

"Okay, I went to get my hair, nails and toes done," I replied.

"That's what's up," he said, not looking up.

"Delonte is dead so we won't have to worry about him anymore," I said and he looked at me.

"Dat nigga been dead for a week now. They just found him?" Pistol asked.

"A week? How do you know?" I replied.

"When will the food be ready? A nigga starving," he said.

"In ten minutes, but how do you know about Delonte? We've been down this road before, remember? His parents will get involved and have the police digging into my life because he told them I was affiliated with gang members when we went to court. They might pin this on me," I replied.

"The nigga had some strippers in his hotel room. They were getting high and he overdosed. One of them was talking about it at this strip party I went to," he said and shrugged his shoulders. I knew GMBAM like the palm of my hand. Delonte's death was not just an accident. He was a lot of things but a drug user wasn't one of them. Delonte was killed and it was framed like an accident but I was somewhat relieved because he turned into a psycho after Beretta bought his building.

"I'm sorry he wasn't the father you were expecting," I said.

"He ain't my father, shorty, so don't bring dat up again. Matter of fact, I don't even know who dat nigga is," Pistol said.

"Are you gonna leave the house every time we argue?" I asked.

"Why are we making this about me, shorty? The real question is, why my shorty can't be open wit' me. I left da crib because I knew shit would've gotten worse if I stayed, plus I had a few things to take care of and didn't need any distractions," he said.

Probably plotting on setting up Delonte, I thought.

"I have talked to Mara and she suggested that we shouldn't have these barriers in our relationship. We have to learn how to communicate better," I said and he chuckled.

"Mara told you dat shit, huh? Shorty ain't got no room to talk or speak on what we got going on over here. Y'all females need to understand that what works for someone doesn't work for everyone else. Communication was what her and Beretta had problems wit'. You knew why I left the house and you also knew why you felt the need to hide the shit from me. Trust is what we need to work on, shorty. I'm not a dumb-ass nigga who walked into this relationship with blindfolds on so don't make me the bad guy, baby girl. Moving forward, come and talk to me and I'll keep it a band with you," he said.

"I won't keep nothing else from you," I replied.

"I was thinking about you, though," he said.

YASSSSSSSS! I screamed in my head.

"Awww, I'm gonna get emotional," I replied with tears stinging the brim of my eyes. Pistol got up from the chair and wrapped his strong arms around me and I melted. The man was everything I prayed for. God sent him in a package for me. He kissed my forehead and the butterflies were fluttering.

"This does look good on you," he said, pulling at my teddy.

"It's a little too tight and da shit itches," I admitted.

"Take it off and get comfortable. I'on really care too much about lingerie. I'm a hood nigga, wear a small tank top and some tight boy shorts and I'm sold," he said.

"Let me go change," I replied and rushed out of the kitchen. On my way upstairs, I cried tears of joy. Nobody else but me would understand the connection I had to Pistol. I told myself every day that Glock's prison sentence was a miracle. I would've never known what real love was like without having to use my body. There were going to be no more secrets between us and I put that on my life.

Poppa

April, 2014

Five months later...

"**U**mmmm, Kamar! Fuck me harder, baby!" Fushia screamed out while I was giving her nothing but hard and big dick against the wall. She wrapped her legs around me and scratched at my shoulders. I thought me and shorty was just going to fuck around when I approached her but she showed me a different world. Museum dates, walks in the park, little ice cream dates; she even took me to church with her a few times. Jasmine showed me that I could love a shorty but Fushia gave me fresh air. She wasn't exposed to the hood life so I wasn't that nigga around her. She didn't even know my nickname and, honestly, I didn't want to be called Poppa anymore. Poppa was a name that made me hate, steal, kill and betray those who cared about me. Poppa was someone who had to adapt to the streets because he was trapped in a world of survival. I detached myself from that nigga. Fushia tried to talk me into going to community college. When I was in prison, I got my GED but that shit was easy. I wasn't a dumb nigga; my attention span wasn't good enough for me to learn so I had to force myself to read. I wasn't ready for college because that was a big commitment I didn't have the patience for. Me and Fushia still had a few things to talk about like me still living with my kids' mother and the deal with her and her daughter's father. It was almost like she was keeping that nigga a secret because she didn't like talking about him. I wanted to know the deal between them so I could decide what I wanted to do with Nika. Speaking of Nika, shorty was always going to the doctor's and she was barely getting out of bed. But I was content with that because it gave me time to spend with Fushia without her being in my business. Odimau was taking care of the kids whenever I wasn't home. Fushia's daughter, Amber, and Hope played together a lot of the time.

"Ohhhhhhhhhh, shit, baby! Pound me just like that!" Fushia screamed. Shorty was a stone-cold freak and into off-the-wall sex. We used sex swings and she loved when I fucked her from the back while I plunged anal beads into her ass. I didn't know where she had been all my life.

"I'm ready bust!" I groaned. She pushed me away from her and sucked my dick until I exploded down her throat. I pulled her hair and bit my bottom lip to keep from sounding like a bitch as she gave me a mean blow job.

"I'm yah dirty bitch, baby?" she asked as I busted.

"Yeah, suck dat shit harder!" I replied and squeezed her face. She sucked the rest of what I had left and I almost snatched her head off her shoulders. The doorbell rang followed by a loud bang.

"Who is that? You expecting company?" I asked as I pulled my pants up. Fushia grabbed her robe off the floor and fixed herself.

"It might be my daughter's father. Fuck! I was supposed to pick her up an hour ago but I lost track of time," she said. Fushia had hickies on her neck and her weave was stuck to her face. I wanted to know how the nigga was going to act seeing his baby mama like that. She opened the door and I was zipping up my pants. Her daughter ran into the house.

"Bitcchhhhhhhhh, you need to learn how to be on time! You got some eyeliner? I'm ready to go out with my bitch and I gotta look goodt, hunty," the nigga Silk said, strutting into the crib. He saw me standing in the middle of the floor while his daughter was pulling at my pant leg asking me about Hope.

"Wait a minute! You fuckin' my baby mama?" he asked.

"Baby mama? Nigga, da fuck is you talkin' about?" I replied and Fushia dropped her head down in embarrassment.

"You had a baby by this faggot?" I asked in disbelief.

"He's bi-sexual and, yes, he's my daughter's father. His lifestyle is his business," she said and Silk rolled his eyes.

"Chilleeeeee, I ought to snatch that weave out yah head. You better hide your purse, car keys and, hell, hide everything, including my child. I had faith in you," Silk said.

"Nigga, shut yah bitch-ass up. That's old news," I replied.

"Umph but living with Nika's ass ain't old news. Nigga, I'll fight you for mine, believe dat," Silk said.

"What is he talking about?" Fushia asked and Silk crossed his arms. I hated that nigga. Even in school, he was starting shit and running his mouth.

"I was gonna tell you but I still live with my baby mama," I said.

"WHAT!" she yelled. Silk picked his daughter up and took her upstairs to her bedroom.

"We aren't together, though. I'm always here witchu," I said.

"Damn it, Kamar. All this time we have been spending together. The least you could do was tell me I was a damn side-chick," she said with watery eyes.

"I'm not sleeping with her," I replied.

"Get out of my house. You're no different than Silk. Straight men, gay men, y'all all cheat!" she screamed at me. Silk came down the stairs with Fushia's eyeliner in his hand.

"Amber is watching cartoons. Anyway, I gotta bounce because my girl is in the car waiting for me. Next time y'all fuck, call me so I can join or watch. My baby mama a freak, ain't she? I taught her how to suck dick, by the way. She learned from the best head master. Thank me lata, toodles!" Silk said, then skipped to the door. I wanted to beat that nigga's ass but Fushia jumped in front of me.

"Yo, you let that nigga raw dog you?" I asked.

"This ain't about him. What about you and your kids' mother? When am I gonna meet her? You said y'all not together, right?" she fired questions at me. I couldn't concentrate on what she was asking because I was still tripping over her baby father knocking a female up like her. Fushia was smart, educated, beautiful and had a phat booty.

"I gotta bounce," I said. I grabbed my shirt, coat and shoes and headed to the door. Shit was all gravy but Silk's glittery ass had to fuck it all up.

"Get back here and tell me what is going on!" she demanded.

"Let's just end this on a good note," I replied.

"Are you freakin' serious? You just walked into my life and gave me everything I looked for in a relationship and now you're telling me it was all a lie? How can you play me like this?" she cried.

"Bye, shorty," I replied and kissed her on the forehead.

SOUL Publications

I'mma fuck dat bitch-ass nigga up when I see him. Naw, I'm not fighting dat fool. That shit will look crazy fighting a gay nigga about his baby mama. A baby mama he shouldn't have in da first place, I thought as I put on my stuff outside of her crib. Nika had to get out of my life but I promised Mara I'd stick around so the bitch wouldn't become bitter and start dragging niggas down with her.

****

When I went home, Odimau was feeding my son and Hope was in her room playing with her toys. I wanted to take a nap before I went to my club. Odimau called out to me when I was walking up the stairs. Shorty was a big help to my family but she always stressed about men in her village back home who took care of their wives.

"Is everything straight?" I asked as I walked downstairs.

"I think Nika is sick," she said.

"Yeah, she has a cold or flu," I replied.

"Not that kind of sick. She would've felt better by now. She doesn't get out of bed like she used to. A few hours ago, I had to help her eat. I'm worried about her and I think you should worry about her, too. She's yah kids' mother, how would they feel knowing their father was out sleeping around while their mother lays in bed sick? I don't want to know who you're sleeping with but a faithful man comes home to his family every night," she said.

"Nika doesn't want a faithful man, Odimau. She just wants a man in the house so she won't be a single mother, and I have been doing that," I replied.

"Go and check up on her," she said sternly. Odimau did a lot for my family so I would never disrespect her. I went upstairs and down the hall to the master bedroom. Nika was sitting up in bed watching TV with a bonnet on her head.

"What's up, beautiful?" I asked to lighten the mood.

"Where have you been?" she replied, looking at the TV.

"The club, as always. Oh, and I went by your restaurant earlier to check out a few things like you asked me to," I said.

"Thank you," she replied dryly.

"What's the matter witchu? You still have the flu?" I asked.

"I don't have the flu," she replied and I sat on the bed next to her. I didn't want to get too close in case she smelled Fushia's pussy on my breath.

"Then what is wrong?" I asked.

"My doctor called me a few hours ago and told me I have multiple sclerosis. What in the fuck am I gonna do? I'm damn-near handicapped! One minute, I was fine, then the next minute, my limbs started acting up. I thought I was just experiencing mood swings, depression and muscle weakness because of your lying ass, so I avoided the symptoms. I waited too late to get help and they found lesions on my brain that they think I had for eight years. Eight damn years!" she cried. I hugged Nika and she cried into my chest. Shorty was a fucked-up person but we all had to get our karma for living reckless and I had mine my whole life. My karma was knocking a bitch up like Nika; they said be careful what you do because it'll skip you and get your kids. I felt like my wrongdoings gave me a daughter with a disability.

"We will be ight," I said.

"No, I won't be okay, Poppa. I'm paying for what I did to Beretta's father. His soul won't let me live a happy life. I have demons on my back," she said as she wiped her eyes.

"I'm gonna get you some help, okay?" I asked.

"No, there isn't a cure for this. Just medicine to keep it from getting worse but I had it for a long time. I'm gonna sign my house and restaurants over to you because I'm gonna eventually become bedridden. I want Omario and Hope to be set for life," she said.

"What about Beretta?" I asked. I spent years despising that nigga because I thought he had it good living in the hood while the rest of us was trying to survive, but the nigga was just like me with a different mindset. He had a mother who didn't like him because of his father and Darcel treated me the same way. She hated my father so much that she hated me and verbally abused me since I was old enough to walk.

"Hope and Omario are my life," she replied.

"I'm gonna ride it out with you," I said and she smiled.

"You don't hate me?" she asked.

"I don't want our kids growing up disliking me because I wasn't here for you. Hope is paying attention to us," I said. She grabbed my hand and squeezed it.

"I'm gonna need a cane or a walker. I can walk but my legs will go stiff and I'll fall if there is nothing next to me I can hold onto," she said.

Damn, I have been up Fushia's ass so much dat I haven't been paying attention, I thought.

"You'll be straight. You're a strong woman," I said.

"I'm gonna end up dying young but, anyways, forget about me, who is the woman you have been seeing?" she asked.

"Why do you wanna know? I don't want you doing nothing to jeopardize my happiness right now," I said.

"The only reason I'm accepting this is because of my condition and the fact that I don't get aroused much. I have no physical use for you which is the only reason I fell in love with you. You treated my body delicately when everyone else was rough with me," she replied.

"She's different but I'm feeling shorty," I said.

"Like how you were feeling Jasmine?" she asked.

"Yeah, but I still felt like Poppa with Jasmine. This shorty doesn't make me feel dat way. Shorty makes a nigga feel free," I said and she rolled her eyes.

"Well, I bet she doesn't look as good as me," Nika said and I chuckled.

"Naw, she doesn't," I replied. Nika looked better than most of the females I knew but her attitude outshined it all. She would've been untouchable if she was a good female. I kissed her forehead and went into a guestroom at the end of the hall to take a quick nap before I went to the club.

****

Five hours later, I was at the bar inside my club getting a shot of Henny. It was the end of the month so Beretta was coming through to collect his cut. A stripper by the name of Pumpkin came over to me and whispered in my ear.

"Are you busy tonight?" she asked.

"Yeah, I am. Go over to your section, baby girl," I replied and she rolled her eyes. I was tired of fucking different bitches. Like clockwork, Beretta walked into the club. A stripper by the name of Apple ran over to him. Shorty had been wanting to fuck that nigga since I opened the club but he always turned her down. Matter of fact, he turned down every broad that tried to take him in a private room. Kemara had Beretta walking around looking like every female's dream husband. He went upstairs to my office and I followed him. Our routine had been the same for over a year, and most of the time, we didn't say shit to each other. I gave him his money, he made sure it was straight then he'd leave, but GMBAM niggas still hung around inside my club.

"We gotta talk, bruh," I said and closed the door behind me. Beretta sat in the chair behind my desk and propped his feet up.

Cocky, stupid-ass nigga, I thought.

"Dis gotta be interesting being as though we ain't on da same level. What do we gotta talk about, nigga?" he asked.

"Nika," I replied.

"Bruh, get my money so I can bounce," he said.

"Naw, fam. This shit is important. Nika got MS," I said.

"She's mentally slow, we been knowing dat, bruh," he replied.

"Multiple sclerosis," I said.

"I know what it is, muthafucka, but I just don't give a fuck. Nika is getting everything she asked for, especially for taking my father away from his seeds. I know everything she did now. She's gonna die alone, and if you were smart, you'd put her in a nursing home," he said.

"Not having parents is tough and I get dat, especially having a mother that doesn't give a fuck about you. I know all about it, but Nika was raped by her father and nobody helped shorty, so she used sex to heal and it became her addiction," I replied.

"Nika ain't my mother, nigga. The streets raised me, clothed me and fed me. She taught me how to survive and conquer all until there was nothing left to take. Even when I've done wrong, she still calls me her son. My mother let another bitch raise me, bottom line," he said. I went into the safe and grabbed stacks of money and put them inside of a backpack. He grabbed his backpack off the desk and left out the door. I sat at my desk and pulled a bottle out the liquor cabinet. The door knob turned.

"I'm busy!" I called out. The door opened and Fushia walked into my office. It was her second time inside. The first time was when she popped up on me wearing a blazer dress with nothing underneath. I gave it to her lil' fine ass right on my desk.

"What do you want, Fushia? I don't have the answers you're looking for right now," I said.

"I think we should talk about this," she said and sat in the love seat.

"Silk was right. I got a lot of shit going on and I should've been upfront, although I wasn't expecting it to get this far," I said.

"Me, neither. It's not easy falling in love with a bi-sexual man. We started out as friends when we worked together, but I noticed he'd look at me the same way a straight man would. One night after work, we ended up sleeping together and I got pregnant. Maybe my self-esteem was low or I enjoyed the excitement of trying something new, but whatever it was wasn't good for me. Anyways, he was sleeping with one of my guy cousins, but the final straw was when he started seeing a lesbian. When I met you, all I wanted was someone to make me forget about Silk for a little bit but you did more. You actually spent time with me and got to know me. I came here because I really want to know if you're not in a relationship. I enjoy dating you," she said.

"No, and my kids' mother knows I've met someone else. Me and her enjoyed the sex, that's all," I replied. She walked over to me and sat on top of my desk.

"I'm still trippin over Silk busting you down and knocking you up. I think I heard he had a daughter but I thought the nigga was playing mommy to one of his friends' daughters," I said and she giggled.

"Don't even bring up his ratchet-ass friends. Especially that Piper girl! And Silk couldn't go a day without talking about Mara and how pretty she is. I didn't like his friends because I knew he would've fucked them if they let him. The situation depressed me for years," she said.

"Mara is my sister," I replied and she covered her mouth.

"I'm so sorry, she isn't that bad, just a little rough around the edges," she said.

"That's my fault," I replied.

"Are y'all not close? You never talk about her," she said.

"We used to be but fuck all dat," I replied, squeezing her thighs. Fushia wrapped her arms around my neck and kissed me.

"We don't have to rush anything. Let's just keep it the way it is until we're ready," she said and I agreed. Shorty was definitely different from the other women I'd dealt with. She was passive with a little sass. She was also a brat, but all those things I could deal with. Nika basically told me I could do what I wanted as long as I made sure the kids were straight and that made me the happiest nigga alive.

Piper

Pistol was in his bench-pressing room downstairs while I was sitting up in bed eating chips.

Everything was back to normal, and just like we promised each other, Delonte's name was never spoken in our house again. I was watching reruns of *House of Payne* and dipping chocolate chip cookies in almond milk. The doctor didn't want me to eat a lot of junk food but fuck it! I was in my last trimester and was only a week and a half away from my due date. We decided to not know the sex of the baby until he or she was born. The baby's room was decorated in unisex colors like pale yellow, white and baby blue. Pistol begged me to find out what we were having but I wanted to be surprised and the anticipation was making the pregnancy a joyful one, although I was feeling like a blimp.

"Damn it! My stomach is in the way," I said aloud when I knocked over the big glass of milk and it splashed onto the floor. In frustration, I snatched the covers off my body and got up to clean the mess. An excruciating pain shot up my spine and caused me to double over when I bent down to get the cup. Warm liquid ran down my leg and I screamed for Pistol to come upstairs. Ten seconds later, he barged into our bedroom drenched in sweat and only wearing baller shorts.

"I think my water broke," I said, leaning forward. He rushed over to me and helped me on the bed.

"You probably peed yourself like you did the other day," he replied. A few days before, I was standing in the kitchen cooking. The baby must've laid on my bladder because by the time I realized I had to pee, I was already peeing. I thought my water broke so Pistol rushed me to the hospital but it was a false alarm.

"I'm having pains in my back," I said.

"But he ain't supposed to come yet. Look, just lay back down and I'll clean this mess up. It'll go away," he said.

"Nigga, this ain't fuckin' period cramps! I'm in labor!" I screamed at him.

"Yo, the doctor said he ain't due for two more weeks! Just calm down," he said. Niggas didn't know a damn thing about pregnancy but was always giving opinions. It was our first child so we were new to everything, but I knew for a fact I was in labor. I held my stomach and screamed at the top of my lungs. Pistol ran to the closet and grabbed my bag. He put on a shirt and grabbed his tennis shoes. I told myself I'd never complain about period cramps again because contractions were ten times worse. He helped me off the bed and down the stairs.

"Just let me sit here and call an ambulance," I said and sat on the step.

SOUL Publications

"Yo, the hospital is right around the corner. We'll have to wait," he replied. He went into the hall closet and grabbed a jean jacket and tennis shoes for me. Pistol put my shoes and jacket on for me as I yelled at him to hurry up. He was nervous and dropping shit on the floor when he helped me back up.

"It hurts sooooo bad," I whimpered. He grabbed his car keys off the hook by the door and helped me out the house.

The drive to the hospital was only three minutes but it was the longest three minutes of my life. The contractions were coming faster and for a second, I thought I needed oxygen because I couldn't breathe. Pistol ran into the hospital and came back out with two nurses and one of them had a wheelchair for me. He helped me out the car and into the chair. My body was covered in sweat and my hair bonnet was soaking wet. I told him to call Mara and the rest of my friends.

"Baby, let's worry about that later," he said as they wheeled me down the hall.

"Call Mara and she'll tell everyone else but please call her right now," I said. Pistol called Mara as the nurses helped me onto a hospital bed. The doctor came in and examined me. I wanted to choke Pistol when the doctor told me it was too late to get an epidural.

****

"Push, Piper!" Pistol was cheering twenty minutes later. Thirty minutes passed since I came to the hospital and I wasn't getting anywhere.

"I'm trying but it's not working!" I said.

"It'll be alright. Just calm down and push," Mara said. She came ten minutes ago and I wanted her in the room with me.

"URGGHHHHHH!" I screamed and squeezed Pistol's hand. He had to be in pain but he kept his game face on.

"I see his head!" the doctor yelled. I was tired, thirsty and weak!

"Just one more big push and they can pull him out," Mara said.

"Take deep breaths first and relax. Count to twenty then give me a strong push," the doctor said. After I practiced the breathing exercises, I pushed as hard as I could.

"He's out!" the doctor said and Mara wiped my forehead. Pistol was sobbing like a baby and it made me emotional; I cried with him. I held my arms out to him and he reached in to hug me. The nurse gave me my baby and he was chunky.

"Awww, congrats! He's so beautiful. I'm gonna go out there and tell everyone," Mara said and rushed out the hospital room. Our son had a head full of pretty dark coils. He got it from Pistol because he had a lot of curly hair when he was younger.

"Are you okay?" I asked, wiping his eyes.

"Yeah, I'm good. Shit snuck up on me after he came out. The best thing that happened in my life besides you," he said and kissed my lips. The nurse took baby Olijah away from me to clean him off.

"This is the beginning 'cause, shorty, we ain't finished. I want a big family," Pistol said.

"Can I heal first before you start talking crazy? Olijah split my pussy in half," I whispered.

"I do, too," he said and winked at me.

Who was I kidding? I'd give Pistol anything he wanted because he gave me everything I needed and more. The nurse gave Olijah back to me and I decided to breast feed. I heard it was healthier and it made the bond between the mother and baby stronger. The nurse showed me how to hold his head and guide my nipple to his mouth. Pistol looked confused.

"I'm breast feeding him," I said.

"Is it good for him? You haven't been eating right," he replied.

"He'll be fine," I said.

The rest of the family didn't come in until thirty minutes later. My room was crowded with people who I'd known for years.

"He's sooo adorable," Kellan said.

"Too cute to be this fool's son," Mara joked with Pistol.

"Yeah, keep talking shit, Mara. Yah husband gonna be mad when I blast you for that wig you got on your head," Pistol replied.

"I'on like it, neither, bruh," Beretta said and we all laughed.

"You weren't saying that last night when you were pulling on it, though," Mara fired back.

"Leave it alone, I like it," I said. Mara was wearing a lace front wig. She wanted to try something quick and easy because she was so busy with school, managing their businesses' finances and taking care of Zalia. Mara didn't have time to go to the salon like she used to.

"I'on remember dat, shorty. You trippin," Beretta replied while holding Olijah. It was Glock's turn to hold him, but he didn't want to. He said baby's necks were too weak but I had a feeling it was something bigger than that. Pistol was ready to interject in the conversation between Glock and Beretta but I shook my head at him. Glock and Pistol were still close, but deep down inside, I don't think he'd ever fully be happy for us. I wasn't expecting him to. I was satisfied with him not causing any drama between us.

"Me and Sniper are next," Kellan said and Sniper scratched his head. Mara was more excited than me it seemed. I thought it would've been difficult for her to be around me and baby Olijah but it wasn't. Her smile was bigger than ever and it reminded me that no matter what she was going through, she'd always be happy for me. That was the friendship we had and nothing could break it.

Part 9:

Karma

SOUL Publications

Kemara

January 1, 2017

"**H**APPY NEW YEARS!" we shouted inside of club Shottaz. It was our newest business investment. We decided to open it up on New Year's to celebrate a new start. At twenty-seven years old, I had it all. A loving husband, a Bachelor's Degree and a beautiful daughter. Matter of fact, the past few years had been some of my best years. Me and Beretta still argued here and there but all couples argued. My husband's style changed along with the way he carried himself. He was still dabbing into illegal stuff but GMBAM wasn't a crime gang anymore, it was a business movement. They gave back to the community and fixed abandoned buildings. A year ago, Beretta had a meeting with the mayor of our city because of the love he had for the youth. I had seen all of him throughout the years. My man went from corner hustling to making business moves. He had a vision of what he wanted and went for it, even if there was blood to be shed. Beretta got finer with age. He was dressed in an all-black Armani suit with soft bottom Armani loafers. He was simple when it came to jewelry. He was sporting a diamond rosary necklace and a plain gold presidential Rolex. Not only did he look good, he smelled good. He smiled at me, showing his diamond bottom row fronts. The nigga was just perfect! The groupies were spreading like the flu and in the beginning, I couldn't deal with it and it made me insecure. But I was secure with my position and them hoes couldn't move me.

"Happy New Year's, baby. We made it," Beretta whispered into my ear then kissed my lips.

Started from the bottom now we're here
Started from the bottom now my whole team fucking
here

Drake's song blared through the speakers inside the club after the ball dropped. Machete popped a bottle of champagne and it got on Jasmine's dress. She socked him in the chest and he fell onto the couch.

"Them two still go at it?" I asked Beretta.

"Machete still loves her. I don't think that will ever change," Beretta replied. Pistol pulled me to the side and he looked nervous.

"What's the matter? Are you about to change your mind?" I asked.

"No, but what if she embarrasses me in front of all these people. This was your idea to do it here," he complained.

"Nigga, it's a new year, so I thought it'd be right doing it tonight. Listen to me, everything will go smoothly. Y'all love each other and you know she ain't gonna tell you 'no.' I'm gonna tell the DJ to cut the music off as soon as you get down on one knee. After she says 'yes,' I'm going to tell him to play her favorite song. We got this," I said.

"I appreciate you. You get on my nerves but it's all love," he said and I rolled my eyes.

"Get outta my face and handle your business. Awww, make me proud," I replied and he grilled me. I left the VIP section and went upstairs to the DJ booth.

"Is everything, straight?" the DJ asked when he took his headphones off.

"When you see that man get down on his knee, turn the music off. Once she accepts his ring, play 'I Will Always Love You'," I said.

"By who?" he asked.

"Troop," I replied and he nodded his head.

"Bet," he said.

I went downstairs, back to the section. Pistol looked at me for approval and I nodded my head at him. He pulled Piper to the center of the room and got down on one knee. Like clockwork, the music stopped. Piper was dressed in an off-the-shoulder silver glitter gown. Her jet-black hair was styled in a deep wave bob and she had a red rose behind her ear. I told her she reminded me of Dorothy Dandridge in the movie *Carmen Jones*. She looked so beautiful and I was so happy for her. I looked over at Glock and he didn't look happy. Maybe I was overthinking it but I always caught Glock staring at Piper and probably wishing it was him she married. Her face was priceless and I told Beretta to get the cameraman so he could capture it. Pistol went into his pocket and opened a velvet box. Piper fanned her face to hold the tears back.

"I want to make this official and give you everything until there is nothing left to give. All I want to know is can you be Mrs. Ramsey and spend the rest of your years with me?" Pistol said.

Piper screamed, "Yes, I'll marry you!" and we clapped for her.

"That's it? What happened to the long speeches?" Kellan asked while sipping the champagne.

"What's understood ain't gotta be explained," I replied. Piper kissed Pistol and the song by Troop came on. Piper was thirteen years old when she told me that was the song she wanted to be played when she got engaged. She said it was for her and Poppa, back when she had a big crush on him. Crazy how life turned out because she hated Poppa and was marrying Pistol, someone she used to argue with all the time.

I looked around the crowd and a face was missing: Emma's. She hadn't contacted me since the incident with her, Quanta and Thickems. I thought I was going to see her in school but she stopped going. Quanta was still around Beretta and his gang. The situation with Emma must've calmed him down because he wasn't out running around with different females. Him and Thickems had a girl and I only saw her a few times at Piper's house. Me and Thickems still weren't talking and I hadn't seen her since I stabbed her.

"Yo, you good?" Beretta asked me.

"Yeah, I was just thinking about Emma. She's supposed to be here," I said.

"You'll see her again. Quanta doesn't even know where shorty's at," he replied.

"It's all of his fault. I still hate him," I said and he chuckled.

"Cut da man some slack, shorty. The nigga is a good dude but he got caught up in the fast life. It happens to the best of us. I bet he'll be a different man if he ran into shorty again," Beretta said.

"I hope so, but I'll still hate him," I replied.

"This party is lit, my nigga!" Carlos shouted out at Beretta. Beretta slapped hands with him then hugged him.

"You better not be drinkin', lil' nigga. I can get in trouble for that shit," Beretta said. Carlos aka Nine, thought he was a part of GMBAM. Beretta kept him around to keep an eye on him, but Carlos worked at the youth center. He looked up to Beretta and had been for many years since he was a kid. He was seventeen years old going on eighteen and was around Beretta's height, just an inch shorter. Carlos was always mistaken for a man but he was still child-like.

"Nigga, drinkin'? I been drinkin' since I was eleven years old," Carlos joked. Beretta walked away when Sniper called him over. Carlos was staring at me from head-to-toe as if he was checking me out.

"What do you want, Carlos?" I asked.

"My name is Nine," he said.

"I'm not calling you that. All I see is the same little kid from Newtowne who couldn't stay his bad ass out the street," I replied.

"Come on, shorty. I'm grown now," he said. He brushed his hand down his waves and licked his lips, the same shit Beretta did when he was annoyed.

"No, you're not grown. Beretta is only allowing you to stay here until twelve thirty so you only have ten minutes," I replied and he smirked.

"Ight, cool. You look beautiful by the way," he said.

"You look handsome yah self," I replied. He kissed my cheek before he walked away and Silk came over to me.

SOUL Publications

"Stay away from that boy, Mara. I'on trust his lil' bad ass," Silk said.

"Boy, what in the hell can Carlos do to me? I don't pay him no mind," I replied.

"He tries too hard to be like Beretta," Silk said.

"All of the hood niggas look up to Beretta. Chill out and stop acting paranoid," I replied.

"Umm hmmmm, you know I hate dat little boy with a passion. I'm surprised he ain't dead yet. That bitch is a bad seed," Silk said.

"He'll grow out of it. Beretta did and we both know Beretta was off the damn chain when he was his age," I replied. Piper walked over to us after she finished dancing with Pistol and I congratulated her.

"Thank you so much! Girllll, I knew you helped him out. Awwww, it was perfect! Bitcchhhhhhh, I'm getting married now," Piper sang and flashed her rock at us.

"Let me see dat ring," Silk said and grabbed Piper's hand.

"Chillleeeeeeee, I'm ready to trade Roneisha in and get me a GMBAM nigga, shat!" Silk said.

"They don't want you," Piper replied.

"Glock might because, honey, he done ran through every female in da city. He needs something fresh," Silk said, feeling on his ass.

"Where is your baby mother?" I asked.

"Which one?" he replied.

Silk knocked up Roniesha and she was six months pregnant with a boy. We were concerned about him raising a son, but we had faith in him.

"Damn sure ain't Fushia. She done moved on with her life," I teased. Silk was still mad about Poppa and Fushia but they were happy. Me and Poppa talked once a week but we didn't talk long. He called me to check up on me. I was shocked at how much he was involved in church and Fushia's father was helping him a lot with guiding him in the right direction.

"I can still fuck her if I want to," Silk said and we bust out laughing.

"Chilleeeee, get over it! Fushia getting banged out by Poppa. He turns bitches out with his dirty-dick ass," Piper said and Silk rolled his eyes.

"My New Year's resolution is finding new hoes to hang with because y'all bitches are cursed," he said and I blew him a kiss. Jasmine walked over to us with a tray of drinks. I was already buzzed but I wanted to get drunk and have off-the-wall sex to finish the holiday off.

SOUL Publications

"When you and Machete gonna stop playing and be together already?" Piper asked Jasmine.

"Never, I'm celibate," Jasmine said.

"Since when?" I asked.

"Since the last time I slept with Poppa and that was a few years ago. I'm focused on my acting career and I don't have time to be going crazy over these fuck-niggas. Machete will ruin my life, I don't care how fine he is," Jasmine said. Kellan walked over to us and Jasmine rolled her eyes.

"Get over it, Jasmine. Zain has moved on from Machete and you're still holding onto da hurt. Let dat pain go, sis," Kellan slurred.

"Bitch, who you talkin' to?" Jasmine asked.

"I got twenty on Kellan," Silk whispered to me and I looked at him. Kellan got busy with her hands but Jasmine was busy with her guns. Fists couldn't stand a chance in a gunfight.

"I'm talking to you. I'm tired of my man complaining to me about how his sister doesn't come around much and we all know why. You still hurt because of Machete cheating on you with my little sister. Y'all were how old again? Machete is a grown-ass man now and Zain has moved on. Get da fuck over it like I said, bitch!" Kellan yelled back.

"Can we not do this right now? Kellan, you're drunk, so chill out," Piper said.

"Drunk or not, that little hoe needs to hear da truth. She thinks because she's a Z-list celebrity she's too good to visit her brother!" Kellan spat. Sniper walked over to us and got between Kellan and Jasmine.

"Yo, why you trippin?" Sniper asked Kellan.

"'Cause I'm tired of you being in yah feelings around the holidays 'cause Jasmine doesn't want to bring her funky ass around. She's still holding on to dat hurt and it's time to let it go," Kellan said.

"You talking about me to that bitch?" Jasmine asked Sniper.

"It wasn't like dat, so chill," Sniper said.

"Naw, fuck you, too!" Jasmine said to Sniper and they started arguing. Beretta came over to calm his siblings down. Kellan walked away like she didn't start anything.

"Chillleeee, they got so much drama and I'm mad 'cause I want to be in it, hunty," Silk said.

"Let's go hit the dance floor," I replied and grabbed a bottle of champagne out a bucket of ice. We went downstairs to the main dancefloor. The club was three levels, and each floor had a big bar wrapped around the dance floor. The black marble floors brought out the red leather furniture. The majority of the walls were made of fish tanks with beautiful tropical fish. Our club looked like an aquarium. There were six bartenders at the bar and the drink line was still long.

"I gotta tell you, this place is da shit!" Piper said.

"And so is that ring. Flash it for me one time," I said and she waved her hand.

The rest of the night, we partied, laughed and argued, but that's what made us family.

Beretta

"**M**y feet hurt," Mara said as I drove through the gate of our new home after we left Shootaz. We lived in a seven-bedroom mansion-style home in Chevy Chase, Maryland. Behind our crib was a lake where we could go fishing. I promised Mara I was going to put her in a big house with a big backyard. We moved into the house five months ago. I surprised her with it on her twenty-seventh birthday. I'd been with Mara for almost ten years and it didn't feel like it. Time was moving fast but I wasn't tripping. I parked my Rolls Royce Wraith in the garage next to Kemara's Bentley truck.

"You getting old, baby girl. You gotta hang the high-heels up," I replied.

"Shut the fuck up, Z'wan. I'm still young and feeling better than ever. You'll be thirty soon so I know you lying," she said and I chuckled.

"But I still make that thing cream," I said.

"Why you gotta be nasty all the time?" she replied.

SOUL Publications

"'Cause my shorty is sexy, fuck you mean?" I asked and she blushed. My shorty was bomb. She was wearing a black long gown with sparkles in it and her hair was styled into a high ponytail that stopped at her ass. She was still thick, but her hips were a meal on their own. Kemara's face still looked the exact same from when she was nineteen but she matured in her body instead of her looks.

"I betta be," she said and got out the car. She took her heels off and walked into the crib through the door in the garage.

"You betta wake up 'cause I'm tryna see what's under dat dress," I said, feeling on her ass.

"Stop before Gwen sees us," she said. Gwen was the babysitter. She was an older lady, around fifty-five years old. Mara wasn't going for a younger babysitter hanging around the house. Gwen only watched Zalia for us whenever me and Kemara had to go somewhere with adults only. Earlene used to do it but she spent most of her time at Queen's Den.

"Gwen is asleep," I said. She walked up the spiral staircase and I lifted up her dress.

"Stop it, boy!" she giggled.

"I'm a grown-ass man so stop playing. You knew what you were doing tossing them shots back. You were getting ready for me," I said. Mara peeped her head in Zalia's bedroom and she was knocked out, head hanging halfway off the bed. I went into her bedroom and fixed her so she wouldn't fall off the bed. Zalia was short for her age. She was five and a half and had the height of a three-year-old, but other than that she was healthy. Having another baby was long gone from my mind. I was busy making moves and always coming up with ways to legitimize my money. Kemara never checked to see if she could have kids or not because she was tied up with work and Zalia. Basically, we coped with it by burying ourselves into what we wanted out of life. I kissed Zalia's forehead before I left out of her room. Our master bedroom was at the end of the hall behind two ten-feet-tall heavy brass double doors. Mara pulled the doors open and the scent of her perfume spilled out into the hallway. Her perfume lingered around our bedroom for hours.

"Tonight was fun. Are Sniper and Jasmine cool?" she asked.

"Yeah, they're straight until Kellan brings something else up. Shorty miserable or sumthin. I don't know why Sniper still fucks with shorty," I replied.

"Because she knows too much," Mara said. She went into her walk-in closet and placed her shoes on a shelf. Kemara had her own closet because she had too much shit. I didn't shop much, and if I did, I only bought a few things. Mara, on the other hand, was ridiculous. She came out of the closet only wearing a G-string. In the corner of our room was a stripper pole. It was Mara's idea to get one because she liked dancing for me on a late night. A lot of females wanted me to step out on my wife; a few of them begged me to and told me they'd sign a nondisclosure paper to fuck me. Pistol called it, "rich nigga problems." I didn't need to step out because she possessed everything a nigga could ask for. She was a freak in the bedroom, educated, beautiful, had a phat ass, big titties, bomb pussy, she cooked and cleaned. Besides, I didn't want to go down that road again. Mara was younger when I cheated and still in school. I was taking care of her and she still mustered up the strength to leave me if she had to. At the time, I felt like she needed me so she wasn't going anywhere. Now, Mara was finished school, more mature and her name was on everything I owned. She'd leave me and take everything with her. I came too far to throw it away over some random pussy.

Mara laid across the bed and I bent down to pull her G-string off with my teeth. Her two meaty cheeks jiggled when I gave it a hard smack. I took off my clothes and she stuck her ass up in the air for me.

"Hurry up before Gwen wakes up," she said.

"Fuck Gwen! She doesn't pay shit in here," I replied and she bust out laughing.

"How she gonna hear us in this big-ass house and she's down the other end of the hall?" I said. I spread her buttocks and dove straight in. Back in the day, eating ass would've sent me to an early grave, but with Mara, I didn't give a fuck. Her body was like a buffet and a nigga stayed hungry.

"Yeesssssss, baby. Right there!" Mara groaned as I ate her from the back. She reached between her legs and opened her pussy lips for me and that pink eye stared at me. I latched onto her clit and squeezed her cheeks as I sucked on her pearl. Pussy juice burst from between her slit and ran down her inner-thighs. I used my thumb to tease her entrance and she fell forward on the bed.

"UMMMMMMMM!" she moaned and my dick swelled. I was high and a little tipsy from the party so I was ready to dig in her guts. After she came on my tongue, I stood up and pulled her to the edge of the bed. She arched her back and I rubbed my head between her sloppy wet lips. Mara's nails dug into the mattress when I pressed my head into her, stretching her pussy. With one hand pulling her ponytail and the other gripping her ass cheek, I pounded her spot. We made love all the time but she knew what type of night it was—straight fucking.

"Go deeper, baby! Pound yah pussy!" she hissed when I slammed into her. Her walls gripped my dick and I bit my bottom lip to keep myself from moaning like a bitch. I pulled out only leaving the tip in so I could watch her asshole wink at me. Mara's body spoke to me when she didn't have to; I curved my thumb and slid it into her anus. She cried out my name and stuck her face in the mattress while I banged her back out.

"Yo, you a nasty lil' bitch," I groaned when she threw her ass back. Her legs trembled and her moans got louder when she squirted and that shit splashed against my lower abdomen. I pulled out of her and rubbed the tip of my head around her asshole. Mara occasionally let me fuck her in the ass, especially on a drunk night.

"Be easy!" she yelled out when I eased the head in. It took me a while to fit just half of my dick in but it was worth it. While I was in her ass, two of my fingers was playing in her pussy.

"I'm ready to cum again!" she squealed as her legs trembled. I wasn't trying to stick my dick back into her pussy after it had been in her ass so I pushed myself a little further in and nutted inside of her.

"ARRGGGHHHHHHH! UMMMMMM!" I groaned. I pulled out and put the rest of my seeds on her ass cheek. Shorty was stretched out and snoring.

"Wake up, Mara. I'm not done! Let's get in da shower," I said.

"Wipe me off. I'm too tired," she said. I went into the bathroom to get a rag for her. Sperm was coming out of her ass and it was across her back. That shit looked nasty after a while. It took me five minutes to clean Mara off. She would've woke up yelling at me and wanting to fight if I left her like that. I took a shower then got into bed with her and went to sleep.

****

The next day, I went over to Sniper's crib to pick him up. We were going to a basketball game at the Capital One arena in D.C. It was the Wizards vs. Golden State. I rang the doorbell and Kellan opened the door.

"Sniper is in the shower. Come on in," she said. I stepped inside the crib and followed her into the living room. She sat on the couch in front of me and crossed her legs, exposing her bare pussy.

"Oh, my bad," she said and closed her robe.

"Why weren't the girls invited?" she asked.

"The niggas just hanging out on this one," I replied.

"I want to thank you again for that night when those men ran into our home. I'll never forget the way you came in there and cradled me. Your arms are very strong," she said.

"Can I use your bathroom?" I asked.

"Sure, it's down the hall," she said. I got up and went to the bathroom. Kellan was flirtatious and that was her attitude, but over the years shorty was dropping hints like she wanted me to fuck her. Sniper loved his shorty regardless of how many females he had other relationships with, but Kellan was on some other shit. I didn't know how to tell my little brother I thought his girl was trying to come on to me because I thought it was her personality.

Maybe she talks to the rest of the niggas like dat, too. I gotta pay attention before I say sumthin because it might not be personal. But, damn, would dat make me a snitch? I thought. After I finished peeing, I washed my hands and left out of the bathroom. I went back into the living room and shorty was bending over dusting the entertainment center with her pussy smiling right in my face.

SOUL Publications

"Tell Sniper I'll be in my whip," I said and stood up.

"It's cold outside," she replied. I walked right out of the living room and out of their crib. When I got inside my whip, I texted Sniper and told him I was waiting for him outside. Five minutes later, Kellan walked out the house wearing leggings, a coat and UGG boots. She knocked on the window and told me to put it down because it was important.

"Did I make you feel uncomfortable?" she asked.

"Yo, what's up witchu? What type of games are you playing? This shit gotta stop," I replied.

"I see the way you have been looking at me for the past few years. You don't have to lie about it. I knew you was feeling me by the way you came over here and saved me. If I'm wrong, I apologize. Please don't tell Mara or Sniper, it won't happen again. Maybe I read your body language wrong," she said.

"Yo, are you crazy?" I replied.

"No, I'm not. All niggas in GMBAM cheat. You can keep pretending to be the perfect husband but I know you still got it in you. Besides, pay attention to your wife. She might have a thing for young niggas," she said and walked into the house.

What in da fuck is dat crazy bitch tryna say? I thought.

****

"Yo, fam. You good, bruh?" Carlos asked me while he sat next to me during the basketball game. When I did shit with my niggas, I invited him out. He wanted to push dope but I wasn't letting it happen, and any nigga who gave him drugs to sell had a price on their head. He reminded me of myself when I was his age and I didn't want him going down that same path. I didn't have anyone to look out for me so the lil' nigga was lucky. He stayed in a three-bedroom condo with his younger sisters. I paid their bills and made sure they had everything they needed.

"Yeah, I'm just thinking about some shit," I said.

"Wifey problems?" he asked, stuffing popcorn in his mouth.

"Da fuck do you know about those types of problems?" I asked.

"Bruh, you treat me like a kid. I'm grown, fah real. All females are the same," he said.

"Nigga, you don't know what you talkin' about. You fucking sixteen-year-olds," Glock said.

"Nigga, I fuck grown women. I was banging a twenty-two-year-old last week and she's been on my nut sack since, nigga," Carlos said.

"Bluffing-ass nigga," Machete said.

"I'm tryna see what's up with Jasmine, though," Carlos chuckled and Machete grilled him.

"Nigga, get yah bread up, muthafucka. You talk all dat shit and still having wet dreams," Machete said.

"Yeah, whatever, nigga," Carlos replied.

Kemara sent a text telling me that she was cooking dinner and she invited people over to our crib—well, the people in our circle.

"We can go to my crib when we leave here. Mara and Piper cooking dinner," I told my niggas.

"Good, 'cause I'm starving," Pistol said.

"Nigga, you always hungry," Sniper replied.

"Scrawny-ass nigga," Pistol joked back.

"I'm all muscle, muthafucka," Sniper said.

We kicked back, had a few drinks and enjoyed the game. Sniper was talking about his on-and-off side-chick, Brittany. That nigga had too much going on, especially with Kellan.

"Wait, nigga. She's pregnant?" Machete asked.

"We don't know yet. I hope she ain't because I'on want no kids and we've been careful," Sniper said.

Is that why Kellan's starting to trip? I thought.

"Kellan gonna fuck you up if Brittany is pregnant," Glock said.

"She already knows Brittany might be carrying my seed. I told her last night after the party because Brittany kept blowing me up. Shit was smooth when all three of us was together. Those bitches are crazy," Sniper said.

"Nigga, you making them crazy. Why not pick one?" Machete asked.

"I know you ain't talking. Yah bitch-ass be knocking all kinds of broads down," Sniper replied.

"I'm single, I can do what I want. I'm waiting for Jasmine to take me back and stop all her bullshit," Machete said.

"She's on da grind, bruh. You ain't right for her right now," Sniper said and Machete grilled him.

"I'm a changed man," Machete said.

"Since when?" Carlos asked.

"Yo, if you don't mind yah fuckin' business! Grown niggas are talkin'," Machete said.

"Fuck you," Carlos snarled.

SOUL Publications

"Yo, chill da fuck out and have some respect. Machete gonna knock yah lil' ass out, then what? You ain't dat tough," I said.

"He keeps playin' me like I'm some sucka," Carlos said.

"Nigga, you a wanna-be thug. You in da presence of some real niggas so all dat lil' tough hood nigga shit will get you kilt. Keep playin' wit me and watch what I do to you," Machete said.

"Yo, that's a kid," Glock replied to Machete.

"Nigga, I'on give a fuck what he is to y'all but I'll body slam his bitch-ass if he keeps talkin' to me. I'on like dat lil' nigga, fam," Machete admitted.

"I'on like you, neither, muthafucka," Carlos said. Machete was ready to get up but Sniper and Pistol held him back. I wanted to fuck Carlos up myself but we would've been a distraction to the game since we had courtside seats.

"Yo, I'm not coming around if that bitch is around. I should put a slug in his dome. That lil' nigga thinks he got stripes or something. Muthafucka ain't never put in no real street work. Bitch-ass boy," Machete snarled.

"Chill, fam. You trippin' over a teenager!" Glock said.

"Nigga, how about you take an ass whipping for him then," Machete said.

"Y'all niggas acting like some straight busters! I'on wanna hear shit else! The whole conversation is dead!" I said. Machete had temper issues and once the nigga started, he couldn't stop. At that moment, he probably wanted to shoot Carlos and Glock.

After the game, we all went back to my crib. Soon as I walked in, the house was smelling like soul food. My mouth watered from the smell of cornbread. Pistol's son ran to me and I picked him up. He was two and a half years old and always asking me for my chain.

"Can I have this?" he asked.

"Naw, you can't. Aye, Pistol, get my lil' man a chain," I said.

"Yeah, right. He tryna floss already," Pistol said. Olijah was Pistol's twin. He had long cornrows like his father had back in the day. I put him down and playfully punched his father in the leg.

"Chill out, boy!" Pistol said, trying to calm him down. Olijah was known to fuck up somebody's crib. He was hyper and Piper couldn't do shit with him.

"Look what Mommy brought me," Zalia said when she came to me. She pointed at the pink diamond earrings in her ears. Mara was still hardheaded. I told shorty stop buying Zalia expensive jewelry when all she did was lose it and give it to her friends at school.

"I hope they fake, too," I replied.

"Mommy said I'm too pretty to wear fake diamonds," Zalia said. She was a bougie little girl and she talked proper. She was the only kid I knew who thought they were too good for Kool-Aid. Kemara was responsible for that bullshit, but other than that, she was a good kid and had manners.

"Can I borrow a dolla?" Olijah asked Sniper.

"You can tell his parents from Newtowne," Machete said and we bust out laughing.

"What you gonna do with this?" I asked when I handed him a dollar.

"Put it in my jar," he replied then stormed off.

"That boy bad as shit," Pistol said and shook his head.

"He probably got two g's in his jar already. I gave him twenty dollas last week," Machete said.

I went into the kitchen and wanted to walk back out. Kellan was sitting at my kitchen island drinking a glass of wine. Mara walked over to me and kissed my lips.

"Y'all had fun?" she asked.

"Yeah, it was aight," I replied. Kellan blew me a kiss and winked at me while Mara's back was turned towards her. Shorty was on some get-back shit because Sniper possibly knocked up his side-piece. I heard noises coming from the living and I walked out the kitchen and down the hall.

"Baby sis," I said and hugged her.

"You're taking me to the airport tomorrow morning, right?" she asked me. Jasmine lived in Maryland but she was always traveling. She was doing commercials, TV gigs and many other things. She was getting her own money in a positive way and I was proud of her.

"Yeah, I'll drop you off," I said.

"Why you ain't ask me?" Machete asked.

"Well, do you want to?" Jasmine asked.

"Of course. Anything for my queen," Machete replied.

"I can sleep in then," I said. Carlos was chilling on the couch and texting on his phone. I sat next to him so I could talk to him. He was quiet since him and Machete got into at the game.

"What's up witchu?" I asked him.

"Nothing," he said. I took his phone away from him.

"Seriously?" he asked.

"Yo, I need your full attention when I'm talking to you. What's good? All that gangster talk back at the game wasn't even cool," I said.

SOUL Publications

Welcome to the Lowlife 3   Natavia

"You were like me when you were my age so I don't get why you not tryna put me on. You got me out here working at clubs and shit like I'm a servant," he said.

"I'm tryna get you off the streets. You're still young, so you can change," I replied and he chuckled.

"I'm a man, Beretta, and I'm already in the streets," he said.

"If you're a man then you don't need my help. Do what I did and get it on your own. You ain't like me and will never be like me. Talking gangsta and having a street name don't make you me, muthafucka. I neva went to another nigga and asked him to put me on. I got it the hard way. We ain't da same, Carlos. You have someone that cares about you and is tryna help you. I didn't have that, so my hunger for it was deeper than yours. Go to school, get an education and do the right thing, bruh. I am putting you on, I'm giving you real knowledge and I gave you a job," I replied.

"Yeah, you right. I apologize for that earlier, though," he said and I slapped hands with him.

"My boy," I said.

Mara came out into the living room and brought me a glass of Henny.

"Can I have one?" Carlos asked.

"Boy, hell no," Mara said.

"Just give him a shot Mara. He's chilling with us so he's straight," I replied and she rolled her eyes.

"Bruh, you lucky. Mara is perfect," he said.

"Yeah, get you a lil' shorty that's down to earth and she'll stick with you forever," I said.

"No doubt," he replied.

****

A few hours later, we were chilling, eating and drinking. The kids were upstairs with Jasmine watching a cartoon movie. Jasmine was like a big-ass kid and Zalia loved her. Zalia called Jasmine her best friend. We were sitting around in the living room and Piper came up with an idea to play some stupid game.

"Okay, so what are the rules?" Kellan asked.

"Someone has to say, 'never have I ever' then call out something. If you did it, you have to drink. For example, never have I ever had a threesome. You had one so you have to drink to it. Now do y'all understand?" Piper asked.

"Chilleeeee, I'm about to be drunk 'cause I did everything," Silk said.

"Babe, are you playing?" Mara asked me.

"I'll participate for a few minutes," I replied.

"Okay, I'll go first. Never have I ever had an STD," Mara said.

Me, Mara, Carlos, and Silk were the only ones who didn't drink to that.

"Damn, y'all niggas nasty," Mara said.

"Man, I was sixteen when I got one," Sniper said.

"Yeah, I was young, too," Machete said.

"This lil' bitch burned me a few months ago," Glock said.

"Okay, it's my turn. Never have I ever had anal sex," Kellan said and took a shot. Mara, Piper and Silk took a shot.

"It's your turn, Machete," Kellan said.

"Never have I ever jerked off to midget porn," Machete said and I took a shot. I was the only one but fuck it. The midget had a phat ass and I was seventeen at the time.

"Niggggaaaaaa, you serious?" Glock asked me.

"Yeah, her ass was too phat," I replied.

"I can't believe you, Beretta." Mara fell over laughing.

"Yeah, whatever," I said.

"Okay, Silk, it's your turn," Kellan said.

"I should close my ears," Machete replied.

"Nigga, I fuck bitches, too. You ain't gotta do all dat," Silk said and rolled his eyes as he cleared his throat.

"Never have I ever wanted to fuck my friend's girlfriend or boyfriend," Silk said. The room got quiet and everyone looked at Pistol.

"Da fuck y'all niggas looking at me for?" Pistol asked.

"Well, take a shot," Kellan said.

"For what? Piper wasn't Glock's girl," Pistol said.

"But she was fucking with him," Kellan said.

"Okay, we shouldn't play this anymore. This game is getting messy," Mara said.

"I mean we're all family, right? Why can't Pistol take a shot?" Kellan asked.

"Leave him alone," Piper said to Kellan.

"Oh, so we gotta avoid certain questions, huh? I mean we already know the truth," Kellan said.

"Exactly, which is why he doesn't need to take a fucking shot!" Mara yelled at Kellan.

"I'll ask another question. I forgot all about that," Silk said.

"We all forgot about that," Piper said.

"I'll take a shot," Carlos replied.

"Nigga, who shorty you tryna smash?" Sniper asked.

"None of y'all shorties," Carlos said.

"And Pistol still acting like a punk," Kellan laughed.

"Yo, get yah girl," Pistol said to Sniper.

"Yo, why you gotta start shit with my niggas?" Sniper asked Kellan.

"Y'all too sensitive to me," Kellan replied.

"You always start shit when you start drinking. Put the alcohol down," Mara said and snatched her drink out of her hand. Kellan rolled her eyes and crossed her arms.

"She betta chill out before I forget we're friends and whip her ass," Piper said.

I got up to use the bathroom. The door opened while I was pissing. I knew it was Mara because of the scent of her perfume. She was always wanting a quickie and it didn't matter who was around.

"Take them panties off, shorty," I said, shaking my head off. I flushed the toilet then took off my shirt. When I turned around, it was that bitch, Kellan, and she was naked from the waist down.

"Yo, what in da fuck are you doing in here?" I asked, fixing my pants.

"They're too busy arguing to notice we're gone. It'll be quick," she said, dropping down to her knees. I snatched her up and she wrapped her legs around me. We fell into the sink and hit against the door. The hallway bathroom was small so shorty was wrapping her legs around me and pulling me into her.

"Chill da fuck out!" I whispered.

"Sniper and Mara don't need to find out," she said. She was still on me so I slapped her dumb ass. I wrapped my hand around her throat and the door opened. The shit looked suspect because Kellan was on the sink with her legs around me and my pants had fell down. It looked like we were fucking.

"What in da fuck!" Mara screamed and I pulled my pants up.

"Baby, it's not what you—" I was cut off when she slammed her fist into my face. Kellan tried to sneak out of the bathroom but Mara caught her by the hair and it got crazy.

"Bitch, you tryna fuck my husband in my house!" Mara screamed. Kellan punched Mara in the face and

Mara almost slipped on the floor. I got in between them but Mara dug her nails in my face and started kicking me. Shorty kicked me in the nuts and I didn't think it hurt that bad but it did. Kellan screamed for Sniper when she ran down the hall but Mara caught her and slammed her head into the wall. Everyone ran into the hallway to see what was going on.

"He tried to rape me!" Kellan screamed.

"Y'all were fucking! How long has this been going on for, Beretta?" Mara screamed when she ran up on me. I held her arms and tried to explain myself.

"Shorty was tryna get me to fuck her. I swear I didn't touch dat girl!" I replied.

"You tried to rape me!" Kellan cried. Jasmine came down the stairs to see what was going on.

"What happened?" Jasmine asked.

"Your piece of shit brother was fucking Kellan in our house!" Mara screamed.

"I didn't touch dat girl, Mara. You know I wouldn't fuck one of your friends! She's my brother's shorty, and why would I fuck her in our house?" I asked. Sniper was angry and I couldn't tell if he was mad at me or Kellan.

"Baby, I was going into the kitchen and he pulled me into the bathroom. Look at my face! He tried to take advantage of me," she said. Her lip was bleeding because I slapped her dumb-ass, but it made me look guilty.

"You're lying. You believe her, Sniper?" Jasmine asked. Kellan spit on Jasmine and started yelling at her. Jasmine hit Kellan so hard she fell into the wall. Kellan was screaming for help as Jasmine sat on top of her and pounded her fists into her face. Sniper grabbed Jasmine and took her upstairs. Mara ran up the stairs, too, and came back with a gun.

"Mara, don't do it!" Piper begged her.

"Why did she feel comfortable trying to seduce you in my house?" Mara asked me.

"I don't know! But I didn't touch that girl. I swear I didn't touch her," I said, damn-near begging her to believe me.

"What happened, Kellan?" Piper asked.

"He tried to come on to me. He's been doing it for a long time. Why won't nobody believe me?" Kellan asked. She was trying to cry rape to make herself look innocent. Shorty wasn't expecting to get caught. Mara pointed her gun at me. She was drunk and wasn't thinking clearly. Zalia came downstairs and Mara hid the gun behind her back. Kellan was still naked from the waist down and Zalia looked at us in confusion.

"What's the matter, Daddy?" she asked.

"Nothing, baby girl. Go upstairs, I'll be up there soon," I replied. Piper took her hand and walked her upstairs.

"Get out," Mara said to me.

"Fuck no. You can leave because I'm not leaving my fucking house! That bitch is lying and you're gonna believe her over me?" I asked.

"I don't think you tried to rape her but I know you have a history of sticking your dick where it doesn't belong," Mara said.

"That was years ago! Out of all bitches I can have and you think I want her? Why would I fuck her in our house?" I yelled at Mara. Pistol told me to chill out but I was mad! My own fucking wife was letting a bird come between us.

"Naw, bruh. Fuck that! This bitch wanna leave, she can leave because I'm not going anywhere," I replied.

"This marriage is over! I caught you between that hoe's legs with your pants down to yah fuckin' ankles. Why would you wait until you got caught to tell me she was coming on to you? I invited that bitch into my house and you knew she wanted you?" Mara asked.

"It wasn't that easy to tell knowing how my brother feels about her," I said. Mara left out of the house. Piper and Silk ran after her. Kellan was crying and still saying it was my fault. Mara came back into the house seconds later.

"NO, MARA!" Piper screamed. Mara pointed the gun at Kellan and pulled the trigger. The bullet pierced through her shoulder and she screamed for help. Machete took the gun from Mara when she pointed it at me. Shorty was trying to kill us.

Kemara

I just knew Beretta was going to cheat on me again but I wasn't expecting him to fuck someone I considered a friend. It made me think back to the conversation I had with Kellan a month prior…

"You smell good. I got the same perfume," I said to Kellan while we were shopping.

"Thank you, my man got it for me," she replied.

"Beretta loves that scent," I said to her…

I wasn't thinking much of it because I wasn't the only one who wore Creed but what a coincidence. When I saw them, I snapped. Beretta's dick was out and her legs were around him. Now all of a sudden, the bitch was coming on to him. Both of them were guilty.

"Chill out, Mara! Yah daughter is upstairs," Machete said and took the gun from me.

"Get her out of my house!" I said. Sniper came downstairs and saw Kellan bleeding out on the floor. He picked her up and rushed her outside. Beretta was mad at me because I was mad at him.

"So, you really don't believe me?" Beretta asked.

"Why would she make a bold move like that if she thought you didn't want her?" I asked.

"I don't know! Maybe her and Sniper going through some shit, but I never gave her the impression that I wanted her," he said.

"I need some air," I replied. I grabbed my purse and keys in the living room and stormed out of the house. I got into my car and the passenger-side door opened. It was Carlos.

"What are you doin'?" I asked.

"Can you take me home?" he replied. I didn't answer him. I just drove straight out of my driveway and through the gate.

"I gotta tell you sumthin, Mara," he said.

"Not now, Carlos. Just shut da fuck up and ride!" I replied.

"Kellan and Beretta have been creeping for a minute. He told me he'd put me on if I didn't say nothing," he said.

"WHAT!" I yelled.

"Yeah, they set that up. I saw him nod his head at her towards the hallway before he got up. That nigga is bogus," Carlos said.

"Why in da fuck are you telling me this?" I replied, speeding down the street.

"Because you're too good for dat nigga. I'm always around him and he be schooling me on how to play bitches," Carlos said.

"That doesn't sound like my husband," I replied.

"How well do you know him? I bet you didn't see him and Kellan hooking up, did you?" he replied and I refused to answer.

"I should take everything!" I yelled out in frustration with tears falling from my eyes. Beretta was calling my phone but I didn't answer. I just needed time to think. Why would Kellan do that? Why wouldn't Beretta tell me she was hitting on him? Which one of them was lying? It was just too much for me to take in.

****

Thirty minutes later, I was pulling up to Carlo's apartment building. He was quiet as he sat in the passenger's seat.

"Get out, Carlos," I said.

"Do you want to come up and cool off?" he asked.

"No, I don't," I replied.

"You can talk to me," he said.

"You're a child," I replied.

"I'm more than a child, shorty. You need someone who can appreciate you. That nigga always got bitches throwing themselves at him and he never checks them. Look, just keep this between us because that nigga will have me kilt," Carlos said. He kissed me on the cheek before he got out of my car.

What is going on? I thought.

I drove around the city for almost two hours thinking about everything and how Beretta took me through a lot in the past. They say history repeats itself, but I wasn't trying to believe it. I begged God to send me a sign, telling me I made a mistake and my husband wouldn't drag me back to that dark place again. My eyelids grew heavy and I needed to sleep. I checked into the nearest hotel on the outskirts of the city. It was a small old place but all I needed to do was sleep off the liquor and my anger. Hopefully, rest would give me a clearer vision. My phone rang as I laid across the full-sized bed and I stared at the ceiling. It was Piper calling me.

"I'm fine," I answered the phone.

"But Beretta isn't! He's so mad, Mara. I know you caught him red-handed but you should hear him out," she said.

"I know my husband," I replied.

"Kellan and Sniper have a weird relationship. How can you trust a bitch that lets her man sleep with other women?" she asked.

"I don't trust her. I know Beretta didn't try to rape her. But I also know he would've told me about her if she was coming on to him. I do think he was trying to push her off in the bathroom, but I feel like they had something going on prior to that. Why would she feel bold enough to make a move like that if she knew how he was going to react? And the bitch is wearing the same perfume as me. I bet she knows how much Beretta loves it. Shit just ain't adding up right now, Pipe," I said and wiped my eyes.

"Where are you?" she asked.

"I'll call you when I wake up. We can talk then," I said and hung up. A couple minutes later, Beretta texted me. He wanted me to come home so we could talk. Maybe Carlos was right about Beretta and Kellan. He was always around him and would know more than me. What would Carlos gain out of snitching on someone who helped his family out if he wasn't telling the truth? My head was spinning from doing too much thinking. I closed my eyes and let sleep take over me.

****

I spent a whole day from home. All of my friends were calling me, including Ms. Baker. We had developed a close bond over the years; me and Beretta even called her our grandmother. She seemed to have the answers to everything and I was feeling bad for not answering her calls, so I called her back.

"Hey, Mara. Where are you?" she asked.

"I'm at a hotel, watching TV," I replied.

"Can you tell me which one? I only want to talk to you. I won't tell Z'wan where you're at," she said.

"I just want to be alone. I kinda feel sick like I'm coming down with something. The hangover I had was a terrible one. It's sorta why I'm still in bed," I replied.

"Send me the address and I'll bring you some soup," she said. I hung up with Ms. Baker and I sent her the address. My stomach was spinning out of control and I jumped out of bed and ran to the bathroom. I had diarrhea all morning and I was vomiting. It was some uncomfortable feelings. Maybe it was my nerves because every time I got depressed, I'd get sick to my stomach or have bad headaches. After I finished spitting up phlegm, I stepped into the shower. The hotel soap dried my skin out but the water was refreshing. I didn't know how long I was in the shower before I heard knocking at the door.

"I'm coming!" I called out.

SOUL Publications

I grabbed a towel and went to the door and it was Ms. Baker with a brown paper bag and a can of ginger ale.

"You look terrible," she said, feeling my forehead.

"I'm never drinking vodka again," I said.

"Are you sure it's vodka?" she replied.

"What else could it be?" I asked.

"Just asking," she said.

"Me and Beretta aren't thinking about having any babies, and truth be told, I don't want any by his cheating ass," I replied. Ms. Baker took off her pea coat then laid it across the chair. She sat down and crossed her legs, the same way she did when we had our sessions. I opened up the soup she got from Panera Bread and the aroma made me nauseous.

"Wait a little bit. Drink the ginger ale first then try to eat," she said.

"Z'wan called you?" I asked.

"First thing this morning. Y'all had a fight yesterday?" she asked.

"I caught him screwing my friend in our bathroom," I replied.

"Tell me about this friend," she said.

SOUL Publications

"She's flirtatious, cute in the face and has a nice slim body. Attitude wise, she's a little loud but I can always count on her to make everybody have fun. Over the years, I've noticed a slight change in her attitude but not towards me. Her remarks come across a little shady and all she does is drink a lot. She's Z'wan's brother's girlfriend and I've been around her for years and not once did I think she'd screw my husband in my house," I said.

"Interesting. Tell me about the relationship she has with your brother-in-law," she said.

"They're swingers—well, she has girlfriends with him but this girl named Brittany has been in the picture for quite some time now. Tiko spends a lot of time with her and Kellan gets jealous. Brittany might be pregnant," I said and Ms. Baker laughed.

"Tiko is quite the man, huh?" she asked and I giggled, too.

"Tiko is a sweetheart but Kellan shares him and she hates to come second," I said.

"Kellan needs counseling it seems. Do you think she's trying to hurt Tiko by going after his brother?" she asked.

"I thought about it, but why wouldn't Z'wan tell me about her coming on to him? He should've come to me. Now I don't know what to believe. Z'wan has a history of cheating and you know that. Back then, everyone was telling me I was overreacting when I suspected him doing something and it turned out I was right. What if I'm right this time, then what?" I asked.

"You have some good points but I've talked to Z'wan. He's not a habitual cheater. He had an affair one time and he's learned from it. Why would he cheat with his brother's girlfriend? She's loud, makes snide remarks and seems bitter. Seems to me she would cause a lot of problems if he slept with her, and he's a smart man. I can't picture him cheating with the type of woman who can blow his cover and ruin a relationship with his brother. It just doesn't sound right to me," she said.

"Z'wan saved her from getting raped a few years back. I keep asking myself why she called him and if she really tried to get in contact with Tiko the night it happened. She told Z'wan Tiko wasn't answering the phone and he got out of bed to check up on her. The intruders left when they heard him pull up," I said.

"And she's been acting different since or when Tiko was spending time with another woman?" she asked.

"It all happened around the same time. Kellan realized Tiko couldn't leave Brittany alone before the intruders came into her house. That's why Tiko wasn't answering because he was with Brittany," I replied.

"Z'wan came to her rescue while her boyfriend was with his side-chick?" Ms. Baker asked.

"Exactly," I replied.

"Maybe she has a case of hero syndrome," she said and I laughed. Ms. Baker looked at me as if I had lost my mind so I cleared my throat.

"What is hero syndrome?" I asked.

"Oh, honey, I had a lot of clients who became obsessed with people who saved them from all kinds of crisis. It's gotten so bad, they would stalk the person. A lot of police officers and firemen deal with people with hero syndrome. Her almost getting raped probably traumatized her, and every time she thinks of that night, she remembers Z'wan coming in to save her. She might be attached to him. You said yourself that she got the same perfume as you because she knows how much he likes it. Maybe she's obsessed with him. But I can be wrong, it just sounds like a case I had before with a patient. A man saved her from drowning and she stalked him for years. Each year, it got worse, and when he moved out of the state, she went insane. She developed Munchausen Syndrome. She purposely drowned herself at a pool or beach so a lifeguard could rescue her," Ms. Baker said.

"People are sick, but you might be right. Kellan said Z'wan tried to rape her," I replied.

"Maybe she wants Tiko to save her the same way Z'wan did for sympathy," Ms. Baker said and shrugged her shoulders.

"I gotta admit, that sounds accurate but I want to know for sure so I won't look like a fool again," I replied.

"I understand, but what if you push him away by assuming he did something when he didn't? Are you really capable of walking away from your husband?" she asked.

"No. Does it make me weak?" I replied.

"No, it makes you a better woman to trust your husband," she said. My phone rang and it was Beretta calling me for the tenth time. Ms. Baker nodded towards the phone and I answered it.

"Hi, Mommy, when are you coming home?" Zalia asked and I could hear Beretta telling her what to say in the background.

"I'll be home soon, okay? I promise," I said.

"Okay, love you," she replied.

"Love you, too, baby," I said and she hung up.

"Do you think I should tell Zalia I'm not her real mother when she gets older?" I asked.

"You are her real mother. Some secrets you take to your grave," Ms. Baker said. She looked at her watch and grabbed her coat.

"Well, I gotta go. I have a session starting in an hour. Take care of yourself and go home to your family," she said. She kissed my forehead then grabbed her coat.

"Thank you for everything," I said.

"Anytime, baby," she replied.

I laid back in bed and stared at the ceiling. Maybe Ms. Baker was right. Kellan could've been plotting on my husband, so did that mean Carlos lied to me?

Beretta

Five days later...

Kemara's ass still hadn't come home yet and Sniper wasn't talking to me. That nigga lost his mind if he thought I wanted Kellan's funny-looking ass. Jasmine didn't think he was mad at me personally but mad in general and even embarrassed. I hit him up twice to talk to him and he didn't return my calls. I got fed up with Mara's bullshit so I had niggas looking for her. Ms. Baker said she didn't know where Mara was but she wasn't trying to tell me. I looked everywhere for Mara and checked her bank statements. She had to have been using cash because the last time she used her visa was six days ago and it was for gas. Just when I thought I was starting the new year off right, some dumb-ass bullshit happened. I could've told Mara about Kellan but it was something I was trying to avoid because a bunch of shit would've got started even though it did anyway.

"Yoooo," Pistol said, knocking on the door to the office of the Boy's and Girl's club. Mara usually was the one sorting out the funds so they could go on fieldtrips and shit like that but I had to do it.

"Come in, bruh," I said and he sat on the other side of the desk.

"Mara got you working, I see," he said.

"You never know how much your life changes when your wife leaves you," I said. Mara used Microsoft Excel a lot and I couldn't figure out what to do with it. Computers just wasn't my thing.

"How in da fuck does Mara keep track of all this shit? I got a headache, bruh," I said.

"I'on know, fam, but I came down here to talk to you about something. Word on the street is Carlos robbing old church ladies and shit," Pistol said.

"Nigga, what?" I asked.

"Yeah, Flo told me. I know the nigga lie and all but you gotta check him. You got the mayor speaking highly of you and shit, and Carlos is always with you, so it ain't a good look," Pistol said. I leaned back in the chair and scratched the hair in my beard.

"I told him real niggas get it on their own and he must've thought I meant robbing old ladies. I would've had more respect for that nigga if he robbed a nigga who was hustling. What da fuck!" I said in frustration.

SOUL Publications

"You can't save him, bruh. Let the little nigga be hardheaded. He's gonna end up dead or in jail," Pistol said.

"Do me a favor. Find out which old ladies he robbed and give them 5 g's a piece. I'll talk to Carlos," I replied.

"Okay, bet. He just walked in," Pistol said. Carlos came into the office and grabbed the trash out of the trashcan next to the desk.

"What's good?" he asked us.

"Shit, just chilling," I replied.

"I'll get up with you later. I gotta pick up Olijah from Earlene's crib," Pistol said. We slapped hands before he left out of the office. Carlos sat across from me.

"Yo, where Mara at?" he asked.

"Home," I replied.

"So, everything cool with y'all?" he asked.

"Yeah, why wouldn't it be?" I replied.

Pay attention to your wife. She might have a thing for young niggas, I remembered Kellan saying to me.

Mara and Carlos? Fuck no! Mara would never fuck with that lil' immature-ass nigga. But why he always asking about her and saying he want a girl like Mara? What am I thinking about? I'm trippin', I thought.

"Yo, Mara took you home the night that shit when down, didn't she?" I asked.

"Yeah, why what's up?" he replied.

"You know where she went afterwards?" I asked.

"I'on know. Someone called her phone and told her to come through. I thought it was you," he said.

"Oh, word?" I asked.

"Yeah, but anyways, I got work to do. I'll see you later," he said and grabbed the trash.

"Word on da street is dat you're robbing old ladies," I said.

"It wasn't me, bruh. The nigga Ron I be wit' be doin' dat bullshit," he replied.

"Tell his lil' bitch-ass I got sumthin for him if I hear about it again," I said.

"No doubt," Carlos said before he left out of the office.

Something clicked in my head and I don't know why I didn't think of it at first. I could track Mara's whip through an app she downloaded to my phone a while back.

****

SOUL Publications

Twenty-five minutes later, I was pulling up to a run-down motel. Mara must've hit her head or something when her and Kellan got into it. The motel was so fucked up she could probably only use cash. I was from the streets but I didn't even want to park my Wraith in the parking lot in case someone tried to take my shit. Back in the day, I used to ride around with a gun in the whip but I couldn't risk my life like that so I got bulletproof windows instead. I opened up the door to the front desk in the lobby and a chubby white woman was sitting behind the desk playing Candy Crush on her phone.

"How can I help you?" she asked, never looking up.

"I'm looking for Kemara Jones," I said.

"I don't know who that is," she replied.

"You don't have a system for shit like dat?" I asked.

"Nope," she said.

"Who drives that white Tesla that's parked outside?" I asked.

"Oh, her? The mean girl with the big butt? I know who you're talking about. She almost got me fired. Are you here to take her home?" she asked, finally looking up.

"Yeah, can I have the key?" I asked and she gave it to me.

*Damn, I could've been here to kill Mara. Shorty trippin'
big time for staying in this dump,* I thought.

I walked outside and walked up the stairs to the
second floor. She was at the end of the hall. I could hear
the TV from outside.

"Mara!" I called out after I unlocked the door and
walked into the room. The toilet flushed and I went into
the bathroom. Mara was throwing up in the toilet and she
looked sick. She had dark rings around her eyes and her
lips were dry.

"I'm sick," she said. She tried to get up and almost fell
over but I caught her.

"I'm gonna take you to the hospital," I replied.

"Nooo, put me back in bed. I'm too weak to go," she
said. She was very weak and her body was trembling. She
was only wearing a bra and panties. In the corner of the
room was her clothes. I grabbed her sweater, shoes and
pants and got her dressed. Her breathing sounded fucked
up and I was nervous. My wife looked like death. I grabbed
her purse and looked for her coat and remembered she
left out of the house without one. After I put my coat
around her, I helped her out the door. She could barely
make it down the steps so I picked her up. Shorty wasn't
light, but I wasn't a weak nigga, neither. I carried Mara all
the way to my whip. The hospital was twenty minutes
away.

****

Three hours later...

Mara was in the hospital bed asleep. She had the flu and her fever was at 105. Her cell phone was dead and she couldn't call anybody. She said the lady at the front desk told her their phones weren't working so she cursed her out. The doctor came back into the room and told me Mara had to stay in the hospital for a few days for observation because she had pneumonia, too. Not only that, shorty was pregnant. When the doctor told me Mara was pregnant, my mind drifted off. She checked Mara's blood pressure and wrote it down before she left out of the room. Mara woke up and was talking out of her head.

"I want to go home," she said.

"You gotta stay here so they can monitor you. You're knocked up, too," I replied and she opened her eyes and looked at me.

"I'm pregnant?" she asked.

"Yeah," I replied and she started crying.

"I don't want a baby, Beretta. Oh, God, I'm gonna go through it all over again," she sobbed.

"Don't think like that," I said and she shook her head.

"When have we ever had good luck? Don't you see how shit be fine one minute then the next everything is falling apart? This baby won't survive in my womb. I don't want it because I know I'll be heartbroken and you will be, too," she said.

"Da fuck you gonna do, get an abortion?" I asked.

"How far am I?" she replied.

"We don't know yet but what da fuck is wrong witchu? You ain't killing my fuckin seed! You crazy if you think I'm gonna let that happen. This is something we gotta deal with to see how it turns out. It's okay to be scared, shit I was scared, too, when the doctor told me you were pregnant," I said.

"I wasn't saying I wanted an abortion. I'm saying I don't want this pregnancy right now even though I have to deal with it," she replied.

"Let's talk about this once you feel better. I think you're overwhelmed because you've been wanting this for a while and suddenly you're changing your mind," I said. Mara mumbled something else then went back to sleep. I called Piper and told her where Mara was at because she was worried about her, too. Fuck what Mara was saying, I was happy she was carrying my seed despite what the outcome might be.

SOUL Publications

Poppa

Nika was sitting in a wheelchair staring out the window in her room when I brought our kids to an assisted living home to visit her. The place was very expensive but it had everything she needed. Over the years, her condition worsened. Shorty went from using a walker to not being able to get out of bed, so she stopped taking her pills. She stilled looked good, though, and the facility took good care of her. I felt bad for her when she told me she had to wear adult pampers. Me and Fushia got a big house together and she welcomed our kids like they were her own. Odimau moved in, too, and I had something I never really had which was a family.

"How are Mommy's babies?" Nika asked and held out her hand to Omario so he could sit on her lap. Hope kissed her cheek and a tear slid out of her eye. She had been in the assisted living home for a year and still wasn't used to it. She called me and complained about how the food tasted nasty and them not helping her change. She met Fushia one time and it was horrible. She threw her food in Fushia's face, so Fushia didn't want any parts of her.

"Where is your holy girlfriend?" Nika asked.

"Home. Don't you think you should be positive in front the kids? I don't want them picking up your attitude," I said.

"You think you're the shit now, huh? Well, you're not!" she spat. I thought Nika was going to change for the better but shorty's attitude was worse. Hope stepped away from her and stood next to me.

"What's the matter, Hope? You don't love me anymore because I can't walk? You're handicap, too," Nika said. Hope dropped the flowers she was going to give to her mother on the floor and Nika began to cry.

"Take me home. Please, take me home! You're trying to kill me so you can get my restaurants. Beretta paid you to do this to me, didn't he?" she asked. The MS was affecting her mind. Omario got down off her lap and I picked him up. Nika started screaming and carrying on. It was her forty-third birthday and the kids wanted to spend time with her. Omario colored her a picture and Hope wanted to bring her flowers and chocolate.

"Yo, I can't bring them here anymore. This is the last time. Say what you want to me but don't treat them like they did something to you! Bitch, you crazy," I said. Nika wheeled herself over to me and tried to hit me but I kicked her wheelchair back and she slammed against the wall.

"I hate you! I hope you die, bitch! All of you can go to hell!" she sobbed.

SOUL Publications

"And I hope you find someone to push your stupid ass right down there with me," I replied. I grabbed Hope's hand and walked out of Nika's room, never looking back.

"Mommy's mean," Omario said when I put him in his car seat.

"She's just sick," I replied. Hope buried her face in her hands and sobbed.

"She doesn't love me anymore. She said I'm handicapped. Why would she say that?" Hope asked me in sign language.

"I love you and you're an angel created differently than others, but even better," I replied in sign language.

"I hope Mommy feels better," Hope replied back.

I hope that bitch just hurry up and die already so I can stop burning my gas to see her shitty ass, I thought as I got into the driver's seat.

✳✳✳✳✳✳✳✳✳✳✳✳

"She's evil. Half of her soul is in hell, that's why she sees demons. Nika is on her deathbed," my wife said. Me and Fushia had been married for six months. I didn't tell Nika because she would've made it harder for me to bring the kids to her. Nika was cool with me moving on but when I put her in assisted living, all hell broke loose. She lost her mind if she thought I was going to take care of her.

"What time will Silk be here to pick up Amber?" I replied.

"In a few minutes," Fushia said, folding clothes in our bedroom.

"What are you going to do about that strip club? You're a man of God now and that's not a good look for the church. You were supposed to sell it months ago," Fushia said. When we got married, Fushia committed herself to God, too. We had good communication and she changed me completely—well, we changed each other.

"I'm going to give it to Kemara's husband," I said.

"I thought y'all didn't like each other," she replied.

"We're cordial but enough about that. How is my baby doing?" I asked, rubbing her stomach. Fushia was seven months pregnant with our son. I was glad it wasn't a girl because me and Omario were around a lot of women in the house.

"Kicking my ass," she replied.

The doorbell rang and I went downstairs to get the door. Silk was standing in front of me dressed like one of those new-age rappers with tight clothes and colorful tennis shoes.

"Amber, yah mother's here! I mean yah father!" I called out to her. Silk stepped into the house and threw his imaginary hair back. That nigga made me sick to my stomach.

"Big house, nice cars and a nanny? When y'all marrying me?" he asked, sitting on the couch with his legs crossed.

"Gay-ass nigga," I said and went into the kitchen.

"But my bitch looks better than yourrrsssssss," he sang.

"And she got a bigger dick than me, too," I said.

"And? You mad?" he asked. Talking to that nigga was straight-up dysfunctional so I tuned him out and poured myself a glass of tequila. Amber ran downstairs with her backpack and jumped onto her father's lap.

"Chilleeeee, those shoes are cute!" Amber said to Silk and she smiled.

"There is a pair in your room at my apartment waiting for you. Let's hurry up because our nail appointment is in thirty minutes," Silk said.

"We are getting pink on our toes?" Amber asked her father.

"Yup," he replied.

"Can we stop at Starbucks? I want a hot chocolate with caramel drizzle," Amber replied.

"Tell baby mama I said call me later. Toodles," Silk said as he and Amber left out the door.

"Amber has two mommies," Hope said in sign language.

"I know, baby. I know," I replied and she laughed.

****

Two days later...

Beretta came into my office at the club and sat in the chair on the other side of the desk. It was his day to collect but I was also walking away from the strip club. Nika had two restaurants and I was going to expand and rename them.

"Your money is in the envelope and so are the papers," I said. He opened the big manila envelope and flipped through the stacks. He pulled out the papers and read over them.

"This is the deed to the club," he said.

"Yeah, I'm giving it you. I'm planning on being a pastor in a few years and I can't have this shit tied to me," I replied. He leaned back in the chair and scratched his chin.

"A pastor, huh?" he asked.

"Yeah," I replied.

"And you giving me this club?" he asked.

"Yeah, you invested in it, so it wouldn't be right if I sold it to you. Besides, you were the brains behind it, I was just running the shit," I said.

"The fuck is you up to, nigga? We don't fuck with each other and all of a sudden you wanna give me something?" he asked.

"I want out and this is the only way. You said I'd have to pay you a percentage for the rest of my life, so here is your percentage plus more," I said. I didn't want to give it to the nigga but it was my only way out of the deal.

"Cool, since it's mine now, go home, bruh," he said and stood up. I grabbed my coat from off the chair and headed to the door.

"I know about you keeping in contact with my wife, too," he said and I turned around.

"She's my sister," I replied.

"Yeah, I know. I hope your intentions are good, though. Nigga, don't hurt my wife," he said.

"I won't," I replied and left without looking back.

I'm finally free from GMBAM for good! I thought.

SOUL Publications

Kemara

Two months later...

I was in the hospital for three days before they released me. Beretta nursed me back to good health but I was still mad at Kellan for the shit she pulled. Sniper broke up with her and moved Brittany into his house. We thought Sniper was upset with Beretta for what Kellan started but he said he was embarrassed. She didn't rat me out but I didn't care if she told the cops I shot her. My gun was registered and I would've told them she was trespassing and I feared for my life. That lil' hoe know she don't want it with me. I sat down and talked to Beretta and he told me everything about Kellan coming on to him and when it started.

"Heyyyyy," Piper sang as she stuck her head around the corner of the door. I was on the computer setting up events for our sports program.

"Hey, what are you doing here?" I asked and she held up Chipotle.

"Ohhhh, give me!" I said and she sat the bag on my desk.

I was ten weeks pregnant and I worried every day that I was going to see blood in my panties. The doctor told me everything looked great and not to worry but I couldn't help it. My morning sickness wasn't as bad as it was with Zyira or the second pregnancy. I was pretty much feeling great.

"Pistol told me he wanted another baby this morning. Dat nigga lost his fucking mind," Piper said.

"Give him another one so we can be pregnant together," I said.

"Gurrlllll, Olijah is going through his bad stages. I can't right now. That chile is bad as fuck!" Piper said and she wasn't lying. I watched him one time and it drained me for three days.

"Beat his ass, he's old enough," I replied.

"I do beat his ass but he doesn't care," she said.

Carlos came into the office and grabbed three bottles of water. He had an attitude with everyone lately and I didn't know what it was about. I heard he robbed some old ladies but one of the ladies told Pistol they didn't know who it was because the boy had on a mask.

"Ewww, what's the matter with you?" Piper asked him.

"Nothing," he said and walked out the room.

"That boy has issues," Piper said.

"I think he does, too. He told me Kellan was sleeping with Beretta but I know he was lying. I think he knew Kellan wanted Beretta and added to his story," I replied.

"You gotta be careful. He's young but that doesn't mean anything. He's old enough to hurt someone," Piper said.

"He's conniving, but I don't think he has the heart to do anything to anyone," I replied.

"I gotta go before I get stuck in traffic. Call me later," Piper said. She kissed my cheek and left out of the office. I sat back and worked for a few hours and it was getting late. The clock read eight o'clock at night. Beretta texted me and told me he was on his way to his club and Zalia was with the babysitter. Carlos stuck his head inside my office and knocked on the door.

"Aye, Mara. Can I talk to you about something?" he asked.

"I hope it's not more lies," I replied.

"I didn't lie, Kellan told me Beretta was pushing up on her," he said.

"Why would Kellan tell you anything?" I asked. He sat at my desk and leaned back in the chair.

"You can't tell nobody about this and I mean it, Mara," he said.

"What is it?" I asked.

"The night after the New Year's party, I met Kellan at a hotel and we fucked," he said.

"WHAT!" I said.

"Yeah, then that's when she started telling me shit about Beretta. Look, I didn't mean no harm. I thought I was looking out for you because I care about you," he said and his eyes landed on my breasts.

"Do you understand that lust can get you killed?" I asked.

"I know but I can't help my attraction to you. Since I was a little kid, you looked out for me. I got older and realized I want a girl like you. You said you wanted to take everything from Beretta, remember?" he asked.

"I was hurt, saying all kinds of shit that day, and I was drunk. Hell, that's what couples do. They say things they don't mean sometimes. What are you hinting at, Carlos?" I replied.

"I think I can replace Beretta if you let me," he said.

"Replace Beretta? Honey, did Kellan feed you these lies? I can't believe I'm having this conversation with you. I'm damn near ten years older than you," I said.

"You used to be hood, Mara. What happened to you?" he asked.

"I moved on so I could have a better life. Maybe you should, too. You're trying to have things that's not meant for you to have. You're trying to be everything but Carlos. I wanna see you win so bad but you gotta see it for yourself," I said.

"Y'all gonna see that I'm dat nigga, watch. I bet you'll want me then," he replied and stormed out of my office.

At that moment, I didn't want Carlos around me, especially since I was carrying a baby. I texted Beretta and told him that I was on my way home and we needed to talk about Carlos.

Beretta

Present Day, August 2017...

*T*hey rushed Mara into the hospital on a stretcher and blood was everywhere. Piper was screaming and Pistol was holding her back.

"Who did this, Beretta? Who did this to Mara?" Piper screamed.

"Carlos did it," I said, still in disbelief.

They wouldn't let me go back in the room with Mara. I should've seen the signs. I didn't think Carlos was bold enough to run into my crib and shoot us, and Kellan was with him. She was still lying on the floor with a gunshot wound to her head but Carlos ran out the back door when Pistol came in.

"Sniper and Machete are on their way," Pistol said after he got off the phone. Sniper's girlfriend, Brittany, went into labor so they were at the hospital. I was glad they were late to our anniversary dinner because shit *would've been worse. Pistol took the seat next to me when I sat in a chair in the emergency room.*

"This shit keeps happening, bruh. Mara warned me about that nigga and I let him live. I should've had his ass merked. He shot my fuckin' wife," I said.

"We gonna get him, bruh. He ain't going too far. Let's just pray for Mara and the baby. Revenge ain't important right now," Pistol said. I looked down at my clothes and I had my wife's blood on my shirt and pants. She stopped breathing on our way to the hospital but Mara was a fighter—she was always a fighter. Two hours later, the doctor came out into the waiting room and all I heard was Piper screaming and my heart almost stopped beating. Kemara stopped breathing but they were able to save my daughter...

Carlos

August 2017

(Four hours ago) ...

I stood in the middle of my room, pacing back and forth in the middle of the floor. My sister, Kiara, barged into my room and I yelled at her.

"Bitch, you can't fucking knock?" I asked.

"We don't have any food!" she replied. She was fifteen years old and old enough to work but the bitch was just lazy. My other sister, Mina, who was thirteen years old was staying at her friend's house because we didn't have any food or electricity. My mother was roaming the streets and I hadn't seen her in two months. We had an eviction notice and I had to figure out something quick.

"And? Go out and get some," I spat. Kiara was a whiny, lazy brat!

"This is all your fault! You ruin everything. Beretta was helping us out and you ruined it by coming on to his wife! You're lucky he didn't kill you!" she said. I wrapped my hand around her neck and squeezed until I couldn't squeeze anymore. She tried to fight me off but I wouldn't let up until she stopped moving. I hated my life and the people in it. There was only person I loved and that was Kemara. She used to smile at me and everything seemed like it was going to be alright. I had this obsession with her. I didn't know where it came from but I couldn't shake it. Many nights I laid in bed jerking off to the thought of her pretty lips wrapped around my dick. If I could be like her fuck-nigga, Beretta, she would look at me the same way. I dropped my sister's lifeless body on the floor and covered her up with a blanket. Seeing Mara's post on Facebook angered me. It was their anniversary and my eighteenth birthday. Why were they celebrating that bullshit when Mara could've been spending her time with me? She said she wanted to take everything from Beretta. I heard all her hateful words she said about him when she took me home that day. She said she was angry and that's what people do when they vent, but she was crying out to me so I could save her. I hadn't seen her in months because Beretta's bitch-ass told me he was done with me and if I came anywhere near her, he was going to merk me and my family. I knew he was serious so I stayed away but I had a plan. He told me a real man didn't ask for handouts so I was going to take it. Six months, I stayed cooped up in my room thinking of a master plan. They should've never let me into their home. The day had come, and after I took him out, everyone would respect me and crown me the new king. I called the one person who hated Beretta as much as I did.

"Kellan, where you at?" I asked.

"I'm at my sister's house," she replied.

"Are you ready?" I asked.

"Wait, are you serious? You really want to rob Beretta? I thought you were just talking out of your fucking head," she said.

"He's the reason you got kicked out yah house! Bitch, you know what we planned on doing, so stick with it!" I replied.

"I can't stand none of them but I'm not going up in that house! I thought you were joking. Look, come over here and we can cuddle," she said and I hung up on her. I grabbed my weapons and mask before I walked out my bedroom and out of the apartment. I wasn't ready to be homeless and I didn't have shit to lose.

****

Twenty minutes later, I was banging on Kellan's sister, Zain's, door.

"Where is Kellan?" I asked.

"In the room," she spat and walked away.

Stupid bitch! I thought.

I went into Kellan's bedroom and she was lying in bed watching TV while eating popcorn. I grabbed her by her hair and snatched her onto the floor. She screamed for her sister to help her and Zain ran into the room. I pulled out my gun and put a bullet right between Zain's eyes. She fell onto the bed and Kellan screamed. I took the butt of my gun and smacked her in the face with it.

"Bitch, you gonna get in yah fuckin' car and take me to Beretta's house! We had a deal!" I said.

"I didn't think you were serious! You're crazy!" she screamed and I backhanded her.

"Bitch, do you wanna die, too?" I asked and she sobbed. She looked at Zain's lifeless body and screamed out to her. She tried to grab her sister but I snatched her back and dragged her down the hallway and out of the apartment door. Zain lived on the bottom floor and I parked behind the building so nobody would see me. I opened the door to Kellan's car and tossed her inside. The stupid bitch always left a spare key underneath the seat because she always got drunk and forgot her keys. I grabbed my backpack and told her to put on the black clothes I had for her. It was a black hoodie and pants I got from out of my sister's closet. It was a little big on Kellan but it worked.

"Put on this mask!" I yelled at her. Her hands trembled as she put on the mask.

"I'm gonna rob that nigga and escape the country," I said. I killed my sister and Kellan's sister. It was too late to turn back now. I sped through the streets of Annapolis before I got on the highway. We had almost an hour ride to get to Beretta's crib. Kellan sobbed all the way there.

****

We made it to Beretta's neighborhood fifty minutes later. I turned off the lights to the car and grabbed my backpack. Kellan was still crying and I slapped her head into the window.

"Shut da fuck up, hoe!" I yelled.

"We can't just go in there and rob them! GMBAM is in that fucking house, retard!" she said.

"Do you expect them to have guns sitting around at their anniversary dinner? This is the perfect moment. I saw Beretta punch in the code to his garage door. All we got to do is figure out how to get inside through the garage. Now, take this gun," I said. I handed her a gun with an empty clip because I didn't trust the bitch with one. She would've probably shot me.

"The clip is empty but use it to scare them. It's not many cars in the driveway so everyone didn't show up yet," I said. We got out the car and Kellan tried to run but I caught her and dragged her up the street. A car was pulling up to the gate so I pulled Kellan down behind the bushes with me. It was Glock. He had perfect timing. I pulled Kellan up and we went in behind his car. Glock stepped out of his whip and went up to the door and rang the bell. He waited almost a minute before an older lady opened the door. I pushed Kellan in behind Glock and the lady was ready to scream but I placed my hand over her mouth. Glock was ready to pull out his gun but I shot him in the head with my silencer then picked up his gun.

"Go upstairs and find the safe!" I barked at Kellan and she ran upstairs. I had a device that could read the passwords to safes. I bought it from a white kid off Craigslist. All I needed was for Kellan to find it. I dragged the old lady down the hall and into the dining room area and there she was. Mara looked so beautiful in her long black dress that hugged her curves. Her baby bump angered me! That should've been my baby! Her hair was in big curls that fell down her shoulders and her make-up was elegant. She was setting the dining room table for her stupid little dinner.

"You look beautiful," I called out to her. She froze when she saw me. The look of fear she had in her eyes gave me an arousal.

About time I get a reaction out of this bitch! I thought.

"What do you want?" she asked.

"Get down on your knees," I said.

"Let her go. Please, just let her go. I'll do whatever you want, just don't hurt her," Mara begged.

"Mara, I'll be fine, honey," the lady said.

"Where is Beretta?" I asked.

SOUL Publications

"He's not here," she replied.

"Who else is here?" I asked.

"Nobody, just us," she replied.

"Get on yah fucking knees, Mara!" I yelled at her. She slowly got on her knees while holding her stomach.

"There is money here," she said.

"Bitch, I know y'all have money in here!" I replied.

"Aye, Mara. I can't find the wine opener," Beretta said when he came out the basement door. He froze when he saw me. He looked between me and Mara. He tried to get to her but I fired a shot at the ceiling and the old lady screamed. Kellan ran downstairs and told me she couldn't find anything.

"Bitch, go back up there and look!" I barked and she ran back upstairs. The old lady bit my arm and tried to make a dash towards the kitchen but I shot her in the back three times and she dropped. Mara screamed and got up to run to her but I pointed the gun at her. Beretta tackled Mara to the floor and I let off the whole clip at him. I saw blood coming from Beretta's head as he laid next to Mara and she was begging him to get up.

"How could you?" she cried.

"You crossed me, Kemara. You fuckin' crossed me! Look at you! You've got this fancy-ass mansion and

Bentleys and shit. What do I have, huh? I have nothin' and it's all because of that fuck-nigga! He took you away from me, Kemara," I said. Blood was seeping from her body and I wanted to help her but it was too late.

"I moved on with my life! I wanted a better life! I'm not the girl I used to be!" she screamed. Mara knew it was me, but she couldn't bring herself to say it. She must've thought if she played dumb I wouldn't kill her.

"A better life? So, what I offered you wasn't good enough? You chose that nigga over me. Sorry, I gotta do this. You should've let me in on the deal when you said you wanted to take everything from him. It was cool when y'all split up but because he begged you to come back, you switched up. Naw, fam, it can't go down like that. You gotta die," I said and pointed the gun at her head. Kellan came down the stairs and looked at the bodies lying on the floor. I saw tears in her eyes as she looked at Mara's bullet-riddled body.

"What did you do, muthafucka? That's Mara!" she screamed. I guess she finally realized all the shit she helped cause the past few months.

"Fuck her, she's against us. I guess you love her now but this was your idea in case you've forgotten," I said. It was Kellan's idea to get rid of Beretta and the bitch was having second thoughts about all of it! She was the one who put the thought in my head that Mara liked me, too. Mara was telling Beretta how much she loved him and I couldn't hear it anymore. I walked over to her and pressed my gun to her head.

SOUL Publications

"Don't do this! Please, don't do this! I didn't want anybody to die and you know I didn't. Mara is pregnant and I can't watch you kill a pregnant woman," Kellan said.

"Bitch, you should've thought about that before you tried to ruin her marriage," I replied.

"I was hurt and you know that! I don't want anybody else to die! Please, let me get her some help. I'm begging you," Kellan cried.

"Bitch, didn't she shoot you?" I asked.

"Yes, but she didn't kill me. I deserved it. Let's just leave. They didn't see our faces," Kellan said.

"Bitch, you crazy if you think Mara don't know who we are!" I yelled at her. Kellan lunged into me and grabbed my arm. A bullet fired from my gun and she began fighting me. As soon as Kellan pulled my mask off, a bullet flew past my ear and pierced through her head; she fell onto the floor. I turned around and Beretta was holding a gun. He killed Kellan. I thought the nigga was dead; his head was bleeding and his upper body was riddled with bullets. He had on a bulletproof vest. He aimed a gun at me and I was ready to pull the trigger but he shot me in the stomach and I fell into a glass table. When I got up, he was cradling Mara. I aimed my gun at him and pulled the trigger and it went over his head.

"My nigga, you really lost your fuckin' mind! My fuckin' wife?" he seethed.

"I loved her! When you cheated on her, she cried on my shoulder! I couldn't wait to get older to merk your bitch ass, anyway," I said.

"Nigga, you did all of this for a woman you'll never have?" he asked.

"Oh, I had her, muthafucka. I banged dat pussy out a few times. You ain't know about dat, did you? I appreciate you for puttin' me on and all dat other shit you did for me, but your time is up. You wanna know what's crazy? I wanted to be like you when I was a lil' nigga, but dat shit changed once I realized I could be betta than you," I gritted.

"Let Mara get some help, bruh. Take whateva you want. I'll give you the code to anything you want. Just get some help for my wife," he said and I smirked.

"Naw, nigga. That bitch can die witchu," I said.

He held onto her and I saw the pain he had in his eyes. Tears fell down his face because he knew he let the bitch down. She spoke so highly of that nigga and he couldn't even save her.

"I bet you thinkin' about how much you love her now, huh?" I chuckled.

"Go ahead and do it, muthafucka. I'll never beg a nigga for my life. Shoot me, bitch. Just remember, you gotta kill to get it but be killed when you keep it. Take my life but another muthafucka like you gonna steal it from you," he said. Bullets flew from behind me and over my head and I dropped my gun. Pistol was shooting at me. I heard his voice but my back was turned towards him. I got caught slipping because I didn't hear the nigga come into the house. The sliding doors in the dining room to outside shattered when I jumped through it. The pieces of glass got into my face and I couldn't run far because of the gunshot wound in my stomach. I ran until I collapsed by the lake behind some bushes and passed out.

Carlos

Hours later...

I woke up, gasping for air. I was in the trunk of a car. All I remembered was running from Beretta's crib then falling behind some bushes. I kicked the trunk, screaming for help.

"Get me out of here!" I yelled. I was weak from my wound and lost a lot of blood.

"Somebody, help me!" I screamed. The car slammed on its brakes and I heard a door open. The trunk opened and Jasmine was smiling down at me.

"Help me. I didn't mean to do it," I said, holding my stomach. She pulled out a razor and slashed me across the face. Machete appeared from behind her and pulled me out the trunk. He wrapped a chain around my neck and dragged me across the soil into an old abandoned house. I was trying to get away but Jasmine slashed me across the face with a razor and it burned. My cheek was hanging and blood dripped onto my shirt.

"We followed your blood trail when you ran out the house and it led us right to your stupid ass! You thought you was gonna get away with what you did?" she asked.

"Where is Mara? I didn't mean to do it!" I cried. Jasmine slashed my face again and I screamed from the pain.

"Please, stop!" I begged.

"Do it again, baby," Machete said. She cut my face again and the razor cut my eye. Machete's phone rang and he put it against my ear.

"I did love you like a lil' brother and I wanted what was best for you. But, nigga, you fucked up and it ain't no coming back. Peace, fam," Beretta said and Machete took the phone away from me.

"Please, noooooooooo! MAMAAAAAAAA!" I screamed out when Machete began slicing me alive. Blood came out of my mouth and I started choking. Jasmine dumped gasoline on me.

"I hope you burn in hell, bitch! I didn't like you, anyway!" she said, then dropped a match on me...

Beretta

October 2017

I stood in front of the grave, not knowing how to feel because I was numb. A tear didn't fall— nothing. But I knew I had to do it so I could let the past and hurt go.

"I don't know what to say to you. I wish shit could've turned out better than it did, but I do know if you didn't treat me the way you did, I wouldn't be a better man or father. Sorry I couldn't give you a final goodbye a few months ago. A lot of things were going on in my life," I said and placed flowers on a tombstone. I wasn't the type of nigga to give long speeches; I kept it short and said what I meant.

"Hopefully, she'll find the peace she was looking for when she was here," someone said from behind me and it was Poppa and his two kids. I never had a chance to meet Omario so he didn't come to me but Hope hugged me and I picked her up like I used to do when she was a baby to kiss her forehead.

SOUL Publications

"I'll give y'all some time alone," I said and walked away.

I got into my whip and Zakia was crying in her carrier while Zalia was trying to give her a pacifier. I looked over to the passenger's seat and Mara smiled at me.

"I'm proud of you," she said.

"Appreciate you," I replied.

I picked up her hand and kissed it. Kemara stopped breathing on the operating table from her gunshot wounds. After the doctor told me she didn't make it, a nurse ran out to the emergency room and told me she was breathing again. Come to find out, Nika had a stroke the same night Kemara was shot. It was almost like she gave her life so Kemara could live. I wasn't sure how life worked but I knew I was thankful. Crazy how a lil' nigga tried to kill me for my wife. Out all the shit that could've happened to me, a little nigga I took under my wing was my biggest downfall. I definitely didn't see that one coming, but I also couldn't kill him. Carlos was a scared kid. He acted tough and tried so hard to be something he wasn't until it ate him up. He felt like he had to prove a point and went about it the wrong way. Deep down inside, I knew the lil' nigga was lost. I always knew.

Mara was a trooper. Shorty escaped death twice. She was shot four times. One in the side, two times in the left arm and one time in her thigh. Mara lost a lot of blood when the bullet hit the main artery in her thigh and it almost killed her. If I hadn't tackled Mara the way I did, she would've been gone. I don't think she would've survived. I caught most of the bullets in my back. Something told me to wear a bulletproof vest. Intuition was a muthafucka. If Mara wasn't pregnant, I would've made her wear one, too. My nigga, Glock, was dead and so was Ms. Baker. Kemara cried every night for a month after witnessing Carlos kill her. I shed a tear for Glock, but I cried with Kemara one night over Ms. Baker. I loved her and she helped me to become a better man and husband. She didn't have to die like that but I knew she was looking down on us. When the police came to my house that night, I told them it was one intruder, which was Kellan who was dead. I didn't mention shit about Carlos because I didn't want to give that nigga credit for turning our dinner into a massacre.

"Can Poppa come over for dinner one day?" Mara asked when I drove away from the cemetery.

"Wait a minute, shorty. Baby steps, please. You can't just toss that nigga on me like dat," I said.

"But he changed," she said.

"We all did in a way, shorty. I know I told you I wanted to be out the game by age thirty, but I'm done with it. From this day forward, I'm done, shorty," I replied and her pretty face lit up in excitement.

"And we can have more babies?" she said.

"Yeah, I want son," I replied.

Zakia started crying in the car seat, and she was screaming at the top of her lungs. My baby girl came out looking just like Mara and was already acting like her with a sassy attitude.

"Awww, shit. Mara, what you do to my baby girl? You let that mean-ass attitude rub off on her while you were pregnant," I said and she laughed.

"You just have to deal with a mini-me. But let's hurry up and get to Piper's wedding rehearsal. I'm hungry and I know Earlene ain't gonna leave me a turkey wing," she said and I kissed the back of her hand again. Since the night she was shot, I hadn't let her out of my sight. On some real shit, Beretta ended that night, but I'd go back to that nigga if I had to over my family, on God! GMBAM type of shit.

The End for Now...

Up Next From Natavia...
DAMAGED

SOUL Publications

CPSIA information can be obtained
at www.ICGtesting.com
Printed in the USA
LVHW081703201219
641253LV00011B/433/P